We All Fall Down

Colson Creek Series, Book One

Erin FitzGerald

Cover Design & Formatting: Erin FitzGerald

Contents

Sometimes you're blessed with a bestie who's like a sister, one who'll support you no matter what but still give it to you straight. She may even have once owned a suicidal cactus named Pedro (R.I.P.).

Heidi, you're the best friend every girl should have.

Chapter One

Judah

Someone was gagging.

"For the love of the sweet baby Jesus, Judah. You keeping goats in the house? Smells like unwashed ass in here."

My left eye cracked open and the low evening light stabbed my eyeball with the blades of a thousand red-hot knives.

"No goats in the house." I snapped the eye shut again.

"No reason *you* should smell like that, then." Levi sounded pissed and I heard the rapid slide of glass across the floor, then a splintering, shattering noise that told me he'd kicked the bottle across the room.

"Wastin' my booze, dickhead?" I grumbled, no will left in me to raise myself from where I'd landed on the sofa some hours earlier.

"Saving your dumb ass from yourself," he snapped. "This stops, brother. It's been more than a year and you're doing your damndest to put yourself in the ground with them. I won't let you do it."

"Something you know a few things about, Army boy." I chuckled, a sound completely without humor, and the dead stillness of the room told me my oldest brother was murdering me with his eyeballs. Because yeah, Levi knew a few things about suffering—probably more than any of us.

"Even Dawg can't stand you. Poor thing's sleeping on the front porch because you smell like a monkey butt."

"Thought it was a goat," I mumbled, turning my back to him.

"I don't discriminate against species. Equal opportunity offender." His voice was moving further away from me, something that made me suspicious.

"Seems like discrimination to me," I called, careful not to upset the headache that was threatening to rage. Hair of the dog was the only thing for it. "Pickin' all the smelly ones—just sayin'."

There was the muffled thud of his boots on the hardwood floor and then a jolt of miserable cold that jackknifed me into a sitting position, sputtering, my hands running quickly over my face. "You just douse me with water, asshole?"

"Worked, didn't it?" Levi stood there with a drinking glass in hand. "You're lucky I didn't put ice in it."

"Fuck you." I staggered to my feet and followed him toward the back of the house. I was pretty sure he was headed that way and I liked my odds.

"Hey!" I protested. Levi stood at the sink, chugging down the last of the remaining fifth I had in the house. "That was mine!"

"Not anymore." He slammed the empty bottle down on the countertop and winced. I couldn't remember the last time he'd had a drink; the man was practically a Quaker these days. I knew that meant I should have asked him if he'd had a bad day too, but I didn't have the energy.

"Yeah, well ... my lips were on the bottle, so it was mine. I licked it first. Now you've got my cooties."

I was going to have to eat a whole bottle of pain pills, a searing pain starting to take over my left eye.

"What are you, six?" Levi looked at me incredulously. "I recall that being your logic with that cheerleader Dan was seeing in high school."

I snorted, though it felt like the action had driven an ice pick all the way through my eye. "Nah, the two of them had a difference of definition. He thought he was dating her; she was just playing the field. You should thank me; I took one for the team with that one." As far as I was concerned, I really had. "Dude, I'm serious." I hiccuped and burped at the same time, and that shit burned like hell. "She had a bush on her only Moses could've burned. I had to wander around in the wilderness to get to the Promised Land—and in the days before

GPS. Felt like our ancestors, wandering in the desert for forty years."

The look on Levi's face suggested he was not following my logic and he shook his head. "Heard she's single again; no update on the bush, I'm afraid. Probably worse these days. Chewbacca status, maybe."

"Hell, no." I crossed myself, which made even less sense, because I was pretty sure I did it backward.

We were not Catholic.

I'd knocked off early for the day and went home to a bottle of bourbon for dinner. There was nothing in my stomach to absorb the liquid stupidity. "You hear of the freshman fifteen?"

Levi smirked and turned to grab a glass from the cabinet, filling it with water. "Yeah, I heard she put on a little weight. Having five kids will do that to you."

That had been my one and only indiscretion, during a time Cait decided she wanted to play the field. Both of us had decided it wasn't worth it.

"When's the last time you fed Dawg?" he asked, and I was surprised he was letting me off the hook.

"Pretty sure I did this morning."

"Bullshit." He snatched the empty glass from my hand. "Couple of mangled cans out on the front porch. Poor thing's so desperate for food, he's turned into a fucking can opener."

Come to think of it, I wasn't sure the last time I'd fed him. Maybe the poor old boy was better off at the Rotti rescue I'd picked him up from three years earlier, when he'd been a gift for the boys. They'd have been so mad at me for the way I'd neglected him lately, incapable of taking care of anything.

"Don't make me take him home with me. I'd take you home too, but I don't feel like waking up in the primate house. Maybe if you'd shower once in a while, you'd be welcome in polite company."

Levi's house was a freaking sanctuary and I was afraid to even stand on his front porch. He was a neat freak and I'd have blamed the Army, but the truth was that he'd always been. He'd been good at everything right from the start. He was the only Benson brother who had his shit together, even though he should've been a mess.

Me? Pffft, I was average. Right in the middle, just like I'd always been: the middle child, three of five.

Not the top and not the bottom.

The middle of my class.

Not too great at anything, but not total shit either.

Nothing special.

Except for Cait: she'd made me special, when I hadn't deserved so much as a second glance from her.

"No, Jude." Levi's voice was soft. "You're doing it again."

It was my face that gave me away, starting to slide downward into the scowl I'd worn the last few hundred days. It usually preceded some pretty unmanly things; things I wasn't about to allow to happen in front of my brother, so I swallowed hard and did my best to man up, even if my best wasn't very good.

"I miss them, man. This house was a home with them in it. Those wild little boys were pure, wonderful chaos." Fuck, I was losing the battle. A tear slipped out and I watched Levi's throat bob like he was trying to swallow a cactus—and failing.

"Pretty sure she wouldn't want you suffering like this." He turned away to open the refrigerator and I was surprised to see there was food in it. I'd been living off easy pantry shit for months and my stepmother saw to it I got a solid noon meal every day at the farm.

"Who put that in there?" I asked, surprised when Levi turned around and set a loaf of bread, then some eggs and cheese on the wide butcher block-topped island. It was the one he'd made for Cait and me as a wedding gift.

"Donna did, dipshit. She's worried sick about your worthless ass. I blame you if she dies young."

Dad deserved Donna, but we didn't. We'd made her life a living hell for years, doing all the things that a group of adult brothers did to stress out the woman who wasn't quite their mother but still gamely took on the responsibilities.

Donna was good people. She'd been trying to save us from ourselves for almost twenty years and clearly lived in perpetual hope, but not so much in reality. She was delusional in the most hopeful, kindhearted way.

"What is this?" I asked, gesturing toward the food he'd dumped on the counter and sinking down onto one of the stools.

"Cooking for you, stupid." He rolled his eyes at me before I heard one of the deep drawers roll open and there was the clang of cast iron as he pulled out a pan. "Been cooking for myself long enough; I have a pretty good idea of what I'm doing." He pursed his lips, an expression my sister used when she thought I was being an idiot. Those two had some kind of weird telepathic link.

"Don't feel like writing your obituary anytime soon; writing one for the boys was enough."

He was right, but it made my eyes fill again and he reached across the island to squeeze my shoulder with one massive hand. It fucking hurt, mostly because after all these years the guy still didn't know his size.

"Wish I'd been with them." My voice scraped and I lifted a shirtsleeve to wipe at my cheeks while he fished a bottle of pain pills from a cabinet, probably so he didn't have to watch me cry like a little bitch.

"They didn't suffer, Jude." His voice was soft as he slid a pan onto the stove, the air thick with grief while he twisted the dial and I swear I saw him lift an arm to swipe at his face. "You're the one doin' all the suffering."

Maybe I was, but it wasn't enough. My sister said it was something called survivor's guilt, when we had video chats. She was a trauma therapist, something I'd never understood—never wanted to understand—and now I did all too well. She'd gotten me hooked up with a therapist friend of hers who left no stone unturned when we met, and it hurt like hell. It was guaranteed that, by the end of our sessions, I'd be blubbering like a baby. He just sat there waiting for me, letting me fight it, then give in, and finally let some of it out.

Ashley and I had never been real close and that was my fault. I was a tease and she said I was a mean one. Because I liked to pick on her, she thought for a long time it meant I hated her and it had only been over the past year we'd mended a rift I hadn't realized was there.

"You're gonna get something besides bourbon in your stomach and then you're gonna shower." Levi slid a plate full of cheesy eggs and toast in front of me and my stomach lurched dangerously. "You do that while I feed the dog—I've changed my mind, by the way. I'm taking him home with me. He needs to be saved from you."

That really would be the end of Levi's sanity: a giant, slobbering hairball shedding all over his pristine house. He'd have to mist liquid Xanax through the vents to keep from losing his shit, because Dawg would absolutely sit on his sofa and sleep in his bed.

"Gonna make you a green juice while you shower, so you don't end up with rickets or scurvy or something weird and pointless and completely avoidable."

I snorted, carefully chewing and swallowing, finally deciding I was actually hungry. I'd forgotten what that felt like, having called the sick feeling in the pit of my stomach by another name for a long time.

Levi had always been our mother hen, as much as he could be, after we lost Ma. He got his shit together the fastest of any of us and he'd never complained about all the laundry, the cooking, or the chores around the house that kept the place from falling apart.

"Thanks." I pushed the plate slowly toward him, struggling with the words I knew were wildly insufficient. "Suppose I'll go see if I have any clean towels."

"Go on." The tiniest smile touched his mouth. "I'll clothes-pin my nose and throw in a load of laundry while you're in the shower."

Chapter Two

Beckett

"Can I help you?"

The blond giant walking out of the cattle barn was not what I'd expected. The man I'd been corresponding with had been interested in estate planning and business management. This guy looked close to my age, which was typically not an age when estate planning was considered in such thoughtful detail.

"Uh, I'm here to meet with Levi Benson?" I squinted against the sharp autumn sunshine. The rays no longer had the golden-yellow filter of summer, and the bright blue-white of an early fall day pierced my eyeballs.

"That would be me." The big man looked suspicious. "I don't have any meetings today."

About that...

"I have a funeral to attend tomorrow, so I'm a day early."

He looked at me like I'd grown another head.

"Beckett?"

I nodded. "In the flesh and at your service." I stepped forward, my right hand shooting out like I'd released a spring.

"Beckett." He looked dazed. "Uh ... shit. Beg your pardon, but ... didn't realize you were a lady."

"I get that a lot." I shrugged. "My parents thought it would be cute to name me after my grandpa. It didn't seem to bother them when I made an appearance as a girl. The name stuck anyway."

He nodded, like that settled it. "Well, I suppose we'll see how this goes. Just give me a minute to fetch my brother. He's the one taking over; I'm just facilitating for the time being. Gonna take a minute to get him back on his feet."

I didn't ask why that was the case, because it didn't feel like any of my business, and I tried not to wince when he put a thumb and middle finger to his lips and blew a shrill blast.

"Fuuuck off," rolled out of one of the sheds a bit further back on the property and I watched as another blond man emerged, wiping his hands on a rag. "I'm not a damn dog."

The man in front of me grinned. "That would be Judah, the boss man—eventually."

Neither of them were what I'd expected. Levi was attractive in a rough sort of way, a man who was clearly used to hard work. But Judah was gorgeous. He was a little shorter than Levi, his features similar but his cheekbones softer, his lips a little fuller.

His eyes, though—I noticed those immediately, because his crystal-blue eyes were flat and dull. There was no soul in them.

This was going to be a problem. I had what my sister sneeringly described as a "fallen angel complex," and Judah looked like one, a grease smear on one sharp cheek that my fingers itched to wipe off.

Working with this man, in any capacity, would not end well.

"You Jehovah's Witness?" Judah eyed my soft shirt, buttoned all the way up to my neck, bootcut jeans and work boots on my feet. I should probably have shown up looking a little more professional, but it was a farm for God's sake, and I'd been driving for the last two days. I was barely able to see straight any longer, let alone coordinate a feminine outfit. Pink plaid had been the best I could do under the circumstances.

"This is Beckett," Levi offered helpfully, and I caught the smirk on his face when he turned to the man who was obviously his brother.

Judah scratched his head slowly, the thick fingers of one big hand sliding through golden-blond hair that was just a little bit too long. He looked at his brother with some suspicion. "Okay, who's Beckett?"

"Bec," I supplied helpfully, and two sets of cold blue eyes swiveled back to me. "Most people just call me Bec. I'm a consultant—applied for the full-time management position your brother posted." I gestured toward Levi.

"Management position." Judah's lips tightened as he shot a look at his brother. "Babysitter."

"Business management," I reiterated, "and I'm damn good at what I do. I take hobbies and turn them into real money." I stood a little straighter, annoyed. Most people were more professional about this. "I worked with a consulting firm in Texas until recently."

"She did." Levi confirmed it in a strong voice. "Ash told me about it. Said her neighbor hired a manager from the same outfit a while back."

Ah, so that was how he'd found me.

"Will." I smiled when I said it. I'd worked with Will DeSantis in the past, but he'd made a beeline for Montana in the midst of what I'd teased was a midlife crisis. It seemed to have worked out well enough for him though, considering he'd landed the woman of his dreams.

"And what brings you to Minnesota from Texas?"

It was becoming remarkably clear that Judah Benson had no idea I was coming, or that his brother had already hired me.

"The transfer of ownership is what brings me." I shrugged. "Levi said you're taking over the farm from your father. He wanted some help with the general estate planning and transfer and said you needed to get things in order if you were going to go bigger."

I'd worked with plenty of commercial farms in the past. This would be a little different, taking them from a family-run operation to something of real size.

This family was going to fight diversification, I already knew it.

"Dad's retiring?" Judah looked over at Levi, his handsome face wrinkled up in confusion.

"Something you'd have known if you'd really been here and not slumming it with your buddy Jack all these months." Levi's voice was soft and I saw something pass between the two of them that seemed to hint at grief and remorse.

I thought better of asking who Jack was, since I had a suspicion.

Judah huffed and folded thick arms over a not-inconsiderable chest. "Been here the whole time."

"No." Levi's voice was still gentle. "Not really."

My eyes ping-ponged between the two of them, hoping for an explanation I knew I wasn't going to get.

"Well." I shoved my hands into my back pockets, fully aware that Judah was refusing to look at me after his initial assessment. "Like I said, I have a funeral to attend tomorrow. If it's of no difference to anyone, I prefer to unpack today so I can return the trailer."

Judah's lip curled a little. "Do *not* tell me you're putting her in the cabin. That pile of shit should be burned in a training exercise."

Well, this sounded promising. I should probably have asked a little more about the accommodations when I'd been offered an on-site house. It had been something that made up for the fact the intriguing offer fell a little short of my salary expectations, but I didn't have better options. It had been announced only a few weeks earlier that my employer was relocating the base of operations to South Dakota—immediately—and there was nothing and no one waiting for me in Pierre.

As of the prior Friday morning, I'd lost the reason I'd taken a job in Minnesota. It was only days after I'd committed to an offer from Levi Benson, the Benson farm being a mere fifty miles from where my father lived. The timing had seemed fortuitous and when my employer asked if I'd relocate to South Dakota, I knew what I had to do. Dad hadn't been well for the past year and it seemed it was in the stars to follow the random job offer that would put me just over an hour's drive from him. And now I was here ... and Dad wasn't.

He hadn't even known I was coming.

"The cabin probably needs a little work," Levi admitted. "I promise I'll get to it. This was kinda ... last-minute." He swallowed hard and I wondered what it was he wasn't saying.

Whatever it was, Judah hung his head.

"Okay, well ... sorry I'm a day early. I hope I haven't thrown a wrench into your plans. Do you need to go through anything with me, since I won't be here tomorrow?"

"We'll sort it out on Friday. If you want, I'll drive you back to the cabin and help you get settled." He turned his head sharply. "Could use your help, Jude—you comin'?"

"Fine." The man glared at me like I was the enemy and started marching toward the truck and trailer I'd left parked on the driveway that ran up to a lovely farmhouse with a manicured hydrangea border. A woman lived in that house, I had no doubt.

No man I'd ever met would have given a shit about the pretty blue flowers.

"It would seem the new boss is a bit..." I was searching for a combination of words that didn't include or even imply the word *asshole*.

"Prickly? Standoffish? A total dick? Yeah." Levi cleared his throat. "I should have warned you about that, but to be fair, I honestly thought you were a dude. Would've probably made things a little different."

Apparently that was what happened when you conducted the entire interview process over the course of exactly three emails.

"Never been a dude, with no plans to be one." I grinned at him and he cracked the smallest smile.

"Apologies in advance, Ms. Beckett; we're a little rough around here." He gestured in a semi-circle and I presumed he was talking about the people, because the farm itself was well kept from what I could see.

"Don't got all day!" Judah hollered from where he stood near the truck and I fished the key fob from my pocket to unlock the doors. It was pretty obvious this guy was going to be an enormous pain in my ass, so it made sense to brace myself now.

"He's not usually like this." Levi cleared his throat and started a slow walk toward the truck, indicating I should follow. "He's ... uh ... been through a lot lately."

Great, so I really was a babysitter.

I gestured that Levi should drive, since I had no idea where this cabin was, and he carefully backed the loaded trailer down the drive and twisted the wheel to pivot. "House is a little way further—got your own driveway, at least." He smiled tightly at me without meeting my eyes and I could feel Judah's gaze burning into me from the backseat. There was something acrid in the cab, something that smelled like hostility, and I couldn't decide whether it was directed at Levi or at me.

From a distance, the little house was charming. It was a small two-story with a front porch. It could use a fresh coat of white paint, but I didn't see any holes in the roof and everything seemed solid.

"We try to come out and check on it every now and then," Levi said as he pulled into the short driveway. "This was the original house on the property—belonged to our grandparents."

The surprise probably showed on my face, because I'd assumed the farmhouse was the original homestead.

"As long as it has running water and electricity, I can probably make it work." My voice sounded far more confident than I felt. I'd learned in the past few years how to be reasonably self-sufficient and there were very few things that I couldn't figure out with the help of YouTube.

"Well..." Levi winced. "Electricity's on tomorrow, but I suppose Donna's got some flashlights and candles up at the house."

Oh good, I could spend my first night in a strange little house without electricity. Probably not the time to tell either of them a grown-ass, middle-aged woman was afraid of the dark—and certainly not why.

"Maybe there's a fireplace?" I asked hopefully. I wasn't worried about staying warm so much as I was about maintaining some kind of light source.

"Gotta have the chimney swept." Judah's voice was rough. "Probably got a family of squirrels living in it and I don't suppose Gramps was able to do much upkeep the last few years he was around. Hasn't really been used much since then."

Levi made a sound like a hum and removed a key from a ring that held only five other keys, passing it to me without a word and I popped the door open, stepping off the running board to take in my new surroundings.

The sound of the trailer door rolling up snapped me out of my reverie and I turned toward the little house, half-listening to Judah grumble as Levi gave him instructions and boxes and furniture began to appear on the driveway.

The storm door creaked on its hydraulic arm as I pulled it open, and by instinct I tried the knob before inserting the key. The door swung open, a foul smell rushing out to meet me and I took a step back in alarm, letting the storm door wind shut.

"That's weird." Levi was right behind me with boxes in his arms. "That should've been locked."

"Something's dead in there," I said, immediately certain I'd just made the worst decision of my life.

"Could be." He shrugged and nodded his head at the screen door like I should open it. I swung it wide to let him through and followed closely behind as he stepped through and gagged. "Dear Lord above us. Septic must have gone."

I knew enough about septic systems to know this smell was indicative of very, very bad things.

I held a hand over my nose and mouth as I followed him through a small living room and into an eat-in kitchen. The place was small and dark and I hurried to the window to slide the lower pane up on the track.

"Holy fucknuts!" Judah shouted from the living room and the door creaked behind him as I heard the muffled thump of boxes hitting the floor. I'd never heard this expression before. "Who's living in the primate house now?" He started laughing, something that sounded a little unhinged and maniacal, and I heard boots begin to thump up the narrow center staircase. Then a gagging, coughing fit and a run-on series of *fuck-fuck-fucks* that mumbled off into something nonsensical, then, "Found it!"

There was another thing I knew about septic systems, and it was that the problem was usually identified at the lowest-lying drain in the house. Whatever this was, it was really not good if it was upstairs.

Levi opened the rest of the windows on the ground floor before he too stomped up the stairs and I leaned against the dusty formica counter with something that felt like tears scratching at my eyeballs.

"Good news." Levi was back just before I could succumb to a breakdown and his expression made me think the words were filled with false bravado. "It's not the septic."

"That's the good news?"

It didn't matter what it was; it was clear to me I'd be sleeping in the truck tonight.

"Uh, well..." He lifted a hand to scratch the back of his neck. "Looks like someone broke into the house a while back and had a party upstairs."

My eyes narrowed.

"We got some neighbors down that way—" he pointed with two fingers toward the refrigerator. "Not real fond of us. Didn't get any better when they asked to buy some of our land a couple years back and we told 'em we didn't have any to sell."

That seemed like a fair point from the Benson side, if you asked me. "If you weren't looking to sell..." I shrugged.

"Exactly." He nodded. "But the two oldest took offense. They wanna sell their land for development; been shoppin' it around for a while."

"Let me guess." I leaned my face toward the window to take a gulp of fresh air. "Their land borders yours somewhere, so they want more to really sweeten the offering."

Levi nodded slowly. "About a half mile from here."

Great, so now I was in the middle of a turf war and the boss already hated me. Things just continued to improve.

I could hear a slow trickling sound from somewhere upstairs and Judah's coughing was punctuated by sharp noises I knew to be dry heaving.

"Seems the boys must've gone hunting sometime last fall," Judah called, and I waited for the other shoe to drop. "Filled up the bathtub with what was probably deer guts. Left that shit there to marinate, those fuckers."

I patted my pocket to make sure the truck's key fob was there, before realizing it was still in Levi's pocket. I was entertaining the idea of loading my stuff back into the trailer and driving straight back to Texas, where even less waited for me.

I shook my head slowly. "You knew I was coming tomorrow, but no one bothered to check the house to make sure it was livable?"

"Sorry." Levi hung his head again. "Had my hands a little too full lately, with that one." He pointed to the ceiling, where the sounds continued. "And the farm. Truth is that once we get the paperwork settled and things humming along, I'm stepping back. Away. Whatever. That's why you're here."

"What do you suggest I do about the smell?" I asked, choosing not to address that very heavy confession, one surely loaded with details to come.

"Well ... Judah's doing what he can now. Suppose we'll finish unloading the trailer and leave the upstairs windows open overnight. While you're away tomorrow I'll see about getting a new bathtub in here. Not sure it's a one-day job, but we'll give it a look—call in the cavalry if we have to."

I followed Levi back outside and while he single-handedly carried in several large pieces of furniture, I gulped the fresh air and then followed him back inside with box after box. At least we could unload and I could return the trailer.

"Fuck me with a rusty pitchfork." Judah was clomping back down the stairs, his arms smeared with something mysterious and his eyes bloodshot. "Worse than pig shit—and ain't nothin' worse than pig shit."

"Chickens," I offered, and Judah's eyes raised to meet mine—really meet mine——for the first time. They were a clear ocean blue, the color you only saw on the intracoastal side of the Atlantic. It took me a second to pick up the thread I'd dropped so suddenly. "There's a huge chicken farm and processing plant twenty miles from where I lived in Texas. They liquefy the droppings because they're so acidic, then spray them on the fields after the crops are off. God save the person driving past those fields on the day they're spraying."

Levi nodded. "Got a few chicken operations here, too. You're right about that. Pretty vicious stink; burn your sinuses right out."

"She can't stay in this." It was Judah, who'd stepped past me to wash up at the kitchen sink, and I was surprised when water trickled from the faucet. "Probably got some tools in the garage." He looked over his shoulder at Levi. "Need to get that tub out of there and gonna have to repaint, too. Smell's probably seeped into the walls."

I rubbed a hand slowly across my face, feeling incredibly small and defeated.

"We'll get the tub out," Levi said firmly. "Jude, you'll put Beckett up at your place tonight."

Judah froze at the sink at the same time I lifted my arms to cross over my chest. *Absolutely fucking not.* "Not necessary. If I can't handle the smell, I'll sleep in the truck. Or find a hotel. Or something."

"You'll do no such thing." Levi sounded annoyed, his eyes swiveling to me. "He's got a perfectly good house and he lives the closest of any of us. Plenty of room. Reasonably clean. I can vouch for him; you're safe."

That didn't make me feel any better, but it wasn't for any of the usual reasons.

Judah still hadn't moved from where he stood at the sink, the water still trickling, his hands braced on the countertop. I had no idea what was this guy's problem, but I knew one thing: My new boss was about to make my life a living hell.

Chapter Three

Judah

There was a stranger in my house.

I rolled again in my bed and punched at the pillow.

Beckett hadn't said a thing as she'd followed me inside. It had been late, because it took Levi and me a long time to clean the tub, then remove the cast iron monster and flip it on its side to lug it down the stairs. We left it beside the garage, upside down for the time being, and I could tell Levi was steamed those assholes had broken into the house. There was no doubt it had been them. There was the greasy smear of a livestock marker across the open stretch of wall by the sink, more *fucks* than I'd ever seen in my life, the only thing I could read and about the only thing they could actually spell. I was pretty sure it was all derogatory, probably something about the Bensons being selfish dicks, but those two were hardly literate, so the scribbles were probably nothing more than pointless vandalism.

I'd managed a couple freezer pizzas and a few beers and she hadn't put up a word of complaint. Then I showed her to the guest room that hadn't been used since the memorial service. I hadn't even thought to check if the bed had fresh sheets, but the room was pristine and I knew I owed Donna some flowers.

Hell, I owed my stepmother a lot more than just flowers.

I knew why I couldn't sleep, and it was because I hadn't had my customary five fingers of bourbon. It was the only sleep aid that had been working the last several months, and by one I gave up and heaved myself out of bed. I was exhausted, but sleep was nowhere to be found and the memories of my wife, the few sweet ones that haunted me in the dark, were crawling into my bed to wrap cold fingers around me.

"Fuck!" The exclamation was loud and I heard the sharp intake of breath when I barked the curse. I hadn't expected the shadowy figure at the small kitchen table, and she startled when I shouted.

"I'm sorry." Her voice was raspy, like she'd been crying, and immediately I felt like an asshole. The beautiful woman with the mahogany hair that I'd been trying not to look at all day was sitting at my kitchen table in thin pajamas, all of that glorious hair finally loose and falling down her back in soft waves.

A lightning bolt of shame just about took me out at the knees. I'd just been thinking about my wife and now I was ogling this woman in my kitchen. *Get it together, asshole.*

"Nothing to be sorry about." I sounded like I'd been swallowing rocks. "Guess you couldn't sleep either."

She drew in a deep inhale through a sniffle and I tore a couple paper towels off the roll to drop onto the kitchen table. This was awkward and I didn't know what to do. I'd never been good with tears, even when they'd been Cait's, and I was even more awkward with a stranger's pain.

"Thank you."

I heard her sniffle again as I turned toward the cabinets and dug around for a minute. I was pretty sure I had an emergency bottle stashed in there somewhere and this qualified as an emergency, since I hadn't gotten the chance to replenish my stash and the meager groceries in my fridge that afternoon.

"Ha!" The sound was sharp and victorious and I winced. "Sorry—found what I was looking for."

Her eyes were huge in the dim light from the stove hood and I held the bottle in the air. "Liquid sleep."

"Liquid lots of things—poor decisions, mostly," she said, wiping her nose with the scratchy paper towel.

Taking two mismatched glasses from the cabinet, I poured what I considered two generous portions before putting the bottle back. Levi would kill me if he knew I'd held out on him, purposely decanting and mislabeling a bottle so he wouldn't find it when he swept the house.

I really had stooped to new lows.

Sliding one glass across the table to her, I lowered myself into a chair and stared down into my drink. Looking at her didn't seem like a good idea at the moment and she wasn't real comfortable around me to begin with—could be that was my fault. I'd been told more than once that I gave strong asshole vibes, even before opening my mouth to remove all doubt.

"Why can't you sleep?" Her voice was low and pleasant and she turned the glass slowly on the old wooden table.

"Don't sleep much at all anymore," I admitted slowly. "Got too much to think about when I shut my eyes."

She nodded slowly, tucking her bottom lip under her top teeth. Then, "Yeah. I've always been an insomniac, but it's gotten worse lately." She lifted the glass to her lips and took a fast, hard swallow, coughing into her fist. "Yuck," she hissed. "Cinnamon."

"Yeah." I hung my head a little. "Emergency bottle. Not my first choice."

She snorted a little. "Toothpaste-flavored whiskey. Been a while."

There was a question I wasn't going to ask, and I choked down my own swallow of liquid fire.

"Not something I need to make a habit," she rasped and I raised my eyes slowly, because my guilty conscience was poking me in the ribs. "This stuff has killed a few people in my family; we seem to have a hard time staying away from it, even when we know it's putting us into an early grave."

I nodded slowly. Levi had given up drinking years earlier and Ashley had confessed she struggled with alcoholism for a very long time. The signs were all there: When the going got tough, the Bensons turned to the bottle.

"Understand that," I said. "Having my own struggle with it lately." I couldn't believe I'd said it out loud, because it was something I hadn't even admitted to myself, and now I'd blurted it right out to a stranger. Maybe that was what Donna called self-awareness, or progress.

"Everyone thinks they have a good reason." She lifted her glass for another swallow and I wondered what was her reason.

"Yours?" I asked, and she shook her head. "Sorry, that wasn't fair. None of my business."

"My dad." She cleared her throat and leaned back in her chair. "He drank hard his whole life, but he upped his game when my mom passed. I should've been here to save him."

"He was an adult; made his own choices." It was out of my mouth before I could stop it and I winced again, because so was I. What was my excuse?

"An adult who couldn't cope." She swirled the glass a little. "He was lost without my mom; they got married when they were still kids."

I didn't ask what took her mom, choosing to take another chug of poison.

"She was only fifty years old," she said slowly. "Still had so much life left to live."

"Damn." That was all I had. I wasn't the only one suffering and the realization was a little humbling.

"What's your story?" she asked suddenly and I realized her glass was lower than mine. It was against my better judgment, but I stood to retrieve the bottle, pouring a few more fingers into her glass. Just for tonight we could exercise a little bad judgment, even though we'd probably pay a hefty price in the morning.

I wasn't sure I could find the words—the ones that didn't turn me into a blubbering mess—and I pointed toward the pictures clipped to the fridge with farm implement magnets. Two finger paintings and a memorial card. That was all I had left of them, other than a few photo albums and some framed pictures hanging in the living room.

We hadn't been able to find enough to bury.

"When did it happen?" Her eyes held mine, something that made me immediately uncomfortable, because I couldn't have looked away if I wanted to. Something about her captivated me against my will.

"A year and nine months ago, take a little." I cleared my throat. "It was on the way back from my sister's wedding in Montana."

"Fuck." Her voice was soft, and she clapped a hand over her mouth like she couldn't believe she'd said it.

"My wife was a pilot." The words tasted weird even after all these years. Cait had been in the Air Force for a while; it was how she paid for her schooling.

Beckett's eyebrows raised slightly but she didn't push, even though I wasn't making sense yet.

"I begged her to quit, because I have a fear of flying." I was going to need more and I splashed additional liquid into my glass. "She begged me to quit farming; she had a healthy fear of the machinery." My face twisted up into an ugly smile. "I told her I'd quit when she did."

Beckett waited.

"She took a new job a few years ago. Private pilot, I guess. Some big businessman." I shrugged.

Beckett nodded. I didn't have to tell her I hadn't upheld my end of the bargain.

I took a huge chug of the fire left in my glass, steeling myself for the abbreviated version when Beckett held up a hand, her palm facing me. "It's okay," she said softly. "It's too soon and you're not ready to tell the whole thing. I get that." Then she nodded once and slammed back the rest of her drink. "I have to be up early to make the drive. Thanks for the sedative."

She rinsed the cup and tucked it into the dishwasher, then lifted her hand in an awkward wave before disappearing through the framed opening that led to the hallway.

I'd wanted to scare her off earlier in the day—meant to, but she'd done it all by herself. *Look at that,* I thought, pouring myself what amounted to a shot before I slammed it back and stood to put the bottle back in the cabinet.

The floorboards of the old house creaked under my not-inconsiderable weight as I made my way through the kitchen, drifting down the short hallway toward the bedroom where I slept alone. The house was silent, far too quiet for my liking, like it always was, and I hoped the whiskey hit me before the memories crawled into bed with me and tried to snuggle up once more.

When I dragged myself out of bed at six, I could smell coffee. It was a weird thing, something that tricked me as I woke, telling me things were normal. That Cait was up making breakfast before she saw the boys off to school and disappeared to the little office cabin I'd built for her, set back from the house.

The stab of grief was sharp and painful when I realized it wasn't my wife at all, and I choked down the bile that threatened to fill my mouth.

There was no one in the kitchen when I finally drifted out, well aware I smelled like a water buffalo—or maybe it was a musk ox. It was ripe and unpleasant, but I'd made the conscious decision to seek out coffee before a shower, so there was no one to blame but myself.

There were no notes, which might have been weird, but there was a pan of still-warm scrambled eggs and potatoes on the stove, and for that I was grateful. My breakfasts in the past months had been cold cereal or protein bars, and coffee with a generous pour of bourbon.

It seemed like cinnamon whiskey was going to be my additive today, because something needed to take the edge off the elephant sitting on my forehead, a dull, pounding weight.

"Look what the cat dragged in."

I held a hand over my head, middle finger fully extended, as I got out of my truck. Ben was the only one who didn't treat me with kid gloves, because my youngest brother's asshole setting was his *only* setting. Ben had no filter and we'd all known for years that it was a crapshoot as to what came out of his mouth next.

It also meant that he'd been the most insensitive asshole of all my brothers in the past months, and I'd come to suspect it was because he didn't know how to handle what I was going through.

"About time you showed up," he called, and I grabbed the travel tumbler out of the truck's door compartment before turning to face him.

"It's seven in the damn morning, Benjamin. Fuck off."

"Morning milking's at five and you know that."

I could hear the sounds in the distance, the chug and whoosh of the pipeline that fed the milk from each machine into the enormous bulk tank in the milk house. The morning milking was drawing to a close. Someone was already in the milkhouse, hosing things down, performing cleanup. The enormous tanker truck would be here soon to collect it, hauling it to the processing plant, something run by the cooperative with whom we were contracted.

"Not sure what you're doing out here." I gave him the hairy eyeball.

"Waitin' on you, boss man." He grinned and ran a hand over his scruffy beard. If he let that thing go on much longer he was going to need a lawnmower to take it off his face. "Heard Tweedle-Dee and Tweedle-Dum were at it again. Levi said to catch you first thing so we could go pick up a new tub. You got measurements?" I sighed. Of course I didn't have measurements, which meant we'd have to go back to the cabin and then drive all the way into the city to pick up a new one from one of those big box stores I hated with a passion.

"Heard you got a new boss. Bet Levi's afraid puttin' you in charge will have this place going tits-up in no time."

"Fuck off." I opened the truck door and put the coffee right back into the holder. I wasn't ready to talk about Levi's massive overstep, or the fact that no one had told me Dad was retiring and I was taking over the farm.

No one had asked if I wanted it.

"Heard she's real pretty, too. That should make the days around here more fun."

"What *are* you doing, Ben? Don't you have somewhere else to be?"

Ben had his own repair business that he ran out of the gigantic machine shed on his property. Farmers towed broken machinery to his shop and he repaired the mangled, welded the broken, and forged new parts from the aether when he couldn't salvage something from his junkyard stash. The three of us called him a prehistoric surgeon, his talents employed on aging, ailing machinery.

"Corn's finally startin' to dry out—seems awful late this year," he said as he opened the door on the opposite side and dropped into the truck.

He was right. I'd noticed on my drive over that the tassels were finally brown, which meant harvest was coming up soon. I preferred to get it off the fields before they turned muddy with late fall rains, but some farmers left theirs standing until the ground froze over. Crops were unpredictable because the weather was a wild thing, and that was always what truly dictated the harvest season.

It was a forty-five minute drive to our nearest big box store and after collecting the measurements of the old bathtub, we made the trip. The two of us secured the huge box in the bed of my truck and made the drive back to the cabin after stopping for a burger and fries for the overgrown baby who was my passenger. Ben ate like he was part wooly mammoth, which is to say indiscriminately—and constantly—always shoving more crap in his mouth, and he was big enough to get away with it.

Ben could have carried the new tub up the stairs by himself, but he let me feel like I was helping and he gagged a little as he kicked the cardboard box back down the stairs. "Smells like a wolverine den in here. The fuck did those assholes do, anyway, that you had to put in a new tub?"

"Deer guts, we think." I was checking the sturdiness of the joists where the newer, much lighter tub would be fitted into place.

"Sick fuckers," he muttered. "What's our game plan?"

It was an unspoken rule that, after all the nasty pranks the Avila boys had played on us over the years, we had to one-up them. Our childish pranks had always bordered on excessive, because we'd never really liked one another, going all the way back as far as I could remember. But it was when they decided it was time to start selling off the family farm so their parents could retire in Argentina that things turned truly ugly. For whatever reason, they'd decided we were standing between them and a return to the land of their ancestors—well, the land of somebody's ancestors, because after a few generations of intermarrying with the local Dutch population, the only thing Argentinian about the Avila boys was their names.

We managed to fit the tub in place and Ben connected all the plumbing while I hauled out the massive box and brought in cans of paint we'd picked up in the city. It occurred to me we should have asked Beckett what color she preferred, but my vote was a plain, boring white paint, so that was what we were putting on the walls.

"Good thing you only gotta oversee the farm," Ben called from the bathroom and the dig was there, that my contributions were not all that meaningful.

I pushed an old vanity table and the solid oak dresser toward the center of the room while I thought about what my life would look like if Dad really wanted me to manage things. I was the only one who'd never forged a clear path for myself, happy to drift along because I had Cait and the boys to focus on, and farm life was good enough for me.

"Good thing I don't have to count on you for any of it," I called back as I poured paint into a tray and started to run a roller over the walls.

"Diana's gone," rolled out of the bathroom in a matter-of-fact tone, and Ben got what he wanted: I froze, the roller only halfway up the wall. "Packed up her shit, said she was done, and drove off madder 'n a hornet."

I had some idea as to why that had happened. Like most women, Diana had stuck around for almost a year and when it became painfully apparent to her that my baby brother would never be tied down, she cut her losses.

"Shame," I called back, coughing. The paint was making my eyes water, even with the windows wide open. "She was a pretty girl."

"Too big for her britches." Ben snorted, and there was a dangerous squeal that sounded like the tensile strength of a pipe being tested. But he didn't elaborate, so I left that one alone, because it took Ben a long time to wrap his head around things and relationships weren't his strong suit—had never been.

Most of us could say that.

"Dan tell you he's gettin' a divorce?"

I dropped the paint roller.

"Yep." Ben carried on like I hadn't just suffered a stroke in the next room.

Dan had been with Lindsey since college and though they'd married much later than she would have liked, that was a breakup I'd never seen coming.

"Turns out she's been carryin' on with some guy from work." I could hear the distaste in his voice. "Got some kinda work transfer to Tennessee or Ohio or Alaska—hell if I know. Somewhere that's not here."

I sank to the floor, knowing what this meant for my other brother: an ugly, looming custody battle.

The Benson boys were falling apart.

Chapter Four

Beckett

It had been one of the longest, most horrible days of my life and all I wanted to do was go home and unpack with the help of the bottle of wine one of the well-meaning ladies brought as a sympathy gift.

Who brings a bottle of wine to the funeral of a man who died of liver failure?

Maybe that was a question for another time.

There was a light on in the house but no trucks in the driveway, and I sat there for a moment with my arms crossed over the steering wheel. I'd been crying the whole way back and I had a pretty good idea of what I looked like: puffy, blotchy, with bloodshot eyes.

The door wasn't locked, something that alarmed me, and I stepped in to strong paint fumes and an enormous man standing in my living room, stacking books into the built-in shelving.

"Levi?" I asked, somewhat uncertainly, and the man turned around with a tight smile on his face.

"Called in some reinforcements today and got most things handled in here." He gestured around him and I realized there were no boxes left in the living room. "Kitchen's unpacked, too—put all your girl stuff upstairs for you to handle."

I couldn't decide whether I was grateful or furious and the look he gave me was nervous. "Hope that's okay. Figured it was the best we could do to help since the place was a wreck." He shrugged.

I nodded slowly and drifted into the kitchen to find the cupboards full of my things, the small table and chairs in place near the window, and I sank onto one of the stools at the small island as the enormity of the day hit me.

"Got your bed set up," Levi called from the living room. "Didn't want to dig through all your master bedroom boxes, though—'fraid you're on your own for makin' it."

"Thanks." My voice was weak and I wondered what was in the pantry that I could turn into a meal.

"Put a gallon of milk and a couple dozen eggs in the fridge for you." Levi's voice was closer and I looked up to see the giant standing in the doorway that led to the living room. "Figured you hadn't gotten to the store yet. Ben's got a couple turkeys he's butchering this weekend; suppose he'll bring some meat by."

That was a brother I had yet to meet and I nodded again, grateful for the act of kindness but incapable of using my words.

I'd used *so* many words today.

"Well, got you mostly squared away." Levi's eyes dropped to the bottle I'd set on the countertop and he crossed the small room to retrieve a drinking glass from the cabinet. "Ain't gonna fault you for not standing on ceremony after a day like today." He plunked the drinking glass down in front of me and twisted the cap off the bottle with a grin. "Gonna have to warn you nothing good comes from a bottle with a screw-off cap or a plastic cork."

I didn't ask him how he knew.

"Shower can be used tomorrow morning; caulk should be dry." He was exceedingly careful to pronounce the *l* in the word, and I clamped down on a small smile.

"Thanks." I could hardly get it out. "This was a lot of work and I'm grateful."

"I'm the one's grateful," he said, turning to leave the room. "Got a fighting chance to pull Judah's head out of his ass, cuz I wasn't gonna get anywhere with that."

I didn't ask how he anticipated I would do that, and there was the sound of a box being broken down in the other room.

"Suppose I'll put the boxes in the garage on my way out," he called. "No rush to get to the office in the morning; just roll in whenever you're ready. We'll get things sorted."

As the door closed behind him, I tipped the bottle into the glass and filled it to the top.

What the hell.

There was some kind of ungodly noise going on outside, something straight out of a horror movie, and I rolled over to squint against the early morning light. The room swayed a little when I got to my feet and stumbled to the open window to look down into the yard. There was a collection of twenty or more crows gathered around something that looked like road-kill, mere feet from the house, and I turned away in disgust.

If that wasn't a bad omen, nothing was.

I'd left the windows open to keep the air circulating through the house overnight and a chill had moved in, enough that it had crept into my bones as I slept, and I hurried to close the windows while I waited for the shower to warm.

The birds were still at it while I brewed coffee and I was grateful to Levi for the eggs and milk. I'd been too tired to attempt dinner the night before, and maybe a little too tipsy, so I mixed up some biscuits to bake while I had coffee, then scrambled some eggs. It was enough to soak up some of the cheap poison in my stomach and finally I had the strength to deal with the cacophony outside. I marched out the front door with a contractor bag and a shovel I'd snatched from the attached garage, ready to deal with whatever remains awaited me.

The birds weren't about to relinquish their bloody prize without a fuss and I took a wild swing with the shovel four or five times before the group scattered. A murder of crows indeed, I thought as I realized the pile of guts and fur was not going to fit in a single trash bag, and I turned my head quickly to throw up in the barren flower bed when I realized what it was. Abandoning the trash bags, I whipped out my phone to take a photo and quickly dug a hole where it lay.

I had a sneaking suspicion the Benson farm was down one Holstein calf today.

I was in the truck moments later, on my way to the small outbuilding I knew functioned as Command Central, and Levi looked up in surprise when I walked in. "Morning, Bec. Didn't expect you for a while yet."

I whipped out my phone and brought up the photo, passing it to him. "That's buried in front of the flower bed now. The birds were making pretty quick work of it."

A thundercloud passed over the man's face as he looked down at the screen and he pushed up from his chair. "Come with me; we'll walk and talk."

I had a pretty good idea where we were going and I followed him back out the door.

"Suppose there are a few things we'll need to go over and one of them is going to involve security, apparently." He chewed at his lip. "For the animals and possibly for you—and I should warn you now, Judah's going to be ... a lot."

Maybe he should have led with that, because he'd never once mentioned Judah when we'd discussed the job. And while I wasn't sure what it was the man could possibly have against me, it seemed like my mere presence was enough.

Levi slid a barn door across the track and I was hit in the face by the unmistakable smell of cattle and shit. For all the time I'd spent on farms, I'd never lived on a dairy farm, and adjusting to the smells as a part of my daily routine was going to take some time. There was a central walkway flanked by large cattle pens on either side, running the length of the barn, and as we passed each pen I could see Levi was counting in his head. "This one," he said finally as we neared the opposite end of the barn, one hand resting on the rail while he ran the other down his face. "We're short. Calves don't just get loose in this setup; someone came in and took him." I chose not to say anything, just nodding instead. "You get a look at what might have happened?" he asked, and I shook my head.

"It was in that shape when I walked out this morning. We can go dig it up if you'd like a look."

"Probably for the best you buried it." He shook his head slowly. "Those damn birds would've eaten the evidence in no time."

There was a shout somewhere outside the barn and I followed Levi back through the open door. Judah was thundering across the large yard, coming toward us from the direction of the house. "You really put training wheels on me, that's why?" he shouted, and I saw Levi's shoulders rise with a deep breath. "You told Dad I can't handle the responsibilities of a farm I've been working my whole life?"

"It was a condition put in place to save you from yourself, Jude." *Uh-oh.* I had a sneaking suspicion I was the condition. "You need someone to help grow this thing and run all the back room stuff. Most days, when you show up, you're half-sauced. You've got me to keep an eye on shit but I can't do all of this on my own, not anymore." He raised one big hand over his head in a gesture of frustration. "I'm building my own business. You know I can't keep an eye on you when I'm traveling."

Judah's face twisted. "Never asked you to be a babysitter." He crossed his arms over his chest and stood glowering at Levi, then at me.

"You leave her out of this." Levi's voice was low.

"Fine by me." Judah huffed. "Should've never brought her into it in the first place. She doesn't belong here."

"I buried the last person I had left on this earth yesterday." I marched toward Judah and poked a finger into his chest. "Maybe I don't belong here, but right now I don't feel like I belong *anywhere*. Get over yourself, asshole. You're not the only person grieving."

Judah stumbled back a step, his arms dropping to his sides, his mouth slack, and Levi chuckled behind me. "I believe the appropriate response is 'Yes, ma'am.'" Judah closed his mouth and raised a middle finger in the direction of his brother, but the look he gave me was absolutely withering. I'd drawn a line in the sand and he didn't like it one bit. That was fine by me, because I wasn't about to let an overgrown toddler with no impulse control trample all over me. Captain Rage Issues could just go fuck himself.

"Believe me—" Apparently I wasn't done. "I've dealt with men bigger and scarier than you." I poked him again. "One thing I don't do is quit and you can't fire me, because I wasn't your call in the first place. You need me here and some part of you knows it, so you'd better get used to this." I gestured toward my face and a little snort slipped out of Levi.

"Come on." Levi gestured we should follow him to his office. "Need both of you sitting in on this; gonna get Bec up to speed on what we do here and what we're looking to change. She's got somethin' to show you, too." I fished the phone out of my back pocket and Judah made a horrified face when I brought up the photo of the mangled calf.

"What on earth does that to a calf that size?" His eyes were wide. "One of ours?"

Levi nodded. "Taken out of one of the pens."

"Fuck around," Judah muttered. "We got a big problem ... willing to bet it's named Avila."

Chapter Five

Judah

My head was spinning by the time Levi suggested we head into the house to see what Donna had going for lunch. The last thing I was going to admit was that Beckett had some good suggestions and she saw the holes I didn't. That didn't make me like her any better, but I could respect that she seemed to be good at what she did. We decided to tackle the potential security issue after lunch and Levi told Beckett there was no time like the present to meet Dad. That was going to be a problem, because I'd never met a single woman who didn't fall immediately in love with Erik Benson. The man was charming as fuck, and with my luck he'd adore Beckett.

No one was going to side with me on this one.

"Judah Benson, those had better not be work boots in my house." Donna's back was turned to me, but I froze in place anyway. The woman had been trying to housebreak me for years and you could say I hadn't exactly taken to it.

"Yes, ma'am. Sorry." I stepped back onto the porch and unlaced my boots, leaving them outside the door.

Levi was grinning at me when I stepped back inside. "See, was that so hard?" he asked, and I knew he was talking about my words, not my boots.

"What's this, Levi?" Dad's deep voice boomed out from the stairs as he descended. "You finally get off your butt and tie down a beautiful woman?"

The look on Levi's face was priceless. I wished later that I'd had the presence of mind to whip out my phone and capture a photo for posterity, but the asshole would probably have broken my phone in retribution.

Honestly, I couldn't remember the last time Levi had a girlfriend—well no, not entirely true. I did remember, because we'd been kids and the woman in question was his daughter's mother.

His *thirty-year-old* daughter's mother, which meant that he'd probably had a decades-long dry spell, because I hadn't known him to be interested in anyone since.

So there was that.

"Dad." Levi coughed and cleared his throat. "Like you to meet Beckett, the consultant we hired to manage the transition and keep Judah on the path to righteousness."

I knew I was making a sour face, even as Dad grinned. Apparently everyone in this family thought I needed a babysitter.

"I'll show you the path to righteousness, because you're about to meet Jesus," I muttered, and Beckett gave me a sharp look that made Levi grin.

"Yeah, she's got him handled." Levi reached over and slapped my back much harder than I thought was necessary.

"Mr. Benson." Beckett's smile was genuine and sweet, something that made me realize just how pretty she really was.

Shut that shit right down. You are not ready for that.

"Beckett." Dad was all smiles. The man was just a natural flirt, he didn't even have to try. That magnetism drew women to him like moths to a flame and he had absolutely no idea he was doing it. "You wasting yourself on us out here in the middle of nowhere? No way these boys are gonna properly appreciate a beautiful woman with a brain *and* a work ethic." He shot me a wicked glare.

It was me. I wouldn't appreciate her.

Donna turned, wiping her hands on a kitchen towel, smiling at Beckett as she shook Dad's hand. "Do you boys some good," she announced. "Keep you on your toes."

I didn't like what that was probably supposed to mean.

"Knock me on my ass," I grumbled under my breath and Donna shot me the fiery eye of Sauron.

"Sorry about saddling you with this one." Ben drifted into the room and gestured in my direction, his eye on Beckett, his mouth already so full of something that the words were garbled and he threw a hand over his mouth to stop the crumbs that blew out when he spoke. "But we're fresh outta ideas."

There was a sharp slap and Levi smirked at Ben's wounded *"Ow,"* while Donna stood there shaking her head.

"This will be good for you, Jude." Her voice went soft when she stepped closer to me, pushing up on her tiptoes to wrap her arms around my shoulders. Donna was tiny and I dropped my head down so she could finish her thought in my ear. "She's lost things, too."

My eyes snapped up to Beckett, to find her watching me as I wrapped my arms around my sweet stepmom. There was something guarded and sad in her expression that made me wonder if she'd lost even more than she admitted to the night I tried to get her hammered in my kitchen.

Donna dropped back down onto flat feet, one hand on the side of my face, reminding me I hadn't shaved in a few days. Her fingers lingered there, scratching through the scruff, her smile gentle. "Time, Judah."

That could have meant anything.

Give it time.

It's time to move on.

You get the time they didn't.

Time was something I'd always thought I'd have more of when it came to Cait.

Time to fix things.

Time to make her love me again.

To my absolute horror, my eyes filled. Those fuckers had been broken for months, leaking at the most inopportune times and this was one of them, because Beckett was looking right at me with clear sympathy written all over her face.

"I gotta go," I mumbled, running a forearm quickly over my face, pushing past Donna and cutting between Levi and Beckett in a blind, frantic stumble toward the front door.

"Judah." Dad's voice stopped me in my tracks, halfway down the porch steps. I sucked in a deep breath and clenched my fists. "This is for the best, son. You're the right man for the job." One of his big hands came down heavily on my shoulder. "You need a sense of purpose."

He knew my purpose had been Cait and the boys, and I loved the farm, but there was no way it would ever take their place.

"When I lost your mom, this was what saved me."

His voice always took on a weird monotone when he talked about mom. Our family didn't do emotion well, something my sister eventually admitted was probably what drove her to become a trauma therapist.

"You still had us," I said, aware it was a total dick move. Our mom had walked out on Dad and left him to raise five kids and run a farm. We had been incredibly fortunate Levi stepped up to keep laundry clean and food on the table, because the rest of us were useless.

"I did." He agreed slowly, hardly voicing what I knew he was thinking.

"Sorry. Dick move." I looked down to realize that I'd rushed out of the house without my boots and I was standing in the front yard in my socks. "I don't know how you managed it."

"Not well." He sounded a little uncomfortable. "But your mom left me, Judah. Cait and the boys did not choose to leave you."

I ran a hand over my face, trying to knit my thoughts back together. Most plane crash victims didn't get to choose the circumstances of their death, I knew that much.

"She was a damn good pilot." My voice was scratchy. "It was my fault—she was mad at me and she left early. She should've waited out that storm."

"Not the first time in this life that you'll ask yourself *what if.*" His voice was uncharacteristically soft, and it seemed weird. Everything Erik Benson did was big and loud, a family trait, it seemed. "You had your differences, like anyone else. Beating yourself up over it doesn't change a damn thing."

I knew that, but no one knew how bad it had been toward the end.

That Cait and I were growing apart.

That she was in the process of packing up to leave me.

"She wasn't ... happy. At the end." The words tasted bitter when I let them fall from my mouth. "She said I had no ambition. No drive." I swallowed hard, the shame heating my face. "She was tired of this life."

It took me a moment to raise my eyes, to notice that his face had fallen. He didn't say anything, just closed the small space between us and wrapped his arms around me. He squeezed so tight, it felt like he was trying to hold me together.

Maybe he was, because I'd been falling apart for a long time.

"Need to do a cattle count." Levi hardly raised his head when I burst into the small office. "Got a real funny feeling we're missin' more than just the one."

That got his attention. His head snapped up. "Why, you find something weird?"

"Nah, just a gut feeling. One that says maybe the Avila boys are finally stepping up their nuisance game and they're starting to play nasty. The best way to hurt us is to hurt our bottom line, and we ain't exactly been flush lately."

Levi looked surprised that I knew that. Trying to stretch the meager earnings of a family farm to cover the financial needs of all five of us and a few hired hands meant there wasn't anything extra to go around. It was one of the reasons Ben had backed away and gone into business for himself, and now Levi was backing away as well.

It didn't take a genius to figure out that Ben and Levi's take were now Beckett's salary.

"You hear anything?" he asked, and I made a note to self to call a guy we were friendly with over at the livestock auction.

"Gonna find out," I said, and he rose from his chair.

“Head out to the pasture and count the heifers,” he said. “I’ll handle the barns.”

My gut was filled with dread as I drove out to the distant pasture. It was a huge acreage, enclosed on three sides by a heavy split-rail and barbed wire fence. The fourth side, the one that ran through the woods, was a thicket of barbed wire, tall enough they couldn’t get any ideas about jumping it.

The heifers were what kept us going year round, when they went to auction. The dairy cows were our bread and butter, but the heifers were what really kept the lights on and anyone with any sense would start there if they were trying to hurt us.

“Son of a bitch.” I released the wire. “They cut the power.”

I was talking to no one, but the thousands of volts that should have been coursing through the wire and knocked me on my ass were nowhere to be found.

“This isn’t going to be good.” I swung a leg through the open space between the two wires and ducked to pass through, into the pasture itself. Cows were curious creatures and typically the herd kept close to the fence to watch the road, if they weren’t wandering around grazing. These girls were grass-fed at this point, something that would have been important if they were going for meat, but most of them went for dairy; our name was good on the livestock circuit, and we pastured most of our cattle during the summer months, since it helped to keep down feed costs and labor.

The pasture was large enough, with trees along one side, that sometimes one didn’t immediately see the herd. When it was particularly hot they liked to meander into the trees and rest in the shade.

I whistled as I walked, like one would call a dog. I was careful to watch my step, though it didn't really matter with my work boots—they'd seen a lot worse.

There was a low hum from a distance, an answering moo, and I felt a tight fist squeeze my gut as I finally made it to the edge of the trees, because where the hell were all the cows?

"Hey, girl." I answered the one who was mooing at me. She was friendly and she ambled over for a scratch. "Where are all your friends?"

The trees were dense here and there was a natural slope, so it was possible some of them were further up the hill. She followed me, my walking companion, as I climbed the gentle hill.

"Fuck me." There were thirty-seven cows. Thirty-seven of what had been a herd of one hundred and fifty-three. I whipped out my phone to text Levi, but he'd beat me to it:

Levi: *Only missing the one in the calf pens.*

Me: *Just about cleaned out the furthest pasture. I'll be spending the night here on the Gator, with a shotgun.*

Levi: *How bad?*

Me: *Got thirty-seven left.*

Levi: *Motherfuckers.*

That was a strong one for Levi these days, and he'd really perfected his sweary game in the military. He'd come back with curses that curled my hair.

"You hold the fort, girl." I reached out to scratch the forelock of the friendly cow. "I'll be back with reinforcements and we'll get to the bottom of this in a hurry."

I called my contact at the livestock auction while I walked back to the truck and left a message asking him to call me back. I was coming back to this pasture loaded for bear and thirsty for blood, because this was a declaration of war.

I walked the fence line carefully, until I found the spot I suspected they'd used. They'd shorted out the fence and disassembled the split-rail at the very corner, something confirmed by the fact there was a deep impression of tire tracks. Someone had backed in a trailer—probably more than one—to haul our girls away.

I was pretty sure they would be back.

Donna was steamed when I got back to the farm. "I always knew those Avila boys were no good," she huffed, handing over a small cooler and two insulated tumblers loaded with hot coffee.

"You packed me a lunch, Ma?" I grinned and she smiled back, temporarily thrown off-course. Secretly, she loved it when I called her that.

"Levi said you're going to be on lookout overnight, so I packed plenty of food for two."

Uh-oh. The hair on the back of my neck stood up when she said it and I turned to see Beckett stomping across the yard, her nostrils flaring. "Please tell me you brand your cows."

I grinned, because we did one better. "They all got ear clips, but those can be removed with a little work, so they all got numbers burned into their hooves too. Small—no one's lookin' for 'em when they see the ear clips. Right rear hoof."

"Good." She nodded shortly and whipped a phone out of her pocket. "I've got friends at auction houses across the U.S., but my guess is they hauled yours into Wisconsin, thinking they could fly under the radar."

That wasn't entirely stupid. The border was less than an hour away and some of the smaller outfits weren't set up with fancy software. They still operated with paper and computers built during the Cold War.

I'd seen someone work an abacus faster than one of those old Soviet-era monsters.

"The Gator's ready to go." Dad came charging down the steps with a pile of blankets in his arms. "Got the kit packed: spare batteries, flashlights, a gas can—should be all set."

Awful lot of blankets in his arms. What was this, prep for a drive-in movie?

"Uh, thanks." That uncomfortable worry was nagging again at the back of my mind. "Suppose I should go home and grab a shotgun."

"Nonsense." Donna shook her head. "You'll come in for some dinner before it gets dark and you can both grab something from our stash."

Dad was an avid hunter. He could be found in a tree stand more often than on solid ground during hunting season, and we joked for a long time that he'd collected more guns than he'd killed actual deer.

"Both of us?" I asked slowly, realizing with a sick feeling in my gut that Beckett had a heavy hoodie tied around her waist, her expression suggesting she was ready to eat someone alive.

"You're going to call the cops when they show up," she said matter-of-factly, "and I'm going to puncture their tires. There's nothing I hate more than cattle thieves and if they've already made off with that much of the herd, they've been at this for a few nights already. They know they're going to get caught—they just don't think you can make it stick."

"No." My brain was slow to fire. "No cops. You'll let the air out of two tires—not flat, just real low. Plant a spike under another, so it blows out. They'll know it's not an accident, and it's gonna slow them down. They'll freak out. They won't go home, because they don't want the evidence on their property, and they'll be running on rims."

Beckett nodded her understanding. "You think they'll lead us right to the rest of them?"

"Lead you to something, all right." Erik huffed. "Think we'd better get a headcount on the other pastures. God knows what they've done to our steers."

Levi winced and I could see the panic starting to rise in him, realizing we were already out a fuckton of money.

"If we can't track this all the way back—make it stick, press charges and get the cows or money back, this is going to have to be an insurance claim." Beckett made a sour face. She was right, and she cast a grateful glance at Levi. "Thank God you've been a halfway decent record keeper."

"Yeah, thanks." He sounded amused. "Better than being a total shit record keeper, I guess."

She twisted her mouth a little, but she didn't apologize and I kind of liked that about her. It hadn't been an insult, but it also hadn't been a compliment, and she wasn't looking to bandage up anyone's feelings.

We had dinner with Donna, Dad and Levi, then Beckett and I climbed onto the Gator and made a mad dash for the pasture. It was a good distance from the house but the Gator reached solid speeds, so we reached the pasture just after dusk. The cows were out of the trees, meandering up to the fence line to see what we were up to and I pulled the vehicle all the way back into the stand of trees, next to the fence. It was easily five hundred feet from the road and Beckett whipped a small pair of binoculars from the kangaroo pocket of her hoodie.

"Ain't gonna see shit in the dark." I laughed at her and wordlessly, she handed them to me. I held them to my eyes, unsurprised to see exactly what I'd expected: nothing.

"Hit the button on the right," she instructed and I groped around, smacking the button and everything lit up.

"You're shitting me. Night vision? The fuck did you do in your past life, Bec? You covert ops or something?"

"Can't tell you or I'd have to kill you." She already had a mouth full of something, and I lowered the binoculars.

"Seriously, like you didn't just eat?"

"Donna packed cookies. Have you tried these things? They're miraculous."

I chuckled, because I'd used that very word to describe Donna in the past. Whether or not any of us said it out loud, she had been the one to save all of us. She had immediately taken to farm life, keeping the house tidy and performing updates, fixing things that had been allowed to fall into disrepair over the years, and the woman was a champ in the kitchen.

Dad had tried to joke years ago about how he needed a few sex marathons to burn off all the good food she was making and I shut him right the hell down, because ... dude. No, thank you. Hard pass on that overshare. That was never going to be a free and easy exchange of information and banter like that.

Gross.

Being stuck on a stakeout with this woman was going to try my patience if she ate all the cookies and spent the whole time chewing in my ear.

"How'd you get stuck on this job, anyway?" I asked, mostly because I hadn't planned on having a sidekick, but it certainly hadn't been her.

"Volunteered. Gotta earn my keep somehow, right?" She grinned in the growing darkness, a flash of teeth.

"Well, settle in, buttercup. Guessing they're not gonna show for a few hours—if they do at all. May as well get comfortable. And keep it down; we don't need the cows clustering over here and alerting anyone to the fact there's something worth watching."

She was bundled up in a blanket within the hour. The humidity had dropped out of the air a week before and once the sun went down it was pretty cool at night.

"Tell me about them." Her voice was gentle, like she was trying not to spook me, and my head practically swiveled on my neck.

"Not ready to talk about it."

"The funny things. The happy parts." She persisted, and I felt a nagging anger growing in my gut.

"Havin' a hard time remembering those parts," I admitted and I felt her nod slowly beside me. It made a rustling noise, like her hair was scraping against the blanket.

"Those are the parts you have to focus on," she whispered. "They're what carry you through the darkness."

I didn't like that at all, but mostly because something told me that Beckett was going to be right a lot of the time.

Chapter Six

Beckett

Three nights and not a single lead.

Judah and I were exhausted, to the point we took turns sleeping while the other kept watch, which allowed at least one of us to be reasonably functional during the day.

"This is bullshit," Judah finally announced. "Either they're onto us, or they're not coming back for those cows and we're just shit out of luck."

None of my contacts on the auction circuit had reported back with anything useful and it made me incredibly angry to think that someone was going to get away with stealing from the little guy yet again. Because that was what the Benson family farm was: little. There were fewer than five hundred steers being raised for meat, the one hundred and fifty cows who had been raised for dairy, their own active dairy herd, and a hundred calves who'd be sorted and used to to replenish both sides.

"Think we should empty out that pasture," Levi said. "Save the rest of the herd by bringing them back home. We'll keep them in the field bordering Donna's garden."

"We were going to plant winter wheat there," Judah said, something that sounded like a protest. "Besides, we'd have to fence in the whole thing, and Donna'll be pissed if they ever break out and trample her garden."

Levi ran a big hand over his face, like Judah was trying his patience. "You got a better idea? Maybe we should just load up the rest in a cattle trailer and drive 'em over to the Avilas—save them some work?"

Judah winced. "You know that's not what I mean."

"Robert VanHassel said he can spare some hands this weekend; he'll send three, and Ben and Dan are already on board. We're going to have a work bee, I'm afraid, digging fence posts and stringing wire."

Judah's eyebrows raised a little. "VanHassel, eh? You two bury the hatchet?"

"There was no hatchet to bury, dipshit. Shut your trap."

Judah shot me a look I couldn't interpret, something both amused and wary, and I realized my eyebrows had begun crawling up my forehead. Levi was nothing but easygoing and affable and whatever this was, it was a nuclear button.

Having napped on the cold, hard seat of a Gator the last few nights, I was more than amenable to Levi's idea. The thought of actually sleeping in a bed filled me with joy. It meant only one more night spent trying to carry a conversation while Judah sat staring sullenly across the dark pasture. In any other situation I might have been happy to be in such close proximity to someone who really was an impressive physical specimen. Judah was handsome, as were Levi and Ben.

I hadn't met Dan yet, but the law of averages indicated that he was likely to be easy on the eyes as well.

"Just sayin'..." Clearly, Judah was looking to eat a fist. "Don't think you've ever forgiven Hannah."

"Shut your fucking mouth." Levi looked like he was about to spit nails, enough so that I took a startled step backward. Enraging a man of Levi's size was a death wish, and he was generally easygoing enough that this was a weird departure for him.

Judah turned to me with a bitter smile. "That's our secret, Bec. All of us Benson boys are cursed. We don't get to keep the things we love—*none* of us." He raised his right hand, middle finger extended in Levi's direction, then stomped out of the building.

"I'm sorry, Beckett." Levi dropped back down into his seat. "There was no reason you had to witness that. Judah doesn't let things go easily, as you might have guessed."

"We all have our sore spots." I tried to smile, but I was finding it pretty difficult considering just how well I was acquainted with that idea. I was fairly sure I suffered from the very same curse.

"Turns out I'm somewhat familiar with it." I sat down across from Levi, aware his expression was uncomfortable. "And whatever your situation is, I'm sorry. I suppose we're all carrying around some kind of baggage."

Levi's shoulders relaxed a little. "Don't expect you to be out there helping with fence posts this weekend. It's hot, sweaty, painful work. We can handle it."

"No, I'm here to work. There's a lot you probably don't know about me, Mr. Benson, and one of those things is that I grew up on a ranch—horses, but I'm no stranger to hard work."

Levi's eyebrows shot up in surprise, but he didn't ask any questions. He simply gave me a single nod. "Suppose you know what you're doing inside and outside the office."

"I do." I set my hands on the arms of the chair, ready to push up on my palms. "The funny thing about this life is that once it gets in your blood, it doesn't matter what happens to try to take it from you, you can't let go."

His expression was thoughtful, like he could somehow glimpse a piece of my own painful past.

"So you didn't let go, exactly, just changed the scenery up a bit?"

"Something like that." I swallowed hard, a dangerous emotion crawling up my trachea and threatening to spill out. "I'd rather start over than give up entirely, even if that's damn hard." I stood quickly, ready to escape, needing to fill my lungs with the oxygen outside of this small room.

"Good choice," was all he said. He understood, and he nodded at me like our conversation was concluded.

Leaving the truck in the driveway outside the farm house, I made the long walk back to my place to shower and have dinner. I sent a text to Judah to collect me when he was ready to head out to the pasture and I brewed some campfire coffee for our evening stakeout.

The truth was that Judah annoyed the hell out of me, even though he was one of the most attractive men I'd seen in my life. He was cantankerous and rude, and it was clear he thought he had the corner on suffering.

"Donna sent apple pie things—like PopTarts, I guess," came a voice from outside the storm door as I rinsed my plate and slotted it into the dishwasher. "That woman's love language is food and she's gonna make you fat."

"Excuse me?" I snorted hard enough that it rattled my sinuses. "Then I guess I'll thank her; it'll make it less of a hardship for you to keep your eyes off my ass."

I knew no such thing, but I *did* know there were two bright red spots burning in Judah's cheeks, even though I couldn't see him, and I grinned to myself. He was plainly the sort who needed to be pushed—and hard. Making him angry, getting him to fight, would draw him out and I was great at fighting, because I thought on my feet.

Cade had always complained that when I argued, I cited my sources, making it impossible for him to win.

Judah's mouth was still hanging open when I walked into the small living room with the thermos in my hand. The sun was rapidly setting and I gestured he should move so I could swing the door open without hitting him.

"Need to be quick," I observed and he finally clapped his mouth shut. I locked the door quickly behind me and zipped up my jacket against the cool evening air. Fall was more than just on the way; leaves were already starting to turn.

"Getting cold," he said as he hurried after me toward the Gator, zipping up his own jacket. "Might hear some coyotes tonight—seem to get closer in the fall, when the weather gets cooler."

I shivered. The sound of a pack of hunting coyotes made my blood run cold. It reminded me of sinister things I'd tried to bury deep.

"So, Bec..." He spun the wheel and we zipped across the gravel driveway, up to the paved road, where he flipped on an overhead light to help illuminate the path. Deer were a prevalent problem at this time of year, that much I knew, and many of the critters who liked to come out at dusk had poorer response times than a sober human—at least, I was assuming Judah was sober. "You gonna tell me one of your happy stories? Maybe a silly one?"

I sighed heavily and thought about it for a moment, chewing on my inner cheek. "My husband used to call me Beast, like the cartoon one, because he said if he tried to wake me without coffee in hand, I snarled at him."

Judah nodded. "Not the knee-slapper I was expecting, but I understand this. I'm not much of a morning person. Husband, though—interesting. Divorced?"

"Widowed." I folded my arms over my chest, because I hated that word. Judah and I had more in common than he knew, from the very little I did know about him.

"Yeah, okay. Sorry I asked." He set his lips in a hard line and spun the wheel to cut across a field that hadn't yet been plowed. The popping and pinging noises from the wheels told me it was a hay field, perhaps recently cut for the last time.

"Won't be mad about getting the cows moved and spending a night in my bed." I yawned as I said it. Both of us were running on fumes after the last several nights spent guarding the small herd.

"Don't do much sleeping in mine," he said absently and I couldn't even turn it into something dirty.

"Night terrors?"

"Yeah. Sleep on the sofa most nights."

"After a hell of a lot of liquor," I mused.

"Yeah."

"I did that for a while, too," I admitted slowly. "But I finally realized it wasn't actually helping. I was waking up every day, waiting for something to change ... I needed to be the one to change, not just because I was tired of feeling like shit."

He grunted at me, because I'd made my point and it had gotten through, even if he didn't like it.

Something told me that change and Judah Benson were not well acquainted, and they certainly weren't friendly.

Judah wasn't a big talker, but he was uncharacteristically quiet that night, sitting with his arms folded while we waited in the deep darkness for any sign of movement. It wasn't exactly uncomfortable sitting with him in silence, both of us lost in our thoughts, until I heard the distant yipping of a pack of coyotes.

"I hate that sound." I shivered, unconsciously moving closer to Judah. It made him chuckle, though it wasn't an amused sort of sound.

"Country girl don't like the country?" he asked, and I wrapped my arms tighter around myself.

"I associate that sound with bad things," I said, my eyes trained on the road as headlights appeared, grew closer, then swept past.

"Fair." He went quiet again, arms folded over his chest.

"You had boys?" I asked quietly, aware that I was pushing. I had only the barest information on him.

"Two." He drew in a slow, deep breath when he said it. "Best thing I ever did in my whole life."

"How old?"

"Four and six." He choked a little when he said it. "Cait had a hard time getting pregnant. She was on bedrest each time and just about lost her mind. She didn't do well with sitting still." That made him chuckle. "That means I just about lost my mind." He paused for a moment and I heard him working on a really hard swallow. "Those babies were a miracle."

I didn't say anything, just let him sit in silence with his terrible emotions, leaning my shoulder into his just enough to remind him that he wasn't alone.

He was quiet for a long time and we finished the thermos of campfire coffee, then dug into the snacks Donna had packed for us. She was like our own little corner Jewish bakery, with all the treats she cranked out: breads and pies and pastries. Every time I opened that little cooler it was like the angels began singing.

"Why do the coyotes bother you?" he asked after we sat in a weirdly companionable silence for so long that I thought he'd dozed off.

"I, uh..." I felt the familiar squeeze of grief around my trachea, something that made me want to throw up the flaky pastry I'd just inhaled. "It's kind of a long story. But ... that night ... the coyotes howled all night long. I wasn't alone for much of it: medical examiner, paramedics, my dad ... but when everyone left, I just wandered around the house and listened to that horrible sound. I've felt *that* alone a lot of times since, but that night was just..."

"Desperate," he finished for me, his voice raw.

"Yeah." I leaned forward to brace my elbows on my knees. It didn't matter how much time passed, because the memories were still so quick to rise to the surface, the flash of recollection a sickening punch to the gut.

"So now you're here," he finished for me, and I was grateful to him for sparing me the inevitable follow-up questions any other person would ask. "Trying something new—smart. I probably shoulda' done that. Just couldn't get myself together long enough to do things like ... shower."

It was unfortunate, but I understood that pretty well.

"You miss him?" His voice scraped on the words and I wondered if he was asking permission to talk about his wife. About his boys.

"Every damn day. He was my high school sweetheart."

"Yeah." He barked out a laugh. "Get that. I asked Cait to be my girl in the sixth grade. Had a few false starts, but we stuck."

"Damn." I could finally breathe around the lump in my throat, and it took work but I was able to get out a chuckle. "You knew what you wanted."

"I've always known." He reached for a second thermos that sat on the floor of the Gator, tucked between our feet. "Problem was I didn't want *enough*, I guess. I was happy here. The land. The animals. The routines. With her and the boys, I had everything I wanted." He poured some of the hot coffee into the small cap and sipped slowly.

There was nothing to say, because I understood it perfectly. A simple life was all I'd ever wanted with Cade: a happy life spent with the man I loved, working hard, having a couple kids.

Sometimes life has other plans.

Brutal ones.

"You think they're onto us?" I asked when he remained silent, and he poured some coffee and handed it to me.

"Doubt it." He stretched his arms upward as another howl pierced the air, and I shivered. "Don't think they're all that smart, to be honest. Probably just got other shit going on. They'll be back, but it's looking like by then these girls will be safe up by the house."

"We're going to find the others, Judah. I'm sure of it."

"Don't go making promises you can't keep, Tex." I could almost hear his smile in the dark and I wished desperately I could see it, because I was certain I'd never seen him really smile.

That was something Judah didn't know about me: I kept my promises.

A strange noise woke me from my sleep and it took me a moment to place it, to realize that the furnace in the small house had kicked on and my sleep-fogged brain tried to remember whether I'd left any of the windows open.

It had just gone fall as far as the calendar was concerned, but apparently Minnesota hadn't gotten that memo, because when I flipped back the blankets to pad across the room it was freezing. The weather had been deep into fall for several weeks already, winter trying to move in much faster than it was supposed to.

The thermostat was in the small hallway between the two bedrooms and when I hurried to check it, there was a distinctly cold blast blowing up the stairs. I crept down carefully, fairly sure this wasn't dream sleep, and I paused at the bottom to listen. The house was silent but for the furnace and I slid a hand silently along the wall for the light switch, blinding myself when sharp overhead light sliced across the living room to reveal the front door hanging wide open. It was the door I had not only shut and locked before going to bed, but I had also locked the external storm door, which lay on the ground, the hydraulic arm severed where it had been ripped from the hinges.

Swallowing hard, I closed the main door and locked it once more—for whatever that was worth. Then I reached into the small closet, fingers curling around the cold aluminum of the baseball bat I'd meant to keep at my bedside.

Prowling the house on quiet feet, I checked every corner and beneath every piece of furniture, even in the upstairs bathtub and the guest room closet, despite the fact I felt my heart might beat out of my chest. The adrenaline sent little lightning zaps down my nerve endings, frigid pinpricks that made my breaths short and my heart hurt.

It did occur to me that I felt like the dumb blonde in tiny white underwear, checking on the noise in the basement in a horror film.

It was only four a.m. according to the blue numbers on my alarm clock, and I checked my closet and under my own bed before trying to talk myself down. *You're safe. It was nothing.*

But it didn't feel like nothing and I sat with my phone in hand, huddled under the blankets with the baseball bat tucked into the bed beside me.

Me: *I'm sorry to bother you this early; I think someone tried to break into the house tonight.*

That was the understatement of the century, because maybe they weren't here anymore, but they'd successfully sent the message that they knew how to get in.

There was no response, something I had kind of expected. It had been foolish to think I could go to Judah for help. The nights spent in companionable conversation and long stretches of silence while we waited in the dark had clearly scrambled my brain. More than likely he'd taken advantage of a night at home by falling into a bottle.

I knew the type, because I had been the type. It was in my blood. Happy? Grab a drink to celebrate. Sad? Here's a bottle of something that'll knock you sideways. It was something I'd worked hard to get a handle on after losing Cade, knowing the tendencies in my family to fall hard for the demon liquor.

I couldn't work up the courage to go back downstairs to make coffee, even though there was no way I'd go back to sleep. Now that I'd used up all the adrenaline, I was exhausted, my eyes watery and burning. I should have been used to feeling scared and alone, but it was a combo I just couldn't seem to normalize.

Headlights flashed through the window and my heart just about lurched out of my body through my mouth. Was it the cavalry, or was someone back to finish the job?

"Beckett." There was a thunderous roar from outside and a hammering set up on the door, enough racket to wake the dead. It sounded like a Benson—a furious one.

"Levi?" I felt my forehead sink into a frown when I finally opened the door. Levi had the storm door in one hand as his eyes assessed the situation and with an awful sound he threw it down, watching it warp as it crashed to the ground.

"You okay?" He looked terrified, not even sparing a second look for the twisted heap of aluminum lying by the front step, his eyes zeroing in on the bat in my hands. "I'll take that as a no."

"Why are you here?" My brain wasn't firing on all cylinders just yet.

"You texted me." He looked thoroughly confused and I fished my phone out of the kangaroo pocket of my hoodie for a quick scroll.

"I'm so sorry. I thought I texted Judah."

"Yeah, well ... you got me. Good thing for you, I'm an early riser."

This was more than early; anyone getting up *this* early had to be mentally unstable.

"Putting in a proper door today," he snarled, finally looking at the aluminum taco on the front lawn. "One with bars."

I'd have suggested that seemed a little extreme, but I was scared, so maybe that wasn't such a bad thing.

"Assholes probably popped that flimsy screen out and busted the tension rod; lock was an afterthought."

It didn't explain why the solid-core door had been hanging wide open, but I kept my mouth shut.

"Come on." He gestured behind me before swiping one enormous paw through a thick head of dark blond hair. "Let's go make some coffee."

Chapter Seven

Judah

Me: *What the duck?*

Ben: *Quack?*

Me: *Duck.*

Me: *Duck.*

Dan: *Everything okay over there? You back on the sauce?*

Me: *What in the actual flying duck.*

Levi: *What am I supposed to say here?*

Me: *FUCK! Stupid autocorrect.*

Ben: *Someone clue me in. Why are we pissed at seven on a Saturday?*

Me: *No one thought it was a good idea to let me know someone tried to break into Beckett's house last night?*

Dan: *The actual duck?*

Me: *See?*

Dan: *Fucking Avilas.*

Finally, someone was getting it right.

Ben: *Bro, you don't even like her. Got your panties all up in a twist.*

Me: *I don't expect you to see the bigger picture here. A threat to her is a threat to all of us.*

Levi: *He's right. Dan, you're going with me to pick up a proper security door this morning. We're installing it before we get started on the fence. Hope you're awake, because I'll be at your house in ten.*

Me: *The fuck you will. Dan's on fence duty; I'm going with.*

I could almost see Levi smirking.

Levi: *See you in five.*

Levi didn't give me a hard time about it, but he wasn't the brother who would—that was Ben. True to his word, he pulled into my driveway five minutes later and honked the horn. "Don't got all day!" He hollered out the window and I pulled the door shut behind me, coffee mug in hand.

"Thoughtful of you," Levi said as I scooted into the truck, reaching over to snag the mug from my hand and taking a chug. "Good, merciful fuck, that's hot."

"You didn't ask. I didn't offer. And you didn't give me time to put it into a travel cup," I grumbled, and he grinned at me.

"You straight?" he asked, something that irritated the hell out of me. My big brother had made it his personal mission to act as my own lord and savior and I knew he'd been stopping by my house the last few days to check my cabinets and make sure I wasn't stowing any alcohol.

Truth was, I hadn't had the time to restock. Being on cow patrol kind of cut into my drinking time and there was no time to restock during the day when there was a farm to tend to.

"First milking of the day should be about done," Levi commented, looking at the battered watch he wore on his left wrist. "Guys'll be out in the field soon to get started on the fence. But you and me, we'll join 'em later. First we're gonna pick up the meanest, heaviest security door we can find."

"Maybe we should be putting bars on the windows," I said, snapping my seatbelt into place and lifting the mug to my lips for a sip.

Fuck, that *was* hot.

We drove in silence, Levi plucking at his lower lip with the fingers of one hand, like he needed the action to reorganize his thoughts, and I stared out the window as the countryside melted into the small town of Colson Creek.

"Called the junior Henderson this morning," Levi announced as he pulled into a diagonal parking spot in front of the hardware store. "Says he has just the thing."

I left the mug on the floorboard and followed him into the store, the bell slapping against the door as it slammed shut behind me.

"Benson?" A disembodied voice floated from the back. "That you?"

Tommy Henderson was our age, the youngest of the Henderson boys. He'd taken over the store from his father a few years earlier when the old man announced he wanted to retire, but you could still find the geezer puttering around in the space most days, mumbling under his breath about how if you wanted something done right, you had to do it yourself.

A disgruntled muttering set up a few aisles over and Levi called "Hey, Tommy," even as he headed toward the row we both knew held the senior Henderson. Levi was a friendly motherfucker—friendlier than me—about the only guy I knew could get old man Henderson to crack anything nearing a smile.

"Morning, Roy. What gives?"

"Arthritis in my damn back, that's what gives," the old man barked, lowering his head to glare at us over a pair of bifocals I could have sworn rivaled the strength of the Hubble telescope. The man's vision was so bad, his driver's license had been pulled two years earlier—but that was something we didn't talk about. It was just an open secret in town.

"Sorry to hear it." Levi clapped a hand on the man's shoulder. "Glad to see you're still about."

"Where else would I be?" Roy made a sour face, about as close to a smile as you'd ever get from him. This was his routine with Levi: bitch about his arthritis, talk about the weather, complain about the big box store three towns over, then ask about Dad. We were still in the preamble.

"You and I both know every day's a blessing," Levi said, something that made Roy's face soften immediately. Something not quite friendly, but he was getting there. He had to warm up to it, given it wasn't his natural setting.

"Damn straight, son. Every day spent topside is a gift."

Levi nodded sharply and my eyebrows raised. He'd gotten the old fart to go off-script. Miracles really did happen every day, right in front of unbelievers like me.

"You old ladies done catchin' up?" Tommy's face appeared around the endcap, a huge smile in direct opposition to his father's perma-scowl. "Hear you got need of a real solid door. Knew I had one, so I pulled it from the back for ya."

"Thanks, Tommy." Levi patted Roy's shoulder gently, twice, before turning to face the younger Henderson. "Glad you had one on hand, or we'd have ended up in the cities looking for one."

"Pffft, no sense in that." It was Roy again. "They ain't got nothin' better than what we got—we just got less of it. Not many people placin' orders these days for something burglar-proof." His craggy old eyebrows raised just a little, like he smelled gossip and he wanted in.

"Microburst," I offered, trying to head him off at the pass. A lie out of nowhere. "Tore the storm door right off the hinges last night; figured if we put something with a little more heft in place—maybe no more problems."

That was bullshit logic and we all knew it. If an actual microburst decided to tear at a real security door, it would probably take the whole house with it.

"This weather sure does funny things; real unpredictable, come fall." Tommy was all affable and smiley. Not the sharpest tool in the store, but a solid guy nonetheless.

Levi trailed after Tommy and I wasn't sure what kept me there with Roy, but I grabbed the box at his feet. The one he was pulling things from, one item at a time, to shelve. Surely there was a better, easier way that didn't aggravate his back.

"No wonder your back bothers you, you old fart," I muttered, standing there for a second with the box held at an easy level for him to reach right in. "Didn't occur to you to put out a step stool or something?"

That finally got a grin out of him. "Nah, insurance." He held up his wrist to display a fancy new smartwatch. "Got me on a plan where I gotta get a certain number of steps each day. Got this thing thinking I'm gettin' 'em all in." He demonstrated by leaning slowly, his arm swinging wide at an unnatural arc.

"Back bothers you but legs don't and you're doing this shit? You make no sense, Roy. Should just be walking the old fashioned way." I shook my head at him before putting the box back on the ground and wandering off to find Levi.

"Box is fucked up," I remarked helpfully as I sauntered up behind my brother. He was waiting on a receipt, something the ancient cash register was coughing up like a hairball.

"Don't suppose it'll give you any trouble." Tommy was still all smiles. "I'm not built like you two—had to drag it up here by myself. The floor tears up that cardboard something fierce."

I chose—wisely, if I did say so myself—not to comment on that. Tommy had a real twink build, something hardly suited to the sort of manual labor we saw.

"You grab that end," Levi instructed and I hoisted it from the bottom while he grabbed it from the top, and we shifted a little to turn it on its side. Tommy rushed out ahead of us to hold the door open and Levi popped the gate on the truck with one hand before we slid it into the bed and Levi held up a hand to wave goodbye.

"Goin' soft in your old age." I chuckled as we got into the truck and Levi turned over the engine. Either one of us could have carried the door by ourselves easily enough, but I knew Levi hadn't wanted to embarrass Tommy, so I'd participated in his little charade.

"Zip it, mouthbreather." It was his favorite insult. "No sense in hurting folks like that. He's a good man."

That was Levi, the softhearted one. Ben teased him about it endlessly, but that was because Ben was admittedly the asshole of the family.

Dan was the hothead and I was the... What was I?

Probably just another asshole in training, if you asked anyone around town.

I'd like to tell you we made quick work of installing the new door, but the truth was that it was a real bitch. Even Levi came up with some new curse words when he smashed a finger and when we finally latched it and stood back to admire our handiwork, he had one hand around the back of his neck, a dubious look on his face. "Never thought I'd see the day we needed to install a security door on this old place." He shook his head slowly. "Got some worries we're gonna need to put a little more into this to keep her safe. Not right to drag her all the way up here to put her in harm's way."

Levi pulled in a deep breath before dropping his hand and turning to me. "You didn't see the look on her face this morning, Jude. I know that kind of scared: foxhole-scared. She's seen some shit."

I was still irked she'd texted him and not me. Maybe he was the safer brother. The protector. The one that, admittedly, the rest of us looked up to, even if we'd amputate our own limbs with a rusty saw blade before admitting it out loud.

"Time for us to pay a visit next door?" I asked, because I was ready to go pound at least one of the Avila boys into the dirt.

"Not a hundred percent it was them," Levi said uneasily. "But thinking our next step might be to install some security cameras to be sure—would go some way to pressing charges if we need to go that route."

My eyes widened at that. "So we'll put her in danger to test a theory?"

"Hell, no." He reached out and gave me a sharp slap before my reflexes kicked in. "Anything else happens, we put her in the big house for a while. Donna would frickin' love it and go all mother hen on her."

"What, I'm so untrustworthy?" My chest puffed out a little, like I was ready to take another hit and once my brain caught up to my mouth, I clapped my jaw shut. I was *not* actually offering to put her up.

"I'm not putting her in that kind of situation." Levi turned a steely gaze on me, zero warmth in it. "Until you get your shit together, she's safer here than she is with you—boogeyman and all."

What a vote of confidence. It hit me like a load of bricks and I struggled to breathe for a second. "You all really think that?" My voice was quieter than I'd have liked, making it obvious that it hurt.

"Course we all think that," he snapped. "We've been watching you kill yourself a little each day, Jude. You refuse our help. You've chosen to wallow and this is our last resort. We can't get you to man up and run the show, then we're out of ideas–except maybe rehab, and you know we can't afford that. Beckett was cheaper."

I swallowed hard. Both he and I knew rehab wasn't going to fix what was really broken inside of me.

"I'll do better," I mumbled, and I was surprised when he didn't push me. He just draped an arm around my shoulders in a side hug and heaved a deep sigh.

"Know you will, Jude. Just need it to be *now.*"

"About time you ladies showed up," Dan called from deeper in the field. "Glad you cut the spa day short to actually help out."

Dick.

I held up a hand, middle finger extended, and laughter rolled across the field.

Dan and I got along just fine most of the time, but he had a mean streak about a mile wide, when he decided to tap into it. I blamed it on Mom, from what I could remember of her. I'd been a teenager when she left, but in my mind she was still kind of a shadowy figure, most of the places that should have contained memories of her filled instead with memories of Donna and Dad. So it was easier to think that all the bad things about us came from her.

It had been cold the night before, but as the day wore on and the sun finally came out from behind the clouds, it beat down mercilessly. By lunch I couldn't stand my own stink, having worked up a vicious sweat while pounding down one post after another. The muscles in my back and arms were already screaming; moving at all tomorrow morning was going to be a challenge.

The dinner bell rang out from the house and there was a collective groan of relief, all of us raising our heads to look around and see how far things had come along.

Dad was walking out from the house, his posture still straight, his movements easy. He was in better shape than most guys my age, let alone his. "Come on in and eat quick," he bellowed. "No wasting any time if we're gonna get the girls moved today."

I knew that was right. Ben had been the one to sit watch over the pasture the night before, refusing to let Levi join him. It benefitted none of us to be this tired all the time and no one would sleep easily until the cows were in their new, secure pasture. Up here they would benefit from the protection of the guard dogs, Skip and Gunar, and the motion-sensing lights installed around the perimeter of the garden––just another of Donna's security measures when it came to keeping out the deer, who were pervasive little fuckers.

"Boots!" Donna barked from inside the house and I chuckled to myself as one of the hired hands scurried back out to the porch to rid himself of the offensive shitkickers. He'd been the first one in and everyone else in line benefitted from his lesson, quickly folding in half to untie laces.

"Best thing on this farm in years." I heard a mumble from somewhere up the line and I looked up to see Beckett climbing the porch steps, a soft sway to her hips.

She really did have a great ... *Stop it.*

"Watch it, dickhead," Ben bellowed, way ahead of me. "Show some respect."

I didn't see who'd been stupid enough to say it, but I watched Levi's eyes zero in on one of the VanHassel brothers. I suspected they were none too friendly with Levi these days. Hannah's brothers had always thought she could do better than him, and then I supposed she had.

Joke was on her, as far as I was concerned. I wouldn't be caught dead saying it out loud, but there was no better man than Levi Benson and there would never be.

"Heard you had an interesting morning," was the stupid shit that came out of my mouth as I came up on Beckett in the dining room. She looked tired and I was still mad at her for just being here, but I had a slightly better tolerance for the woman after a week spent pulling night watches together.

She didn't say anything, just lifted one corner of her mouth to acknowledge my words before she handed me the serving spoon for the green beans and moved on down the line. Donna had assembled some kind of miraculous buffet on the kitchen counter, a feast to rival a Thanksgiving dinner.

I sure as hell wasn't going to follow Beckett and sit next to the woman who smelled like some kind of sexy-ass flower, because that was all I could come up with when trying to describe it. It bugged me. I didn't know if it was her shampoo, her laundry detergent—didn't matter. I'd spent five nights on that Gator trying to keep my thoughts straight every time I caught a whiff of whatever that shit was, because it scrambled my damn brains and I hated that.

"I see you, bro." Ben shoulder-checked me and my plate just about went flying. I managed to save it with some kind of uncoordinated, spastic move, but green beans went tumbling everywhere anyway.

"Watch it, dickslinky."

"There's a visual I don't need," Dad piped up from Ben's other side and I looked around my huge younger brother to see Dad giving me the glare of righteousness. He'd never been a fan of the names we came up with for one another—said we were all each other had and we should act like it, with a little more appreciation.

Dad still didn't understand that terms like *dickdrip* and *sack-munch* were terms of endearment for guys like us. I mean, not that we'd have called them terms of endearment, but we only ever used the weirdest, most offensive ones for each other. It was a constant case of trying to one-up.

Ben snorted on a laugh next to me and I elbowed him hard. "Yuk it up, chucklenuts. Your day is coming."

"Just sayin'." He kept his voice low enough that only I could hear him over the hum of voices in the large room. "See some eyes heading our girl's way and you might want to call dibs—get out ahead of that rush."

My plate crashed to the floor and Donna's lips went tight in my peripheral vision, but she wasn't a yeller. She rounded the island and stooped to pick up the pieces while Ben reached across the counter and snagged the roll of paper towels.

"Son." Dad's voice was stern. "Outside."

I felt like a little kid all over again, getting into trouble for something Ben had done.

He started it, my thoughts whined.

Storming out of the kitchen, I let the screen door slam behind me as I huffed my way across the porch and dropped into one of the rocking chairs, arms folded across my chest. There was howling rage burning in my chest and I blinked hard when all I wanted to do was throw Ben on the lawn and get in a few good blows. That hadn't happened in years, and the last time it had I'd ended up with a mouthful of grass.

It might have been at my bachelor party.

"Sometimes I gotta remember you boys are grown." Dad's voice came from inside the house and the porch door squealed on its hinges as he stepped outside with two plates in his hands, wordlessly handing one to me as he dropped into the next rocking chair.

"Ben said something stupid..." I let it trail off, suddenly aware of how foolish and petulant it sounded. Maybe I really was five.

"I know what Ben said." He lifted a dinner roll and took a small bite, nodding toward my plate. "Your brother's a shit-stirrer and you're easy to rile, Judah."

I didn't have to like it for it to be true.

"I didn't like what he insinuated." My voice was shaky.

"No one would think you were being disloyal to Cait for finally moving on with your life, son."

I lifted an arm to swipe across my face, because suddenly I could feel moisture pooling and trickling, damn it.

It was something I hadn't admitted to anyone, that I'd come home blind-drunk from my sister's wedding to a wife who was already furious.

"We had a few fights." I was surprised to find I'd said it out loud. "She said if I refused to grow up and ... be a man ... she was going to take the boys with her."

Dad's cheeks, above his beard, went a little pale, but he nodded.

"I told her over my dead body, then I went to bed and passed out. She packed up the boys, and ... you know. Left me to find my own way home from the wedding."

"Shit." Dad set his plate on his knee and leaned back, the chair creaking.

"She got the last laugh." I set my plate on my knee as well, my stomach churning violently. Not much that had happened between Cait and me in the months leading up to that moment had been anything but confrontational, and she'd always been the one to push my buttons.

"You need to call your sister," he said quietly, sucking in a shaky breath as he stared off into the fields.

"Conflict of interest and we all know it," I said bitterly. "She can't treat family."

"Not the treatment I'm worried about. Besides, I know she's got you hooked up with her therapist friend," he said, finally swinging his head to fix me with that stern glare he was so good at. "She's someone you'll talk to and conflict or not, she knows how to help. You gotta get this off your chest, son. It's eating you alive and I can't stand to watch it any longer."

I made a sound, something like a strangled laugh, and tried to force a few bites of food into my mouth. That had been an Erik Benson proclamation, which meant there were no other options.

He hath spoken, and so shall it be.

"Mind if I cut in?" There was a soft voice from the other side of the screen door and I groaned, dropping my head back to smack against the siding.

Fuck me, another armchair therapist.

I kept my eyes closed while Dad's rocking chair creaked and his muted footsteps moved away from me. The door squawked and a whiff of that flowery smell made me open my eyes again.

"My mama used to say that hurt people *hurt* people," Beckett said softly, her hands curling over the armrests on the chair.

"I'm fine," I snapped, and her head began to shake back and forth almost immediately.

"I didn't mean you, but I *know* you're hurting. There's no question about that."

Well, that was confusing.

"Ben," she said quietly. "Something's bothering him, so he's picking on you because you're an easy target."

It made me a dick that I hadn't noticed, but Ben was always an asshole. This wasn't out of line for him—nothing was.

"You're still too close to it," she observed, something that raised my hackles. "You can't see the hurt in others yet."

I didn't trust that something cutting wouldn't come out of my mouth if I let words out, so I shoveled in a huge bite of food instead, even though I wasn't sure it would stay down.

"It's not an insult," she said quietly, and weirdly I noticed her knuckles were white. "It's from experience. I'm further out than you."

Supposed it would make me a dick to argue with that, so I didn't. Instead, I finished my plate before taking it inside to rinse. I thanked Donna and followed the group of guys already trickling back out of the house and toward the field, but Beckett was already gone.

Chapter Eight

Beckett

Everything freaking hurt, maybe even my hair follicles, as I stood under the hot stream of water that night and hoped it would wash the soreness of the day from my muscles.

It would be worse tomorrow. I hadn't pounded fence posts in years, but I remembered what happened to a body the next day and I wasn't looking forward to it.

Thankfully, Erik insisted I go home while the brothers saddled up a few horses and headed out to herd the cows to their new pasture. I'd have gone with, but thanks to a week of abbreviated nights, I didn't have the energy to argue with him and after a turkey sandwich and a cup of coffee, I'd gone straight for a hot shower.

Donna had already invited me for Sunday lunch the following day. She said it was family tradition and now, seeing as I was family, I should show up around one. I didn't follow her logic, but I sank into her welcoming kindness like a warm bath, ready to soak up every kind word and hug she had to offer. It had been a long time since anyone had mothered me and I wasn't ashamed to admit that I missed it terribly.

My hair was still wrapped in a towel and I was padding into the kitchen in a fluffy bathrobe when the doorbell rang.

I hadn't even known I had a doorbell.

"Hey." It was Judah, looking incredibly sullen when I opened the door and flipped the lock in order to open the security door. "Didn't want to bang on this giant grate and scare the shit out of you."

It was nearly dark outside, so I'd have definitely freaked out.

"Thank you for installing it," I said slowly. "I can't begin to imagine anyone will get through or around this."

"Not too worried about that now," he said matter-of-factly, and I stood aside to let him into the small space. "More worried about the fact there's another access point through the garage, and these windows are old as hell."

Well, if I hadn't been completely freaked out before, I sure was now.

"Careful, Mr. Benson," I teased as I shuffled back into the kitchen. "Coming to check up on me? People are going to think we actually get along."

"Can't have that," he huffed, toeing off his boots in the small entryway and following me into the kitchen.

Was it weird I liked having him there? He was an annoying jerk, but at least he was a big one. Possibly a protective one. And I felt safer just having someone there with me, talking and distracting me from the stupid things my brain would do in a dark, quiet house.

Revisiting a terrifying past.

"You get any dinner?" I asked and he nodded awkwardly. I realized he hadn't told me why he was here.

"Cider?" I asked, flipping off the burner and holding up the small saucepan. It made him wrinkle his nose.

"So you can pretend it's spiced rum or something?"

"Exactly." I grinned. "And it just helps to have something hot to sip, to help make you sleepy. A bedtime routine to make your brain be quiet."

"Not going to have any problems with that tonight." He groaned, stretching his arms upward, his shirt lifting and exposing what was a very nicely defined middle.

"Bec."

Shit, I'd been staring and gaping at the same time. How completely mortifying.

"Sorry." There was no playing this one off. "I think my brain just powered down; apparently I'm more tired than I thought."

He nodded slowly and took the saucepan from my hand, pouring carefully into the mug I'd left on the counter. Then he grabbed a glass from the drying rack and filled it with water.

"I thought I texted you this morning." I finally voiced what had been bothering me all day.

"If you'd texted me first, I'd have answered." He almost looked like he wanted to smile. "I was kinda pissed at Levi. Guess I thought we had some kind of a ... dunno ... somethin' friendly enough, after all those nights waiting for those damn Avilas."

I felt like a complete idiot. "I guess I was so freaked out, I didn't even notice I hit the wrong contact."

That seemed to placate him, if his feelings had been hurt, and I thought his shoulders loosened just a little.

"Well, don't matter where I sleep tonight—I'm only waking up for breaking and entering—and breakfast, if you're cooking." He grinned, and I realized for the first time that he meant to spend the night.

"I'm ... shit, Judah. You're going to have to give me a minute to set up the guest room. I haven't gotten very far."

"Nah." He blew a raspberry. "I'm sleepin' on the sofa. Those assholes get in, they're doing it on the ground floor and I'll be waitin' for 'em."

There was no way I was going to let that happen. That was ridiculous.

"Absolutely not. I don't need you to be in harm's way."

"Bec." His voice went weirdly soft, but it wasn't gentle or sweet. It was flat and calm, devoid of emotion, which was frankly terrifying. "I'm doing it because it's not fair to leave you to clean up our shit, and let's be honest: I got nothin' to lose."

Apparently he hadn't really caught onto the fact that neither did I.

"Morning, Princess!" came a singsong voice from the front porch and Judah's hand shot into the air, middle finger fully extended. There was a snort and a tittering laugh, and I shook my head at the overgrown giant sitting in one of the rocking chairs with a mug of coffee in one hand and a grin on his face.

"Fuckface." Judah acknowledged Ben finally. "Heard you had a date last night."

The smile dropped right off Ben's face and I could sense the change in Judah. He was like a shark smelling blood in the water. "Pretty sure there are laws against relations with livestock." He *mooed* at his brother.

Ben visibly relaxed. "Well, you know ... no complaints registered. Guess I've still got it—these old hips work just fine." He cackled, taking a sip from his coffee mug.

I waited for someone to enlighten me and Judah made a face. "Chucklenuts here has a bad habit of picking up the wrong sort of woman."

Apparently that was all I was going to get, because the screen door swung open and Donna's smiling face appeared. "Beckett,

I'm so glad you could make it! Come on in; don't pay any attention to these two."

I heard Judah throw himself into one of the chairs on the porch as I followed Donna into the house and I slipped out of my shoes before trailing after her into the kitchen. She noticed immediately, a sly grin on her face. "See? Your mama house trained you. Can't tell you how long I've worked on these boys and it's still hit-or-miss."

"I think you might be the only thing standing between them and cave-dwelling." I shot her a grin before gesturing toward the kitchen island. "Put me to work."

While I chopped vegetables for a salad and she pulled heavenly creations from the oven, she asked me how Judah and I had gotten on the night before.

"Well, we didn't exactly braid each other's hair, and he refused to let me paint his nails." Donna snorted when I said it. "But he insisted on sleeping on the sofa with my baseball bat."

She nodded thoughtfully before sliding another pan into the oven and handing me a pitcher to walk into the dining room. Her voice trailed after me: "That one's a tough nut to crack; it took Cait years to get through that shell. He'll act like he hates you for as long as he possibly can." She snorted when she said it. "Ask me how I know."

Now that was intriguing, because the man didn't talk about his wife. He'd spoken a little here and there about his boys, happy memories sneaking out in small, funny stories he'd sometimes filled space with after we'd been sitting quiet for too long.

But Cait? Not a freaking peep about her. I'd wondered if it hurt too much to even think about her, much less let himself talk about her.

"What was she like?" I asked softly, finally sinking onto one of the island stools and helping myself to some veggies and dip.

"Stubborn." She turned to face me and smiled softly. "Driven. Ambitious. *Hard.* Cait lived a careful, planned out life whereas Judah was just happy to drift along for a very long time. He's no less passionate, he's just..." She had to think about it for a moment. "He lives it on the inside. Quieter. He wants simpler things, I think, and things that are fiercely important to him are kept private; held close. He's intensely loyal and giving, but it's only for the people he loves, and it takes a long time to get on the inside with him because he keeps his circle so small."

I could have guessed some of that, but it was good to hear it confirmed. Maybe it meant he didn't actually hate me, he just hated *everybody*.

"Hi, Bec." A huge arm was slung over my shoulders, a crippling weight as Ben pulled me halfway off the stool in a sideways hug. "Sorry you had to put up with the grumpy asshole last night; the rest of us had shit going on, but tonight I'm on duty. Bringin' a little more than an aluminum bat, though. Hope you don't mind a little firepower in the house."

I had some of my own, but for some reason I always gravitated toward the bat.

I laughed weakly. "Maybe I should move the guest bed to the living room and be done with it."

"Nah." Ben grinned at me, a huge smile that I suspected hid a lot of things. "I can sleep just about anywhere. Get a little Fireball in me and I've been known to fall asleep in a hayfield, in the bed of a pickup truck, and once on a rock—big one. You ever been out to the Grandad's Bluff area?"

I hadn't set foot in Wisconsin, but even I'd heard of the bluffs.

I shook my head, but Ben was already on to something else. "Takin' you out first, though. Bet you never been to our little town here, and Colson Creek is buzzin' about you. The folks would like to meet our girl from the big, fancy outfit in Texas." Another panty-melting grin. "We're goin' to the Machine Shed."

I groaned and Donna nodded. "Yup, Clinton, that half-wit, named his bar the Machine Shed." She shrugged. "It's not all bad, I suppose. He got married a couple years ago and his wife has been trying to class it up a bit."

"Donna!" Ben looked like she'd mortally wounded him. "You been holdin' out on me? How many times I asked you if you wanted to go with me?"

There was an interesting visual.

Donna sniffed, propping her fists on her hips. "I hardly go out to tie one on, Benjamin. You are an absolute menace." The look she gave him should have cowed the man. "Sometimes your father wants to go out and socialize, so I visit with Debbie and have a civilized cocktail or two while the men drink that swill you call beer."

Ben shook his head in disbelief. "That's it. You're coming, too."

There was a groan from somewhere behind me and Levi appeared in the room. "Last thing you need is an excuse to drink, shit-for-brains, especially if you're on duty tonight."

Ben held up a hand in a pledge. "Promise to cut myself off after four."

After four I'd be under the table, but at his size something told me he'd metabolize them like water.

That was how I found myself wedged into the back of a pickup truck between Donna and Erik, Levi riding shotgun while Ben drove. It had been a wonderful afternoon, full of laughter and teasing and more good food than I'd had in ... possibly ever.

How did these people do this every Sunday?

Both Dan and Judah had bowed out of the festivities, though Dan said maybe he'd show up later. Judah said nothing, just stalked toward his truck with the ever-present thundercloud hanging over his head and peeled out of the yard like someone had done him a grave injustice.

"You'll love Debbie." Donna was in my ear. "She's such a sweetheart; did Clint a world of good when she moved here." Erik chuckled beside me and I wondered if he had a different version of the story. "Took right over with those two precious little boys of his."

As it turned out, Debbie was not at all what I'd expected. She was built like a grizzly, all six feet of her, in tight jeans and cowboy boots, with wild pink hair pulled back into a ponytail that very nearly reached her butt. She had the shoulders of an Olympic swimmer, something that should have been terrifying, but I suspected made her very effective bar security.

"Clinton!" She bellowed as we walked in the door and a man several inches shorter and easily thirty pounds lighter hustled out of the back. "Come meet the new Benson girl."

The protest died in my throat when Erik beamed like he'd actually gained a daughter, his big hand landing on my shoulder in a hearty clap three, four, five times. He didn't seem eager to correct Debbie.

The man nodded at me and shook my hand as Ben instructed, "Your finest lager for the newbie, Clinton," and the man hurried behind the bar to draw up a literal two-pint glass. I was going to be in trouble, though this went some way to explain why Ben was comfortable with cutting himself off at four.

"Thanks." I nodded at Clint when he slid it across the bar and I gamely took a large chug, something that delighted Debbie. She laughed and pounded me on the back, something that made me pitch forward and nearly dump the beer all over the polished wood. To be fair, the glass felt like it weighed twenty pounds. Who even made these things?

"Heard you're gettin' the Bensons all squared away." These people were almost irrepressibly friendly and I didn't really know what to do with it. "It's for the best—gives the old man here time to enjoy his retirement." She shot Erik a grin and squeezed Donna's shoulder. "Might keep the boys in line, too." Her gaze drifted to Ben. "Won't have to worry much about Levi, that one's got his head on straight. But the other three?" She shook her head. "I'll light a few candles for you in church."

Well, that was encouraging.

The bar filled up a little more as the evening went on, though I got the impression Fridays and Saturdays were their busiest nights. Tonight it was mostly the regulars and a few stragglers.

Levi took Donna and Erik home about an hour later, but Ben insisted we stay as he yukked it up with a few of the locals hunched over the bar and spread out over the booths. It wasn't hard to see he was the life of the party, larger than life in almost every respect, all smiles and affability and stupid jokes.

"Okay, big guy." I clapped a hand on his shoulder when he started missing his mouth, so I texted Levi about picking us up. "I think it's time to call it a night." Debbie caught my eye and nodded just once, and Ben made his rounds, slapping backs and shaking hands with every person in the bar.

"Come on, chuckles." I steered him toward the door, because it was clear that the self-imposed four-beer limit had been exceeded pretty significantly, and Levi's shoulders drooped when he caught sight of us.

"I'm so sorry, Beckett. I shouldn't have saddled you with this." He huffed out a heavy sigh and scrubbed a hand over his face. "Some days I can't decide which one is the bigger mess."

He helped Ben into the front seat of the truck, clipped his seatbelt and rolled down the window. It took a while to get the big guy situated, and when he climbed into the driver's seat Levi looked at me over his shoulder. "Apologies. I had to be a gentleman with this guy first, or it would have been a much bigger job picking him up out of the dirt."

I waved a hand at him. Ben was already leaning halfway out the window, singing at the top of his lungs as Levi backed the truck out, turned, and headed back in the general direction of the farm.

"Give him five minutes," Levi hollered. "He'll pass out."

"Will not, asshat." Ben cut his song short once he processed the insult. "Hey, you're going the wrong way; I'm on duty tonight." He hiccuped and burped at the same time, groaning.

"Afraid not, my dude." Levi flipped the blinker to make a left turn. "Judah said he'll take your shift. You're in no condition to do anything but sleep this shit off."

He was the one to drag Ben into his house with a "You, stay," in my direction. I got the impression he'd done this regularly over the years, because he seemed to have it down to a science and it was less than ten minutes later that he was back out in the truck.

"I'm really sorry about that." He rolled up the windows. "He, uh ... was doing better for a while. His girlfriend was doing a pretty good job of keeping him in line, but she got tired of being his babysitter, I suppose. She wanted something more and he didn't, or so he says. She left a couple weeks before you got here, or so the story goes. Can't really say I blame her, but he's gotten even worse since."

I hummed, propping my elbow on the window to look out, dark shapes whizzing past as Levi drove: fields, fences, trees, broken up by the occasional dot of light from a farmhouse set back from the road.

"You guys don't have to babysit me," I finally said. "I'll figure something out; I'll be fine."

"Judah's idea," he said roughly. "I told him Ben was out and he said he'd take his spot." He shrugged. "Don't tell him I told you this, but as much as he acts like you get under his skin, I think you're growing on him."

"Like a fungus," I muttered, but we both smiled a little.

The house smelled like warm apple cider when I stepped in and I waved to Levi before securing both doors and stepping out of my shoes. "Honey, I'm home!" slipped out of my mouth and I cringed and bit my lower lip, because I wasn't sure Judah was going to take that in the right spirit. He wasn't the jokester Ben was.

"Whatever, Lucy," drifted from the kitchen. "Guess I'd better put away the apron and your high heels because now that you're home, dress-up time is over."

I snorted. What was that, a joke coming from the world's biggest grump?

"Hope you found the red ones—those are hot."

"Highlights my killer calves," he joked as I drifted into the kitchen to see an actual smile on his face.

He was handsome to begin with, but when he smiled he was lethal.

"You're handy in the kitchen?" I asked, gesturing toward the pan he was stirring on the stovetop.

"Nah, still learning my way around. Cait wasn't much of a cook, something I didn't really realize until recently, just how much we leaned on Donna. She can't be our mom forever." Another smile, this one a little rueful.

"Well, you're in luck. I'm pretty okay at cooking and I love to bake."

His eyes lit up. "Cookies?"

"And cakes, pies, breads. My mom was an amazing baker and I picked it up from her."

Something that looked like deep sadness swept over his face and I wasn't sure what it was I'd done, so I went for misdirection: "Warming some cider?"

"Yeah, figured you were going to need something better than that awful beer Ben likes."

"How on earth can he drink so much of it?" I asked, genuinely shocked by how much the big man had put away over the course of the evening.

"Drowns his thoughts," Judah said, flicking off the burner. "Would like to say I don't understand it, but I do. Our family has always excelled at substance abuse. It's our singular coping mechanism and the smarter ones are off the sauce completely. Take that as you will when it comes to who's figured out their shit." He shrugged.

He pulled mugs from the cabinet and poured straight from the pan, then pulled out a bottle of Fireball I didn't remember putting there, adding a splash to each cup. "My guess is that you had one awful beer that you choked down about four hours ago." He grinned, passing me the mug. "This will help you sleep."

The truth was that I'd slept a little better the night before, grateful there was a man with a baseball bat sleeping on my sofa.

It wasn't late, but I drifted into the living room to unfold the bedding and make the sofa into a makeshift bed. Judah had neatly folded the sheet and blanket that morning and left them stacked, with the pillow on top, at one end.

The fire he'd clearly built snapped away cheerfully in the hearth, making me wonder when they'd had the chimney swept, and the unwelcome thought that I wasn't used to coming home to someone anymore nagged at me as I tucked the flat sheet around and beneath the cushions.

"Mind if I use the shower?" he asked, and I looked up to see him digging through a small duffel bag.

"By all means." I gestured toward the stairs. "I'll just be here." I pointed to the single overstuffed chair near the fireplace.

What I hadn't counted on was to look up no more than fifteen minutes later to see Judah, wet hair neatly combed, his beard trimmed down, in a fitted black t-shirt and … *gulp* … sweatpants. Gray ones.

"Uh…" That was it, my brain had officially flatlined, because suddenly I couldn't remember how to speak English. "Found everything you needed?"

Except underwear, apparently. Because it hadn't been intentional, but that was the first place my eyes had gone.

He smirked at me like he could read my thoughts, probably because I was plainly staring at his crotch and I Could. Not. Look. Away.

Judah Benson was going commando and it made the room about fifty degrees hotter because when faced with that, he seemed very human. He wasn't always a growly bear, was he? And some evil part of my brain wondered how long he'd been going without and if he knew how to use what he was packing.

Bad Beckett.

He didn't respond, just picked up his mug from where he'd left it on the fireplace mantel before he threw himself down on the sofa, one big arm stretched along the back.

What in the ovarian hell was happening? The man had muscular definition I'd never seen before, not gym muscles, but hard work muscles. Packed and defined. The kind that could snap someone in half or assist in fucking a woman through a wall if he decided to put his back into it.

"Gonna take a breath over there, Bec?" He looked completely amused.

"Sorry." I shook my head. Hard. "Spaced out, I think. I should let you get some sleep and get through a shower myself."

"You got some matching sweatpants?" he teased, because he had to know my brain was in the gutter.

Wallowing.

Rolling like a happy little piglet in slop.

"Nah." It was time to knock him a little off-balance and I rose quickly, carrying my mug into the kitchen to rinse and slot into the dishwasher. I couldn't see his face when I delivered the death blow, but I heard him groan softly when I called, "I don't bother; I sleep naked."

I was playing with fire and, with a jolt of terror to my gut, I realized that I liked it.

Chapter Nine

Judah

I listened while Beckett moved through the shower and into her room, the old wood flooring creaking as she walked. She had delivered her kill shot and scurried up the stairs like someone was chasing her, and I wondered if she'd fallen out of the practice of flirting—that was what that had felt like, anyway, but maybe I was reading into things I had no business reading into.

I hadn't flirted with a girl since the fourth grade, when I'd tripped Cait during a game of kickball at recess. What could I say? The charm was strong with me—and apparently it had worked, because eventually she'd married me.

Lying there as the fire burned down, staring at the ceiling and thinking of Cait, I wanted more Fireball. No cider this time. So I crept into the kitchen and poured what I considered a responsible amount into the mug. Not so much that I'd be incapacitated, but enough to help tip me over into sleep. Because the truth was that I didn't want to think about Cait, but I also didn't want to think about Beckett, and her little wisecrack about sleeping naked had gotten under my skin. It had been long enough that it didn't take much to pique my interest.

The drink did the trick and though I drifted off to sleep, I woke at every creak in the old house. As a kid I'd always thought it was haunted, but my Gramps said it was just settling.

It seemed to me like it had been settling for a hundred years.

My phone said it was just after three when something jolted me from a dream, something I didn't think had come from the dream itself. It had been a whisper of a noise, something from the far side of the house where a door led to the single-stall garage.

I jumped up without even thinking, my fist curling immediately around the baseball bat, rushing into the kitchen to snap on the light and throw open the door to the garage. There was no one there, the garage silent and still, and I could hear my heartbeat pounding in my ears as I looked down and realized what it was that had awakened me. A thin sheet of newspaper lay just inside the door, like it had been pushed through the crack. I didn't stoop to pick it up, I stepped over it, rushing through the garage and out the small side door into the yard, trying to quiet my breathing to listen for any sound at all in the deep darkness of the early morning.

The cold breeze rustled softly through the crisp leaves, a papery rattling that set my teeth on edge. It would be enough to hide the sound of soft footfalls if someone were making a speedy getaway on foot.

I held my position for long moments, the bat raised, my adrenaline cranking, but there was no engagement.

Eventually I let myself back in through the garage and, with a deep sense of foreboding, scooped the news sheet from the floor to drop onto the kitchen island. I knew better than to think I was going back to sleep, so I hit the button on the coffee pot to start an early brew and while it hissed and steamed I pulled out a stool and dropped down to read.

The paper was old, a piece that had clearly been handled time and again, repeatedly smoothed out, the date in the banner from twelve years earlier.

"What the..." My eyes skimmed the article though my brain couldn't keep up. I wasn't processing what I knew to be salient details about a home invasion in Texas, a burned horse barn and two outbuildings, several bodies, and a missing suspect.

Cade Langmore, 30, Rebecca Langmore, 4, and Frannie Kingston, 50.

I dragged a hand over my face, realizing the black-and-white photo was one of Beckett standing with her back to the camera, a sheriff staring directly into the lens as he wrapped her in a hug.

Ben was sleeping off too much booze and God knew what Dan was doing, but Levi would be up in an hour, so I tapped into our group chat.

Me: *Got a bigger problem than the Avila assholes. More suspicious activity at the cabin.*

It was another twenty minutes before a response rolled in and, as I'd expected, it was Levi. The voice of reason out of all of us.

Levi: *Pretty sure it has something to do with your dick finally waking up.*

Me: *Fuck off, it's way worse than that.*

I was only reasonably sure it was worse than that, and I hoped Levi would ignore that I'd walked right into his trap. Because hell, no. No part of me was getting involved with another woman like that, not ever.

I took a photo of the sheet of newspaper.

Dan: *The hell are you doing, blowing up our phones at four in the morning?*

Levi: *Our boy's learned how to read. So proud.*

There was nothing more for almost five long minutes, then...

Dan: *Oh, shit. I couldn't read that tiny print, but I found the article online. Why didn't we know this before?*

A tragic past seemed somewhat unlikely to show up in the sort of background check we'd have conducted, and I was pretty sure Levi had taken her at her word and performed only a cursory check-in with a few references.

Me: *Donna was right, she's lost a lot.*

Levi: *Maybe now you'll be nicer to her?*

Me: *I'm not mean to her, dickwad.*

Dan: Kissy face emoji.

Asshole.

Levi: *Gonna have to step up our efforts. Suggest you file a report this morning if you suspect trouble. Fire up the paper trail just to CYA.*

Yeah, there was that. I sighed, running a hand over my face and taking a deep chug of coffee as I weighed the options.

"Morning, Sal." I held open the front door, trying to keep my voice down as one of the two local officers wiped his boots on the doormat before following me into the kitchen.

Salvatore DiAngelo was an oddity in our little Midwestern town, an Italian transplant who'd moved to Colson Creek as a kid. He'd lost the accent, but the dark hair and bright blue eyes made him real popular with the ladies, something that infuriated his wife.

"Um, good morning." Beckett's voice was sleepy and I looked over Sal's shoulder to see her standing on the third stair, her hair a wild mess as she tightened the sash around the fluffiest robe I'd ever seen. She was a delicious little pink cream puff, and I ran a hand down my face to clear some really inappropriate thoughts. These things were starting to spin out of control. "Did something happen?"

"Yeah." My voice sounded like I'd been snacking on gravel. "Gonna have a chat with Sal here and see what we can figure out."

"Good morning, Sal." She held out one hand and I watched his eyes widen as he turned to take her in. That was when I looked at her through the eyes of another man and realized with a bone-shaking start that I wasn't the only one to realize Beckett was an absolute fucking knockout.

Sonofabitch. When had that happened?

"Good morning, ma'am. I apologize for waking you at such an early hour."

Oh, now the asshole was all smooth polish and charm. I gave him a stink eye that would have made Donna proud.

"Would seem we have a few things to sort." He gestured toward the kitchen and I sighed. He had no idea what we were about to sort—neither did she—and this was going to require massive amounts of caffeine.

"Yeah, so..." Where was I even supposed to start with this? I pulled the carafe off the warmer plate and filled three mugs hurriedly while Beckett moved to the refrigerator to fetch some cream.

"Uh, Bec ... hope you slept well." I pasted a grin on my face, a stupid one, because the truth was that I'd had enough time to think about what had happened and it scared the shit out of me. "Sal ... uh, here's how it goes. Bec found a calf carcass in her front yard not all that long ago–buried it. We all wrote that off as something weird."

Sal was blowing on his coffee, one thick, dark eyebrow already hitching up his forehead.

"Got some missing cows we been lookin' into. We're not sure that's at all related."

Now the other eyebrow was crawling upward.

"Someone broke into the house—sheared the storm door off the damn hinges." I was getting worked up already. "Levi and me replaced it, but last night..." There was a bile rising in my throat, something that made it seem unwise to add the acidic coffee to the mix. "Well, really not all that long ago. Less than an hour ago. I was sleeping and something woke me. A scraping noise." Beckett pulled her robe tighter, her eyes going wide.

"Someone shoved a piece of newspaper under the door between the house and the garage. It didn't take me long to get out there, but it was long enough for them to get away." My teeth ground together.

If only I'd been faster.

"Newspaper?" Her voice was thin and terrified.

"Yeah." I rose slowly and fetched the sheet from the far counter, where I'd left it. "Turns out you got secrets, Tex."

Her face went completely white, one hand lifting to cover her mouth and I could have sworn to you in that moment that her eyes filled with tears.

Fuck that. I couldn't handle tears.

"I think you should sit," Sal said softly, and he scooted a stool beneath her butt just as her knees gave out.

"More coffee for the lady?" he asked solicitously, like he was asking her if she wanted some, but he was looking at me. I turned and poured more into her mug before splashing in a stupid amount of cream.

The way she took her coffee meant it wasn't coffee at all, it was a damn milkshake.

"Now let me get this straight." Sal was still looking at me. "You went *chasing after* this person?"

"Didn't think it through so good." I shrugged, pouring another mug for him and then one for myself before resetting the basket and clicking the button to brew another pot. "Just kinda lost my shit and went for it."

"Do me a favor and *never* do that again," he admonished sternly. "You don't know what kind of lunatic you're up against. Only a freak would do something like this—this looks obsessive and weird—and you don't need to get tangled up in that."

Beckett hadn't moved yet and if it was possible, I thought her face was even more pale.

"Doin' okay there, Bec?" I said her name goofily, like I was clucking at a chicken. She was freaking me out a little and I wanted her to at least crack a smile.

"Judah," she whispered, "somebody knows."

What the hell she was talking about was anybody's guess.

"Knows what?" Sal was ready to run with it.

Beckett reached for her coffee with a shaking hand, sloshing a little of it on herself as she tried to get the liquid to her lips. She took several quick swallows before setting the mug back on the counter.

"It means he's found me."

I didn't like where this was going, not at all. "I think you're gonna have to be more specific, sugar lips."

That hiked one of Sal's eyebrows halfway up his forehead, but that didn't get a smile out of her either.

"Did you read the article?" Her voice shook when she asked, and I shrugged slowly.

"Skimmed it. Some kind of tragedy on a ranch in Texas. Some dead folks."

If there had been a sharp knife within her reach at that moment, I think she'd have stabbed me with it—gone for the jugular, too.

"Someone was stalking me, Judah. Someone I had absolutely no relationship with. I did everything right. I documented everything. I secured the property. I got my concealed carry and went to the range to practice at least once a week. I put up security lights, installed a video doorbell, and took out a restraining order."

The hair raised on my arms, because I knew where this was going.

"Those dead folks were *my* people. I couldn't keep them safe." Her eyes filled with tears. "The cops found a dugout on my property. He lived on my property in a pit in the earth for *months*, watching us. Watching my family and our patterns. And while I was away for work for a few days, he decided to eliminate the competition. The things that his twisted brain had decided were keeping us apart."

Now I needed to sit, and I sank down onto the last remaining stool. Someone had taken everything from her, something I could feel in my bones.

"It's been twelve years," her voice shook, "and I still think about them every day. I ask myself what I could have done differently; what more I could have done to keep them safe."

"Fuck me six different ways from Sunday," Sal huffed out under his breath and I couldn't help but cut him a funny look. Where did he come up with this shit? "He out on parole or something?"

Beckett shivered and I shot Sal the meanest glare I had.

It was a good one, I'll have you know.

"He's not eligible for parole. He pleaded in order to avoid the death penalty. As far as I know, he's still in Ellis." Her face twisted. "I did everything right. I changed my last name. I moved away. I sold the ranch and took a desk job. I disappeared." She swallowed hard. "I lived so quietly ... I didn't do anything that would draw attention."

"Hey." It came out harsher than I'd intended, and her head snapped up. "We don't know what's going on yet, so that thing that's going on in there—" I made a winding gesture in the direction of her head. "Stop the doom spiral. We don't know shit yet, so no sense in makin' yourself sick."

The look Sal shot me told me he'd been thinking the same thing I was.

It was two hours and three cups of coffee later that Sal rose to leave. The sun was just starting to come up and he said he wanted to have a look around the property to see if there was anything he could document.

Beckett looked wrecked and I knew she'd relived the worst night of her life about a thousand times in the space of the last few hours.

"Hey." She dragged her eyes slowly up to mine when I said it. "Pack some stuff. I'm taking you to my place and you're going to crash there for a nap so we can both feel like you're safe while I go do the big boy shit."

That got a grin out of her.

"If you don't mind, I think I'd feel safer having other people in the house. Would it be okay if I went with you and just crashed on the sofa in your parents' living room?"

Was she kidding me? Donna would be overjoyed and Bec probably wouldn't get any sleep because they'd end up braiding each other's hair or some weird shit like that. I didn't know what women did when they got together, but Donna could talk the hind leg off a mule once you got her going—and it was obvious she already adored Beckett.

"So no kiddin', huh?" I asked as we climbed into my farm truck. I tossed her bag into the back seat and she pulled herself into the passenger seat with the help of the *oh shit* bar, a huge travel mug of coffee in her other hand. "Guess you really were the perfect person for the job—you got a story wilder than mine."

As far as I knew, she still didn't know my story. My brothers didn't talk about it out of respect for me, but chances were good Donna would fill her in on a few of the details as time went on.

"We need to check the woods," was all she said, and her voice shook.

"Nah, you don't think this guy really broke out and came to finish the job?" I stole a look at her. "Because I would *not* put it past those Avila assholes to do something this shitty."

"Well, it worked." She clipped her belt and wrapped her arms over her chest. "I'm about three seconds away from a panic attack."

"Xanax, take me away?" I tried to tease. "I got some in the glovebox there if you need it—doc keeps prescribing it and I just keep putting it in there."

She turned the knob on the glovebox and about fifteen bottles of pills came pouring out in a rush, something that made her shake her head at me. "You're probably supposed to be taking these."

"*Supposed to* sounds an awful lot like directions to me, and I don't much like being told what to do, in case you didn't get that memo yet."

Her eyes drifted shut as her head shook back and forth. "You are going to be a thorn in my side, Judah Benson."

I'd been accused of as much and worse before, and more than once by my wife. I had no problems with that.

Donna didn't say a thing when I walked Beckett into the house that morning, and Dad looked up from his newspaper and coffee with a wide grin. Erik Benson was a sly old fox who didn't miss a thing and his eyes darted from her face to mine, concern quickly creasing his forehead. "What happened?"

"Donna." My voice sounded weirdly strained. "Okay with you if Bec crashes on the sofa for a while? Kind of a short night last night."

Dad's eyebrows rose suggestively and I gave him a single, sharp shake of my head. Ben was the troublemaker, but Dad was the original mold and he never missed his chance to give me shit, probably because I never took it like a champ, something I would only admit to myself. I was predictable, always growly and annoyed. It was a Benson trait: most of us liked to poke the bear and Dad was the gold medalist of shit-stirring. He was just much more suave and subtle about it. A real connoisseur.

Donna hustled her out of the room and I knew the sofa wasn't happening. She would have Beckett installed in her coziest guest room in no time, probably ferrying up tea and cookies for snacks.

"Got a problem." I dropped into the chair across from Dad. I hadn't brought him up to speed on the weird happenings yet, because I hadn't wanted to worry him. The man deserved to enjoy his retirement, for fuck's sake, even though we were bumbling our way through the transition.

He folded his newspaper slowly and reached for his coffee, leaning back in his chair. Something creaked—maybe the chair, maybe his back—and he fixed me with a sharp look. "Something you should've told me a while ago?" he asked, making me wonder just how much he already knew.

"Maybe. Didn't think it was real serious at the time, just weird."

"Have anything to do with our missing cattle?"

"Not sure." I desperately wanted more coffee. My early morning marathon and the expenditure of all that adrenaline made me wonder how I was going to keep myself upright the rest of the day. There was a lot to get done today, too; no time for a nap in the hayloft. "Had a couple weird occurrences out at the cabin."

"That why you boys been takin' turns babysitting Beckett?" he asked sharply, and I wondered how much he knew about that.

"Thought it was the Avilas stirring up trouble because Levi keeps telling them to go fuck themselves every time they try to push in and buy land."

"Entitled sons of bitches," Dad muttered. "Parents never taught 'em the meaning of the word no. No manners. That field they got behind ours, they always go through it rather than stick to the road—run our crops right down."

That was something I'd never heard him complain about.

"Yeah, well ... not so sure it's them anymore. Had something creepy happen last night and it kinda felt like a warning shot."

"Get a police report filed?" he asked, crossing his arms over his chest.

"For whatever it's worth, sure. Sal came out at the asscrack." I swallowed hard, running a hand down my face and over my tired eyes. "Heard something in the kitchen early this morning and found an old newspaper clipping slid under the door. Went tearing out into the yard trying to catch the sick fucker, but no luck. Not a damn trace."

"And what was this article?" he asked firmly, his eyes fixed on my face.

"Bec says she had a stalker." I blew out a slow breath as it started to really unfurl in my brain what that might mean. "Lived in a dugout on her property for God knows how long and learned her family's routines. Didn't drill down on the details real close, but she says he's in Ellis—I think he killed her family, Dad."

Dad already had a hand over his heart and he sucked in a deep breath, only to blow it right back out. "Just might've found someone with a sadder story than you, boy."

I nodded slowly. "Maybe. At least someone who understands, I suppose."

“Should probably stop being a grumpy dick to her, eh?” he asked, just the corner of his mouth quirking upward.

“Keeps her on her toes.”

Only, now that I knew there was something ugly in her past, I felt a little badly about the way I’d been treating her, like I was the only person who knew suffering. By all accounts, from what I’d skimmed in that article, she’d been through a hell even worse than my own. My experience had been a sudden, catastrophic loss and I was still struggling to adjust to the idea, but she’d had to live with hers every day for the past twelve years, through investigations and interviews, court dates and testimonies.

I knew the worst part came after all those things were over, when a person was left alone with their own thoughts.

“Are we sure we can keep her safe?” he asked slowly. “Maybe best to let her go her own way?”

“Don’t know that she has anywhere else to be.” I shrugged slowly, a really uncomfortable feeling in my chest that I thought might be pity, and I knew she wouldn’t want that. But was that all of it? Maybe there was something else in there, mixed up, tied in, and I couldn’t pick it apart. Like some part of me understood her need to have people of her own—family, like I still had in some way, even if they drove me fucking nuts.

The truth was that I wasn’t entirely sold on Beckett yet, although it was obvious some part of me enjoyed her company, and yet it was weird to think that she might leave. I liked to argue with her and give her a hard time, just because I enjoyed being ornery. It let out a little of the anger every time, and she was willing to give it right back in attitude and smart-assed responses. But I realized now that I didn't really *dislike* her either, not the way I had when Levi introduced the person I knew would turn my life upside down. And that scared the fuck out of me, because I didn't need to make room in my life for anyone. I had all the people in it I needed and I wasn't about to open up my heart to anyone new.

That shit hurt too much.

"Suppose she figured out how to put herself back together," he said slowly and I raised an eyebrow as I watched the thought process play out on his face.

"Not like she wrote the book on it," I said, and he shrugged.

"Had a little longer than you, maybe, but seems to be a productive member of society."

Well, that was something I couldn't claim lately so if that was the insinuation he was making, he had me there.

"Wouldn't be surprised if Donna knows all of it already," I commented, rising to pour myself a cup of coffee and Dad snorted behind me.

"That woman's got the jump on the Almighty when it comes to being all-knowing."

"The baby Jesus heard that, Erik Benson." Donna's voice sailed down the hallway and he was grinning contritely when she floated into the kitchen. "Besides, we have an understanding." She pointed upward and I shook my head at her. Donna was the religious one in the family, the one who dragged my dad to church every week because it was "good for his soul."

Donna was one of the best, kindest people I knew, and I knew for a fact she'd been the one to save Dad when he'd resigned himself to remaining alone forever. She had an ugly past of her own, a no-good gym teacher husband who'd upgraded to a high school cheerleader and left her and their kids. So when Dad started seeing her, she had something of an idea of how he felt, stuck raising kids by himself because his wife decided she was in love with another man.

"That girl can't be left in the cabin all by herself." Donna clucked at me. "Even if there's no real danger, she's going to drive herself mad with worry." She bustled past me to swing open the oven door and the smell of cinnamon and sugar made my mouth water. "You boys can't keep sleeping on the sofa, and it's improper for her to stay at any of your places. You know how people will talk."

There was the squawk of the screen door, a shuffling sound, and a big hand landed on my shoulder.

"Thought I'd check in." It was Levi, dropping into the chair next to me. "Got everything sorted?"

I gave him the abridged version of the morning's events, in addition to what I'd skimmed from the article, and he ran a hand over his mouth. "Can put her up at my place if you need a spot to stash her. Dawg would just about rip anyone in half trying to come on the property—thought he was gonna puncture the tire on the delivery truck yesterday when I had a lumber shipment come in."

Dawg still lived with Levi. Not only had my brother become ridiculously attached to the dog, but the giant Rottweiler was still a tangible reminder of my boys. I still couldn't hack it, but I didn't blame Dawg for that.

"Already got the town in a tizzy." Dad slurped his coffee noisily. "Pretty girl working with the Benson boys; neighbors probably got bets going on which one of you ends up with her." He grinned. "Think there's a few wouldn't mind their shot with her, but they know better."

Levi shook his head and I wondered for the first time in my life if I should have moved away while I'd had the chance. These people had nothing better to do than gossip and poke around in business that wasn't their own. It was a real perk to small town life.

"I'm out." Levi held up his hands, a small smile on his face.

"Never questioned it, you monk." I socked him in the shoulder, hard, and he absorbed the blow with a grunt. It was no secret Levi didn't have time for women, and hadn't for years, since Hannah left for California.

"Has anyone checked on Benjamin this morning?" Donna was sliding some magical confection out of the oven and my stomach roared. She lifted one eyebrow and reached into a cabinet to pull out a stack of plates.

"Need to get him a babysitter, too," Dad said, his eyes cutting quickly to me and then away—but I saw it. He'd absolutely had a part in hiring Beckett, and now I knew it.

Chapter Ten

Beckett

Donna tapped softly on the door hours or days later—I wasn't even sure anymore, I'd fallen into such a deep sleep in the softest, dreamiest bed I'd ever been in. My eyelids felt like they were lead weights, refusing to do more than barely crack open, and I croaked something that sounded like *Come in*.

"Sweetheart," her voice was soft. "If you're hungry, lunch is on. But if you want to catch up on some more sleep, just come down when you're ready and I can warm a plate."

I loved Donna already, so much. She was soft and pliant, sweet and gentle—but if you pushed too hard, and this part I knew intimately—watch the fuck out. This woman was not fooling around. If you dared come for those she loved, payment would be swift and probably pretty awful.

"Mmmfff." My words weren't working yet; that part of my brain didn't seem to be awake yet and I raised my head slowly to give her a sleepy smile. "Probably shouldn't sleep all day or I'll be up all night, freaking myself out." Phew, there they were.

"I don't like it," she said, crossing the space to sit on the edge of my bed, her fingers going to the stitching on the thick, beautiful quilt. "That cabin is just far enough from everyone that I don't have a good feeling about this." She swallowed hard. "Erik and I have been talking about it and we'd like to extend the offer to have you live here until we get this sorted, whenever it is. We want you to feel comfortable and safe; there's more than enough room in this house for you to have your own space."

That would be uncomfortable, disrupting the routines and rhythms of a couple who hadn't had another soul in their house in what was probably decades, and I shook my head slowly. "I really appreciate it, Donna. Thank you. I'll figure something out, but I'll keep the idea on the table." I reached over to lay my hand on her arm. "Judah's probably right, someone's just trying to scare me because I'm an easy target—these Avila guys he keeps telling me about." I tried to chuckle, to fill myself with some kind of bravado, because I didn't feel it at all. "People get weird when money's involved."

I spent the rest of the afternoon in the small office on the property, going through the files Levi kept before I tackled the outdated software as I tried to make sense of the numbers. He'd sent me some cursory information before I moved that I hadn't had much time to review, and my eyes narrowed as I cataloged the figures. The loss of so many cows was going to hurt tremendously. Each spring and fall the Bensons sold a large number of cattle and used a portion of the money to fund the following year's seed purchase. It was going to be tight this next year, the price of seed corn having gone through the roof.

"Lookin' worried there, Bec." I startled as the door opened and Benjamin stepped through. "We done the farm in that bad already?"

I sighed heavily. This was my burden to bear now and there were going to be some hard decisions to make in the near future. "I'm just a little concerned about how the loss of all these cows is going to knock the bottom line. I still don't have a lead on anything from the auction houses."

"Maybe they weren't sold," Ben said simply, shrugging his wide shoulders before folding himself into a chair. "Maybe there was a trade."

I liked that idea even less, not a single footprint to follow.

"The rest seem to like the pasture next to Donna's garden." I grinned, because Donna was out there now, sorting through squash and celery, putting her garden up for the season while the ever-curious, nosy cows lined the fence to watch her and nibble on any scraps she might decide to hand out.

"She did that to herself." He grinned. "She walks out there and feeds them shit and they're just like dogs who come running for treats. They'd live in the house if she'd let 'em, big ol' grass puppies."

I leaned back in my chair to critically survey the handsome, enormous man sitting across from me. These Benson boys had really hit the genetic lottery. I could see why the local women might have opinions about who ended up with them, and it was possible that meant I had a target on my back.

"What's your story, Ben?" slipped out and I tried to hide the wince. Trading secrets seemed a little premature, especially with the happy-go-lucky brother who was clearly struggling and trying to conceal it with a smiling face.

"Eh." He shrugged again. "Not much story to tell. Grew up here. Been here my whole life. Had a couple girlfriends who weren't real interested in sticking around; suppose I was too small town for them—kind of like Judah. Always been happy here, don't need anything bigger or better or ... more." He let it trail off slowly, a troubled look on his face and I waited for him to explain, but there were no more words.

"I used to think that, too." I folded my arms across my chest and leaned back, the chair creaking on its casters. "I grew up in west Texas, on a ranch. We raised show horses." Ben's right eyebrow lifted but he didn't say anything. "It was enough for me. I was content to live there, to take it over when my parents were ready to step back."

"No brothers or sisters?" he asked softly and I dipped my head.

"One sister. We haven't talked in twelve years. She blames me for what happened to my parents and is ... well, we're not in touch."

"Blamed you for what some sick weirdo did?" he asked, and I wondered just how much the Bensons already knew about the event that had destroyed my life, the thing that drove my father to drink himself to death. He had been states away when it happened, on a trip to pick up an expensive horse we'd just purchased to vary the bloodline.

I shrugged slowly. "People process grief in different ways. Hers was to blame those who were still living."

"Sorry, Bec." One side of his mouth twisted into something like a grimace. "People are fuckin' weird."

Ben's phone dinged and he fished it out of his pocket, fingers flying over a small screen as he cursed. "Tiny frickin' screen and big-dick hands." He snorted as he said it. "Judah says I'm supposed to leave you alone, so I gotta give him a hard time cuz it'll make him crazy." He looked up, his standard mischievous grin back in place. "Told him he'd better be quick, because I'm in here stealing his girl."

A rush of heat to my face surely colored my cheeks red and I dipped my head. I wasn't sure how I felt about that, or that Ben had already decided something like that, when it was clear Judah could hardly stand me.

"Bec?" Ben sounded suspicious. "You blushin' over there?"

I lifted my head with a wince. I wasn't sure why I'd blushed over that. "Definitely not." I cleared my throat. "Judah can hardly stand to be in the same room as me."

"Probly cuz you're a knockout." He shrugged easily. "Prettier than Cait was any day, in my opinion—a lot nicer, too." He said it without any particular inflection, just a simple observation, and I felt my eyes widen. Was that why it felt like Judah disliked me, I made him think of Cait?

"Maybe it's the hair." He lifted a hand to the top of his own head. "Cait had real nice hair, like yours–more red, maybe. And she was just as feisty as you." He grinned.

I hadn't been called feisty in a long time, a streak I'd been sure died out twelve years ago when I'd just stopped fighting. Truthfully, it had been because I'd stopped living when I lost them.

"He's real loyal, Bec. That's the problem. It don't mean he dislikes you, but that he has a hard time letting in anyone new. *Anyone*. He's always been that way, but it's gotten worse."

I wasn't sure why that was a problem but I didn't ask him to clarify, and his phone buzzed again. It was something that made a broad, mischievous smile break across Ben's face and he finally pushed slowly to his feet. "Suppose I should go, before he loses the rest of his shit." He grinned at me. "Says if I don't leave you alone he'll come kick my ass, but I'd like to see him try."

I had to agree it was fairly unlikely anyone would best Ben, considering his size.

God had broken the mold after making the massive baby Benson.

I spent the rest of the day performing system updates and I made several more calls to contacts on the cattle auction circuit. I wasn't about to let this go, even if I kept hitting a dead end.

Those cows hadn't vanished into thin air and someone had to know what had happened to them.

"Ready to call it, Bec?" Judah's voice was surprisingly gentle. "Donna says she has dinner ready."

I sagged into my chair with a combination of exhaustion and relief. I had been ready to call it for some time, and the thought of someone cooking for me was almost too good to pass up.

"I'm good," I called, fully aware I was not. Why had I said that?

"Whatever, Langston. Don't even play with me." I startled a little, because no one called me by that last name anymore. "It's been six hours since we ate lunch, so let's go."

Was Judah my babysitter now?

"Nah, I'm good. Thanks, though—I'll head home."

"The fuck you will." He looked annoyed. "Don't make me sleep on your lumpy-ass sofa for a third night, friend."

Friend was said with annoyance.

"You've been relieved of duty." I forced a smile across my face. "Donna invited me to stay in the guest room, so you can head on home—but thanks." And wasn't that a shame, sending the man in gray sweatpants back home all alone.

"The fuck you will," he said again, and he looked mad. "Bec, I'm not playing around. You can go right on ahead and spend the night in Donna's guest room, but we are going to handle this. Tomorrow we're gonna figure shit out."

"Thanks, Judah. I'm just tired and ... I don't know... scared, I guess." I shrugged. I had been exhausted for more than a decade, always looking over my shoulder. More than scared—terrified.

"Fine. But tomorrow we're retrofitting the rest of your place, and if that doesn't work..." He paused for a moment, looking really mad. They were dumping a lot of time and money they didn't have into this. "Well, if that doesn't work, we're going to move you into my place." He held up a hand, an *expression* on his face. "Nothing improper, just ... keeping you away from those assholes."

There was a weird thought, having Judah as a permanent roommate. I wasn't sure that would work out all that well, and I was sure Donna would have something to say about it. And though we were getting along better than we had initially, I knew it would take nothing for us to start fighting like cats and dogs.

I ended up staying in Donna's guest room for the next three nights while the brothers worked on installing security cameras and heavy window locks. Going was slow, since work was done at the end of their workdays, and three of them were doing their own thing now, rather than working on the farm.

Levi was the one around most often, as he was slowly handing over his duties to me. But I knew he was running himself ragged with a custom furniture and specialty restoration business he'd been running on the side for a long time. Now he could throw himself into it fully and while I could see it brought him joy, it was clear he was exhausted.

"Thank you for this." My voice wobbled a little as Levi walked me through the changes they'd made to the cabin.

"Can't get internet this far out–no cables," he announced. "This one's that link thing—some satellite system."

I winced, because I didn't even want to know what that had cost, and I wondered if the brothers were pooling money from their own pockets, because it hadn't been disappearing from my budget.

He showed me how to operate it, how to disarm and reset the alarm, had me key in my own code, and I wondered who would respond if the alarm was ever tripped. Sal had been nice enough, but the fact the tiny town had two police officers on rotating duty didn't instill a lot of confidence in my quaking heart.

"I appreciate everything you've done." My voice shook a little. "I'm sure I'll be fine, now that you've installed the Iron Dome." I tried to smile and Levi cracked one in return.

"You need anything, you just call any one of us and we'll be here in a heartbeat. I'm sorry we dragged you into whatever this is, and we're gonna fix it."

I wasn't so convinced they had dragged me into anything, so much as that something or someone had followed me. It was something that I'd lived in irrational fear of, despite the fact I knew my stalker was locked away in Ellis for the rest of his life.

It wasn't long enough, in my opinion.

Levi patted my shoulder and told me to call him immediately if I needed anything, and I thanked him profusely. I was thankful the eldest Benson was such a kind, generous, giving man. He clearly felt responsible for me, and in a way it was like having an older brother, something I'd always wanted.

"Get some rest, Bec." Levi pulled me into an easy hug. "Things'll get easier, you'll see."

"Hands to yourself, fuckface." It was almost a snarl and I felt Levi tense and then relax, a chuckle rolling out of him when he turned to see Judah standing in the doorway.

Apparently this little house had an open door policy and I was just now getting the memo.

"Awful nice of you to check up on her, Jude." Levi clapped his brother's shoulder so hard, Judah's frame shook a little. "See? You got some thoughtfulness in you. Never thought I'd see the day." His eyes twinkled with mischief and I wondered if each of the brothers was beginning to feel responsible for me, something a little disheartening, because I'd already figured out I wasn't interested in Judah Benson viewing me as a little sister.

Boy, wasn't that just going to complicate things?

"Donna sent some things." Judah's voice was rough and scratchy, something it seemed to do when he was angry. "Told her I'd drop them off on my way over." He leaned over, setting a box on the floor.

"I was just heading out; walked Bec through how to handle the alarm system," Levi said easily, something that seemed to take a little of the ire out of Judah. He was so damn prickly all the time, even with his brothers. I couldn't imagine it had always been that way. "I'm headed out to Montana in the morning," he reminded me, then turned his head toward Judah. "Gonna be gone a couple weeks, at least. Got a contract to do a renovation for someone Ash knows."

Judah's face split with a sweet smile. "May as well move to Montana, with all the times you've been out there. Ash is like your pimp, always hookin' you up. You stayin' with her, then? Be good to catch up."

"Yeah, looking forward to it." Levi suffered that same Benson affliction: When he smiled, he was devastatingly gorgeous. "She's already warned me to lock my bedroom door at night; says their nanny's a real predator." He chuckled. "Haven't met that one yet. She's been away the last few times I've been out there and I kind of wonder if Ash arranged that for my safety."

It had crossed my mind that maybe Levi could use a little distraction. He was too tense and serious, all work and no play, and from the little Donna had let slip, he wasn't interested in dating.

"Do you some good to find a playmate." Judah grinned wickedly, his mind on the same track as my own.

Levi just shook his head at him. "Not happening. Got no time for that foolishness."

Yeah, the three of us in this room knew something about that. A view probably born of a common affliction: grief.

Levi patted my shoulder, then clapped Judah's again before letting himself out the door and Judah and I were left in an awkward silence.

"So..." The single word felt gunfire-loud in the quiet room. "What did Donna send with you?"

"Oh, right." Judah sprang into action, obviously just as uncomfortable as I was. "She said you probably needed more winter things, so she was doing some cleaning and thought she'd send over some shit." He popped the lid off the box to reveal warm flannel sheets and several soft blankets. They looked suspiciously new.

"That was awfully sweet of her." I swallowed hard against the lump in my throat, because I'd commented on the delightfully soft flannel sheets on the guest bed and she'd clearly taken note.

"Donna is one of the best people I know," he answered honestly. "Never understood how she puts up with all us assholes. Probably because she loves my dad an awful lot—she'd have to in order to deal with us, because we're in her hair all the time."

"Everyone deserves to be loved like that," was out of my mouth before my brain engaged, and I watched him swallow hard.

Shit, I'd gone and stepped in it. "I mean..."

"Yeah, I know what you mean." He nodded, his expression sad. "You're right, too."

"Did Cait love you that way?" I asked, because obviously I was batting a thousand. I was really hellbent on digging myself in tonight.

"Dunno," he answered honestly, shrugging his shoulders. "Thought for a while she did, but we grew apart, I suppose. She loved the boys, and that's what matters."

That wasn't enough, but I was smart enough not to say it.

"Kind of funny, isn't it?" I chuckled. "Yours was Cait, mine was Cade."

His lips hooked up just a little at the very ends. "S'pose. He love you like that?"

I thought about that for a moment, the question more than fair. "I don't know that I had him long enough to ever really put that to the test, honestly. We were only married seven years."

"Can't imagine what that put you through." He shook his head. "Tried to decide if I'd feel better there was *someone* I could be mad at, but haven't come up with the answer yet."

I was fairly certain he was still angry with Cait, but I didn't say so, because grief and anger were usually pretty difficult things to pick apart.

"Weird shit." He nodded, the air thick and uncomfortable once more. "You think it ever gets any easier?"

It felt like he was looking for some kind of guidance.

"Yes and no. You never stop missing them, you just get used to the gaping wound."

"Great." He rolled his eyes, because I was clearly killing my motivational pep talk. "Thanks, Tex."

His ridiculous nickname made me grin. It was something he'd let slip a few times already, and I gestured he should follow me into the kitchen. "May as well sit for a while." I didn't want to say anything like *It'll keep you from going home to drown your sorrows*. "I was going to roll out some pie crust."

He hummed and rubbed one hand over his stomach, though it may have been an unconscious gesture.

While he sat at the table, I made hot chocolate. Then he sat quietly, watching while I rolled out the dough for a pie. I had a metric fuckton of apples from Donna and while tonight's project was six apple pies, tomorrow night's project was applesauce before they all got away from me. Cooking and baking had always settled me, something I'd picked up from my mom. When she was happy, she made pie. When she was sad, she made casseroles and brownies. When she was stressed she worked on fussy, tedious projects to take her mind off things, like elaborately decorated cakes.

"Don't think I ever saw Cait make a pie," he mused and I half-turned to look over my shoulder at him, giving him an encouraging smile. I didn't say anything though, wondering if he'd allow the thread of that thought to spool out. "She tried to make a cake once, for Braden's birthday. The kind from a box. She said she'd give being a domestic goddess one good go, and then she brought the fire extinguisher in from the garage—just in case." A small smile, something wistful. "Good thing, too, because that ended with a kitchen remodel when she set the joint on fire."

Fire was my worst fear. The word made me shudder, my memory folding time to take me back to the night I lost everything. I had been too late. By the time I arrived home everyone was gone, including sixteen beautiful horses when a stable was burned down around them.

Judah didn't notice I'd gone still. "We put it out and cleaned up and the next day I drove into town to pick up a cake from the bakery. Thomas the Tank Engine." He fell quiet and I stole another look at him. He was lost in thought, not in a way that appeared sad, but like he was sitting with the memory despite the fact it was uncomfortable.

The oven couldn't manage all six pies at once and after sliding in the first four, I washed my hands at the sink and rinsed our mugs, refilling both with hot tea before dropping down next to Judah. Sitting across from him carried the distinct possibility of making him uncomfortable, like I was obligating him to look at me, so I sat next to him and waited for him to say something.

"You have any memories like that?" His voice was soft and I leaned my chin on one hand. The memories still had sharp, jagged edges that cut me every time I retrieved them, but even I knew it was time to move on.

"Cade and my daughter shared a birthday." I tried to smile, but it felt weak. "He joked that she was his birthday present, like she knew to show up early. She was born five weeks early."

He nodded, signaling that he was listening even as he stared down into his tea.

"Cade was a broker of sorts. He traveled the country collecting orders and selling our horses. He was the one with big ambitions. I just ran the ranch and trained the horses. My parents had moved to the large guesthouse on the property and we lived in the main house..."

He lifted his eyes, probably because I was oversharing. This information was in no way pertinent to a birthday celebration.

"Our daughter loved horses—I suppose it was in her DNA, considering what her parents did. My mom made this ridiculously fancy cake for the two of them the year Rebecca turned three. She airbrushed it and everything. It was like the scene out of a western, with a band of wild horses streaking across the prairie." I pulled in a deep breath. "Rebecca smashed her face in it." I couldn't help but smile just a little at the memory of Rebecca helping Cade to blow out the candles and then, once the candles were removed, face-planting in the cake. "She said the picture was so pretty, she thought she could get inside it. She was so upset when she realized that she couldn't—I don't think she cared about the mess she'd made."

Judah gave me a small smile. "Kids don't give a shit."

The chair creaked as I leaned back and stretched out my legs, surprised to find the silence between us was comfortable for once as we both sat with our thoughts.

It was the timer that jolted me from the memories I didn't entertain often, and I jumped up to swing open the oven door. All four pies slid neatly onto a cooling rack while I placed the other two in the oven and reset the timer.

"So, how'd you end up in management and consulting, or whatever?" Judah asked easily, leaning back in his own chair and I carried one of the pie plates to the table and set it on a hot pad.

"It was actually my dad's idea. He had some distant cousins up in the Dallas-Fort Worth area who ran a firm. They were a decent-size outfit and had a good reputation. I had boots-on-the-ground knowledge of how a successful ranch ran and I was a quick study, so I advanced quickly. I was fortunate to gain a lot of experience in a hurry, because it turns out that between farms and ranches there's a decent amount of carry-over." I smiled at him.

Grabbing plates, forks and a pie server, I returned to the table. There was still nuclear steam coming from the top of the pie, so I sat and gave him another piece of my story.

"I needed to relocate after what had happened. A fresh start. Even though the man who destroyed everything I loved was put in prison for life, I couldn't stay there. I was terrified, fearful he had some way to reach me even from Ellis. So I packed up and disappeared. That's when I moved to the Dallas-Fort Worth area."

"And now you think he's found you?" Judah asked quietly, something that made me shudder even in the warmth of the kitchen.

"That's the first place my mind goes when weird things happen."

"More weird things been happenin'?" he asked slowly, reaching over to sink the knife into the pie.

"My brain makes things up to scare me sometimes." I shrugged. "Two nights ago I could have sworn someone was tapping on the window, but it was just a tree branch. Then last night I thought I smelled gas, so I woke your parents." I winced. "It was nothing and I felt like an idiot."

Judah nodded and plated two pieces of the pie. "No one could blame you."

Yeah, blaming myself was already more than enough.

"You think the missing ever stops?" he asked, his eyes on the pie as he held a fork suspended over his slice.

Twelve years had taught me that no, it didn't stop, but I didn't want him to despair. "Maybe." I cut a piece slowly and sat staring at it as I tried to formulate the words. "I think you learn to focus on the happy things, it just takes a while for your brain to finish sorting. You have to be patient."

He nodded like that was good enough and ate his piece of pie slowly, thoughtfully. When he was finished he stood and collected both plates, walking them to the sink and washing each plate and fork and placing them in the drying rack. The timer on the stove went off as he finished and, turning it off, he grabbed the hot pads and removed the two remaining pies to cool on the stovetop.

"Thanks, Tex." He sounded uncomfortable again. "Pie was delicious."

That made me get up and I snatched a roll of plastic wrap from the drawer, tightly sealing one of the cooled pies to hand to him. "This one's yours. I'll take one to Dan, Judah, Levi, and Donna tomorrow. It's silly. It's little. But this is some small way for me to say thank you for everything you've all done for me."

"Don't owe us nothin', Bec." Judah's voice was rough and scratchy. "Never meant to drag you into our shit."

I wasn't so sure this had anything to do with them, but that they owned it was admirable.

He shrugged back into a coat, the pie plate clutched to his chest. It made me wonder when someone had last made anything, cooked or baked for him, a woman who wasn't Donna.

"Thanks for the things," I said lamely as he shoved his feet back into his big, unlaced boots. "I'm sure I'll be fine."

"You know who to call if you're not." His expression was serious. Stern, almost. "I'm five minutes down the road. You need me, just call. I probably won't wake up for a text."

I nodded and let him out the door, locking the security door as he walked toward his truck. Then, as it started up and backed down the driveway, I closed the main door and bolted it as well. Then I set the alarm and fed the fire once more before drifting back to the kitchen to clean up.

A lifetime of habit had me working nearly in the dark, most of the lights out now that I was the only one in the house, and I wondered not for the first time if I should install shades and drapes on the weirdly bare windows.

Everything cleaned up and put away, I banked the fire, checked all the doors and the window locks, then drifted upstairs to shower and go to bed.

Chapter Eleven

Judah

I thought about eating another piece of pie before bed, but I decided to have some for breakfast instead, so I tucked it into the fridge and took a hot shower. It had been a long, difficult day. I smelled like cow shit, and I refused to drag that smell into my bed.

As usual, sleep was elusive and I was tempted to get up and search the cabinets for something to knock me out. I knew better, though. Levi had really stepped up his game lately, letting himself into my house every day to do a sweep for booze. When he found it he poured it down the sink drain and left the empty, rinsed bottle on the countertop for me to find when I got home. It was almost like he was taunting me, but I knew his intentions were good. It was the big brother version of "*I see you,*" and I knew it was because he cared. It just annoyed the shit out of me.

It bothered me to think of Bec by herself in that little house, probably still scared half to death despite the fact it was Fort Knox. Nothing was getting into that house now, not even a spider.

My phone dinged and my heart was in my throat as I snatched it off the bedside stand.

Calista: *Just checking on you, Jude. I hope you're doing better.*

I heaved out a huge sigh, because I had to admit to myself that I'd kind of wanted the text to be from Beckett.

Cait's sister was struggling with her passing just as much as I was. The two had been oil and water, night and day. Cait was confident and assertive, whereas Calista was friendly but flighty. But still, the loss of her sister had unmoored her almost as much as it had me, and she was still struggling to find her way.

Ben thought it was weird my sister-in-law texted me sometimes. Calista had never liked me because I wasn't good enough for her big sister, Cait being all of a year older. She'd tried to talk her out of marrying me, and when Braden was born she hadn't come to see him until he was almost two months old.

You could say it wasn't a surprise that we'd never been close.

Me: *I'm fine, thanks. Hope you're well.*

I didn't want to encourage anything. Calista could talk a rock to death and she was sweet enough when she wanted to be, but I didn't have the patience for her endless, pointless conversations.

Calista: *I'm as well as can be expected. I saw my therapist today; I go twice a week. She says I'm making progress, but if I was making progress I wouldn't still be going twice a week, would I?*

There was some kind of laughing-crying face emoji, but I didn't really find it funny.

Me: *We're all just getting through it the best we know how.*

Calista: *I've been meaning to ask you if it would be okay to collect some of her things? I'd like to have a few pieces to remember her by.*

An absolutely indignant anger flared to life in my chest. Hell no, she could not go through Cait's things. I'd practically hermetically sealed her closet to preserve everything just as she'd left it. Her dresser drawers remained untouched and her perfume bottles were still sitting on the top, just as they'd been before we left for Ashley's wedding in Montana. For nearly two years, I'd simply not used that side of the bedroom. I'd let it gather dust because I couldn't dare touch anything of hers, and it was why most nights I slept on the living room sofa.: The ghosts had a harder time finding me there.

Me: *I'll think about it.*

I would do no such thing. I tossed the phone back down on the nightstand, angry all over again.

To be fair, I could understand why Calista was struggling. She and Cait had lost their parents five years earlier in a freak accident and Calista hadn't really been the same since. Losing Cait had pushed her over some kind of edge, because the therapist thing was new as far as I could tell.

My phone buzzed several more times but I didn't pick it back up. Calista and I were not close and there was no reason to be. That was something that I had no desire to change.

It was after one when I finally fell asleep and when my alarm went off at five I groaned, slapping a hand over the face of the phone to silence it. It was dark and warm in the room. I had closed the door before going to bed and the bedroom was at the end of the heating loop in the house, making it one of the warmest rooms.

I lay there for a moment and pretended Cait was sleeping beside me, hogging all the blankets, like a feral orangutan sprawled across the bed. If I concentrated really hard I could almost smell her shampoo and the lotion she always put on before bed.

I didn't spend any time analyzing why I still missed the woman who hadn't wanted anything to do with me.

A muffled, single beep from the coffee maker starting its cycle filtered through the closed door and I sighed heavily, my eyes aching with exhaustion as I pushed into a sitting position. I remained there for a moment, head in my hands as I tried to talk myself into getting through another day. This was always the hardest part, the beginning and then the end of each day. The reminder that I was completely alone, and that I'd chosen to remain that way when I isolated myself from family and friends.

I dismissed the continuing barrage of texts from Calista without reading them. That she wanted to be grief buddies now that Cait was gone felt weird to me, and it was terrifying to look at another person and see the resemblance to my wife. It was just too much.

I didn't have a piece of pie for breakfast, I had two—with a huge mug of black coffee. It was the most settled my stomach had felt in the morning in a long time, my body processing pastry dough and apples instead of caffeine and bourbon. It was something that made me feel admittedly better, but I wasn't sure I liked sobriety yet. My thoughts were too loud without the alcohol to make things fuzzy.

"Morning, Jude." Dad's voice drifted out from the kitchen when I let myself into the house around six. The man had never slept late a day in his life and already I could smell bacon frying, bread toasting, and Donna had some kind of magic in the oven. "You already check in on the morning milking?"

I was so used to the sound of the pulsating milking system that it was like white noise to me. "Yeah," I called, toeing my boots off at the tray Donna kept just inside the door during the colder months. "Guys got it under control, as usual. Got a new calf this morning, born overnight in the barn. Nice, big bull."

"Good." Dad's back was to me as he poured a cup of coffee at the counter. "Seems we'll have an uphill battle rebuilding. We can trade him for a few more head next year—make a swap with VanHassel."

I knew Bec was still trying to catch wind of what had happened to so many cows. So far there hadn't been a whisper of their whereabouts.

"Bec already here?" I asked, because no matter how I tried to beat her she was almost always there before me in the mornings.

"Probably." Dad turned, handing me a cup of coffee. "She's a hard worker, that one. Levi did real good picking her up."

I nodded somewhat grudgingly, because she really did pull her weight. She showed up, she was good at what she did, and she wasn't a princess about any of it. That was generally not how things seemed to go with most people, in my experience.

"Things been quiet at the cabin lately?" he asked, as if Bec had been back in the little house for days or weeks rather than just overnight.

"Well, she didn't call me last night and I told her to do that if there was any trouble, so I'm guessing it was quiet."

"I'm guessing she just didn't sleep." He moved carefully to the table, sliding the ceramic mug across the surface with a dull scraping noise. "She's been real twitchy the last few nights. Whatever happened to her marked her deep, son." It sounded like a warning, something I was meant to take to heart, and I didn't like the implication.

I knew a little something of what had happened to her, beyond what she'd been willing to tell me. The past several nights, when sleep had been hard to come by, I'd read every article I could get my hands on about the triple homicide that rocked a tiny town in west Texas. It had taken nearly a year to bring the perpetrator to trial, which dragged on for another eight months.

"She had to live in that hell for almost two years before the piece of shit went to prison," I said, surprised to feel sympathy uncurling somewhere deep inside. It was an unfamiliar feeling, an emotion I hadn't wasted on anyone in a really long time because, admittedly, I'd been way too busy feeling sorry for myself.

"Be careful with that is all I'm sayin'." He lifted the mug to his lips and took a careful sip, and I bristled.

"No danger of *that* happening," I said a little angrily, but I wondered if I was trying to reassure him or myself.

The look he shot me over the top of his mug told me he didn't believe a word I said.

"Beautiful woman—warm, passionate, dedicated," he remarked casually as he returned the cup to the tabletop and settled back in his chair, arms crossed over a wide chest. We were all built like Dad, tall and broad, his blond hair having faded to a silvery white in the past few years.

"You insinuating something?" I finally asked, settling into the chair across the table from him, watching a slow smile curl his lips upward.

"You suppose it's an accident Levi hired her?" he asked, his speculative gaze growing hot and uncomfortable on my skin. "A woman who enjoys farm life, is damned good at it, and can put you in your place?"

"Happy accident," I grumbled, something that made a deep laugh roll out of his chest.

"No such thing as an accident where Providence is concerned." Donna's small hand landed on my shoulder in a gentle pat as she breezed past me, propping open the oven door to peer inside at something that smelled like rainbows.

Anything involving potatoes was magical, as far as I was concerned.

"Not happening." I held my palms up. "No interest in dating anyone, and she drives me batshit."

Dad's lips twitched like he found that hilarious.

"No one's making any such insinuation," Donna announced as she slid a pan from the oven and I hiked an eyebrow in Dad's direction, because maybe he wasn't using the right words to do it, but he sure as hell was making an insinuation.

"I can't with you two." I shook my head, pushing to my feet. "I'm driving one of the wagons over to Ben's today. Got three busted ones we need repaired before the spring and figure I'll get him started on it now—make sure he keeps so busy that it keeps him at least a little straight."

Dad nodded, wisely choosing not to dig in any further, and Donna poured more coffee into a travel mug for me. "I'd take one over now and shake him out of bed," she said. "He's been doing way too much moping since that girlfriend packed up and left."

That was Ben's constant state. His drinking and unwillingness to commit drove them away, then he drank to forget he was alone again. It drove Donna nuts, that he didn't even try to hide it.

"He'll never find a good one," she lamented. "Certainly not if he won't give it up. No woman wants to be saddled with something like that. She doesn't need a man-child."

I swallowed hard, because that felt like recrimination and maybe it was. I deserved it, if it was.

I hitched up the wagon to the 570 Case we kept parked just inside the machine shed. The little tractor was a workhorse, used to haul wagons and loads of manure out to the fields, and I was thankful for the cab Dan had put on when the weather started to turn cold. There was no heat, but the frame would help to keep me from freezing completely through on the drive over.

Driving the tractor over to the bank of fuel tanks we kept at the bottom of the yard, I filled the tank, cursing myself for not putting on thermal wear when I'd gotten dressed this morning. It wasn't more than thirty degrees and there was a nasty little breeze picking up from the east that was eating right through my heavy shirt.

Checking the back of the wagon, I made sure the slow moving vehicle sign was still in place before I pulled out of the barnyard just as the sky began to turn gray. It was seven miles to Ben's place, a slow trip when you couldn't take it at more than twelve miles an hour, and when I rolled into his yard I was frozen through.

"Get up, shithead," I called as I let myself into his house. I tripped over something before I could switch on a light and I pitched forward, banging my shin on something hard before I could catch myself. The light switched on as I stood there clutching my leg and cursing.

Ben stood there in boxers and nothing else, scratching his bare chest and squinting at me. "The fuck you doin' here so early, Jude?" His voice was raspy and he smelled like booze.

Did I always smell like that?

"Donna's worried about you, so I'm on a mercy mission. Froze my nuts off driving a wagon over with the 570."

He grinned slowly. "Gonna have to amputate, you know. That shit goes to gangrene, you'll lose the whole kit."

"Dipshit." I shook my head at him, annoyed, finally looking around and realizing his small living room was a disaster. There was shit everywhere—I still didn't know what I'd tripped over, but it was a miracle I hadn't broken my neck. "Seriously, you ever hear of cleaning? Maybe throwing something in the trash once in a while? You're probably living with rats." I mean, I really wasn't one to point fingers because I wasn't exactly putting on an apron and dusting my house every Friday, but I didn't have an assortment of chip bags and cookie sleeves piled up on my coffee table either.

"Not my strong suit." He shrugged, gesturing I should follow him into the even smaller kitchen. It was comical, really. At 6'5", Ben made the house look even smaller than it was. We'd always joked Mom was snorting Miracle Grow while she was pregnant with Ben, because Dan and I were only 6'1" and Levi 6'3", but Ben was a giant.

"You sound like shit," I offered helpfully as he cleared his throat and coughed up what was either a hairball or part of a lung.

"Late night working on some welding." He winced, one eyelid snapping shut, and he reached around me to snag a bottle off the counter, pouring what smelled like Fireball into his mouth before he grabbed a crusty old coffee pot and filled it with water from the sink.

"You drinkin' while you weld?" I asked, going for casual, but worry crept into my tone anyway. I wasn't one to call a kettle black, but I had a terrifying vision of all the things that could go wrong in Ben's large repair shop.

It was probably a miracle he still had all his fingers.

"Nah." He didn't seem offended, pouring the water into the ancient drip machine. He pulled a paper filter from a cabinet and filled it with coffee from a familiar red plastic tub before pressing a button. The machine hissed and popped and Ben leaned back against the sink, crossing his arms over his chest. "Usually feel a little more focused later in the day, so I head out to the shop after lunch and work until about two in the morning, or until I've finished the job. Whichever comes first. Then I come inside for something quick to eat, maybe a movie and some beers."

Judging by the stack of cans and bottles I'd noticed next to the living room sofa, that had been happening for some time and it had been a hell of a lot harder than just beer.

"Look, Ben." I sighed, running a hand over my face. "You know I'm not one to point fingers, cuz I ain't got my shit together." Where was I going with this? "But you know this is a dangerous recipe, right?"

Ben's face twitched just slightly as something that looked almost like sadness flitted across his expression, gone as quickly as it had come. To blink was to miss it. He was the happy-go-lucky one. The flirt. The jokester. But I suspected that my baby brother had been deeply lonely for a very, very long time and that was something I understood far more than I wanted to.

"You miss her?" I asked slowly, and he reached over my shoulder to pull a mug from the cabinet.

"Sure." He shrugged. "Not like we were gonna get married, but it was nice to have her around. Not like I couldn't live without her, obviously."

It was something of a pattern with him. He'd had a string of girlfriends the last twenty-five years, none of whom lasted longer than a year. When he'd bought this place some twenty years earlier, they started moving in with him, only to move out in the predictable timeframe.

"Seems like that might have been the problem," I observed quietly, and he shrugged, careful not to spill hot coffee on his chest. "Doesn't look like what you're doin' is much living."

"They all know that up front, bro. I tell 'em goin' in that I'm not the marryin' type. They wanna stick around and play house, fine by me. But I ain't got no plans to marry a woman just so she can leave me."

Yeah, we all had hangups about being left behind.

Thanks, Mom.

The problem was, all these women clearly thought they could change Ben. He was an old dog who refused to learn any new tricks–not that he wasn't capable, he just wasn't interested. And the last thing he was about to do was let some woman change him and his comfortable routines, being such a creature of his own inflexible habits.

"You never wanted to settle down?" I asked, genuinely curious. I'd always figured it would happen eventually. Even Levi had managed to have a daughter, despite the fact the marriage hadn't lasted.

"Yeah, no." He dropped into one of two rickety kitchen chairs and it creaked dangerously under the sudden weight. "Never met one that made the heart eyes thing happen." He shrugged. "Never been accused of being a romantic."

That was probably true.

I heard another tractor pull into the yard and craned my neck to look out the small living room window. There was a woman climbing down, a wagon hitched behind it—one of *our* wagons.

"Bec's here. You should probably go put on some clothes."

"What?" His lips curved wickedly above the lip of his mug. "You afraid once she gets a load of this magnificent beast, she'll be off you?"

There was a bright flash of red in my vision, like an artery had burst right behind my eyeballs, and it occurred to me that I had no idea why that made me so mad.

"Fuck off," I muttered. It was too early in the morning to start a fight, which probably just meant that I was getting old. I'd never been very good at picking my battles, because what was the saying? When all you have a hammer, every problem looks like a nail? Yeah, that was me, usually ready to let fists fly at zero provocation.

"Morning, Bec!" Ben sauntered over to the front door and cracked it open to call out into the yard. "Come on in for some coffee; Judah says I gotta put on pants so you don't get an eyeful of the heat I'm packin'."

"Fucking moron." I shook my head at him as he loped toward the back of the house, giggling like an idiot as he went.

The front door squeaked on its hinges when it swung open and Beckett stepped through, her work boots already sitting on the front porch.

She had manners, I had to give her that.

There was no cab on the tractor she'd driven and her hair was wild, her cheeks bright red, and her teeth were chattering.

"You idiot." I couldn't help but chuckle. "I'd have brought that wagon later. Come on, you're probably hypothermic." I switched on the oven and swung the door open so she could warm herself in front of the glowing coil.

"'Bout three minutes too late, Bec," Ben called as he rounded the corner into the kitchen, fastening the last button on his shirt. "Missed the whole damned show."

"Nothing worth writing home about," I scoffed, because sometimes Ben just pushed too far.

"Ass that launched a thousand ships," he said, reaching for the coffee pot and Bec chuckled.

"I'm not so sure that's the saying."

He just waved a dismissive hand and blew a raspberry, always the goofball.

"Sleep okay last night?" he asked her, a concerned expression on his face. He could be serious for brief moments.

"Not really." She shrugged. "I live in Fort Knox now, but I have to sleep with the lights on."

"Got a spare bedroom." Ben hitched a thumb over his shoulder and I knew what he meant, but he was pointing toward the backyard.

"No way in hell she's living with you, not in this primate house." I shook my head at him. "She needs some place to stay, I've got the room—and my house is a hell of a lot cleaner than yours."

He didn't even try to hide it when he nudged me with an elbow and wiggled his eyebrows.

"Knock it off," I hissed under my breath, glaring at him like I could incinerate him on the spot, but it just made him grin bigger.

"Suppose I'll get to your wagon problem today, right after I help out VanHassel with his silo unloader."

We weren't on particularly friendly terms with the VanHassels any longer. The old man was alright, he and dad were still pretty tight, but the kids hated us, and Sally VanHassel hated everyone. I was pretty sure her hatred ran all the way up the ladder to God, Himself.

"There's no hurry." Bec was rubbing her hands together, but her limbs were no longer tight with cold. She'd relaxed in front of the stove as heat poured out and seeped through her clothing. “Clearly we’re in no rush to use them, but it seemed like a win-win. One more thing crossed off the list.”

Somehow she seemed to know that we tried to find projects for Ben during the winter months. His business had grown comfortably, and quickly, but he seemed to suffer some kind of seasonal affective disorder and when the cold came we took turns doing wellness checks on him.

“That why Judah made you change?” she asked, pointing to the chair that sat near the window. A lacy red bra hung from the back by one strap and I smirked. How had I not noticed that?

“Well now, where’d that come from?” Ben looked genuinely intrigued, taking a few steps closer to lift the scrap of fabric. “Oh, yeah.” A slow, wicked grin spread across his face. “Had company a few weeks ago. Guess she forgot some of her stuff.”

I didn’t want to know a single detail about my brother whoring around, especially not who he was doing it with, so I chose to focus on the obvious. “You mean it’s been hanging there for *weeks?* You haven’t cleaned anything in that long?”

“Hey, at least one of us is getting some.”

My jaw practically unhinged when Bec said it and I turned slowly to give her a stern look, even though my brain was screaming at me, *How long has it been for her?*

“Damn straight, sis.” Ben held out his fist for a bump. “Knew I liked you.”

I shook my head at both of them. "Be back for the other tractor tomorrow, when it's not arctic out there. I'll take Bec back with me."

Ben's eyebrows wiggled a little suggestively. "What, in your lap? You know there ain't no room in that thing. I'll drive her back in the truck."

I chose not to examine why that thought made me incredibly angry, and I shook my head at him before stomping out of the house.

Maybe that was my problem. Maybe Ben had it all figured out, taking whatever was thrown his way every chance he got. It was something I'd never done. I'd been a one-woman man since the day I'd met Cait, with *one* deviation because I'd wanted to make her jealous, but toward the end she'd hardly wanted to be in the same room as me.

It had taken me a very long time to progress through the stages of grief, but it seemed I was beginning to observe anger just fine.

"Jude." Ben came jogging out of the house after me. "You mad at me?"

Ben had never been concerned about something like that a day in his life. He lifted one huge hand to scratch the back of his neck. "Lately, when you get mad, you run away."

He was probably right, there did seem to be an emerging pattern.

"Not mad at you." I crossed my arms over my chest and looked down at the boots I'd never bothered to take off when I let myself into his house. "I don't know what I am." It was true.

Before I could stop him Ben's arms were around me in a bear hug, squeezing the life out of me. "No one's gonna blame you for finally bein' mad," he said, and I wondered if I was hallucinating the words due to oxygen deprivation. "Just don't take it out on that beautiful woman. She's too good for you and you don't deserve her, but she seems not to realize that."

Well, now I was going to have to pretend I had no idea what he was talking about.

"Not tryin' to steal her from under your nose, bro. You know I wouldn't—she's too good for the likes of me." He seemed completely serious, but it made a cold knife of adrenaline stab my gut. "She's not mine to steal, anyway. She don't look at me that way." He finally released me, clapping my back so hard it rattled my bones. "Always the last one to catch on, but we love you anyway."

The screen door slapped against the frame and Beckett came clattering down the steps, slapped Ben on the back and unhitched the wagon. She pulled the pin and kicked the hitch to the ground before she climbed back up onto the tractor and fired it up, tearing out of the yard without a word to either of us.

"Think she heard any of that?" I asked him, filled with shame.

"Deaf people heard it, bro." He grinned at me. "Everything you think shows up on your face when you look at her. Sometimes you turn bright red and that's when I know it's dirty."

Fuck me, did I really? This was getting out of hand.

I shook my head at him before climbing up onto the smaller tractor to follow her out of the yard.

Chapter Twelve

Beckett

Levi had finally taken off the training wheels, leaving me to run things and I spent the next few days going over the books, trying to figure out where to cut expenses to make up for the massive amount of unrealized revenue we'd already lost.

I'd gotten a couple leads on the missing cows, most of which turned out to be dead ends, and I was feeling incredibly frustrated by the end of the week. I wasn't sleeping well, locking all the doors and windows each night and setting the alarm as soon as I was inside the house. There hadn't been anything strange since the night Judah chased a phantom, but I still slept with the lamp on in my bedroom and a chair propped under the doorknob. All those old fears I'd worked so hard to suppress over the past twelve years had come roaring back.

The only thing that gave me any peace was that I hadn't received any phone calls from the DA who'd put Jason Bachman in prison for life. I'd been beside myself when she'd presented him with a plea deal rather than going straight for the death penalty.

"Beckett." I hadn't even heard the door open and I looked up to see Dan standing there with a strange look on his face. "You heard anything from Judah yet today?" I looked up, surprised. It was nearly eleven and I hadn't run into Judah. He didn't usually drop into the little office until later in the afternoon.

"No." I pushed to my feet and stretched out my aching lower back. I'd been hunched in a weird position for hours. "Should I be worried?"

"He said he'd be out to the job site this morning to help me out with something and he never showed, so I came here first."

I didn't know much about what Dan did, some kind of construction work, but it was unlike Judah to say he'd do something and then no-show.

Grabbing my coat, I followed Dan out to his truck. It was Thanksgiving week and the ground was frozen hard, the bare, ugly dirt waiting for snow to hide its sins.

Judah's truck was parked in his driveway when we pulled up to his house and I watched Dan's forehead wrinkle with worry.

"Jude, you in here?" he called as I followed him through the front door, and there was a groan from the back of the house. Immediately all the worst visions flooded my mind and without even stopping to take off my boots, I pushed past Dan and rushed toward the sound, terrified.

"Are you okay? Are you hurt?" My voice sounded weird and breathy as I burst into his bedroom to find ... nothing. The bed was a rumpled disaster, and then I realized the light was on in the en suite bathroom.

Judah was curled into a huge ball on the bathmat near the tub, facing the toilet. "Never eat the suspicious chicken," he groaned, just before he bolted upright and heaved violently into the toilet.

"I'm suspicious of all chickens," Dan announced as he rounded the corner. "The living ones, anyway. Most of them are ornery fuckers—the ones Levi keeps are like guard dogs. Like the dead ones just fine, though, with a crispy coating. Delicious."

Dropping to my knees next to Judah, my hand came up almost automatically to rub soothing circles on his warm back. It was hard ... and muscular ... and wide.

Fuck, Beckett. Stay on task.

He tore off a piece of toilet paper to wipe his mouth and I reached up to snag the drinking glass off the counter, quickly filling it with water so he could rinse and spit.

"Thank you." He sank weakly back against the tub surround, his forearms braced on his knees. There were deep circles beneath his eyes and I reached up to feel his forehead.

"I'm not so sure it was something you ate," I said softly. "You have a raging fever."

"You got the shits?" Dan asked helpfully, leaning his big body into the doorframe and Judah's head shook slowly back and forth. "Maybe not food poisoning then. Think Bec's right, you got some kinda flu."

"Came on real fast." Judah's voice was weak. "Middle of the night. Started sweating and shaking and I don't know how there's anything left in me to throw up."

Instructing Dan to help him back to his bed, I finally took off my boots and coat and hurried to the kitchen to look for essentials. There were no bland crackers, no cans of soup, and certainly no electrolyte drinks, so I asked Dan if he'd mind grabbing some electrolytes and I'd figure out the rest.

There was a box of beef stock in the pantry, so I heated it with a few herbs and some salt, then found a loaf of bread in the fridge I was pretty sure Donna had put there. It seemed Judah was good about seeing to the needs of others, but he wasn't very good at taking care of himself.

"Just sip this," I announced as I carried a large mug of the broth to his room, a plate of dry toast in my hand. "It's not exciting, but let's see if you can keep it down."

He looked like hell, his eyes bloodshot, his hair damp with sweat and with some effort he propped himself carefully up against the pillows. I sat next to him and placed my palm against his forehead again. His hands shook as he tried to sip from the mug.

"Fuck, Judah. You're burning up." I waited until he lowered the mug to take from him, placing it on the nightstand next to the bed. Then I rose and grabbed two hand towels from the linen closet in the bathroom, running them under cool water and wringing them out.

I brought a bath towel to place over his pillow before wrapping one cold towel around his neck and instructing him to lie back, draping the other over his forehead.

"Damn, that's cold," he hissed.

"It's only that cold because you're on fire," I said, returning to the bathroom to dig through his medicine cabinet for something that would bring down the fever. "This is dangerous. You should have called someone to help you."

"Couldn't." His voice was hoarse, and I believed him. But I also believed Judah was the type of man who would never ask for help.

There was a rustling sound in the kitchen, something that told me Dan was already back and pulling things from grocery bags, so I patted Judah's arm gently and hurried out to see what he'd brought.

"Didn't find much that was helpful—just ran home and grabbed a few things," he said, but there was pasta, canned soup, crackers, soda and electrolyte drinks on the counter. I grinned at him.

"That's plenty, thank you."

"He never gets sick," Dan said quietly. "This must be pretty bad if it kept him away from the farm today."

"He's burning up," I responded. "I can't find anything in his medicine cabinet to bring down the fever and I think we need to get him into a cool bath."

A light of understanding dawned in Dan's eyes and he nodded. "Yeah, good idea. Used to do that when my kids were little and they spiked a fever. You can change the bed and I'll help him with the bath."

Was it weird that was a little disappointing?

"Tryin' to kill me," Judah hissed from the bathroom when Dan helped lower him into the water and I peeled the sheets from the bed, hurrying down the hall to the small laundry room and dumping them into the wash machine. I quickly remade the bed with linens from the hallway closet, swapping out the duvet cover and bringing a Gatorade and a straw to set on the bedside table.

I took myself back to the kitchen to tidy up a bit, because it worried me that I wanted to stay close and help. It was something I'd have chalked up to a motherly instinct, but it was more than that. Someone I didn't want to care about was hurting and I wanted desperately to fix it, something that scared me half to death.

Caring was dangerous, something I'd learned the hard way.

"All cleaned up." Dan's voice was uncharacteristically soft as he walked into the kitchen. "Madder 'n a wet cat, but some time sitting in that cool water helped. Judah's not helpless, but when he starts to feel like he is, he gets real angry." He crossed the kitchen slowly, flipping open a cabinet next to the refrigerator.

"Think that idiot keeps all the medicine in here somewhere." There was the sound of a turnstile spinning and an "Aha!" from Dan, who produced a bottle from the depths.

"Thank you." I held out my hand. "Whatever this is, it probably just has to run its course. I'll stay."

One of Dan's eyebrows crawled slowly up his forehead. "Not sure I'd recommend that. He's a jackass on a good day, and when he's sick he's probably a polar bear. Might eat you alive."

"Was he a jackass three years ago?" I asked quietly, waiting while Dan leaned against the counter and chewed on his lip.

"No, I don't suppose he was—not like this, anyway. Life's changed him, you could say."

I nodded. That was all the answer I needed. "I think it's changed all of us, sometimes for the worse. Thank you so much for fetching supplies. Once he's better, we'll *both* be out to help with whatever it was you were trying to get done today."

He nodded slowly, like he understood he'd just been dismissed, and maybe even more so that there was no sense in trying to argue the point. "K, Beckett. Thanks for seeing to it." He inclined his head toward the back of the house. "Good to know we've got another set of eyes on him."

Whatever that meant, I wasn't about to address it.

The front door shut quietly behind Dan just as a soft groan drifted down the hallway. I grabbed one of the drinks cooling in the fridge, hoping he'd already downed the one on the table, and walked it down the hallway.

“How are you feeling?” I asked softly, unable to help myself when I reached up to sweep some damp hair off his forehead.

“Not great.” He grimaced. “But I haven’t thrown up in an hour and that’s pretty great news right now.”

“Yeah, about that.” I reached over to the nightstand and grabbed the bottle of electrolytes. “Let’s get some of this into you.” I uncapped it and he waved away the straw, taking it from my hand to take slow, cautious sips.

“You shouldn’t be here.” His voice was hoarse again. “I’ll get you sick.”

“I’m a big girl.” I shrugged, because the truth was that I only felt that confident during daylight hours these days. “You shouldn’t have to do this alone.”

“There are a lot of things I never thought I’d be doing alone.” It must have slipped out, because he winced as soon as he said it.

There was nothing to say to that, but I understood, so I just nodded and waited for him to finish the bottle. It took a long time, but the silence wasn’t uncomfortable.

He cautiously ate some of the dry toast and then took the pills I handed him, uncapping the second bottle in order to swallow them down. It was clear that used up whatever strength he had left and he collapsed back into the pillows with a sigh. “Feeling useless today, and now I’ve taken you away from your duties.”

“More important things to do,” I said easily enough, before I realized what I’d just given away. It made him smile weakly and he patted the top of my hand.

"Thank you. Probably would've died in front of the toilet. Not a great way to go—can you imagine the obituary Ben would have written?"

That made me smile. "I think Donna would make him tone it down, but the original would be a real work of art. He would commission an actual toilet headstone." The corner of his mouth lifted at that.

I waited with him as his eyes drifted closed, his hand still resting on top of mine. It was a strange feeling, something I didn't dislike, because it didn't feel like Judah Benson hated me anymore.

It was late—or maybe it was early, and I rolled carefully. Something had awakened me and I swung my legs carefully over the edge of the bed in Judah's guest room. The house was warm and dark and I'd fallen into an exhausted sleep what felt like only moments before, surprised to find that I felt safe enough in this house to allow myself to sleep.

"No." The word was sharp and alarmed, and I bolted from the bed and rushed down the hallway, only steps from the master.

Judah thrashed restlessly in the bed and I sank to my knees beside him, an unwilling *Shhh* leaving my lips as I leaned closer and pressed a hand to his forehead. His fever had broken, but he was damp with sweat.

With a single swift movement, his arms went around me, pulling me up into the bed with him as he rolled.

"Cait." His voice was tortured, striking both pain and fear into my heart. "Please stay with me. Just ... let me pretend for a minute."

This was wrong. I let him pull me in with him, feeling his hard body mold around mine and fighting tears as I absorbed the fact he thought he held someone else.

Warm lips sought the back of my neck, a tortured sound coming from the man behind me, and I pressed a hand to my mouth. This was everything and nothing I wanted, to be a stand-in for someone else.

His breaths grew almost immediately deeper, the warm weight of his body around mine eventually lulling me to sleep, dragging me under, and despite my better judgment, I stayed.

"I'm so sorry."

There was something wet happening on the back of my neck as I slowly blinked into consciousness. There was a hot, hard body behind me and with a start I realized I was in Judah's bed, his arms wrapped around me, one hand beneath my shirt, fingers smoothing over my ribs.

The worst part was that I wasn't sorry anymore. Something had shifted overnight and I didn't care what it had taken to get us to this point, because this had been my fantasy for longer than I cared to admit.

"Don't apologize." My voice was hoarse, and I cringed. "You needed to pretend for a minute and I could give you that."

Judah's big body shook rhythmically behind me, something that took me a moment to realize he was crying so hard that there was no noise.

My eyes filled with hot tears—this was a pain I knew so well—and I rolled carefully to face him, tucking his face into my neck as I pulled him closer, my arms wrapping around his wide torso. He was closer to loss than I was, and if I could guide him through some of it, I would.

"I know." I whispered it into his hair as he shifted to gasp into my neck. "And I'm sorry. I wish I knew how to help, but the truth is that I don't know anything—just that it hurts every damn day."

His shoulders contracted several more times beneath my grip, telling me the pain hadn't yet passed by and I curled the fingers of one hand into his hair, scratching gently against his scalp.

"Tell me about her," I urged gently. "Let it out."

He shivered for long moments, his breath hot against my skin as he gasped and sucked in more oxygen, and I could feel the hurt and anger emanating from him as I stroked his back.

"She didn't love me anymore." His voice was flat when he finally spoke. "She was leaving me after my sister's wedding. We had agreed to put on a unified front and she was going to move the kids with her when she left."

I hummed softly into his hair, a little terrified that I held my boss in my arms. "But you still loved her."

"Of course I did." His voice was anguished. "How do you just stop loving someone because they can't change into what you want them to be? I couldn't be what she wanted, so she stopped."

How could I even begin to answer that?

"I don't know." I wrapped my arms even tighter around him, aware the moment would break at any given second. "But she loved you in her way, she must have—and your babies loved you."

My voice caught, stopping the flow of words.

"I lost it all." His voice was still flat. "I lost it a long time before she decided to leave me, I just didn't know it. Maybe I was ignoring the reality because it was too much."

I had nothing to say to that, so I just stroked his back.

In slow, halting words, he took me all the way back with him, to the day he met the beautiful young Cait and fought to win her.

The time she spent in the Air Force to pay for her education, going on to become a commercial pilot once she was released. But she wanted more, something she couldn't find in a sleepy little town, and Judah had adamantly insisted there was nothing for him in city life.

The miracle of their children, born after years of struggle.

"For what?" His voice cracked. "It was pointless, all of it, because I lost them anyway. That was worse than her leaving, because now there's nothing I can do to ever get them back. I can't even visit them; we never recovered the bodies."

I understood that so much better than most people, and I squeezed him tighter. Finally he relaxed into my hold, his face still pressed against my neck. My shirt was soaked from the tears he'd shed for them, and I curled my fingers gently through his hair as he continued to speak, in what I hoped was a soothing touch.

"Thank you." He sighed softly, finally pulling away and I released him reluctantly. It felt too good holding another person, something sweet and intimate about it in a way that wasn't sexual. "I'm sorry for making you uncomfortable; I don't really talk about that stuff."

"There's nothing wrong with talking about it—telling people the truth of it. It doesn't make you less, or weak, or any less lovable." I winced when that last part left my mouth, hoping that didn't sound like *I* loved him.

Reluctantly, I rolled to the edge of the bed. "I'll make coffee. You think you can keep it down?" He nodded, pulling himself back up into the pillows and adjusting the blankets around himself with an irritated huff.

"Hate being sick. Lie here all day, thinking of the things I should be doing."

"Fortunate you have the hired help," I said. "I'll check on them after I've gotten some breakfast into you and then I'll be back this evening."

"Don't have to babysit me, Bec." He rolled his eyes, but it was in a good-humored way. The thunderclouds were parting; rolling away.

"Making sure you're not dead is not the same thing," I called as I moved down the hallway and into the kitchen, where I quickly brewed coffee and made more soup and toast.

I left him with tea, Gatorade, crackers, and a puke bucket—just in case—before I drove out to the farm to make sure things were operating smoothly. There were a few employees who largely ran the daily operations, but Judah was always there tweaking feed ratios, fixing things, answering questions, and lending a hand wherever he was needed.

"Morning, Beckett." Erik Benson's voice startled me and I nearly knocked my head on the crude wooden stall. I'd poked my head into one of the cattle barns to make sure they had feed in the long trough, their water cups functioning properly.

"Good morning, Mr. Benson." I smiled, a little embarrassed because I was fairly sure I looked like something the cat had dragged in.

"Heard you got stuck taking care of Judah." That didn't seem like much of a question. "Hope he wasn't too hard on you."

I shook my head slowly. "He was pretty miserable. Some kind of flu, I think. The fever broke, but he's still too weak to do anything but rest today."

"That boy doesn't know how to rest." Erik smiled. "Even hung over, he pushes himself too hard."

"I think work is all he has," I answered honestly, something that made Erik pause, then nod slowly.

"Might be right."

He kept pace with me as I checked the remaining barns, peeking into the milkhouse to make sure everything was washed down and put away. Then he fell into step beside me as I finally made my way to the small office outbuilding.

"Work was all I had," he said finally, something that almost made my steps falter as I looked up my shoulder at him as I unlocked the door. "When their mother left me, that was what kept me straight. Was terrible neglectful of those kids, because I didn't know how to get through each day, much less raise them on my own."

I didn't know how to respond, so I didn't, simply gesturing that he should take a seat as I moved toward the small coffee maker at a station along the wall. I held up a mug and he nodded.

I didn't know anything about Erik's first wife, because no one talked about her. The only reason I had a clue was that he'd mentioned her previously, and the brothers occasionally slipped and referred to Donna as their stepmother.

"When she left us, each of the kids struggled in some way. Levi had to become a mother, to hold the house together. He learned how to cook and clean—he established a chore chart for the others so the house wouldn't fall down around us. Had to grow up way too fast." He leaned back in his chair and I passed him a steaming mug of coffee. He took his black, just like Judah. "Dan turned into a ghost. Judah started fights at school. Ashley had herself convinced it was all her fault and went through a deep depression. And Ben..." He blew out a long breath. "That boy turned into a clown to hide a broken heart."

He took a sip of the scalding liquid in his mug. "Ashley's the only one who's made it out so far. Did a hell of a lot of work on herself to put the ghost of her mother to rest. The rest of them still struggle with it, though I don't suppose they'd ever admit it—my fault, for not shepherding them through it."

I tossed the spent pod in the trash and sat in my desk chair, my coffee so light with cream that Judah had teased it wasn't coffee at all.

"And what about you?" I asked slowly, sure he was going somewhere with this. I just wasn't sure where.

"Got Donna to thank for saving my ass." He grinned, something that reminded me the elder Benson was an incredibly attractive, virile man, though I doubted he was a day less than seventy. He'd done his sons a real favor in handing down such exemplary genetics. "That woman did not give up on me, even though I was a growly bear for a real long time. She just kept showing up with pies and cookies and bread, luring me out. She knew that if you feed a feral dog long enough, it'll let you tame it."

"Is it really that easy?" I teased. I couldn't help but smile at his analogy.

"With Judah it is."

Oh shit, there it was. It had taken a while to get to his point, but I was sure this was it.

"Uh..." That was all I had.

"You're good for him, Beckett."

"I'm his employee, Mr. Benson."

"Psssh." He waved a big hand at me. "Judah needs to be pushed—he hates it–and you're not afraid to push him, but not like Cait. You're gentle with him; make him see the reason, not just diggin' your heels in to be ornery. Your motives are better."

I didn't know what to say to that. I had absolutely no read on what his relationship had been with Cait, I just knew that he missed her desperately.

"He's a wreck without her," I said slowly.

"He was a wreck *with* her, he just didn't know it. Grieving someone who's gone on isn't the same as grieving 'em while they're still alive, and that's what he was doin' with her. They were oil and water from the start and he was the only one determined to make it work. He was just the one clippin' her wings and she was real tired of it." He propped his right ankle over his left knee. "Gotta hand it to her for holding out as long as she did, but what he's got now? That's survivor guilt."

It was quiet for a long moment while I tried to absorb that. Was he telling me the loss was inevitable, just that circumstances would've been different?

"Would've been an ugly custody battle. Would've torn off another piece of his heart every time he had to leave those boys behind again." He shrugged. "Instead, she just shattered the whole thing, all at once."

My face probably gave away my surprise, because I couldn't help but wonder if he'd just implied something terrible, that an accident had been intentional.

"It was Cait who gave up on my boy, not the other way around." He stood slowly and crossed the room to rinse his cup in the small sink. "Judah doesn't quit anything, Beckett. He's solid. Won't find a better man—once he gets his head on straight."

Like a deer caught in headlights, I just stared as he gave me a two-fingered salute and let himself out the door. I blew out a long, hard breath because I had a distressing suspicion that Erik Benson thought I was a miracle worker.

I was pretty sure he was wrong.

Chapter Thirteen

Judah

I couldn't remember the last time I'd felt like such shit, though at least I didn't feel like death was imminent. For a minute there I'd been worried I might actually dehydrate and die on my bathroom floor, something Ben would have carved into my headstone just to be a dick. Beckett was right, too: He'd have ordered an actual toilet for the headstone.

It was long past dark, but I hadn't turned on the lamp next to the bed as I sat with my thoughts in the dark, quiet house. I'd slept on and off during the day, sipping on the Gatorade and water Beckett had left, and I'd worked my way through a sleeve of dry crackers and some ginger candies.

The front door opened and shut, there was a muffled noise, and a light went on in the kitchen. There was a low sound, Beckett humming something to herself as plastic rustled and the fridge opened and closed. It was a weirdly comforting sound, signs of life in a home that hadn't known more than my bare existence for far too long.

"I'm sorry to keep you waiting." Her soft voice preceded her down the hallway and I finally snapped on the bedside lamp, running a hand through what was probably insane hair. "I stopped for some groceries on the way and it took longer than I expected."

I hoped that meant she hadn't stopped for groceries for me, but I chose not to ask.

"Chicken and rice," she announced, "and ginger ale, just in case. Something that will go easy on your stomach, I hope."

At the smell, my stomach roared and a sweet smile stretched across her face. "Sounds like we're in luck, then."

While I ate she brought in fresh laundry, folded it and put things away without asking where they went, like she just knew.

"You're off the clock, Beckett." I tried to keep the bite out of my tone but probably failed.

"I know." She didn't seem to take offense. "Now I'm helping out a friend."

That wasn't meant to offend either, I knew it, but somehow that felt wrong. Like it made me less than in some way.

"Things run smoothly today?" I asked around a mouthful of chicken, the best thing I'd tasted in a long time. Chances were good it hadn't come from the grocery store, but from Donna's kitchen.

"Completely smooth." She smiled indulgently and I knew there was something she wasn't saying. She couldn't look me in the eye, something that was weird for her. Maybe it was because of my massive overstep the night before, I thought with more than just a niggle of discomfort. It made my stomach twist with a sharp pain and I set the fork down for a moment.

"Look." I was just going to have to take the bull by the horns. "I overstepped and I'm really sorry. I made you uncomfortable."

She hadn't turned around. She'd frozen in place, staring at the floor, facing away from me and I didn't like that I couldn't see her face.

What she couldn't ever know was that I had been thinking about it all day and it scared the shit out of me that I wanted it to happen again, not because I was so desperate to pretend it was Cait in my arms, but because something about it had quieted that howling in my soul for those moments she nestled into me.

"It was me who overstepped, Judah," she said softly. She still hadn't turned to face me. "I don't ever want you to think that I'm trying to fill a hole in my life with just anyone who fits, because that would be impossible. I can't replace Cade and you can't replace Cait."

"I don't think I want to replace what I had with her." I was coming into a slow, terrible realization. "I don't ... think we were happy."

She didn't say anything, but she came over to sit on the edge of the bed, near my feet. "I think I've been working really hard to *not* let go of them. I've been living in the past this whole time." She hung her head. "I suppose it's been time for me to move past it for a very long time now."

"So what I'm hearing is, 'Judah, I don't want to pick fights with you anymore. You're a fucking stud and I'm sorry for causing so much trouble.'" I grinned and waited for her response, her eyes flashing with anger when she lifted her head.

"I don't pick fights with ... jackass." She held one palm up to her forehead when she finally caught on that I was grinning at her.

"Nah, to be fair, I've been the prickly one. Ben's made sure to mention that to me about seven hundred times."

She took my empty plate and since I was still weak and dizzy, she ran a bath for me and helped me into the bathroom. I'd have sooner bathed fully clothed than strip down in front of her, all shaky and weak, so I told her I could handle it and shooed her out.

I wasn't quick about it. After I dried off I had to sit on the toilet lid for a while to keep from keeling over, then again after I dressed. I just barely managed to brush my teeth, only because I could hang onto the edge of the sink, and I tested my limits by letting go to put on some deodorant.

Opening the door, I noticed she'd changed my bedsheets again. She was using something different than I did, something fragrant and soft, and it made the sheets smell heavenly.

She'd tidied a little more too, the room feeling weirdly more ... sparkly, a vase of fresh flowers on the dresser across the room.

I tried to appreciate it, but it hurt a little. Cait's dresser had been touched, and I tried not to be irrationally angry over something so small and pointless. There was no going back, no matter how desperately I wished.

I just barely made it to the bed and collapsed into it as she reappeared through the doorway. She had taken a shower and changed into the most ridiculous flannel pajamas with yellow ducks on them. I choked on a snort and she grinned sheepishly. "I accidentally left them at the farmhouse and it turns out that was fortuitous. Donna brought them to me in the office today."

That made me swallow hard, because I knew I'd wanted her to stay but I really didn't want to have to say the words out loud.

She handed me a mug of hot tea and snugged the blankets up around me. I kind of liked this weird dynamic, something I was a little afraid to put into words.

"Stay?" It slipped out in a moment of weakness, when I remembered what it had been like to just lie there and talk with her this morning. It was the first handful of happy moments I'd been able to cling to in almost as long as I could remember.

"Okay." She didn't look at me weird or ask me why. She just rounded the bed to Cait's side and crawled in, flopping into the pillows and rolling to face me. "Tell me about the boys."

I took a sip of tea before settling back, a small smile on my face, and I let all the good memories flow out through my mouth.

It was thanks to Beckett that I was reasonably well by Thanksgiving and was able to attend family dinner. She'd been on what I jokingly called "death watch" all week long, sleeping beside me at night, walking through the happy memories with me as we fell asleep, and I hadn't had a single nightmare all week.

Ben was on fairly good behavior, though he was on his phone an awful lot. I suspected he was working on the installation of another girlfriend, maybe Ms. Red Bra, but I really couldn't handle all the details he typically liked to share, so I didn't ask.

"Whew, that one's a looker—I'll save that screenshot for you for later, bro." Ben was grinning at me like the cat who just ate the canary.

"I'm sorry, you what?" I shook my head to clear the ringing in my ears. I could have sworn Ben just said he'd created a *dating profile* for me.

"You heard me, dipshit. It's time you got back out there and started thinking with Small Brain for a while—had some fun."

I held a hand over my eyes and pulled in a deep breath.

Counted to ten as I tried to tamp down the murderous rage.

Sometimes I could blame Ben for making me want to drink.

Thank God Donna and Dad were in the kitchen, because they were Ben's salvation.

"I am not going to swipe right just to fuck around," I finally hissed angrily. The truth was that I hadn't been able to stand the idea of being unfaithful to Cait, and those feelings had been getting a little ... fuzzier lately. I knew what that meant, that somewhere deep in my subconscious, my brain was sorting, processing, getting things figured out and trying to push me forward.

And for the first time in a long time, I knew exactly which direction I wanted that to go.

"Eh, don't worry." Ben waved a big hand at me. "I didn't activate it yet, but if you don't get off your mopey ass, I sure as hell will."

Beside me, Beckett chuckled and Ben's twinkling blue eyes turned on her. "Don't be too quick to make fun, missy. I made one for you, too."

Beckett sputtered and choked, folding in half as a coughing fit overtook her.

"Yep, doing the Lord's work." Ben leaned back in his chair, looking inordinately pleased with himself. "Any day now I'll take them live—bet you two will be a match." He gestured between Beckett and myself, and I reached over to clap her on the back.

"I'm going home," I announced angrily, pushing up from my chair and Beckett lifted a hand to squeeze my forearm, gently encouraging me to sit again.

"Don't worry, AssAttack76, I'll send you a screenshot of your profile tonight for your approval."

AssAttack? Was he kidding me?

"I'm just giving the ladies a taste of what they're really in for when you hit the market."

"Don't you dare tell me you're into that kinky stuff, Judah Benson." Donna's voice drifted in from the kitchen, something that made Ben giggle. She'd been looking at me suspiciously ever since Ben had gifted me a vibrating butt plug at family Christmas five years earlier and told me he was just looking out for Cait and me. Donna had asked what it was and Cait told her it was a wine stopper, but I knew from the look on Donna's face she'd never seen a bottle of wine that could take that thing.

I wanted to storm off to my truck and drive home in a huff. The thought of anyone swiping in any direction made me irrationally angry, and I started mentally cleaning and organizing the garage because I was mad and wanted to throw stuff, even if it was only in my imagination.

I was definitely lifting weights tonight. I'd been flat on my back most of the week, losing strength and feeling helpless, and it was time to burn off some of the frustration that had been building up in my gut.

Beckett was going back to her place tonight. There was no reason for her to stay, since I could finally walk on my own and hold down food, and the thought of going back home by myself was the most depressing thing I'd considered in days.

After showering and crawling into a softly-scented bed, I picked up my phone to watch a few stupid videos when the screen lit up with a message from Ben. It made my stomach lurch uncomfortably, pins and needles of adrenaline prickling along my skin as a dating profile flashed up on my screen.

Me: *You fuckwit, that's not even a photo of me.*

Just the thought of having a dating profile out there gave me heartburn.

Ben: *It's better than any photo you'd take—and check out the bulge on this guy. Ladies will lose their minds.*

Me: *I consider gray sweatpants formalwear? Are you even kidding me? That is not a personality trait or an interest.*

Ben: *Oh no, it's a whole thing—ask Ashley. She's in a dirty book club and she says the ladies looove a man in gray sweatpants. Gets them all worked up, especially if he's going commando.*

I groaned and slapped a hand over my eyes, because I remembered walking into Beckett's living room wearing gray sweatpants once, and I was fairly certain her eyes had zeroed in on my junk.

Fuck my life, Ben could *not* be right. He'd never let me forget it.

Me: *I am* not *doing this, Benjamin.*

Ben: *You're not getting any younger. Better get out there while the equipment still works.*

Me: *My equipment's just fine, don't you worry about it.*

Ben: *You sure about that? When's the last time you got laid?*

I swallowed hard. Cait and I had been sleeping in separate rooms toward the end.

When *was* the last time I'd gotten laid?

Ben: *Yeah, that's what I thought.*

I hadn't told anyone but my therapist and Beckett that Cait and I were having problems, but Ben was like a service dog, picking up on and interpreting even the smallest twitch. Sometimes I thought he could actually read minds.

Me: *You just let me worry about myself. You've got your own shit to work on.*

The truth was that I'd had my head up my own ass for so long, I hadn't noticed Ben was going off the rails. He'd always been the prankster of the family, the one who hid suffering behind humor. Usually I just gave him a hard time for being an asshole, but I'd caught the tail end of a few worried conversations between Donna and Dad, and something was definitely going on with him.

Me: *Better watch yourself or I'll set up a damn dating profile for you, too.*

Ben: *Nah, I'm off it. Gonna join the priesthood.*

Me: *Converting because the ladies no longer want what you have to offer?*

Ben: *Taking my personality where it'll be appreciated. I've tapped out this small town.*

Me: *How has your dick not fallen off?*

Ben: *I'm wounded. I didn't say I'm indiscriminate. I've just seen all I want to of the ladies who are even an option in this town—and you know I always wrap it up.*

Me: *I'm going to bed, idiot. Don't you dare post this shit. I am* not *dating again, not ever. Have you seen what a shit show it is out there?*

There was no response from my brother, because apparently he'd been doing the legwork and had come to the same conclusion.

Ben had been on the market, intermittently, since he was a teenager. No woman had ever been able to lock that one down. And while all of us had our issues, Ben's commitment issues were positively legendary, and I blamed it on losing our mom. It had really fucked with Ashley's head, but Ben hadn't been the same since.

I couldn't sleep knowing Beckett was back at her own place, all alone. There was a nagging worry in the back of my mind that no matter what we did to secure the cabin for her, it wouldn't be enough. Part of me knew it had nothing to do with the Avilas, that it was a separate issue altogether. I didn't know how to keep her safe from one threat, but I had no idea how to keep her safe from what was potentially two—and even more worrisome was the realization that I felt like it was my responsibility.

Beckett pushed me, if I had to name a reason. She was smart and she looked at things a different way than I did. She had a better head for business, whereas I just wanted to put my head down and work. Lose myself in the daily chores until I'd beaten my body into submission and collapsed into the blessed relief of an elusive, hard-earned sleep.

I enjoyed poking at her, flustering and irritating her by finding her weak spots and exploiting them, and oftentimes she quickly turned the tables on me, putting me in my place with a well-timed observation.

For her part, Beckett said the new security measures seemed to be working—nothing new and weird to report at her place over the next several weeks—and we settled into a less adversarial working relationship as hard, repetitive frosts killed off everything else, finally turning the landscape a uniform gray and brown. Donna's mums and pumpkins froze out on the front porch of the farmhouse and Dad continued to take his coffee out there each morning, bundled up in a thick Carhartt while the rocking chair creaked back and forth. He was clearly bored, not adjusting well to such reduced responsibility, because almost every day I found him in the office with Beckett, discussing the price of seed corn, feed ratios, the latest visit from the vet or the nutritionist, and charting birth dates for the calves we needed to replenish our herd.

There was still no word on our missing cattle, though I knew Beckett hadn't dropped the baton. She was still in touch with her guys on the auction circuit, and once a week she'd been making a habit of driving out to neighboring farms, a little further each time, to put out feelers. The woman was on a mission, that was for damn sure.

Donna had roped Beckett and me into dinner late that Friday evening, since the two of us had been fixing a broken water pipe in one of the cattle barns most of the afternoon. Beckett was covered in shit and she could swear like a sailor—I was impressed, because this seemed like a new development, maybe Ben was rubbing off on her—but she had replaced the section, watered the cattle in that barn, and then drained the pipes for the night since we were set to freeze again.

We were in the office, warming our hands over the space heater and brewing shitty coffee when Donna poked her head around the door. "You two are coming in for dinner; it's late and you're just going to go home and eat garbage anyway." Beckett looked guilty when she said it, but I didn't. It was no secret I ate crap most of the time, and the only thing standing between me and malnutrition was Donna.

Beckett was sent off to the shower the instant we got into the house, and Donna hauled her filthy clothes off to the laundry room. I chuckled when Bec came back down the stairs wearing an old university sweatshirt and a huge pair of sweatpants. The sweatshirt had been my sister's, but I suspected the sweatpants were Dad's.

"Zip it, mister," Donna warned. "From the state of you, it's clear who was doing the heavy lifting today." She hiked an eyebrow, and she probably wasn't wrong. I'd been working on a silo unloader all morning, and Beckett's discovery of the flooded cattle barn meant a huge job cleaning it out before repairing the pipe. She'd been halfway up to her knees in semi-frozen shit even before I'd found her taking out a section of pipe with a blowtorch.

To be fair, I hadn't expected her to be so hands-on. I'd thought she'd be the business end, sitting in the office with her spreadsheets, barking orders at me. And now that I was finding she was not only a hard worker, but one who was not afraid to get dirty, it surprised me to realize how much I liked it. She wasn't just an employee or a manager, but someone who acted more like a partner who gave a shit.

Cait had nothing to do with the farm and hadn't wanted much to do with me after a day on it, smelling like hay and manure. It was funny, the painful clarity that was coming with time and distance, that I could see how she might have viewed it as a stepping stone. Maybe she had hoped one day I'd get tired, sell off my share, and follow her big dreams—the ones she'd forgotten to share with me along the way.

I slept like shit that night and when I pulled into the yard and parked early the next morning, Bec's truck was already there, a light glowing in the little office building. Tapping on the door gently, I pulled it open to find her sitting at the desk with her head in her hands, her hair loose and wild for once, rather than pulled back into her standard bun or braid, and she jerked backward when the cold draft of air blew across the room. "Sorry—think I fell asleep sitting up." She pushed her hair out of her face and I could tell she'd gotten even less sleep than me.

"How long you been here, Tex?" I asked gently, moving across the room to brew a cup of the weak shit she called coffee.

"Since about eleven." Her voice wavered dangerously and I turned sharply to look at her.

I watched with absolute horror as her eyes filled and I was across the room in a heartbeat, pulling her from her chair without even thinking, dragging her into my arms. "Tell me what happened."

The obvious answer was that I was going to cut someone.

"I don't know, I don't know." She was shaking her head slowly, her hair making a rustling sound against my coat. "I haven't been home all week, so things were right where I left them. The alarm was on. Everything was locked. It was fine." She convulsed like she'd managed to hold in a sob. "When I went up to bed, there was a doll on my bed–right in the middle–a little girl's doll."

My blood ran cold in my veins. "Did it look familiar?"

"No, it wasn't one of Rebecca's. But I have no idea where it came from; how it got there. I ran right back out of the house. I don't think I even turned off the lights. So I came here."

Motherfucker. I'm going to use a rusty fucking blade.

"This ends today." I could hardly get the words out, I was so mad. "We're doing a perimeter sweep and we're having another chat with Sal." She moved like she was going to protest and I shut her up with a "No. This is enough, Bec. This sick fuck has got to be stopped. You're calling the DA today to make sure there ain't been no jailbreaks, yeah? New people fall down on the job all the time. Me and the boys are gonna be real thorough once the sun comes up." I helped her settle back down into her chair so I could grab the phone from my pocket and fire up the group text.

Me: *Beckett found a doll on her bed last night.*

Ben: *Aw cute, Jude. You been leaving her little love gifts? Guess I don't have to fire up that dating profile no more.*

Levi: *Do we have any idea how someone got into the house?*

Dan: *What's Ben doing awake? It's not even six.*

Ben: *I was working on a project. Haven't been to bed yet.*

Dan: *Did that project have thighs around your ears two minutes ago?*

Levi: *Stop fucking around, you two. This is a problem and we're about to lose a damn good worker because of it. This will drive away the one person that can save us.*

Me: *Yeah, thanks a lot.*

Ben: *You'll never admit it, but she's taming you, bro.*

Dan: *Willing to bet she spent the whole week at your place, taking care of you.*

Ben: *Judah and Beckett, sittin' in a tree...*

Levi: *All of you do what needs to be done this morning. We're meeting at her place at eleven, with Sal. We're doing a full sweep of the house* and *the woods. Someone else must know the alarm code.*

To be honest, I knew we should have done a full sweep of the woods that first night she had trouble. The house butted right up against a dense collection of trees, a beautiful forest filled with majestic old-growth, only a few hundred feet from her back door. It was peaceful. Serene. Idyllic.

Until it was like living in a M. Night Shyamalan movie.

I didn't say a word to Beckett. I leaned down and scooped her out of the chair and she put up no fight when I carried her across the office, killing the light and closing the door behind us. A fresh snow crunched under my boots as we crossed the yard, her arms going around my neck for support and I felt hot liquid trickle beneath the collar of my shirt as she sniffled.

It took some doing to get both our boots off at the front door, then I picked her back up and carried her inside. Dad was coming down the stairs as I carried her up. He didn't stop me, didn't ask any questions, just raised one eyebrow with a knowing grin.

Walking her down to the guest room I knew she'd been in before, I set her on her feet and helped her out of her jacket. She was shivering and I flipped down the blankets on the bed. I didn't wait for her to invite me. I tucked her into the side furthest from the door, walked across the room to close it, and then crawled in right beside her, hauling her up against my chest.

She sniffled, curled up against me with her palms on my chest, and in just a few short moments she was asleep.

Chapter Fourteen

Beckett

There was a sharp blast of cold air and the bed dipped, startling me awake. Judah stood there stretching slowly, rubbing one eye. "Go back to sleep," he murmured. "You're safe in here; me and the boys are gonna take care of a few things."

I heard Donna look in on me, then Erik—that man wasn't half as sneaky as he thought—and I heard low voices downstairs. Judah's voice was angry and Donna shushed him more than once.

When I woke again, it was to find Erik sitting in the chair in the corner of the room, watching the door. "Sounds like all that retrofitting's been worthless." He sipped coffee from a travel mug, meaning he'd been here for a while.

"It seems I've been an expensive nuisance." I felt a shameful blush rush to my cheeks as I slowly pushed myself into a sitting position. "I never meant to bring this trouble to your family, Mr. Benson. It's probably best if I just resign and try to disappear again."

"Now, who accused you of bringin' anything on us?" His expression was genuinely kind. "We got some whacko doing this to send a message and it would seem we're not real clear on the message part. Got some mixed signals goin' on. Trashed the house." He held up one finger. "Killed the calf, or at least made sure a dead one showed up in your yard." Another finger. "Busted your door." A third finger. "And a newspaper article slid under your garage door. Not sure all these things are related. Would guess the newspaper article and the doll to be the nearest matching things, so we got some process of elimination to go through. Until then, Judah says you're stayin' with him and he's not gonna hear it any other way—argued with Donna over it, and he never raises his voice to her."

A soft warmth filled my chest, something that felt an awful lot like relief. I felt safe with him in a way I hadn't in years, comforted by his ferocious protective streak when it seemed I was in harm's way. He was the grizzly bear who would step between me and danger, I knew that now, and the gratitude that filled my spirit for that was something I could easily confuse with something much bigger and scarier.

"You come on down when you feel ready and Donna will get some food into you. Work's done for the day, young lady. You're shot."

What did it say about me, that I was such a twisted mess over this? I'd wasted more than half the day when I could have been tracking the cows.

"I'll do better," I promised, startled to feel a tear bolt down my cheek.

"Sweetheart." He rose slowly and came to stand near the edge of the bed, wrapping one huge hand around my jaw as he stared down at me with kind eyes. "You're one of us now, part of this family, and we take care of our own. You're not goin' this alone."

Then, maybe because he knew the dam was about to break, he patted my cheek, turned, and left the room.

I cried until I had a migraine, but knowing he meant what he said, some of those tears were of relief.

Judah showed up at the house around dinnertime, the brothers trailing after him one by one. Donna was in her element, putting more plates on the table and bringing out dish after dish of food. I didn't know how she did it. She'd cooked for a handful of people, but she was pulling some kind of biblical loaves and fishes miracle in the kitchen, because more kept coming out.

"Got things sorted, boys?" Erik asked as each of them lowered themselves into what seemed to be their assigned spots.

Levi gave a short, sharp nod and I noticed Judah looked grim. Dan looked like he wanted to murder someone and Ben wasn't smiling, which I was pretty sure meant he felt the same way. A somber expression on his face was something I'd never seen before.

"I'm sorry, Dan." I finally spoke up. "I told you once Judah was better we'd both be out to help you."

He waved a hand at me. "Had one of the guys do it. Couldn't wait a week; I always subcontract the electrical work out to Jude." He clapped his brother hard on the back. "Trained to be an electrician while Cait was in the Air Force—he ever tell you that?"

Judah ducked his head like he was uncomfortable. "Didn't turn into nothin'. Don't go makin' it a big deal."

"It's something to be proud of, Judah." Donna smiled at him, reaching over to squeeze his forearm. "You have two potential careers open to you where most people don't even have one."

"Wasn't enough for her." The table fell silent as the words dropped from Judah's lips like little IEDs. He pushed the chicken across his plate with a fork before he looked up at me and I gave him a small nod. "Told me electrical engineering was the way to go and tried to get me to go back to school. Wanted me working for the military industrial complex." He snorted. "Had my position all lined up and everything, one-fifty a year."

"The fuck pays that kind of money, some kind of shell running heroin for the three-letters?" Ben chuckled and Judah leveled him with a sharp look.

"Sellin' your soul, either way. Pretty sure she fucked someone to hold that spot for me."

Donna's fork clattered to her plate and she crossed herself. She *was* the only Catholic in the house.

Erik looked stricken as he stared down the table at Judah. "Son ... there some things you weren't telling us?"

"Shit-ton of things he wasn't tellin'," Ben muttered under his breath and I caught a glimpse of just how quick Ben was to pick up on things and store them away, something I wondered if people overlooked because he was such a big clown. It was an asset in its own way.

"I did a stint with the Army," I offered quietly. "Four years so I could put myself through college for agricultural management. I understand that she wanted to better your lives." She wasn't alive to defend herself anymore and though I carried no sympathy for her, I understood her devotion to her career path even if I didn't understand why she'd tried to choose her husband's for him as well.

"You some kinda special ops sneak-attack super-commando, Bec?" Ben teased. "Got a JSOC operative sittin' at the dinner table?"

"Hardly." I folded my napkin and laid it next to my plate. "If I was, I don't think we'd be having this conversation because if

I knew what to look for, trust me, I would have eliminated the problem."

Erik's eyes sparkled and I knew it was because he appreciated the can-do attitude.

"Cait was leaving me."

Everyone froze when Judah tossed out that bomb and Ben's fist fell from his mouth to the table, his jaw slack with surprise. "What d'you mean, she was leaving you?"

"She landed a new job, something in Minneapolis. She was gonna pack up the boys and leave me and she had no real interest in figurin' out where that left us." He shrugged those wide shoulders and more than anything I wanted to reach under the table and take his hand, but I wasn't sure we were that kind of friends. "So I started a fight with her when I got back from Ash's wedding, and the next day she flew my boys into the side of a mountain."

Dan looked like he was going to be sick and he leaned back quickly with one hand over his eyes.

Levi nodded slowly, like he'd either suspected the whole time or wasn't at all surprised.

Ben's face was turning from red to purple, an interesting variegation I'd never seen him sport before, his expression twisted up in something that looked like fury and finally he spat, "You mean to tell me she took those precious babies from you cuz you wouldn't do what she wanted?"

All the fight had left Judah now that he'd laid waste to the dinner table, and he nodded wearily. "I don't know what she was thinking, but I know she should never have left the ground with that storm coming in. She was smarter than that."

Ben was muttering something under his breath about headstones and spit, and I finally reached over to place my hand on Judah's knee, squeezing gently. It made his eyes soften and his features relax, and he lifted his head to give me a grateful look. It made my stomach trip over itself in a very not-employer-employee-relationship kind of way.

Donna was muttering something under her breath that I thought might be a rosary and finally she reached over to place a hand on Judah's arm, squeezing gently. "You didn't have to carry that burden alone then, and you don't have to now. I know we're a poor substitute, but you are a loved, valued member of this family."

I expected a smart-assed remark from Ben, but nothing came as he sat there nodding in what appeared to be agreement.

"And now we have some more family." Erik smiled warmly at me. "Like the way this is going. Wouldn't mind adding some lady Bensons." He gifted each of his sons with a loaded look and I blushed uncomfortably. The look he gave Judah was somehow softer and more understanding, like something had been decided without words.

We all helped to clean up after dinner, the brothers quietly insisting that Donna relax while they put up the kitchen, scraping and rinsing dishes before stacking them into the dishwasher and wiping down the counters.

Because it went without saying that the Benson brothers ate like a horde of locusts, there were no leftovers to put away tonight.

"You'll be safe with him." Erik pulled me into a one-armed side hug as the brothers began to drift out into the night. Ben was the first to go, with a bone-crushing hug and a "We got this, Bec," followed by Levi, who simply squeezed my shoulder in what I supposed was solidarity.

"Got a load of shit in my truck," Dan announced. "Follow you back and help you unload."

The statement seemed to be directed at Judah, who had Donna wrapped up in a tight hug. She leaned up to kiss his cheek when he released her and he moved to his father, exchanging a back-slapping squeeze with him.

"Ready, Tex?" His voice was gentle, a teasing smile on his face and I rolled my eyes, grabbing my boots from the enormous tray near the door and shoving my feet in just before stepping over the transition and onto the porch.

He kept a hand at the small of my back as we walked toward his truck. Mine sat parked in the yard, but I made no move toward it, letting him guide me toward the passenger side of his.

I didn't ask why Dan was following us or what we were unloading, and the drive to Judah's house was quick.

"Whoa." Dan's voice was explosively loud and Judah paused, halfway through the front door with a load of boxes in his arms—boxes I was fairly certain came from my place.

"What?" he called through the door, where I stood waiting for him.

"Got a declaration of intent on your kitchen table," Dan called back and my eyebrows raised slowly.

Judah stepped into the entryway and closed the door against the sharp wind, leading me toward the back of the house. There was an enormous basket on the table, filled with breads and cheeses, jams, olives, pickles, and mustard. "What the fuck?" he murmured. "Door was locked. How'd this get in here?"

"More like *who* put it here in the first place, bro." There was a huge, wicked grin stretching across Dan's face as he threw an explanation over his shoulder for me. "This is Midwest for 'I'd like to fuck you,' and ... oh. Oh, my." He turned slowly, something in his hand.

I choked, turning it into a cough as Dan's eyes swept over my face. Whatever he saw there, I couldn't be sure, but I knew I wasn't going to like it.

"Manchego?" Judah took the block Dan held in his hands, and he swapped it out for another. "Tipsy Goat."

"Oh, that's the one. Someone wants to wine and dine and bed you, man. Better start thinkin' on who you got in your circle tryin' to put the moves on you—maybe you too, Bec, if that's any concern of yours." Dan wiggled his eyebrows. "Bet you'll find your answer here, though." He handed Judah a small envelope.

I held up my hands quickly, palms out, just before a horrifying thought occurred to me. "Is this seriously how you people interpret cheese? I brought a block of smoked gouda to your dad last week. What was I saying with that?"

"Whoa, Tex." Judah turned with a wicked grin on his face. "You proposition my old man? You got some balls on you, woman. Might have to be a little jealous."

I had a hand over my mouth already, horrified by this cheese etiquette of which I'd known nothing about.

"Well, your secret admirer got one thing right." Dan reached into the basket to pull out a bag of smoked string cheese, removing one and snapping off the end with his teeth.

"Monster," Judah teased, snatching the bag from his hands and handing it to me.

That was it, I was never giving anyone cheese ever again. Not until I got my hands on some kind of chart of intentions so I could decode what I was suggesting by giving someone a block of aged milk.

"Got a few more loads to bring in," Dan announced suddenly and Judah nodded, following him back out into the yard, shoving the envelope into his back pocket without a second thought. The two of them proceeded to walk in a tremendous number of boxes, piling everything in the dining room before Dan dusted off his hands and announced, "Well, that's not quite everything, but it's most of it. Enough that you shouldn't have to go back anytime soon."

"She's not *going back*." Judah's voice was low and dark, almost threatening. "She'll stay right here, where she's safe, and we're going to find this sick fuck and deal with him."

I wasn't sure when this decision had been made for me. It seemed a family powwow had taken place at some point during the day and all of them were on the same page, but I was just now being read in on the most basic details. It surprised me to find that it didn't anger me, the incredible amount of presumption taking place right in front of me.

I was too emotionally spent to care anymore.

"Make yourself at home." Judah swept an arm out, but both he and I knew I'd done just that during the days and nights I'd already spent in his home. I was familiar with his kitchen and I'd fallen into the easy domestic routines of laundry and meals, things I'd have done for myself anyway. Judah had been too ill to put up much of a fight, though I suspected he didn't mind the fussing and the care.

"What did you find today?" I asked, something that made him shake his head in a short, sharp motion.

"Don't worry about it, we're working on things."

"Judah." My voice was sharper than I'd intended. "What did you find?"

His shoulders deflated a little. "The alarms were fine, but the cameras were all offline. Alarm was tampered with. There was a new tree stand built in the woods, about a hundred feet back into the tree line. Surprisingly clear view of the house."

The hair rose on the back of my neck. Someone was watching the house—watching me, since there were no window coverings.

"No evidence of anyone having been there in a while, but the tree stand's not one we put up. No one in their right mind would hunt so close to the house and the wood isn't weathered yet, so it's not been there long."

One of my hands shot out blindly to grab onto something to hold myself up. I was thankful to find the back of a chair within easy reach.

"I called the DA's office today." His expression was grim. "Your forwarding information wasn't processed, for whatever reason, and since your old employer has relocated, your office phone number has been reassigned. Apparently no one thought it important enough to call your personal number."

I yanked the chair toward me and sank into it, a buzzing setting up in my ears.

"Bachman and five other inmates managed to escape nearly two months ago and only three have been apprehended. The DA suspects the rest have crossed into Mexico."

Judah sank into a squat in front of me, elbows braced on his thighs, loosely-folded hands hanging between his knees. "You're safe with us, Tex." His crystal blue eyes searched my face as I struggled to take deep, calming breaths. "No way he knows you're here and no way he's gonna find you, and if he shows up I'll be burying a body next to that calf in the front flower bed–bare hands, if need be." He bit out the last part of the sentence vehemently, something I had no doubt he meant.

"And if it's not him?" My voice shook. "Or if it's more than just him?"

"We'll figure it out." His voice was hard. "And in the meantime, you don't leave my sight."

"Who's the babysitter now?" My voice was still wobbly.

"Training wheels." The softest smile crossed his handsome face. "Made me so fuckin' mad. Went and wasted money we didn't have, hiring someone who was going to be *my* babysitter." He lifted one hand to cup my face, his expression going soft, and it made my heart catch. "Shoulda found you sooner."

I had no idea what he meant by that, whether it was a regret or a compliment, and I let my eyes drift shut, swallowing hard. I wasn't used to tenderness from another human any longer, especially not from him—not yet and maybe not ever.

"Come on." His voice was still gentle. "Go clean up and put on your pajamas. I'll make the tea."

He'd gotten used to my nightly tea ritual quickly.

I was sitting on the edge of the bed in the guest room when he drifted past the doorway with two mugs in his hands. I didn't ask where he was going, because I knew, and when his big frame filled the doorway I raised my eyes, feeling weirdly nervous and vulnerable.

"Bedtime, Tex." His smile was sweet as he flipped off the light and crossed the room, scooping an arm beneath my knees and banding one around my back to lift me, carrying me down the short hallway to his room.

Chapter Fifteen

Judah

It was weird that Beckett had become my new emotional support human. I didn't have nightmares when she slept beside me, and I suspected it was because when we crawled in and turned out the lights, we were talking about all the deep, dark things we'd kept buried for a long time.

Shining a light on them and chasing away the ghosts.

As the weeks went on we continued the pattern, like a married couple getting ready for bed each night and crawling in to talk about our day.

It hadn't escaped my notice, and probably not hers either, that there was no sex. My brain and my body were different pages about that issue, something I found a little alarming to realize I wouldn't mind exploring with her. It had to be something she suspected, because each morning I woke painfully hard, her back pressed to my front, and I wondered about the *what if.*

The family knew she was staying at my place while we tried to smoke out the creep, but they didn't know she was sleeping in my room. No one even suspected—and trust me, Ben would have asked for details just to watch me squirm.

There was a comfortable familiarity with her by now. I knew exactly how far I could push her before she blew up and she knew how to calm me when I was having a meltdown. And each night after we turned out the lights, we traded stories with her tucked up against my side, my arm beneath her head, my miserable dick hard as stone and my brain screaming at me about all the reasons why we shouldn't—the first being that I was pretty sure she'd shut that shit right down, and I couldn't risk losing what was easily becoming my favorite thing.

Bec took over the place in the next few weeks, my entire dining room table swallowed up by her mess as she made things for each of my family members for Christmas. I had to remember that she hadn't had family to celebrate with in a long time, so I just kept my mouth shut. It was a given that she'd celebrate Christmas with us and I think Donna might've had a coronary if she didn't.

Things were still tight with the books, but she'd found a couple interesting ways to cut costs and she'd done a couple swaps with neighboring farms to trade for things we needed rather than having to splash out on new stuff. I had to hand it to her, she was inventive and seemed totally unafraid of being told no. Every problem was a challenge for her, a puzzle to solve.

Donna and Dad were completely in love with her. Dad lit up like a fucking Christmas tree every time Beckett was a topic of conversation. She'd been pulling long hours on the farm, between her work in the office and lending a hand wherever she could, and I was impressed by the fact she was willing to brave the elements. Minnesota winters are no joke, but she Carhartt'd right up and went out to help Ben fix the chain link on the feed trough, ran the skid loader when it was time to clean out the calf barns, and crawled right into the back of the manure spreader to literally break up frozen shit with a shovel when the weather was so cold that it started freezing before I could get it spread on the fields.

Damn, this woman could work. She wasn't a princess. She didn't whine. Most days she ended up covered in shit and smelling just as bad as I did, but she didn't seem to care. She just showered it off and started all over again the next day, and I loved it. It gave me something with her that made me smile a hell of a lot more than I had in a long time.

There were easier, cleaner, faster ways to get these tasks done, but that involved a lot more money than we had, so we stuck to the old ways. We paid for it in time, frustration, broken machinery and cursing, and closer brushes with frostbite than we'd have liked, but it was just as well. Dad would never have gone for the expensive equipment or fancy automations. He said that family farms had soul, where all the cows had names and a life expectancy three to four times that of the factory farms. It was something Bec backed up, having done some consulting for large dairy operations in the past. She said she'd turned down a job offer in North Dakota, paying considerably better than whatever she'd negotiated with Levi, because she preferred the family setting. But when I considered that she'd never even conducted an in-person interview with us, I had no idea how she'd thought we would be a good fit.

If she'd met us, I was pretty sure we would have scared her away.

Thank God she hadn't conducted an in-person interview. Levi would have turned her down the instant he knew Beckett was a *she*. That was a complication I knew he hadn't counted on, even if it seemed to be making a pretty positive difference.

That thought pulled me up short, the realization that I was thankful for the biggest disruption in my life since losing my family.

"I still don't know what to get your dad." Beckett sounded distressed, her voice preceding her as she moved down the short hallway. "I was going to put together a huge cheese basket, but ... well, in light of the fact there's apparently some kind of weird cheese etiquette here–or cheese wooing, which is really freaking me out, by the way–" she threw up her hands in an adorable gesture of frustration, "I'm rethinking this."

I couldn't help the snort. I didn't mean for it to go beyond that, but the hilarity set in. Suddenly I couldn't stop laughing, doubled over, clutching my stomach with one hand while I braced myself on the bed with the other.

"Not funny, Benson." She was standing right in front of me, her lips curving just a little at the edges. "I really don't know what to get him."

"Tex." I wheezed. I wanted to hug her more than I wanted my next breath, and that was terrifying. "We were pulling your leg, baby."

She froze at the same moment I did, but apparently it was for a different reason, because I'd just realized I'd called her *baby*. Where had that come from? Her eyes flared with indignation. "Judah Benson! I would expect as much from Benjamin, but you played along? You should be ashamed of yourself, you bully!"

Was I? Uh, no. Absolutely not. The look of absolute horror on her face had been both hilarious and adorable.

"Sorry, Bec—but not really. It was so stupid-cute when you freaked out." I couldn't catch my breath. "You actually thought you'd put the moves on my dad." I hadn't laughed this hard in *years*. It was unfamiliar, but it felt good.

Her expression flattened out. "So you just hung me out to dry, that's how it is?"

"Not exactly..." I swallowed suddenly, a little alarmed.

She moved closer, pushing an index finger into my chest, her face only inches from my own as she leaned up, eyes blazing. "You thought it was hilarious to let me think I had just propositioned your father. I was *mortified*."

She folded in half all of a sudden, hands braced on her knees. Her shoulders were shaking and there was a weird wheezing noise coming from her general vicinity.

"Tex." I was alarmed. I placed a hand on her shoulder, smoothing gently, afraid she was suffering a panic attack. Then the tiniest fart of a laugh came from her mouth.

"You piece of shit." She straightened quickly, one hand over her eyes, her shoulders still shaking, the sound of her laughter still not audible. "I should have known you were just like your brothers. They're all out to get me—killing me with kindness most of the time, maybe, but still assholes." She finally dropped her hand, her head shaking back and forth. "Thank God I love you anyway."

Suddenly she stilled, like she'd just realized what she said.

"Bec." It died in my throat, because the way she was looking at me was...

I stumbled back when she lurched forward, both of her hands coming up to cup my face. "Judah." Her voice was low, urgent, and a little terrified. And then she pushed forward, her mouth pressing against mine.

I couldn't have responded if I'd wanted to. I was thunderstruck, absorbing the softness of her lips against my own. So hot and sweet and ... hesitant, like this was something she hadn't practiced in a long time. And I let her lead the charge for a moment, her lips moving against mine. Because holy shit, I wanted this. How many nights had I held her in my arms and dreamed of this very thing?

There were no words from her, only soft sighs as I let her deepen the kiss. It was beautiful, magical, delicious ... I had no words beyond that. It was something I'd never thought I'd feel again, that powerful rush of desiring and being desired.

Suddenly she broke away, reeling backward, hands flying up to her mouth as her cheeks went the most adorable shade of pink. "What the hell was I thinking? I'm so sorry." Her eyes were suspiciously shiny and I couldn't help but think this was not the time for tears.

"Hey." I held up my hands, moving toward her slowly so as not to spook her, circling my arms around her shoulders and gently pulling her against me, one hand coming up to cradle her head. "No harm, no foul. Got zero complaints about being kissed by a beautiful woman—ten out of ten, would do it again."

I left it at that. She was having a meltdown, somehow convinced she was in the wrong. She was shaking, but my words had put a tiny smile on her lips.

"Take a breath, Tex." I kissed the top of her head, unable to stop myself.

"I'm sorry." Her voice was thick with tears. "I forgot myself for a minute."

Oh, I knew what that meant. For a minute, she'd forgotten *him*. The man to whom she'd dedicated all her grief, remorse, and longing this past twelve years.

"They're gone, Bec." I couldn't believe it when the words left my lips. They were words I hadn't allowed myself to say, not even once before. "We're what's left." I hated that, but some small part of me had to admit that as angry as I'd been when Beckett had arrived, she had quickly become what got me through every day. When that had happened, I wasn't sure I could say, but it was an uncomfortable truth.

"It never really goes away." Her voice was a little calmer. "By now I think it's mostly guilt. I brought it to them, Judah. I'm the reason they're dead and I just can't let that go."

I squeezed her a little tighter, feeling her melt into me as I stroked her hair. "Someone you told to leave you alone. Someone you took every precaution with, to keep him away and keep your family safe. That person was unwell—is unwell. There was nothing you could have done to stop him."

"Yes, there was." Her voice went cold and hard. "And if I ever see his face again, I'll do it."

No sweetheart, I'll do it.

I straightened a little, sobered by the realization that there was no doubt in my mind I would eliminate anyone who threatened her. Somehow she'd wound herself around my heart in just a few short months, pushing aside the self-pity and suffering I'd been marinating in for the last several years.

We were instituting an elaborate game, beginning tonight, trying to flush out the person making Beckett feel unsafe. Levi had been the one to drive her truck back to her place, keeping the lights low in the house but spending the night in hopes someone might tip their hand; might try something stupid and get caught.

To this day I didn't know what Levi had done in the Army, because he wouldn't talk about it. But I knew it made him the perfect person for the job. He was used to waiting patiently, then seizing the moment.

"He'll never get that close to you." My voice was ice, and it was enough to make her pull back just enough to look up into my face.

"My battles aren't yours, Judah."

"Yes, they fucking are."

Way to tip your hand, big man.

She shook her head at me, a tiny smile tugging at the corners of her mouth. I wanted her to kiss me again, so desperately that I could taste it. I leaned down, tipping my forehead to hers, and repeated the words right up against her lips. "Yes, they are."

She sucked in a deep breath and placed her palms flat on my chest, but she didn't push me away. She waited for me, like we both needed time to wrap our heads around the fact that this was intentional. She may have just acted on the spur of the moment, but this next move was a conscious decision on both our parts. I brought one hand up, catching her chin with my fingers, my thumb pressed into her bottom lip. And I'll be damned, she kissed it, puckering her lips around it.

"Life's too short for regrets. I don't want any more of them," I said quietly, just before I leaned down that last inch and kissed her hard. She sagged into me like she was relieved, her hands going up to hold my face before one slid into my hair, holding me tight.

Fireworks exploded behind my closed eyelids when she opened to me, letting me kiss her like I really meant it, something I could feel all the way down to my toes. It made her sigh softly, a little whimper that went straight to my dick. I wanted more of those noises and suddenly I didn't care what it took to get them.

Sliding one hand down her spine, I flexed my fingers into her ass, bringing her flush against my body. I felt it when she registered what she'd done to me, her breath catching for a second. It changed something in her, made her bolder, her hands drifting down to grip my hips, holding me tight to her.

Everything about Beckett was soft and warm, and maybe it was just that I was starved for a woman's attention, but whatever it was, this felt like coming alive again. Her tongue dipped into my mouth in a slow, seductive dance, twisting and hungry, something that threatened to draw out my soul.

We kissed until we were breathless, dragging ourselves apart, gasping. I wanted to draw the oxygen in faster, to get back to the magic happening with her lips.

She was the one to break the kiss again, panting, and I tipped my forehead down to hers. She didn't have to say it; I could feel what she was thinking. It was too much, too fast for either of us, unfair to ourselves or loved ones past, or maybe just one another. I didn't know and couldn't sort it out, my brain fuzzy and buzzing with what I knew was lust. That animal had been awakened after a long hibernation and was roaring, starving for a taste of her.

"I don't think it's a good idea for me to sleep in here tonight." Her voice was timid, and it took a minute for the words to sink in. To hurt a little. Then, "I think you would be the perfect gentleman."

"What are you saying, Bec?" I wanted to hear the words, and I watched as she chewed on her bottom lip for a long moment, her eyes downcast.

"I'm saying I don't trust myself."

"Okay." I almost couldn't believe I said it and it sounded far more measured and calm than I felt. "But you know I'll be here if you need me." That was the best I could do, even if we both knew how I hoped she might need me.

She slept in the guest room the rest of that week and I just about lost my mind. Without her wrapped up in my arms I was sleeping like shit, tossing and turning for far too long before finally letting exhaustion pull me under. And when it did the nightmares were different, a disturbing blend of loss and conjecture. In these dreams she was in danger and I was helpless to stop it and I often jolted awake, sweating, my heart racing. It meant that more than once I'd crept from my bed, telling myself I'd get a glass of water from the kitchen because what I really needed was to peek into her room to make sure she was safe.

My phone dinged just moments after I'd fallen asleep the night before Christmas Eve. I'd struggled with the urge to dig through my small basement stash of liquor—the one Levi didn't know about—to help me sleep. But in the end, I didn't. It had been weeks and while a weird part of my brain craved it, it wasn't about the unbearable loss of a coping mechanism, but that having companionship made me a little less lonely.

Calista: *Merry Christmas, Judah. I'm sorry we can't celebrate it with Cait and the boys, but I hope you're finding your way through the darkness.*

I groaned, not at all willing to respond to that, when another text rolled in.

Ben: *You bringing Bec to Christmas Eve dinner tomorrow night, fucknuts?*

Me: *I swear you've become completely nocturnal, Benjamin. It's unnatural. You're part possum.*

Ben: *Things are quieter at night. I can get shit done without interruptions.*

He kind of had a point.

Me: *You bringing the new mattress buddy to meet the parents?*

The dots bounced and stopped, then bounced and stopped again. Then finally,

Ben: Ah, that would be a hard no. Not a good idea. Don't need her getting attached.

That was typical for Ben and unfortunately for him, women seemed to get attached quickly. Maybe they thought it was that they thought they could fix him, that he was redeemable in some way. I couldn't say. Women quickly became addicted to him, something he didn't even try to explain.

Honestly, I'm not sure he understood it, but he definitely took full advantage.

Me: *Kind of have to bring her, don't I? Dad and Donna have obviously welcomed her into the family.*

Benjamin: *Clearly you have, too. You just haven't figured it out in the awake side of your brain yet.*

I had nothing to say to that, so I left it and tossed the phone back down on my nightstand and tried yet again to go to sleep.

The phone buzzed again and I heaved out an angry sigh and snatched it back up, because clearly I wasn't allowed to sleep tonight.

Levi: *Called the fire department. Cabin's on fire.*

Chapter Sixteen

Beckett

There was a quiet sound somewhere in the house, something that made my hair stand on end, and my eyelids snapped open like they were spring-loaded. Whatever it was, it had awakened me from what had been a warm, comfortable sleep and I held my breath while I tried to figure out what it had been.

The furnace kicked on, blasting a current of hot air through the floor vent next to the bed and I held a hand over it, thankful Judah kept the temperature settings at a non-polar bear level. He was a hot sleeper, something I now knew from experience, and I knew he was keeping the thermostat higher for my sake. I had complained only once that I'd spend the entirety of my first Minnesota winter in a state of hypothermia and mysteriously, the thermostat bumped up by eight degrees.

I lay there for a long moment before swinging my legs over the edge of the bed and sliding from beneath the warm cocoon of blankets to move down the hallway on quiet feet.

"Judah?"

There was no answer from the bed and I moved to the edge, aware that I couldn't hear him breathing. I lifted the edge of the blanket and slid in, surprised to find the sheets were warm but there was no warm, sleeping man in the space. I wasn't willing to travel back down the hallway to retrieve my phone, so I curled into the warm spot, my head on a pillow that smelled like him. It was soap and woods and comfort, and I allowed that false sense of comfort to eventually lull me back to sleep.

It must have been hours later when I felt the bed dip and I scooted a little as Judah slid in behind me, warm and smelling a little of smoke. He didn't seem surprised to find me there, just wrapped himself tightly around me and pressed his face into my hair. Something about it felt fearful, and he slid one arm beneath my pillow while wrapping the other around my middle to hold me tight, his lips pressing to the back of my skull.

I didn't fall back to sleep for a long time, the weak gray light of dawn starting to filter into the room by the time my eyes drifted shut. The dark winter nights were long in the north, something I was learning the hard way, but it had been a fractured night and my eyes felt gritty when I opened them again, the room almost fully light.

"Shhh." Judah's hold was firm and comforting. "I turned off the alarm. Dad's going to keep an eye on things this morning so we can get some rest. Go back to sleep." He hummed contentedly into my hair a moment later, his hand folding over mine, fingers intertwining, and I felt my eyes fill with tears. It wasn't guilt. It wasn't remorse, regret, sadness, or any of the other emotions that had been plaguing me for years.

It was peace.

It was hours later when I woke to realize Judah was no longer in the bed behind me, and I rolled into his still-warm spot, certain this was my new favorite place.

"You're like a kitten." His voice was deep, his chuckle soft, and my eyes snapped open to see him walking into the room with two enormous mugs of coffee. "You know where to find the warmest, most comfortable spot in the house."

"You're admitting your side of the bed is more comfortable." I grinned at him before scooting back just a little and he set both mugs on his bedside table before crawling back in.

"To be fair, no one's slept on that side in a long time, so yeah, maybe."

The mortification probably showed on my face, when I realized I'd just essentially called his wife's side of the bed my own, but it didn't seem to bother him, if it registered at all.

He leaned over and grabbed both mugs, carefully passing one to me and we settled back, propped up by pillows. It was a weird, wonderful feeling, something that I'd missed with an unidentifiable ache in my heart.

"Merry almost-Christmas." He clinked his mug against mine, a soft smile on his face. "Looks like you'll be stuck with me for a while."

I didn't know what that meant, but he didn't look too upset about it.

"Something you need to tell me?"

"Cabin caught fire last night. Saved most of it, but the fire marshal's coming out this morning to take a look. Scared the shit out of me." The smile was replaced by a faint crease in his forehead and I knew he was thinking of what might have happened if I'd been alone.

"Levi said he went through the regular routine: went home to feed the dog, then went sneaking back to the cabin, kept the lights low, locked up. He took a shower and went to bed–said he wasn't sleeping yet when he smelled something weird."

"Did it start in the garage?" I asked, certain the last time someone had tried to get into the house, that was the way they'd done it.

"No." There was a strange look on his face. "Chimney fire."

"From the ... furnace?"

"No, fireplace. And I know it was swept and repaired, because you've been using it, but you'll like this part even less: Levi didn't start a fire last night."

I was perfectly warm, but the thought made me shiver. "We're never going to get to the bottom of this, Judah. Not if we keep playing it this way. Someone's going to end up dead, and it might not be me—and your family would never forgive me for that."

He cradled the mug close to his chest with one hand, the other arm slipping around my shoulders to pull me close. "Not gambling with you and using you as bait if that's what you're suggesting, Tex." His voice was all scratchy and emotional, something that almost made me tear up, because what was this thing? What were we doing? I was fairly certain we were getting attached, and how could anything good come of it?

We stayed that way for a while, cuddled up close, sipping our coffee, the fingers of his right hand rubbing up and down my arm. It was something deeply comforting, something that made me feel precious and like I belonged to someone again. It was an addictive, dangerous thing.

While I made breakfast he helped me wrap the last of the gifts I had either made or purchased for his family, then he piled everything into laundry baskets to load into his truck.

I was a little nervous. It had been more than a decade since I'd spent a proper Christmas with anyone. Usually it was just me with a rotisserie chicken and store bought mashed potatoes, some kind of cloying holiday drink, and a Christmas movie.

"I'll do the evening milking with you," I said as I drifted back out into the kitchen, dressed for the day. "We can give the guys the night off to spend with their families." I knew he'd already given them Christmas Day.

He nodded, a small smile on his face. "Good idea. Probably the best thing we can give them." He whipped out his phone.

"I'll let them know. Dad said morning chores went off without a hitch and to expect dinner around seven."

"Suppose we should get going then." I reached behind my head to pull my hair up into a knot I secured with a soft elastic band. "You know Donna's going to want dinner by six, not seven."

It was nearly three when we rolled into the yard and Judah helped me carry the baskets of gifts into the house to unload before we headed out to the barn. We conducted what had become a very careful daily head count, then distributed the evening feeding with a little extra, since it was earlier than usual. I fed the calves while he hauled wheelbarrows to the heifer barns and distributed the silage. The cows had only been allowed out into the barnyard a few short afternoon hours since it was so cold, and when he opened the huge door they snorted and shoved their way into the space, each cow trained as to which stall was hers.

We worked together quickly, efficiently, and we met in the milkhouse to carry the milk machines into the barn. He started up the system while I hauled a pail of hot water in to wash udders before the milk machines were put into place and we developed a quick rhythm, moving down the line with ten machines between the two of us. We moved as quickly as possible and while he hosed down the milkhouse I grabbed the grain chart and gave each cow her allotted amount, turned off and drained the water to the back barns, and added more bedding to a few stalls.

"Work good together." I jumped at the sound of his voice so near me. I hadn't heard the barn door slide open or shut, an unmistakable sound on such heavy rollers, and he locked the gates to the alleys that led up in front of the cows. Then he checked the electrical current to the outdoor fence before nodding at me. "Snug as bugs and with ten minutes to spare. Donna will be pleased." Then he leaned down and brushed a soft kiss across my lips. It was an easy, routine gesture, something that seemed almost habitual, but the smile on his face told me it was anything but. It was purposeful, something that made him seem happy, and when Judah was happy he was a beautiful man.

I was willing to bet there were a number of things we'd do well together, but I didn't respond. I just nodded at him and flicked off the lights, following him out of the barn and sealing the door tightly behind me.

"Bec, I missed you!" Ben sang as I tripped over the transition strip and into the house. My boots were an abomination and I'd left them on the front porch, padding into the house on thick wool socks just as Ben caught me in a huge hug. He released me quickly, just in time for me to observe a warning glare pass between Judah and Ben, something that made me smile.

Dan looked remarkably subdued and I knew without asking what was going on with him, his family wasn't attending.

Levi's smile was small and tight and I drifted over to hug him. "You're taking too big a risk for me."

"Nonsense." He waved a hand in the air. "Anyone's trained to handle that piece of shit, it's me."

I didn't ask about his experience. All a person had to do was look at Levi to know he was dangerous in the right situations, simply from the way he carried himself.

"Why don't you all spend the night?" Donna asked almost hopefully. "Got plenty of room." Her eyes darted between Judah and me. "You wouldn't have to drive back in the morning for breakfast and chores."

"Ma." Judah chuckled as he leaned over and scooped the tiny woman into a gentle hug. "Live like a mile away."

"Got to feed the dog," Levi offered matter-of-factly.

"Got a date," Ben chimed in, and I watched Donna's shoulders sag just a little.

"On Christmas Eve, Benjamin?"

"Well..." I fumbled for the words. "I mean, we could probably stay." I could tell it meant something to her and I gestured between Judah and myself, a little surprised at my own presumption. One of his eyebrows raised slightly, but her face lit right up and I knew it was the right thing to do. I knew from a conversation with Erik that her kids weren't out to visit often, even though they didn't live all that far away, and all three of them had informed her they wouldn't be able to make it home for Christmas this year.

Ben's right eyebrow raised slightly and he shot me an absolutely wicked grin. I wasn't sure what it meant, but knowing him it was loaded with some kind of dirty innuendo, because one thing I inherently understood was how Ben's twelve-year-old boy brain worked.

"You bring the smoked gouda?" Dan's smile was slight when I shot him a sharp look and heat rushed to my cheeks.

"Oh, the cheese tray!" Donna spun to open the fridge while the boys burst out laughing.

"The card, Judah." It was almost an afterthought, something that I'd forgotten to ask him about the night he'd tucked the card from the gift basket into his pocket. It made him raise an eyebrow at me, like he wasn't following. "From the basket in your house."

"Don't know." He shrugged. "Forgot to open it and I think it went through the wash."

My mouth dropped open as I remembered the inordinate amount of green lint and paper chunks I'd pulled from the dryer screen a few days later.

No one seemed to care that Judah and I smelled like cows and pickled forage, and as I put more and more of the delicious food into my stomach, my eyelids grew heavier. Conversation continued around the table, good-natured teasing and a few potshots.

"Gonna head out," Ben announced, pushing back from the table as I struggled to take the last few bites of cherry pie. "Meeting my date at the Machine Shed for a Christmas nightcap."

Dan rolled his eyes. "Seriously. Just call it a booty call and be done with it, you man whore."

"Benjamin." Donna's voice was disappointed. She was going to try her luck one more time. "I was really hoping you'd join us for midnight mass."

"Uh..." Ben's laugh was nervous. "Don't think my date's Catholic, Ma, but thanks. Maybe a raincheck?"

"We'll go." Judah's voice was soft, and he grinned at me. "Bec might need a nap first, though."

I showered, grateful for the sweatshirt and sweatpants Donna put out for me, and I collapsed on top of the soft mattress, promising myself I'd close my eyes for just a moment.

The bed dipped moments later and my eyes snapped open, the room warm and dark. There was the slide of clothing being removed and a chuckle I recognized as Judah tucked me beneath the blankets and crawled in beside me.

"But ... Mass," I protested sleepily, which was met with soft laughter.

"You slept through Mass, Tex. I went with Dad and Donna." He scooted me over a little more and from the intense heat radiating from him, I could tell he was leaning over me. He leaned down, dropping several soft kisses on my face, then turned me so he could spoon me, his arms caging me in.

"Favorite part of the day," I mumbled, my social filter weak thanks to exhaustion, and he sighed softly into my hair.

"Me too, baby." His breathing evened out almost immediately, and happiness filled my heart.

The room was still dark when I woke again, minutes or hours later as Judah groaned uncomfortably and stretched out, rolling onto his back. I rolled with him, twisting myself to hook one leg over his and press into his side. It was frightening how quickly I'd become dependent on this man to help me sleep at night, and I suspected it was the same for him.

"You know this was my bedroom when I was a kid?" It was almost a whisper, and I wondered how long he'd been awake.

"Donna had me sleep in your bedroom?" I was a little horrified. Surely the devout little woman would have thought that through.

"She's an evil genius." His chuckle was warm, amused. "Then again, she probably thinks I'm sleeping in Levi's old room, but that monk had a twin bed. No way in hell."

"I definitely wouldn't fit in a twin bed with you." I snuggled a little closer. Judah already took up a huge portion of the queen-sized bed, and he sometimes starfished in his sleep.

"Wouldn't have been mad if you'd tried." He squeezed me gently, one arm wrapped loosely around my shoulders, his hand curling down around my ribs. "Always sleep better."

I knew the words were hard for him, but I needed to know what this was. I'd been unsettled the last few nights we'd slept apart, puzzling over what it was that I meant to him. It was more than friendship; friends didn't snuggle. And for the most part, he didn't fight with me anymore when I pointed out things I wanted to institute. It made me wonder if I'd proven myself, so he was just letting me be.

"What are we doing, Judah?" My voice was so quiet, it was barely more than a whisper. I was terrified of the answer.

"What you need us to be, Tex? You eager to have Ben activate that dating site profile for you?" I heard the tease in his voice, but it also contained a note of hesitation. Maybe it was worry.

"I'm never dating again." I blew out a raspberry. "Have you seen what's out there?"

He snorted. "Pretty sure Ben's fucked ninety-five percent of what's out there, at least as far as my potential landscape is concerned. Not interested in doing that homework."

"I don't want to be a replacement." I knew as soon as the words left me, that was what had been bothering me. It was the truth.

"I don't either." The words came out of him slowly, like he'd just come to a similar realization, and a thrilling rush of adrenaline coursed through my limbs.

"So, we're agreed that we're not replacements? We ... do this thing clean?" My voice was still hesitant.

"How on earth could anyone replace *you*, Beckett?" His voice was tender, his arm tightening around me, and I pressed my face into his side. I'd never expected to feel all these big, scary things for another human again, not so long as I lived. It was lighting up something inside me, something long dead and forgotten, and I pushed up on one arm in order to find his face in the darkness, turning his head just slightly toward me so I could press my lips to his.

"Knew the instant I saw you, you were gonna be my undoing." He rumbled the words between kisses. "Probably why I was so damn mad at you—not ... mad anymore."

Something that astonished me was the deep well of tenderness in such a big man. He was so careful with me, so gentle, when I'd been sure he'd be angry and feral. His arms went around me as he turned onto his side, pushing me carefully to my back and looming over me. One big hand came up to cup my cheek, to hold my face just so as he leaned down and turned the kiss into something deeper, something that made my toes curl when his tongue stroked against mine, leisurely licks like I was something delectable to be savored, a soft rumble in his chest.

For once, I turned off my brain and simply felt. I let my fingers trail up beneath his t-shirt, to explore the smooth, soft skin of his bare back and chest. His muscles twitched as my fingers explored, his body tight with a tension I understood.

He broke the kiss slowly, rubbing his nose gently against mine, our bodies nearly flush with one another. "Gonna stop myself now so that we don't get a lecture from Donna at breakfast about fornicating under her roof on the baby Jesus's birthday."

I snorted so loud, he laughed too, and he held me close as we giggled together.

"Didn't have this before," he whispered into my hair when we finally calmed enough to stop wheezing and I wiped tears of laughter off my cheeks. "Wasn't ever easy with her. Everything was a fight. A negotiation. I just figured that was normal, that everyone had to compromise, but it was over *everything*."

There was such sadness in his voice, such remorse, and I wondered if the rest of the family had opinions of Cait they hadn't found fit to share.

"Did your sister like her?" I whispered, and he snorted just as loudly as I had.

"Ash fuckin' *hated* Cait, and Ash doesn't hate anyone."

"She wanted what was best for you then, and maybe didn't think Cait was it."

He hummed what might have been agreement and wrapped himself around me, his head on my shoulder for a change. He yawned quietly and pressed his face into my neck, breathing me in as his inhalations quickly began to slow and deepen. I kept him gathered close, my eyes beginning to drift despite the aching discomfort of being so wildly turned on.

If he could control himself, so could I.

"Angel sent to save me, Tex." His words were slurred with sleep, soft against my skin. "Angel makin' me fall."

Chapter Seventeen

Judah

"Awful lot of giggling going on at two a.m." Dad's voice carried down the hallway as I walked into the kitchen to find him fixing me with a disapproving look.

What was I, fifteen?

"Hey, wasn't no funny business under your roof. Scout's honor." I held up a hand and Dad snorted.

"You weren't no boy scout, son—didn't have time for it, with all that farm work."

Donna tucked under my arm and kissed my cheek with a little grin tugging at the corners of her lips. "Happiness looks good on you, sweet boy—good on Beckett, too."

That made me blush. She had no idea how happy I'd wanted to make Beckett the night before, but I hadn't been able to bring myself to do it in the room directly beneath theirs.

"You best be serious about this, son." Dad was fixing me with his best hairy eyeball and it was a good one. It made me squirm. When had he learned that?

"Can't not be serious about her," I admitted half under my breath, but they both definitely heard it.

"Good." Donna's tone suggested we'd finalized that and gotten it out of the way. "Get some coffee in and grab a cinnamon roll before you head out for chores. Everyone will be here by nine for breakfast and we'll open presents after."

A hand trailed slowly across my back and Beckett moved past to fill a mug with coffee. Her hair was crazy, a wild tangle she hadn't even tried to tame, and when she turned to face me I saw Dad's grin get even wider. Her face looked like she'd been attacked by a belt sander and Donna snarked, "You'll be pleased to know Judah's getting razors for Christmas, my dear."

That made Beckett's face turn even more pink, and I shook my head at Donna. "You two don't think I overheard some things while you were dating?" I wiggled my eyebrows. I hadn't exactly been a kid when they'd started dating, I'd already been into my twenties, but I had lived at home until Cait and I were married.

Dad's mouth opened and then closed several times, like his words were broken, and I grinned at him. "Yeah, that's what I thought you'd have to say."

Beckett gulped down her coffee before disappearing to change back into the work clothes Donna had laundered the night before. She collected her heavy work coat from the garage and carried her boots out onto the frigid front porch, where her teeth chattered while she sat in one of the rocking chairs and laced them up. I waited for her, then stood as well, taking her hand in mine to walk down the steps and across the yard. Out of the corner of my eye I saw the little smile that tipped up the corners of her lips and I didn't let go of her hand until we were in the milkhouse, out of anyone's line of sight, when I could tip her face upward and press a soft kiss to her mouth. "Tonight we're back at our place," I said, watching understanding start to dawn in her eyes. "No Donna and Dad overhead." It made her swallow hard, her breaths picking up a little. "If..." I couldn't even finish the sentence.

"Yes." She nodded slowly, then pulled my face back down to hers for a hard kiss. Her lips remained unmoving, just a tight seal of her mouth against mine. A promise.

We worked together quickly, knocking out the chores much the same way we had the night before, slipping through each of our duties like a well-oiled machine. We didn't need to use words to communicate, something I was starting to realize. She knew what needed to be done and she did it quickly, then jumped in to help me as I finished up the morning feeding. We tag-teamed the milking process, then moved through cleanup quickly, and I linked my fingers through hers once more as we hurried toward the house. Ben, Dan, and Levi's trucks were already parked in the driveway and I grimaced when I realized Lindsey's car wasn't there.

"Looks like Dan's on his own for Christmas," I said softly to Beckett. "Don't know what's going on there, but I'm worried about him. Might try to pull him aside today and see what I can get out of him."

She nodded thoughtfully, folding to quickly unlace her boots and shrug out of her jacket before stepping through the front door.

"Just coffee for you this year." Levi appeared in the hallway that led to the kitchen with a mug in his hands, whipped cream piled over the top. Donna's Christmas coffee was legendary and if you weren't careful it would knock you sideways in a hurry, more liquor than caffeine in it. I knew why I wasn't getting the spiked version, too. It was no secret that I'd been all the way off the wagon for a long time.

"That looks like a good idea." Beckett's eyes were wide and Levi grinned at her.

"You want the real Christmas version or the kiddie one?"

Bec's eyes shifted over to me, making me smile. "Yeah, fix her the real deal and see what she thinks."

"Oh, I see how it is. You just want to get me tipsy so you can take advantage." Her hands flew to her mouth the instant the words were out, her eyes wide, and Levi cut me a sharp look. He turned slowly, throwing a shoulder into mine, two fingers raised to his eyes then swiveled to me like *I see you*.

"Shit," she muttered under her breath as he stalked away. "And that's *before* any alcohol. I really didn't mean to let that slip out."

I couldn't help but chuckle. Eventually I'd have to put a name on this and announce it to the family, because it was about to hit the fan before we'd even begun. Donna and Dad were already in on it and now Levi had an inkling. Once it got to Ben it would be shot to shit.

It was probably my imagination, but I could feel eyes on us throughout breakfast. Bec sat beside me, admirably keeping her hands to herself, and she didn't fuss when Dad brought her a second doctored coffee. It was starting to loosen her up, her posture more relaxed, her eyes bright. She was quick to smile and laugh, to jump into the conversation, and Ben was delighted when she teased him right back.

Dan sat across from me, deep shadows beneath his eyes. His hair looked like he'd forgotten to brush it, the blond waves crazy and rumpled, stubble on his face.

Now that I was looking closely, I could tell he'd been losing weight, and it wasn't a good look.

Levi was quiet, happy to let Ben direct the circus, while Donna was in her hostessing element.

Dad was watching Dan too, catching my eye once with a look of concern. I knew there had been some bullshit excuse about Lindsay and the boys going to visit her family for Christmas and going through recent memories, I realized I couldn't recall the last time I'd seen her. There had been a similar excuse at Thanksgiving, now that I thought back a little...

We opened gifts after breakfast and at one point all of us uncomfortably ignored the fact Dan's elbows were on his knees, his head hanging down. He was so checked out, he didn't respond when Donna softly called his name several times, and finally Ben got up to make him one of Donna's vicious coffee concoctions.

"How'd the date go, son?" Dad was venturing into incredibly brave territory, clearly soliciting information he didn't actually want from Ben. It was something to fill the air. Something to distract from the fact it looked like Dan was about to burst into tears.

"Great." Ben was eating something again. "Turns out we have a lot in common." He shrugged and Levi was the one to snort, but he didn't say it out loud. He was thinking the same thing I was. *Were there any words involved? Bet the list was short and naked.*

"Will you be bringing her for our New Year dinner?" Donna asked hopefully and I couldn't help but shake my head as Beckett tried to cover a snort.

"Not sure we're there yet." Ben cracked a grin. "Don't want her gettin' the wrong ideas about my intentions."

"Benjamin Winchester Benson."

"Winchester?" Beckett squeaked, a fart of a laugh sneaking out, and I shushed her with a kiss before I realized what I'd done.

"Holy shit." Ben's eyes went huge. "Did you just lay a smooch on my best girl? You fucking sneak—right out from under me! I didn't even have a chance!"

I was only mostly sure he was teasing me. When he employed it, his deadpan expression was terrifying.

"Glad that cat's finally all the way out of the bag," Dad muttered, standing slowly. "Believe I'll have another coffee. Anyone else?"

In true Benson fashion, we were going to be ripped before noon. This was where some of our worst ideas and our greatest mishaps generated: with alcohol. One year it sent Ben and Dan to the ER with grease burns when we tried to deep fry a turkey in the yard. Apparently neither were impressed that they needed to thaw the turkey first, and the resulting fireball when they dropped that frozen-solid chunk of bird into the grease was biblical. Dad swore the pillar of fire in the wilderness, that which led our ancient forebears to freedom and safety, was less impressive.

In the past, holiday imbibing had led to some truly spectacular displays of stupidity: tractor races. Snowmobile chicken. Testing whether the lake was truly frozen all the way across—only Ben fell in that time, but I'd been the one to fish him out and I was hypothermic for a week.

Ski golf had been the most catastrophic—worse than the deep-fried turkey, if you can believe it.

It had been said, more than once, that the Benson boys did not mature beyond the age of twelve–except Levi, apparently. It seemed all the common sense had been used up on him.

"Get it, Bec." Ben leaned over to fist bump Beckett. "Makin' him a happy man and we're all seein' it. He can't even help himself no more." He chuckled to himself.

Well, there was no more sense in hiding it. I leaned over and dragged her closer, right up against my side. She squeaked a little when I did it and it made me smile. I turned my head and pressed a kiss into her hair. She smelled like cows and hay and shampoo, and she'd just agreed to be mine.

Best Christmas ever.

Chapter Eighteen

Beckett

We stayed on through lunch and completed the evening milking a little earlier than was normal, working together in a silence that wasn't uncomfortable. There was the weight of expectation pressing down on both of us, something that seemed to steal all of our words.

He kissed me again in the cattle barn, like he couldn't bear to keep his distance any longer. He walked up behind me, spun me around, and dragged me right up against him—not like I was complaining. He snatched the pitchfork from me and leaned it against the wall, grabbing my cold hands in his and placing them under his heavy flannel shirt, directly on his warm sides. I tried to ball up my fists; it was my own fault I'd forgotten my heavy gloves at his house. "My hands are freezing, Judah."

"Take any chance I can get to have your hands on me." He smiled down at me. "Couldn't wait another minute." Then he leaned down and gave me a searing kiss, the sort that made me warm all over, and I unclenched my fingers, letting them slide up his back to keep him close. He kissed me breathless, then stepped back. "Know better than to start something I can't finish here." Another smile lit his handsome face and I was reminded of how much I loved to see him smile. "You all finished up here?" I nodded, letting him lead me back into the main barn and he sealed the door for the night.

We locked the gates, made sure the pipes were drained, and I followed him out to his truck. Mine remained parked outside the cabin, something I hadn't been back to see just yet. I would have no choice the following week, when repairs began.

We drove the short distance to his house in silence, unlacing our boots in the garage. I hung my jacket on one of the wall hooks and followed him inside, thankful for the warmth.

"If you need something to eat, grab it now." The look he gave me was something dark and promising and it made my stomach flip.

"Not interested in food." I barely managed to get the words out before he had me pinned to the wall, both hands cradling my face.

"Fast and rough or slow and gentle?" he demanded and I almost giggled, but I realized he was completely serious.

"I'm impressed." I couldn't help but smile. "You have a menu of options?"

"Whatever you need, I'll be the one to give it to you."

"I presume that's within reason." I was wasting time teasing him, because he was clearly in no mood to be teased.

"Beckett." He was clearly frustrated. "I'm guessing it's been a lot longer for you than it has been for me, so I need to know how you want this to go."

"Free rein," I whispered, swallowing hard. "I trust you."

"Not sure that you should," his voice was like sandpaper, "but I'll never hurt you."

It made me wind my arms around his ribcage and lean my face into his neck, overwhelmed by the things this man made me feel. His arms went around me, one big hand cradling my head and he twisted to press a kiss to my hair. "Feel things for you—should probably tell you that—and it scares the fuck out of me."

"Yeah." My hair made a scraping sound on his shirt when I nodded and I leaned back, looking up at him. "Kind of managed to worm your way in, too."

He placed his palm over my heart and I thought his eyes looked just a little shiny. "Good. Think you probably know I'm not..." He broke off with a laugh. "Uh, well, I'm not like Ben."

I chuckled. "You and your brothers are some of the most loyal guys I've ever met. Ben just hasn't let anyone in yet."

The way he was looking at me made my heart skip a few beats, something that I thought might have been adoration, and he pressed a kiss to my forehead. Then he took my hand and led me through the house and down the hallway to his room. He was breathing like he'd run a marathon and when he turned to reach for me again, his hand shook just a little when he scooped my hair over my ear.

He hadn't turned on the lamp, a beam of light from the hall slicing across the bedroom. My fingers shook too when I lifted my hands to his shirt, starting at the top button and slowly working my way down. I had obviously seen parts of him before, but the thought of seeing this man completely naked made my mouth go dry.

He let me slip the shirt from his shoulders before he tsked at me. "My turn, Tex. It's only fair." He lifted the thick sweatshirt's hem. "Arms up." I did what I was told and he stripped it quickly over my head, apparently baffled to find a thermal henley beneath it, and he made short work of that as well.

Thank God I'd worn a decent bra, and I watched him swallow hard as he looked down, one thumb trailing along the edge of the lace cup. He looked like he'd frozen in place and I reached behind myself to undo the clasp when he stopped my hands. "Don't rush me, woman." A sweet smile. "Let me enjoy every second of this."

If someone had told me months earlier that I'd be happily undressing the hottest grump I'd ever met, I'd have laughed until I passed out.

"I like this." He bit his lower lip as he said it, then slipped his fingers beneath the straps, letting them fall down my shoulders. "Pink lace is my new favorite." Then he reached around me to unhook it, dragging the straps slowly down my arms, his eyes hot.

Without a word he pulled me down to the floor with him, piling me into his lap so that I was straddling him. His hands went to the back of my head, pulling my face down to his and kissing me deeply, like a man dying of thirst. Then suddenly he broke away, trailing tiny kisses across my jaw, down my neck and across my chest. "Hurts to look at you," he whispered, brushing the pad of one thumb over my lips. "Prettiest thing I've ever seen—can't stop looking." Then he tipped his head down, hoisting me up on his lap to draw a wet trail with his tongue over one of my breasts, circling and teasing until I thought I'd combust. Only then did he draw me between his lips, the sweet suction sending a jolt of sensation between my thighs. The noise that slipped from my throat was something long and low and his hips bucked beneath me.

I knew what I was in for. I'd been unable to stop staring the night he'd worn the gray sweatpants, and I was desperate to get my hands on all of him. I needed to drive him at least half as wild as he was driving me, the gentle suction of his lips and tongue winding me higher.

He rolled me quickly, scrambling to his feet before leaning down to scoop me up, carrying me into the bathroom with him and setting me on my feet. He reached into the shower to flick the dial, then reached for the button on my jeans and peeled them down my legs, leaving me in thick socks and the most ridiculous pair of underwear I owned.

"Woodstock?" he asked incredulously, taking in the pattern of little yellow birds. My cheeks were burning, and I shrugged.

"Good thing I led with the pink bra?"

"Definitely the right idea." He chuckled before removing my socks, then slowly dragged down my underwear, helping me step from them. He blew out a soft breath, his eyes roaming my body with an undisguised hunger as he sank to his knees, something that made me think he liked what he saw.

"Look at you." He looked dazed, staring up at me from where he knelt, his hands coming up to rest on my hips. "I don't think I've ever been so hard in my life."

That made me blush even more and he shook his head slowly. "That's not something to be ashamed of, baby. You're breath-taking." He let his thumbs smooth over my hip bones several times before pushing to his feet and I swatted his hand away when he reached down to undo his jeans.

"My turn." I grinned at him, tipping my face up so that he'd lean down to kiss me, something he did willingly while my greedy fingers popped the button and carefully unzipped his fly before reaching into the back to squeeze with both hands. It made him chuckle and his words were soft, said right against my mouth.

"All that time you just couldn't wait to get your hands on my ass. All you had to do was ask, you know."

My words weren't working anymore and I tipped my face into his neck to kiss my way down his chest the way he'd done to me, carefully peeling down his jeans so he could step from them.

Then I reached for the band of his underwear, my hands shaking a little. He noticed, misinterpreting what it meant. "Don't worry, sweetheart, we'll go slow."

"No." I swallowed hard. "I'm not afraid. It's..."

"Adrenaline." He smiled at me, brushing my hair over my ear. "You make my hands shaky, too."

To say I couldn't breathe was an understatement. Completely naked, the man was magnificent, lean and defined, his arms, chest and thighs thick with the muscle that came from brutally hard work.

He reached behind himself to pull open the shower door and a billow of warm steam enveloped us. He waited for me to step in before following behind, arms going around to hold me gently as I stepped into the spray.

Without a word he turned me so that the water ran down my back, filling his palm with shampoo and working it carefully into my hair. There was no conditioner in his shower, something I could hardly blame him for, and when he poured body wash into his palm and began to run it over my skin, I relaxed into his touch, letting my eyes drift shut. He washed me carefully, his rough fingers gentle on my skin as he stroked, kneaded and smoothed. Then he turned me again so that I faced the water and I could feel him against my backside, hard as stone.

"Let me wash you," I whispered, and he hummed softly as he pressed a kiss to my ear.

"I'm not done yet." His fingers slipped between my legs to cup me gently. "I need you soft and relaxed, Tex." Another kiss pressed to the side of my head. "That means plenty of time playing with some of my new favorite toys." A soft chuckle before he started kissing my neck, fingers gently seeking out the most sensitive places on my body, his other hand smoothing over my breasts.

"I don't think you'll need to spend much time," I panted, my body winding up quickly. His fingers slowed and he turned me to face him once more, his lips taking mine in a hungry, desperate kiss just before he dropped to his knees in front of me.

"Hold onto something." His voice was rough and I reached out to brace myself against the wall just as he lifted my right leg over his shoulder and closed his mouth over me.

"Holy shit." That was the best I could do, the fingers of one hand slipping on wet tile and I reached down to slide my fingers into his hair. Then I had no more words, only sounds while he worshiped my body in ways I'd forgotten existed.

"Let go, sweetheart," he whispered softly, lifting one hand to find mine, linking our fingers as my vision began to tunnel. I tipped my head back and let my eyes drift shut, welcoming the winding feeling wrapping itself around my spine before it began to radiate outward, the powerful waves shaking my body as I melted into Judah's arms. They came up quickly to wrap around me, holding me upright.

He stood slowly, pulling me into his arms and I sagged weakly against his body. "Give me a second," I whispered against his chest.

"Have all the time in the world." He squeezed me gently, rocking slowly back and forth and I felt my eyes fill with tears. I wrapped my arms around his ribcage and squeezed ferociously.

"My turn," I finally whispered, leaning to grab the shampoo and he smiled down at me while I worked it into his hair. Then I filled my palms with soap and glided them over his body.

"Go easy." His teeth ground together when I slipped a soapy hand between us. "Got to last a while yet and that's not gonna help."

"That's not fair," I whined and he shuffled forward a few inches, just enough to let the water run between our bodies, rinsing himself before he reached behind me and snapped off the shower.

"Has nothing to do with fair, baby." He kissed the top of my head and yanked a towel from where it hung over the frame. "Has everything to do with getting you ready, because once we really get started..." He shivered when he said it, his eyes glazing over just a little as he wrapped the towel around me. "By then I can't guarantee I'll have much control left. I promised I wouldn't hurt you."

The thought of Judah losing control was enough to make me shiver too, a delicious shudder of anticipation, because I was going to make it my new mission in life to bring this man to his knees every chance I got.

We brushed our teeth together and he dropped a kiss to my shoulder, tugging off my towel to hang up while he wiggled his eyebrows at me.

"You're a different man when you're happy." The words slipped out before I could stop them, something I meant to sound sweet but I wondered if it sounded accusatory.

"Been unhappy for a long time." He didn't sound upset, just thoughtful. "Still got a lot of anger, but I'm not lonely anymore." He smiled at me sweetly, a crooked little tip to his lips that made him the most beautiful fallen angel I'd ever seen.

"Yeah." I hummed a little as I gave that some thought and he reached over to swat my butt.

"Hope some of those are dirty thoughts."

"Happy ones, but I could get on board with dirty."

"Good," he pointed toward the door, "because we have work to do."

"You do realize this isn't exactly what I'd consider work, right?"

He grinned at me. "Well, you're not up yet. All you've got to do is relax and, you know, get off a few more times."

I wrinkled up my nose and reached into the hallway to turn off the light before turning on the bedside lamp. I froze as I stood staring down at his bed, something he seemed to pick up on because he came up behind me and wrapped me in his arms, his words soft against my ear. "It's been so long, I don't remember the last time she was actually in this bed with me."

"Will her ghost be here with us?" I asked hesitantly, not sure how to ask him what I was thinking.

"No, sweetheart." He turned me gently, catching my chin in his hand to make sure I was looking into his eyes. "This isn't hers anymore. *I'm not.* I don't have the room in here—" he tapped the side of his head, "or here—" he tapped his heart, "for more than one woman."

I didn't trust my words at that moment, my eyes feeling suddenly and dangerously full. Somehow this man knew exactly what I needed to hear.

He lifted the blanket and then crawled in after me, lying on his side and propping his head up on one arm, the other hand smoothing over my face and hair while he stared down at me.

"You ever ... think about this?" I asked, suddenly nervous, and the slow grin that stretched across his face convinced me that I was an idiot. Of course he'd thought about this before, probably a lot.

He didn't answer, just lowered his face to mine and kissed me, his hand trailing softly across my skin until I made a frustrated sound and tried to pull him to me. "Not yet." His eyes were dilated when he lifted his head to smile down at me. His body was tight with restraint, the heat rolling off of him like a blast furnace, and he watched my face intently as his hand slipped between my thighs.

"Please, Judah," I finally begged, closer and closer to insanity with every gentle stroke of his fingers. He shook his head at me, testing me gently.

"You're not ready yet."

I growled in frustration and twisted quickly, throwing a leg over his hips and settling the center of my body over his. He had been hard for so long, it had to be painful, and I lowered myself carefully. He hadn't allowed me to touch him, but I was fairly certain he wouldn't be able to resist this and I worked my hips carefully, my body just barely touching his. His eyelids drifted shut at the contact, his mouth falling open with an expression of pleasure. It made me feel powerful, to make him lose himself, his hips beginning to follow the motions of my own.

"You first," he ground out from between his teeth and I let the pleasure build, my muscles beginning to shake just before a powerful release. I moaned nonsensical words through it, hardly able to hold myself upright, and he caught me when my arms gave out, chuckling as he rolled me onto my back and settled between my thighs.

"I should warn you, Tex..." He looked terribly conflicted. "I don't have any condoms in the house—haven't needed them in years."

I shook my head at him. "Judah, I've been with one man my entire life. I'm not exactly..." I let the sentence trail off, because what on earth was I telling him, that I was ready to lock him down? I waited a beat, sure he'd bolt from the bed and run for the hills.

"It's something I take pretty seriously," he said quietly. "Don't have much of a body count myself." A lopsided grin, something that made my heart hurt with what I felt for him, something intense. Overwhelming. Something that threatened to pull me under and drown me in emotion. "Don't want one. Just this—just you. Want it all with you."

I hugged him with my whole body, arms around his shoulders, bringing my legs up to wrap around his hips. It made him chuckle softly and he dropped a series of kisses into my hair and across my cheeks, something that I realized later meant he could hide his face from me. Something that let him dash his forearm quickly across his eyes before he nuzzled his face into my neck. It was something tender and sweet, a shared moment that made my heart hurt, it was so full.

"Not interested in sharing you, Tex, just so we're clear on that." It was a vulnerable admission, his expression open and unguarded, and I reached up to hold his face with both of my hands.

"You'll never have to." I said it with a ferocious conviction.

The relief that flooded his expression was almost heartbreaking to see, and I wondered if he'd truly had to share Cait. Perhaps there was more to the story of her leaving than he'd ever let on.

He dropped down to brace himself on his forearms, one arm wrapped protectively over my head, his hand in my hair as he pressed his lips to mine. It was soft and slow, an outpouring of something tender that made me ache. This man could transport me with the touch of his lips, wiping away everything but him. It was a revelation, to lose myself so completely in another person, something that should have terrified me.

"You'll tell me if it's too much?" He looked worried and I wondered if he'd been told that before, that he was *too much*. Too intense. Too needy.

"Not enough." I wiggled a little beneath him, reveling in the feeling of the partial weight of his body. He kept himself braced on his arms, careful not to crush me, and when I reached between us to guide him I watched his eyes drift shut, the sweetest expression of bliss on his beautiful face.

"Easy," he hissed when I lifted my hips to take him, welcoming his body into my own.

"You're not hurting me," I whispered, wiggling just a little, and his eyes flew open.

"Need this to last more than fifteen seconds, sweetheart."

I slowed, letting him catch his breath, a shudder wracking his big body as he leaned down to kiss me again. He kept himself so tightly in check, I wondered what it would take to get him to let go, and I waited for him.

It was excruciatingly long moments later that he began to move again, slowly, his eyes on my face watching for any signs of distress. It was fair; nothing about Judah was small and I was years out of practice.

"Oh." A delicious shiver ran through me and he looked panicked.

"What?"

"Whatever that was, do it again." I grinned up at him, watching his face relax with relief and he carefully swiveled his hips, something that made me gasp. I watched the realization dawn on him, something that seemed to fray his control just a little, and I knew the best thing I could give this man was my enjoyment. I let my eyes drift shut, my hands going to his hips to knead and squeeze, little whimpers of pleasure leaving my lips. It made him bolder, his movements becoming a little wilder, his breaths faster.

"Tell me," he demanded, and I smiled at the frantic note in his voice. He was losing it.

"Soon," I panted, my back arching, and I wound one leg around his hips, a movement that made his eyes roll back in his head.

"How soon?" he demanded, his teeth grinding.

"Judah." I slowed and pulled his face to mine to kiss him. "Stop keeping score. Stop worrying. I'll always catch up."

"Old habit." He hissed the words, a brief expression of pain flashing across his face.

Oh, those demons were hanging on by their wicked claws, ready to steal and ruin.

I lifted my hips to him again with a sigh and he made a broken sound, something desperate and hungry, and when I clenched my muscles around him he groaned. I let my hands drift up and down his sides, tugging and urging him, seconds away from the blinding pleasure he finally let himself chase. His movements became frantic, more uncoordinated, and a cry burst from my lips just as I felt the first telltale jerk of his body. A sound rumbled out of his chest, a groan or a sob, something that was a sound of surrender and he collapsed on top of me, rolling quickly to his side and taking me with him.

Then he pressed his face into my neck and wept.

Chapter Nineteen

Judah

It scared the fuck out of me, to fall apart on Beckett after what had been one of the most intense experiences of my life. Being with her was consuming, something that made me feel incredibly alive and powerful.

She didn't freak out on me, just held me in her arms while she dropped kisses into my hair, the fingers of one hand smoothing up and down my back.

"I'm sorry." I finally managed to choke out the words, humiliated. "I don't know what that was—weird, though."

"I do." She hummed softly. "You have a lot of guilt over things you couldn't control." Her fingers drifted through my hair. "Now something in you is trying to let it go."

Taking a deep breath, I shifted her against me and sighed into her hair. She was probably right. Women seemed to know these things.

"My sister will love you." She chuckled when I said it, but I meant it. Ashley was going to adore this one, though Cait had set that bar pretty damn low if I was being honest.

"I think you grieved the only way you knew how, by ignoring as much as you could." Her voice was soft when she said it and I closed my eyes for a moment. Looked like we were going to talk about this anyway. "There's no time limit on it. Your brain doesn't just one day decide that's it, you're done. You can experience happiness and still be sorting your way through loss. They're not mutually exclusive. Sometimes I'm still sad for what I lost—for what I thought I'd have for the rest of my life."

The weird part was that I realized it wasn't that I missed Cait in the way I had for so long. I felt regret that she'd wasted so much time with me when she wasn't happy, and we'd dragged two little boys through the struggle with us.

We lay there for a long time, touching gently and leaning to kiss arms, necks and shoulders, relaxed in our warm little cocoon, wrapped up in one another.

I spent the night with my skin pressed to hers, holding her close, taking comfort in the circle of her arms, drinking in the soft sounds she made when something felt good, drifting from one catnap to the next, each of us waking the other repeatedly.

The farm hands were on duty the following morning and there was no need to rush, so we took our time, waking with gentle touches and whispers. It was something completely foreign and unfamiliar, to wake with someone next to me. Someone who smiled and snuggled into me, and it made me sad to realize this was what it should have always been.

There was a slam and my eyes flew open.

All of my family members had a key to my house. Levi had taken it upon himself to have keys cut and distributed when he felt I needed people checking on me daily, and my brothers had gotten into the habit of letting themselves in without knocking.

"Jude, I need coffee," Ben croaked. "Had to run away from my own damn house."

Beckett winced and I shook my head at her, holding a finger up to my lips. I tucked her in quickly and snatched a pair of sweatpants from the dresser drawer, slipping into them at the speed of light. Then I called quietly down the hallway, "Shut up, you barbarian, Bec's probably still sleeping," just before hurrying out and swinging the bedroom door nearly shut behind me.

Ben was standing in the kitchen in clear view of the hallway and a Cheshire grin spread across his face when he saw me close the door as I left the room, something I never did. Dead giveaway. "Yeah, you would know, since she's in your bed."

If looks could kill, I'd have given him third-degree burns at the very least.

"You're lucky I didn't come walking out here naked," I shot back and his eyes went immediately to my crotch.

"Still free-ballin' it, bro—bad enough."

I scoffed. "Like I haven't gotten an eye full more times than I can count."

"Just jealous I'm hung like a horse."

"Not really making your case for free coffee, Ben. Just sayin'. Now, what possessed you to drive all the way over here for it?"

There was a weird mark on Ben's neck, something that looked a little like a bruise and I squinted at him. "Is that a fucking hickey? What are you, fourteen?"

"The … ah … well, you remember the woman I was seeing?"

That was a euphemism for *dicking* if I'd ever heard one.

"Turns out she's a stage-five clinger." He shivered. "Had to sneak out of my own house to get away from her this morning."

I just shook my head at him, filling the carafe with water and transferring it to the reservoir. He was never going to learn. The man was the textbook definition of shitting where he ate.

"Think I need to just take some time and figure shit out by myself. Can't live in this … fog … all the time."

I hummed, filling the filter basket with coffee grounds and sliding it into the machine to begin brewing. "Alcohol and hoe-ing it up will do that to you."

He didn't say anything else, just dropped down onto one of the island stools, which groaned in protest. There was a deep red welt running down the other side of his neck and into his shirt and I leaned closer, pulling his shirt away from his chest to see where it led. His chest was a mess of welts and my mouth dropped open. "Holy shit, you sleep with a literal cougar last night?"

"Maybe." He grimaced, but he didn't offer any more information.

"If that's what's out there, I'm glad I'm not on the market." I shook my head as I said it and realized entirely too late that there was a wicked gleam in his eye.

"You don't say." He steepled his fingers on the counter. "Went through creating those profiles for nothin', then?" He was *so* onto me. "Guess somebody swiped right on our boy, huh?" Another wiggle of his eyebrows that made it seem dirty.

"Good morning, Benjamin." Bec drifted down the hallway in a perfectly acceptable pair of flannel pajamas, her hair pulled into a ponytail. He turned his head at the sound of her voice and held his arms open, like he expected her to walk into a hug. She did, slapping his back when her arms wrapped around him and I laughed when he winced, because now I knew his back was covered in claw marks as well.

"Mornin', baby." He patted the seat next to him. "Surprised you can walk at all this morning. Cervix of steel, apparently."

Beckett's cheeks went a violent shade of purple and Ben giggled like a little girl.

"Coffee?" I poured quickly and scooted a mug across the counter to Beckett, fishing through the fridge for cream.

Ben looked ridiculously pleased with himself. "Good on you. Glad you two got in some Christmas cheer—haven't seen this grumpy dick smile so much in years." He gestured toward me and it stopped me in my tracks for a second, because maybe he was right. "Cait sure didn't make you smile like this." His expression was completely serious.

I slid a mug over to him and he took a noisy slurp of the boiling liquid, hissing. "Told Dan I'll take him out tonight; take his mind off this Lindsey bullshit."

Beckett cut him a sharp look and his shoulders folded forward a little. He shook his head slowly. "Kept that shit all to himself. She left him for some guy from work. Packed up the boys, transferred them to a school in Ohio or something—been gone for months and he ain't said a *word*." Ben actually looked stricken. "Spent most of Christmas all by himself and we didn't even know it."

Beckett made a soft sound of disbelief and I ran a hand over my face. "You two need a babysitter; can't trust either of you will get home after a night of tyin' one on."

"Nah, Levi's picking us up after last call." He tapped the side of his head and Beckett rose from her seat, pulling a few things from the fridge and a cast iron pan from beneath the stove. Ben watched her quietly, a thoughtful smile on his face as he gave me one of those *I see you* nods.

"You should come." I realized with dismay that he was inviting Beckett. "Introduce you to Roy; old man would *love* you."

Beckett didn't even turn around. "If you're not careful, Benjamin, you're going to turn into Roy and it'll be sooner than you think."

"Oof." Ben and I made the noise at the same time, because that had been a solid burn. She had a point, though. Roy's wife had passed on so long ago, I couldn't remember her face. Dan always joked she'd died in order to get the last laugh, because Roy was such a grumpy old fart.

Beckett cooked a quick breakfast and the three of us ate at the island, refilling our coffee a few times, and Ben rose to help clear the dishes and wash up.

"Any word on the cows?" Ben asked conversationally and Beckett's shoulders stiffened.

"Nothing solid yet, but I've found a livestock hauling service that claims they took an order of cattle from Minnesota to Texas a few months back." She hadn't breathed a word about that and I shot a funny look at her back. "They gave me a delivery address I'm familiar with, in hill country. Dispatch said it was an unusual order but wouldn't give me anything more than that."

"You're not chasing a herd of cattle all the way to Texas by yourself." My voice came out sharper than intended. "We'll eat the loss, Bec, because you're not putting yourself in harm's way." Because somehow I knew that was what she would do. "Someone knew you would uncover their tracks eventually, because you're good at what you do—you're relentless."

She still wouldn't look at me and I wondered if it meant I only *thought* I knew all the details of her past. Maybe there was something else she hadn't disclosed.

We drove to the farm together in silence. It wasn't a long trip, but she was lost in thought and when she didn't reach for me, choosing to fold into herself, I had to work hard to keep my shit together. She was all about helping me overcome my demons, but what about hers? It was becoming clear to me that I was operating with only a piece of the information.

I pulled the truck up near the office, but I didn't get out. She finally looked at me, probably realizing the engine was still running, and I offered something half-assed. "Gonna go see Dan and find out what's going on." She nodded, the door squeaking as she got out and walked toward the small building, her shoulders slumped.

Dan had a commercial project going some thirty miles out, closer to the city, something I knew only because it was one of the largest contracts he'd ever landed. He'd been the first one to step back from the farm, concerned it wouldn't bring in enough revenue to comfortably support all of us, and he was right.

I wasn't the numbers guy, I was the worker. I showed up every day and put my head down, convinced that if I just worked hard enough I could fix everything. Save us money. Find another way to turn a profit because I didn't have to hire out another job if I could do it myself.

The truth was that our hired hands had been meant to fill a temporary gap. Levi had brought them on when he started to consider stepping back, and they'd been with us for the better part of a year while I wallowed. So that was on me. There was nothing to keep me from stepping in to do the milking each day, something that took them a few hours each morning and evening. And in truth it was still cheaper than supporting all of us, but with Bec's help things were starting to tighten up.

I kicked things around in my brain for a while during the drive, finally pulling up to a construction trailer on a huge job site, an area that had been fenced in with razor wire and dotted with security lighting.

"Looking for your boss," I told the men standing around a work truck, laughing and smoking, and one pointed in the direction of the elevated trailer.

Dan was on the phone when I let myself into the small space, a stack of paperwork in front of him, his fingers over one eye like he was fighting off a headache. I realized with a start that his ring finger was bare and I dropped down into one of the chairs in front of his messy desk, waiting for him to conclude his call with a few clipped, frustrated words.

"When were you gonna say something?" I didn't shout, but I may as well have tossed a grenade into the room with the way his face blanched. "Know we've all been assholes, wrapped up in our own shit, but you didn't think it was important to tell your brothers that your life had gone to hell? You know we'd have been there."

"Not today, Judah." His voice was as weary as his eyes, the same deep shadows visible that I'd noticed the day before. He looked like he hadn't slept in months. "I have a load of I-beams stuck on a ship in the middle of the ocean; they've had to take a different route thanks to increased pirate activity. My building inspector is scheduled for a walk-through on a space I can't complete, and I've got to explain to someone that his project is delayed somewhere between six weeks and six months, depending on when those I-beams finally come in."

I sat quietly, arms crossed over my chest. I could smoke him out and I knew it, thanks to our mother's gift of the hairy eyeball. It had been her genetic legacy, something she'd passed down to me.

"She left late this summer, before school started, so she could get the boys settled." He took a long chug from the insulated tumbler sitting on his desk. "Finally got around to filing for divorce around Thanksgiving, because she decided she was going to need child support for the boys."

If anyone had an inkling of what he was going through, it was me, and to some degree he knew that.

I tried to think back, wondering when it was I'd first noticed the signs. Lindsey had been removing herself from family functions in small degrees for almost as long as I could remember. She hadn't ever been one of us though, so it hadn't been a surprise. She'd been something Dan picked up while he was in college—he was the only one of us to get a degree–and my guess was that she'd not been a particularly willing transplant.

"Surprised she didn't head back to New York," I said, recalling that her extended family lived upstate.

"Nah, her fuckboy's got some contract in New Jersey, so that's where they are now." He swallowed hard.

It occurred to me at that moment that it was a good thing Ben wasn't married, because it looked like the Benson track record had just taken another hit. Between Levi, Dan, and myself, we were zero for three.

"Any custody arrangements in place?" I asked slowly, a dull ache starting to spread across my chest. My brother was living a nightmare.

"Boys will be here for the summer, but for now that's all we can agree on. Lindsey thinks it's important we don't disrupt their school year." He couldn't look at me when he said it and I knew it was because he was right on the verge of losing his shit in front of me.

"Least you won't have to make payments for long?" I offered, holding up both palms. I was trying to be helpful and failing. Dan's kids were only a year apart, sixteen and seventeen years old.

"Not going to abandon them because she made a shit decision." He shook his head at me. "Have to get them through college yet."

"Sorry." I shook my head as I said it, the word filled with the weight of meaning. I knew he understood and he nodded at me, still not meeting my eyes. "Careful tonight," I warned. "You and I both know Ben's a menace." It went without saying that Ben would try to talk someone into a pity fuck for Dan, though I was pretty sure there'd be some willing volunteers.

"Only going out to get him off my back." He picked up a pencil and snapped it with one hand before tossing it in the trash bin beside his desk. He sighed and ran his hand back over his face. "Be out later in the week to work on cabin repairs with a small crew."

Yeah, about that... "No rush, I suppose. Got Beckett staying at my place." It made his eyebrows crawl up his forehead, and finally his eyes fixed on mine.

"Got her *staying* at your place, or fucking her brains out?"

Had he not been paying any attention yesterday?

"Uh..." There was no right answer for this. "You could say we've come to an understanding."

"Does this understanding involve you sleeping with the help?"

I squirmed uncomfortably in my seat. Beckett was so much more than that, but I didn't expect him to understand. It lit a little flare of anger in my gut. "You know it's more."

"Take your word for it." He nodded. "Suggest you don't mess it up."

Yeah, I was trying not to, but apparently I didn't know what the hell I was doing.

"Bec seems to think she has a lead on the cows."

"Too much drama." He groaned and leaned back in his chair, the casters creaking ominously. "Missing cows, fire, some freak stalking her—you notice all our troubles started when she got here?"

Not all of them, he knew that, and I leveled him with a glare. He just sighed and shook his head at me. "Thanks for coming to check on me; I'll make it if you did." He stood as he said it and rounded the desk, holding his arms open. Dan had always been a hugger. I stood and leaned in, squeezing and clapping him hard on the back. It wasn't a proper hug unless I suffocated him a little, then left him with a few welts.

Beckett's head was bent over a ledger when I let myself into her office and she looked up with a smile, pushing to her feet and crossing the room to drop a pod in the coffee maker.

It was like the woman could read my mind.

"Might have a way to cut some expenses," I said slowly, dropping into a chair. "Involves more work on our part."

"I'm listening." She reached into the small refrigerator to remove a carton of half-and-half before carrying both mugs toward her desk and setting one in front of me. She dropped into the chair next to me, plainly aware that I'd feel scrutinized if she sat across from me.

"Find the guys different positions—locally. You and me take over their duties." I shrugged. It really was that simple in my mind.

"I've worked out a few different scenarios." She reached across the desk for her ledger. "That was one of them, but there are a few other implementations that I think could really make a huge difference." She pulled the book toward us and pointed to a column, launching into what I knew was going to be the equivalent of a university lecture.

"Bec give you the run-down?" Dad asked when he found me an hour later, welding a new paddle into the track in the barn gutter.

I could no longer feel my toes.

"Yeah, some good ideas. Lot of hoops to jump through and a lot of money to lose if we're not careful—just not sure where we're going to find enough yet."

I knew better than to think she wasn't careful. She had a head for numbers where I didn't, and a more entrepreneurial spirit than myself. She was a hard worker, but she had a different and more innovative perspective than I did, something I could admit without grumbling.

"Liked the artisanal idea—something different," he said conversationally, and I felt like he was fishing for more.

"Yeah, definitely some room for it. Probably means expanding the herd quite a bit. Cancelling our contract with the co-op and putting in some serious hustle, which should be interesting. Felt like we were busy enough already."

He nodded. "She seems to have some experience and success with innovation, but I think she's really pushing on this one. She's invested."

I wasn't going to ask him why he thought that, because I knew my father. He had never been Mr. Innovation; he was dead-set against it. No, he was looking for an in, to crack that door open just an inch so he could crawl right into my business. Instead, I went straight in for the kill. "Yes, it's serious," I barked without even looking over my shoulder. "Or at least, I'd like it to be."

"Good." I just knew he'd crossed his arms over his chest. "Donna will be pleased."

Donna, my ass. Dad would never admit to it, but he was becoming incredibly meddlesome in his later years, now that he had nothing better to do. I thought briefly about suggesting he start a matchmaking service to stave off boredom.

Bec and I had a late lunch with Dad and Donna, and after a few more lively discussions in her office and a sweep of all the barns, we left the hands to manage the evening milking and headed home. Donna had invited Beckett to Mass with her the next morning, so I planned to spend as much time defiling her as possible. She could atone for it in the morning, if she really felt confession and repentance was necessary.

I let Beckett boss me around in the kitchen while we fixed dinner and we ate together at the island in our filthy clothes, laughing and talking about the farm, sitting closer than we had any real right to.

I knew I was doing this wrong. I'd never brought her flowers or asked her out to dinner—this was all backward—but every moment spent with her was like being able to take a deep breath after my oxygen tank had run dry. The world had color again, something I'd never expected to happen.

We washed the dishes and while I made tea she put in a load of laundry. It was so weirdly, comfortingly domestic. Such a ridiculously simple routine, but something I hadn't had in as long as I could remember. Cait hadn't cooked, and she'd demanded I wash my dirty farm laundry separately from everyone else's clothing.

The memories contrasted to my new reality were almost jarring.

I started a small fire in the fireplace and because it wasn't a decent hour for bed, even if that was the only place I wanted to be, I asked her if she wanted to watch a movie. She grinned at me and spun, racing down the hallway. It took me a moment to realize she was racing for the shower and I took off after her, nearly tripping over the shirt she'd already managed to peel off and toss on the floor.

The water was already on and she was hopping to get out of her jeans, laughing as I rounded the corner, my shirt already off as well.

It was official, showering was one of my new favorite things, for entirely new reasons.

There was a naked woman in my shower, all slippery, smooth skin and long wet hair. It was like a dream come true, something I hadn't even dared to hope for as long as I could remember.

"I've never looked forward to the evenings at home this much," I admitted as I stepped in with her and she grinned up at me. We knew we were living in a little bubble, that this perfection wouldn't last forever, but while it did I wanted to shut out the rest of the world and devour her.

She pulled me down to her and into a kiss that stirred everything to life. It tugged at something in my chest, reached right in to squeeze tight until I wondered how I'd ever been able to breathe without this woman in my arms.

Showering took longer than it should have, because I couldn't stop kissing her, and finally she turned off the water and snatched a towel from where it hung over the frame. She handed it to me before grabbing the other for herself, quickly squeezing water from her hair before running the towel over her body, winding it around herself and tucking it between her breasts.

We brushed our teeth side by side, her hand squeezing my butt, until I growled and threatened to back her up against the wall to give her what she was clearly asking for. It made her spit and rinse quickly, dropping her toothbrush and then her towel, and my toothbrush clattered to the countertop. I rinsed at the speed of light and backed her up against the wall, crowding her close and stretching her hands upward, over her head, leaning down to take her mouth. I was so much bigger than her, but she gave as good as she got, pushing up into me and meeting my tongue stroke for stroke.

It was an awakening, and one that didn't terrify me, to realize that I had already fallen for this woman—hard. She showed up for me, with words and actions, on a daily basis. She worked as hard or harder than I did, proving to me that she was equally invested. I loved that, that she wasn't fussy. She wasn't afraid to get dirty or to break a nail. She was beautiful and determined, hardworking and fun. She teased me right back, gave it to me good, and now I knew that she was sweet and giving and passionate in a more intimate setting, too.

"Tex." I said it against her cheek, aware that I'd taken her hard the night before. "Is it too much?" Her responding laugh was low and sweet against the skin of my neck.

"Oh, Judah. Everything about us is too much. We're too old, too wrecked, too jaded. It's the perfect story because of the way we get to write it, isn't it?" She lifted a hand to my face, her expression tender and sweet as she invited me down to her mouth. I took it gratefully, thankful for every moment she allowed me. Her presence calmed me, turned off the angry whirling of my brain, and I was at peace when she was near.

"You make me happy," I admitted quietly, pulling her tightly against myself and whispering the words into her hair. "Took me a while to accept that."

"You drove me nuts." She laughed when she said it. "Always so angry and hostile. Always second-guessing me and my decisions. Why'd you have to be so damn hot?"

"Huh?" I pulled back, confused, to look down into her eyes. "You were attracted to me?"

"From the moment you walked out of that shed scowling at me, I thought you were the most beautiful man I'd ever seen."

I scoffed. "Even after meeting Levi? All the ladies go for him." It was something that had always low-key bothered me as a kid.

There was a light of understanding in her eyes as she stood there looking up at me, her hands cupping either side of my face. "You were all I could see." Her eyes were a little shiny and something cracked open in my chest, warmth and contentment flooding me. I had never felt chosen before, not intentionally or unconditionally.

Without another word I scooped her up and carried her into the bedroom. I knew I had to find a way to keep this woman; to bind her to me.

I kissed her until we were both panting and needy, clawing at one another as we tried to get closer, as if we could crawl into one another. Then she took me by the shoulders to guide me over herself, opening herself to me and taking me into her body.

It was overwhelming, the feeling of acceptance, being desired, someone who'd opened her heart to me and let me see inside. I moved slowly with her, hardly eager to rush while I savored every moment of her nearness. It was a moment of intense intimacy I wasn't sure I'd ever experienced with another human, and when I felt her body tighten around mine, soft sounds of pleasure drifting from her mouth, I let go. I chased that euphoria, the world turning silver behind my closed eyelids as we flew together, and I rolled to pull her on top of me, my arms banding her tightly against myself.

Don't say it, don't say it, don't say it.

"Want you with me always," was what came out anyway and I winced. It was worse than telling her I loved her, and now she would probably run for the hills.

"Would like to stay with you always," was her soft response against my chest, and she rolled her head just a little to press a kiss to my skin. She didn't say anything else, just cuddled against me and eventually her soft, deep breaths told me she'd fallen asleep.

Maybe it was weird, but eventually I rolled to the side so I could watch her sleep in the low light of the lamp. She felt safe with me, at peace, something I knew to be a gift. If I had anything to do with it, she would continue to sleep next to me for the rest of our lives. It was a thrilling, terrifying thought, and while she slept I mulled over how I was going to convince her to do just that.

Chapter Twenty

Beckett

A satisfied man is a happy man, something I'd known for a long time and with regular meals, gentle teasing, and nights spent in Judah's bed, I watched him become the man I'd known he could be. I wasn't the only one who saw it, either. Benjamin bumped my shoulder a few weeks later and commented on how loved up Judah was looking lately, that the fool couldn't stop grinning from ear to ear.

Things had been quiet and peaceful for the weeks I'd spent living in his home, my nights spent in his arms, something that had quieted my howling soul.

"Headed out to the cabin." My head snapped up at the sound of Erik's voice. It was an unseasonably warm day for the middle of February, and work on the cabin had been prevented by weeks of brutal weather. "Got no plans to install you back in there, from what Judah tells me." He grinned. "Thinkin' maybe we'll rent it out once it's fixed. Maybe some vacationing folks will want the full agricultural experience."

I nodded slowly. That wasn't a terrible idea, and it could generate some steady income, so I scribbled down a quick note.

"You like to come with?" he asked easily and though it made dread curl through my gut, I pushed to my feet and put the small desktop to sleep.

"Morning, Beckett," Dan called as I stepped out of the truck and stood surveying the damage to the cabin. It was far worse than I'd anticipated, and Dan nodded once as he watched me absorb the information no one had shared. "Some structural damage, as you can see. Real glad you weren't here when it went up."

There were still so many unanswered questions and though the past few weeks had been quiet and peaceful, part of me was waiting for the other shoe to drop.

"Bec!" Ben came tearing out of the cabin with a grin on his face. Sometimes he reminded me of a Labrador. "How come you didn't say hi last night?"

Dan's eyes narrowed a little as he looked at his brother and I felt my face screw up in confusion. "What do you mean?"

"At the Machine Shed. Me an' my date saw you, but you didn't come over—hightailed it right on out of there like you were busted doin' something bad." He grinned at me while I tried to process the information that was making my brain overheat.

“I didn’t go out last night.” My voice sounded funny to me and I looked up to see Erik watching me with some concern. “I was...” I couldn’t very well tell him that I’d spent the evening getting fucked through a wall and my face heated when I remembered the passionate, dirty things Judah whispered to me when he pressed me up against the bathroom wall and took me from behind. “I was home with Judah all night.”

Ben gave me a look that said he didn’t believe me. “Yeah, right. You two probably sneaked out for drinks—it’s about time Judah started taking you out and showing you off. But I can see why you wouldn’t want to get caught. Keepin’ your dirty little secret.” He grinned.

There was a loud ringing in my ears as something started to click into place in my subconscious mind. “Ben, did she... Did I walk with a slight limp?”

“Yeah, maybe.” He thought about it for a moment. “On your way out I thought you looked awful sore.” His eyebrows danced on his forehead. “Just figured our boy was giving it to you something good.” He howled when he said it and I watched Erik’s face blanch.

“Shit.” I breathed the word so quietly, I knew Erik read my lips when he took a step closer.

“What is it, Beckett?” He put one hand under my elbow to steady me. “You’ve gone completely white, sweetheart.”

“It wasn’t in the papers.” I had to work hard to get the words out, reliving just a portion of the nightmare as my brain compressed time to take me back. “I’ve only told Judah about her in passing." The man himself appeared from the front door of the cabin as I spoke his name, like I'd summoned him, and he marched immediately toward me, concern written all over his face.

"What is it?" His voice was commanding and when he reached me his arms went around me.

"She's found me," I whispered, something that made his forehead furrow.

"What in the hell is she talking about?" Ben asked, a concerned expression creeping across his face as well.

"Something you need to tell us that'll shed light on some of the weird things happening around here?" Erik asked gently, moving to stand right next to Judah.

"I have a sister." I swallowed hard. "She hasn't spoken to me in twelve years. She was institutionalized for a while after ... things ... happened. She didn't take the news well. She took a bottle of pills and jumped off a parking garage in Dallas."

Ben's mouth dropped open. "Survived it, I'm guessing?"

"Some reconstructive surgery and a metal rod in her left leg, but yes, she survived it. She was put under observation and I had her committed. She wasn't safe—to herself." I swallowed hard. It was only one of the reasons she'd never forgiven me. She'd completely cut me off. "She obviously wasn't ... uh, well after what happened." Though in truth, I wasn't sure the last time she'd been truly stable.

Judah pulled in a sharp breath. "And you think she's tracked you down?"

She had always threatened that one day she would find me and make my life the hell I'd made hers, something I'd written off as the ramblings of someone who was ill.

"I think she's tracked me down and she's brought Jason with her to finish the job."

Judah's face went completely white. "Why would she do that?"

This was another part of the story I hated telling. It was the part that had been miraculously excluded from press coverage, and I sank into a slow squat, my knees threatening to give out.

"Jason was seeing my sister not long before things went to shit."

"I don't understand." Ben was shaking his head, and Judah squatted down beside me.

"You said you had a restraining order filed against him; that he was living on your property, observing the family's patterns." Judah sounded completely confused.

I didn't have any answers for them, but I knew where to start looking, and it was in the hill country of Texas.

"I don't know how yet, but this is connected to the cows. The hauling company wouldn't share any of the information with me from the shipping manifest, beyond confirming the delivery address." I swallowed hard. "The next time I called back it was a different person working dispatch. He wasn't quite so friendly or helpful."

The address was a property Cade and I had considered purchasing to start our own outfit just after we'd married. Instead, my parents had talked us into buying them out over time, allowing them to retire, and my sister had been livid.

"Beth thought I'd stolen her inheritance." I shrugged. There had been no reasoning with her, not then and not years later, when she'd been hopped up on painkillers and in traction.

When the property sold, money had been put into a trust for her, something that hadn't assuaged her anger, because I'd been appointed her guardian.

Judah's jaw set so hard, I thought he'd start cracking molars. "You're telling me this ghost we've been chasing might be your own family?"

I had no idea. For the better part of nearly twenty years, I hadn't known her. She'd married and divorced young, a wild child who wanted to see the world rather than stay home and help with the family business. But that business was what she expected to fall back on when she ran short on money, which she did frequently, always calling home asking my parents to wire her funds.

"You have a sister." Ben was still shaking his head in disbelief.

"A twin," I said softly, and I watched Judah's expression go stony.

"Doesn't seem like you two got all that much in common, except maybe the same color eyes and hair. But if she's here and she found a way to bring that piece of shit with her..." Judah looked like he was going to eat someone alive. "You're not safe here, Tex. Not if the two of them are working together." His eyes went soft when he lifted a hand to cup my face.

"Gotta flush 'em out." That was Ben, looking determined and just as angry as Judah. "Need to bait a trap and catch him—no doubt law enforcement will be real interested in knowing an escaped felon's here in Colson Creek."

I wasn't sure I wanted to know what he had in mind. From the stories Donna had told me, Ben was typically the one with the harebrained ideas.

"Not using Beckett as bait." Judah was looking at me when he said it, biting off the words to throw over his shoulder.

"Not suggesting we do that." Ben had a hand on his chin like he was entertaining something. "But we gotta do something, because this person is unhinged. Kinda feel bad for blaming those Avila assholes—knew they weren't all that smart."

"I wouldn't totally rule them out," Dan called from where he stood surveying the work several of his guys were doing while he clearly had an ear trained on our conversation.

"Can tell you what we're gonna do right now," Erik said firmly. "Judah, you two need to go have a talk with Sal. Get everything documented you think will help and read him in on your suspicions. Town will be crawling with feds in no time, and that'll bring this to a head real fast."

Judah nodded. "Force the issue. It might be the only way at this point, because we're going to need the manpower."

He wouldn't let me out of his sight for the rest of the day. We worked on the farm together. There was no shortage of work to keep us busy, but I knew he was doing it to keep me from spiraling while he could keep close watch over me. And when we drove home later in the evening, there was a weighted silence in the truck. He parked in the garage and sealed the house up tight, doing two rounds to make sure the windows were locked, the doors were bolted and the alarm was set. I wasn't sure when he'd had the alarm installed, but I knew it had been since I arrived in Colson Creek.

Donna had seen to it we had an early dinner before leaving for the night and once we arrived home, Judah led me to the bathroom, where he started the shower and pulled me in with him. He just held me close for long moments, and I knew he was battling his own fears now that it seemed we had shared some direction.

He wrapped his body around mine and let me fall asleep shielded by his arms, and when I woke early the next morning to smell coffee brewing, I was still wound up in him.

Instead of driving to the farm that morning, he drove me into town, where we parked outside the tiny police station and he led me inside. Salvatore sat listening with one eyebrow permanently arched as I walked him through the complicated family dynamics and shared information that hadn't been made public knowledge.

"You're telling me you think this Jason fellow who escaped *Ellis—*" his eyes got big when he said it, "is holed up somewhere in our little town. He and your sister have rekindled their romance and they're here to tie up a loose end?" He looked incredulous.

I shrugged, because it did sound fantastical, but it was all we had to go on.

"Why the cows?" he asked, as stymied as I was. "What did she stand to gain by stealing cattle?"

That was where I was still hung up as well and I shook my head. "That's the part that makes no sense to me whatsoever."

"Maybe it wasn't her," Judah offered. "Maybe it was him—and maybe it was someone else entirely. We still don't know without a doubt that the cattle ended up in Texas."

"One way to find out," Sal said, "but I don't want you two doing the detective work." He paused, clearly entertaining a thought before he pointed at me. "You piss off anyone in town?"

Truthfully, I'd spent very little time in town or getting to know any of the locals. Aside from my trip to the Machine Shed with Ben, my only other interactions had been when I went grocery shopping. I wasn't the sort to make daily trips to the coffee shop, the bakery or the florist. I had never been to the little diner or to the one sit-down restaurant in the town, one Donna said she didn't recommend anyway.

"I went to the hardware store last week?" My voice lifted at the end like it was a question. "Maybe I pissed off Roy." That made Sal grin and lean back in his chair.

"Old man hates just about everyone, but I very much doubt he took offense to a beautiful woman. That one's an old hound dog."

Judah's phone dinged with an incoming alert and he fished it from his pocket, his features flattening out as he read. It was a hard expression and all the color left his face as Sal gave him a searching look he ignored.

"If you'll excuse me for just a moment." Judah cleared his throat as he pushed to his feet. "I need to make a phone call—Bec, I'll be right back."

Sal shook his head at me as Judah let himself out the front door, stepping out onto the sidewalk that ran in front of the building. "I don't like it, Miss Beckett. There's too much conjecture in this."

I sat back in my chair and thought over the chain of events, an odd collection of occurrences that I'd have never attributed to my sister. It was too much work for someone like her.

"I'm going to make a few phone calls and gather whatever information is available," Sal said slowly. "I would suggest keeping a low profile while we try to sort through this and nail down some facts. If we can determine this Jason fellow is truly in the area, we have a much bigger problem." His lips turned downward and I knew he was thinking of the town being overrun by FBI agents.

Judah marched back into the room, his face still pale, his expression tight and when he sat down next to me and I put my hand on his thigh, I felt his entire body tense up.

"What was that?" I asked softly, and he ignored me while he reached across the desk to shake Sal's hand.

"Expect we'll be in touch," was all he said and the burly cop nodded at me, something Judah took to mean we were dismissed, because he hauled me out of my seat and practically carried me to the door.

We sat in the truck for a long moment before he turned over the engine and backed out of the angled parking spot, pulling a careful three-point turn on the street to head back toward the farm.

"Judah." I kept my voice soft, fearful I'd spook him again. "Is everything okay?"

"Just had an unpleasant reminder of something, is all." His voice was like gravel and he ran his free hand down his face, eyes blinking rapidly. I had no idea what that meant, but in my gut I knew it had something to do with Cait and a tiny tendril of concern started to curl through my gut. She was the ghost he couldn't seem to shake.

It wasn't more than a fifteen-minute drive to the farm, but Judah's eyes stayed resolutely on the road. I could see him chewing on something, his expression tight and angry, and when he pulled into the yard I invited him into the small office for coffee.

He was putting up a wall, shutting me out while he tried to process something on his own.

"Dad," he barked across the yard and I watched Erik rise from the rocking chair on the front porch, bundled in a heavy winter coat. The weather had tanked overnight, dropping nearly thirty degrees, and last night's rain was today's ice. "Need you to keep Bec with you for a while; something I gotta do."

Whatever it was, Erik didn't look surprised. He ambled off the porch and pulled me in for a quick hug before asking whether I wanted to head into the house or out to the little office. I knew that nothing would distract me like work, even if I had a babysitter on guard, so I pointed toward the small outbuilding and he nodded shortly.

Judah didn't hug me. He didn't kiss me goodbye, smile at me, or even look at me as he hurried back to the truck and tore out of the yard.

"Expect he forgot," Erik said softly, shaking his head as he watched the truck swerve wildly onto the road. I didn't ask what that meant, because if he'd really meant to say it out loud I had a feeling Erik would have finished the sentence, and it left me unsettled.

"Is he going to be okay?" I asked finally, my voice a little shaky, and Erik smiled down at me.

"He will be, mostly thanks to you, and some thanks to his sister and her patience." He chuckled. "Patient. Stubborn. Whatever you want to call my girl."

I hadn't met this Benson yet, the last sibling to whom I had very little connection but for the stories the family told about her. She was the one who'd escaped small town life for the big city, the nation's capital, before she gave it all up to move to Montana and lock down the love of her life. I knew almost nothing of that story either, just that the brothers had the biggest man crush possible on Ashley's husband. Judah had let it slip once that they had a running group text, all the Benson siblings and Ashley's husband, Travis. I wondered if perhaps one of them had sent up the bat signal earlier in the day and that was why Judah had disappeared.

"He's the hardheaded one." Erik laughed, mostly to himself as we walked into the office and I flicked on the desk lamp and the space heater. "Would feel sorry for you, but I think you're handling him just fine." His expression softened a little. "Be patient with him; doubt he's done pushing you yet."

I didn't ask for more details, just fired up the desktop and started reviewing some things I'd saved for later. Between reading and frequent coffee breaks, the day dragged toward early afternoon and finally Erik tucked his phone into his shirt pocket and announced it was time for lunch.

Judah's truck was still missing as I followed him into the house, where it seemed Donna was expecting me—and only me, if the place settings on the table were any indication.

I sent Judah a surreptitious text when Donna directed me to sit while she finished chopping a salad, and I wasn't surprised when it was marked delivered but remained unread.

"Might be a difficult day of it, dear." Donna's voice was gentle when she leaned over my shoulder to place a basket of warm rolls on the table. "Wouldn't expect him to be real talkative—go a bit easy on him."

What was with these people and their tiptoeing and riddles?

"Does it have anything to do with why he looked so stricken at the police station?" I asked her softly, water running in the background as Erik washed his hands at the kitchen sink.

"Don't know anything about that," she said, pausing, her eyes locked on mine. "But last year was a bad one; expect he's still adjusting."

I shook my head at her, tipping one palm upward to indicate I had no idea what she was talking about.

"Wedding anniversary," she said quietly, and I wondered if it was so her husband wouldn't overhear. "Would have been eighteen years today if my math is right. Remember it because Levi's was last week—has a real hard time with it, too."

That was definitely something I'd be asking Levi about one day, because it was clear to me that the man was resolutely single, even though there was often talk of his grown daughter who lived in Boston.

I struggled to swallow any of the delicious food Donna had made, only half able to process the lively flow of conversation between her and her husband.

I felt the other shoe hanging over my head, ready to drop.

Chapter Twenty-One

Judah

It was late when I returned to the farm and Dad said everything had been seen to for the day. The hired hands were finishing up the evening milking and Beckett was nowhere to be found. He said she'd insisted on making the walk to the cabin to pick up her truck and I very nearly blew a gasket when he admitted to letting her out of his sight. It took me a minute to breathe, to count backward from ten, to remind myself that I hadn't read him in on quite everything I suspected, but I hopped into the truck and tore out of the driveway to get to the cabin.

It was all fine and dandy if Beckett wanted to face her fears, but to leave her alone for a second was irresponsible.

Her truck wasn't at the cabin and, frantic, I sped down the road toward my house, finally able to breathe a deep sigh of relief when I found it parked in my driveway. It was an advertisement, telling the world that the woman was staying at my house, but at that moment I didn't care. I quickly parked in the garage before rushing into the house to find her stirring something on the stove and I bit back the angry words about irresponsible behavior. It would only make her shut down and pull away.

"Thank God." The words out of my mouth were more from relief than anger, and she looked up at me with a soft smile. Something smelled delicious, and I realized that her presence had given my home a soul. I loved this, coming home to her or with her, going through the easy rhythms of an evening routine together, and it terrified me to think of losing that. It was something I'd only just begun to have, only weeks into something that had changed my life in the best ways.

"Dan and his crew were still there," she said gently. "I was fine."

"Don't much trust anyone these days," I admitted. "Got my mind running wild with all these possibilities. Why didn't you tell me all that stuff about your sister?"

She shrugged slowly, flipping off the burner before turning to the island, bracing herself to lean on wide-spread hands. "Water under the bridge, or so I thought. She was a non-issue and I didn't in any way think it was connected to what's been happening. I still can't wrap my head around how she was responsible for bringing Jason into our lives."

"About that." I'd been mulling over some of that weirdness over the course of the day. "She's your twin?" That was a weird thought, two women who looked like Beckett running around in the world, one of them totally unhinged. "Why did Jason fixate on you when he already had someone who probably looked a lot like you?"

"Don't think I haven't asked myself that question a million times over the last twelve years." She dropped her eyes. "I've never come up with an answer that didn't involve some kind of incentive."

"Well, if she's here we have some idea of who's likely causing trouble. That's a start. I'll talk to Sal again in the morning; have a strong suspicion Colson Creek will be crawling with FBI in the next couple days, so if he's here, they'll flush him out."

She nodded, her eyes still downcast, and it bothered me to think she looked subdued. This was stealing her light, and for that I felt justified in hating people I didn't know.

We ate dinner in strained silence that night and I kept one hand on her thigh. Part of me worried that if I let go of her for a second, she'd bolt. She'd pack up and disappear and I'd never find her again.

She slept wrapped up in my arms again that night and I whispered the things I felt for her into her hair once I was sure she was asleep. I was terrified to admit to her that what I felt for her was just ... too soon. There was no way she wanted to be saddled with some small town farmer living out in the middle of nowhere. She'd make us profitable and move on again because it was the nature of her job.

Maybe I had her sister to thank for slowing progress and keeping Beckett here longer.

"What was the phone call?" Her sleepy voice startled me and I felt my cheeks grow hot. How much had she heard? "The one you took while we were talking to Sal. You seemed spooked—angry, even."

I swallowed hard, because this was something I didn't want to talk about, even if it solved an awful lot of problems.

"Cait's life insurance policy was paid out this week. Donna must've filed all the papers for me, because I've been useless." There was a terrible lump growing in my throat as I realized how much my family had done to keep me upright even when I'd repeatedly tried to check out. "Deposit cleared and the bank was calling to confirm a very large transfer."

"I'm sorry." Her voice was small and she burrowed into me, her lips pressing to my chest. "That had to be a terrible reminder."

I still hadn't wrapped my head around it. Ten million dollars, the price of her life and that of my boys. There had been just enough doubt the crash had been an accident that while the investigation had delayed the release of the payment, they hadn't been able to deny it altogether—and at the time I hadn't cared one bit. There was nothing bringing them back and the money meant nothing.

"It's blood money," I said quietly. "But it's more than enough to save the farm. We can implement your plans without taking on an investor or taking out loans." It was an ironic sort of gift, financing the very thing Cait had fought so hard to get away from for years.

"Donna said she thought it was your wedding anniversary."

"Yeah." I squeezed her a little tighter. "Ironic, isn't it? Used to be, I guess."

"Oh, Jude." She wrapped her arms tighter around me, as if she could hold me together, and I realized when she did it that the worst was past. Because of my family and because of her, I was moving on.

Thank God.

When we pulled into the farm driveway that morning, there was a familiar extended-cab pickup truck in the driveway. It made me smile, but it was a little rueful. There was only one reason my sister would show up unannounced, and it had something to do with Dan's news.

"Get your hands off my sister, you filthy caveman," I hollered when I walked into the kitchen to find Travis's arms wrapped around Ashley. His face was pressed into her hair and I recognized the way he held her, like he feared letting go.

"Coffee's hot," Travis announced without letting her go and without another word I marched over and threw my arms around both of them, squeezing tight. I was beyond grateful that Ashley had ended up with him, all stern bluster to her sunshine, and he loved her fiercely. I could see it every time I watched the two of them.

"Jude." Ashley lifted her face from Travis's shoulder to lean up and kiss my cheek. "You're looking much better." A smile lit her beautiful face and I stepped back just far enough to observe the adoring way Travis looked down at his wife.

"Got someone to introduce to both of you," I said, remembering Bec was standing behind me, just at the edge of the doorway.

"Oh, I already know who this is." Ashley disengaged herself from her husband's arms and marched toward Beckett, giving her no time at all to react when she threw her arms around her. "Levi's told me everything about you, Beckett, and I'm just so pleased you're setting our boys straight." There was a little mischief in her voice. "This one especially, it would seem." She stepped back then, her hands on Beckett's shoulders as she surveyed her with absolutely no shame.

"Whew, Judah." Ashley whistled. "I can see why her methods were effective. Woman, you are *stunning*."

I knew Beckett was blushing, though I couldn't see her because Ashley was still blocking my view. There was a soft noise that I thought might be a laugh from Beckett and I stepped around my sister to slide an arm around Bec's waist. It made Ashley's grin stretch even wider. "That's what I thought." She nodded. "Yes, that's perfect." She nodded once before turning back to her husband and he happily tucked her into his side when she drew near.

"Imagine you're here for Dan," I said quietly and her expression flattened out just a little before she nodded.

"Sebastian's had his hands full with our family," she said quietly, referring to her close friend to whom she'd referred me for therapy. "I've been trying to get Ben and Levi to talk to him for years. Levi insists everything is fine and Ben just denies he needs any help." She shrugged. "Levi doesn't feel the need to change, but Ben absolutely refuses. Hopefully Dan's smarter than those two."

Donna breezed past us, giving my bicep a quick squeeze before she flipped down the stove door and the smell of potatoes, sausage and onions filled the room. Beckett and I had already eaten, but my mouth watered at the smell.

"Gonna head out and get some chores done," I announced. "Bec's got some big plans for this outfit. Might not recognize the joint the next time you're here for a visit."

"This kind of change is good," Ashley said gently, her eyes warm. "All four of you were just marinating in misery all these years. Now you have something to work toward. Something to build with this beautiful woman." She gestured toward Beckett, and that time I was the one who blushed.

We made our rounds, feeding the calves and the heifers, checking to make sure all the equipment was functioning properly and nothing needed repairs. Then I backed a manure spreader under the conveyor that ran from the barn and Beckett watched the paddles carefully for ice, knocking some with a shovel as the putrid load was dumped into the spreader. Then we spread a layer of bedding in the gutters while the farm hands cleaned up the milkhouse, and each cow received her allotted portion of grain. We worked quickly, as it was too cold to let the cows out and if we didn't work quickly the contents in the spreader would freeze before we could get it on the field.

I didn't like to clean the gutters on such frigid days, when things were liable to freeze and snap, but it had been bitterly cold the past few days and the cows had spent a great deal of time indoors. They were going to be swimming in it soon, if I didn't literally get shit handled.

Beckett rode with me inside the tractor cab, her gaze trained on the manure spreader as I fired up the power takeoff and cow shit rained down on the field. The earth was frozen solid and I drove carefully, trying not to hop over some of the deep ruts left in the earth, marks left in the fall. The tractor had absolutely no suspension and I didn't want to test the strength of the hitch holding the manure spreader.

There was a little heat in the cab, but hardly enough to combat the frigid air outside and Beckett's teeth chattered as I finally lowered the hatch and directed the tractor toward the road. It wasn't a long trip back to the farm, and I carefully backed the spreader and the tractor into the machine shed. It was too cold to clean anything and though the shed didn't offer much warmth, it was better than leaving everything parked outside in the direct blast of the elements.

The two of us hurried into her little office space and she rushed to turn on the heat while I made coffee with half-frozen fingers. Then we sat and drank our coffee together, shivering as the little space heater worked to warm the room.

"I'll fix it," I promised her with something of a nebulous idea forming in my mind. "We'll make the necessary improvements to the farm. We'll get things up and running. And you'll have a proper office, something with central heat and a bathroom. A small kitchen area. We'll do this thing right."

Her eyes softened with something I hoped was affection, but part of me wondered if she was biting back an admission, that she'd only stay until she knew I was on my feet she could move on.

"Don't waste your money on me, Judah," she said gently, but there was a sweet smile on her face. "This is perfectly workable and honestly, it's more than I expected. This was a pleasant surprise when I arrived—and so were you." Her grin turned wicked and I quickly stood, rounding the desk to lean down and press a hard kiss to her mouth.

"Fuck's sake, you two can't be left alone for a minute," Ashley teased as a cold blast tore through the room when she stepped into the office, rubbing her hands together. "I've had at least four cups of Donna's coffee and I swear that stuff has nitrous in it. Why do I want more?"

"Because you have an addictive personality," I offered, and she rolled her eyes at me. All five of us had that, and three of us had been through our fair share of struggles with the bottle. Levi's addiction was the woman he still obsessed over, and Dan ... Come to think of it, I didn't know what was Dan's chosen poison. He usually seemed to keep himself pretty straight.

"You going to see him?" I asked and she nodded, a solemn expression stealing across her pretty face.

"Don't care to watch him spiral like I watched you," she said softly. "Want to get him hooked up with Sebbe as quickly as possible, because this family's response to stress and grief ... well, obviously we can't be trusted."

There was far more truth to that than I wanted to admit.

Beckett was still sitting quietly behind the desk and she rose slowly. "Be right back; I'm going to head up to the house for a moment."

I nodded, as did Ashley.

"She's been your therapist lately," Ashley observed as the door closed. "Be careful with that."

"What the fuck are you talking about?" I asked her, aware that just about made my hair stand on end.

"Judah." She leaned closer, kissing my cheek gently, making me soften into the kindness she'd always had to offer. That wasn't from our mother, and it wasn't a part of Dad. I didn't know where it came from, but I loved her for it. "Something I should have told you long ago, except that I don't know that I understood it then. It's hard to explain."

"Give it to me straight." My voice was hard.

"I know I pushed Sebbe on you, and I hope it's helped. All I can say is that some people enter therapy looking for a reason—something or someone to blame for what they have experienced or are experiencing—and fewer yet enter it looking for a cure. Typically, no one establishes their *why* up front and that's an oversimplification, but there you have it."

"And?" I asked leadingly, reasonably convinced my sister had the answer. God knew she'd searched for her own "cure" for almost thirty years.

"Jude, you know this already. Some people don't want to get better, even if they don't recognize that. It involves more work than they're willing to put in."

My heart lurched. "Do you mean that about Bec, or about me?"

"No, she is impressively self-motivated. I think she wants to improve—to move beyond, and not everyone has that motivation. But you have to be on the same path as her. You can't hold her back. A lot of people dwell in the past and they can't move beyond it, mostly because they're not really led beyond that point."

"You admitting to some professional shortcomings?" I teased, and she rolled her eyes at me.

"There are definitely some less-than-stellar therapists out there, and I should know. I've worked alongside a few of them."

Ash had always known she wanted to go into trauma therapy, something that impressed me, that she'd been so driven and focused. I knew I didn't have the stomach for something like that.

"Well, Sebbe's done some pretty heavy lifting to this point." I had to give her that much, because the friend she'd hooked me up with had been working pretty hard to get me sorted out. "Got to hand it to the guy: He doesn't give up."

"Neither do you," she said, patting my cheek. "You just took a little detour for a minute. And I think being able to focus on something larger than yourself has been good for you. Dad's told me about all the drama surrounding Beckett and I know it's a weird thing to say, but it's given you a new direction. You've been concerned about someone else, and that someone has come to mean something to you."

I hadn't really thought of it that way, but I thought it made Beckett sound like a distraction.

"Are you saying that once the danger's past, the honeymoon's over?"

"Not with that one." She grinned. "I think it'll be the beginning. The way she looks at you..." She trailed off, her smile growing softer. "Cait never looked at you that way, Jude. Not ever."

That was a sobering, somewhat terrifying thought, that my sister had seen the end from the beginning with Cait, and could see it again.

"The hell you come from, woman?" Ben bellowed from the doorway and I turned to fix him with a vicious glare.

"You live in a barn? Shut the damn door. It's colder than fuck out there."

"Pffft." Ben latched the door before crossing the room in two huge strides and crushing Ashley into a hug. "Don't know who you been fuckin', but it ain't supposed to be cold. Lemme know if you need me to have a chat with your lady." He shot me an evil grin at me over Ashley's shoulder and I lifted my hand to give him the finger.

"I suppose your girlfriend with the lacy red underwear's a bit chilly without her accoutrements."

Ben stared at me and the use of a big word he clearly didn't know.

"Never gonna let that go, are you?"

"Not until one of us is dead," I promised, quite satisfied with myself.

Ben rocked Ashley back and forth until she squeaked a little and he had to release her so she could catch her breath. Then the two of them sank into the chairs in front of the desk and Ashley demanded details about Ms. Red Lace, while I excused myself to step outside and make sure Beckett was on her way back. I knew I was being paranoid, but I could have sworn something unsettling was in the air. There was a malicious intent that felt closer than ever, something heavy and foreboding.

"Saw Sal on our way in this morning," I heard from behind me. "Donna wasn't expecting us and I didn't want to drop in on her for breakfast, though you know she managed a feast anyway. I thought I was going to burst. I tried to tell her we'd already stopped at the diner." Ben made some kind of noise of affirmation while I debated walking up to the house to make sure Beckett was okay. "Told me we could expect a lot more law activity around here later today."

"Here?" Ben sounded alarmed, and it was enough to pull me back into the small building. I hadn't considered that the property would be swarming with agents looking for every possible hint. It meant they would check *everything*: outbuildings, the barn, the farmhouse, Beckett's cabin—probably Levi, Dan, Benjamin's, and my houses as well. Not that I would blame anyone for being thorough, but that was an unwelcome disruption, even if I did want answers.

"Least I'll sleep knowing someone's keeping watch," I bit out. I hadn't slept much the past couple nights, winding myself with the *what if* while Beckett slept in my arms. The reality of loss for me was that I had a very clear understanding of what it felt like and what it did to me. I was just smart enough to know that to experience it again would do me in.

"You stayin' for a minute?" Ben asked, and Ashley nodded slowly.

"The ranch is on slower rhythms during the winter and Travis trusts his foreman. He has the same guy who's been running things the last thirty years; safe to take some time off now and then."

Ben popped up, his eyes alight. "You brought the boys?"

It was no secret he was just a big kid and he adored Travis's twins, who worshiped him like the sun rose and set on Benjamin Benson.

"They're inside." Her smile was sweet and he whooped, shoving me aside to tear out the door in the direction of the house.

"Check on Beckett," I called after him, his long strides eating up the distance as he ran. He held a hand over his head to acknowledge he'd heard me.

"Suppose this means we'll be having some family dinners every night for a while." I grinned at her, because I'd miss some of the quiet time with Beckett, but nothing made Donna happier than feeding an army, and we may as well have been one.

"Might be the only quiet time we get if we're being overrun by an investigation," she said quietly and I pursed my lips, nodding.

The sooner we could put this behind us, the better.

"I'm so stuffed, someone's going to have to drive me home." Ben burped loudly, leaning back in his chair on the frozen front porch. We had decamped while Ashley put the boys to bed after yet another family dinner cooked by the tireless Donna, coffees in hand. The sun had set moments earlier but the waning light of day was still visible, illuminating each of us.

"You look sick." Dan reached over to place a hand on Ben's forehead and Ben groaned again.

"I wish I was. Then I'd have a real good excuse not to be here."

Levi looked amused, leaning back in his rocking chair and crossing one ankle over his knee, a signature Benson move, like there was just too much going on in our pants to risk crushing things by pulling a full leg cross. "What did you do this time?"

"Gonna stop drinking, that's what I'm gonna do."

"About time." Dan huffed and Ben shot him a viciously hair eyeball.

"Gonna start going to church with Donna and make whatever that thing is for my sins."

"Recompense?" Beckett offered and Ben raised one eyelid to look at her, his face squinty.

"Sounds right."

"The hell did you do?" Dan asked, reaching over and shoving Ben's shoulder hard.

"I accidentally sexted Dad."

There was a sharp snort from Levi, who pitched forward, unable to hold in a raucous laugh. "Come again, now?"

"Yeah, that's exactly what I told him to do."

"Holy shit." Dan was pale and Beckett had a hand over her mouth.

"Turns out after a couple of the Machine Shed's specialty Boilermakers, uh ... *Dad* starts to look an awful lot like *Dara* on your phone."

Beckett pitched forward over her knees, holding onto her knees, her shoulders shaking violently.

"She the one with the red underwear?" Levi asked, an evil grin on his face.

"Nope." Ben bit off the end of the word like that was all he was willing to say about that, and Beckett wrinkled her nose.

"Benjamin, I say this with love." She clamped her lips together for a second, like she was trying to formulate a diplomatic way to tell my brother he was the biggest whore she'd ever met. "Perhaps it would make your life ... easier ... if you were to confine all of that love to one woman for a while."

"Pfffft." Ben blew out a raspberry. "More than enough of this man to go around—and around and around. Might've liked to keep some of those details from Dad, though." He winked at Bec, who maintained a stern expression.

"Ben." Her voice was soft. "You're hurting yourself. You're not actually happy."

Every eye on the porch went wide. No one had ever really called him on his shit before.

There was a soft snort from the doorway and I looked up to see Ashley leaning against the frame. She had opened the inner door silently and stood with the screen door in front of her. "I knew I was going to like you," she said in Beckett's direction as she let herself out onto the porch, coffee in hand. "Finally, I'm not the only voice of reason. Maybe these dipshits will actually listen to you."

Beckett shrugged slowly, an exaggerated movement. "I watched my sister chase men she didn't really want for years. She wanted the attention, but she had no intention of keeping them. Of course, that made her a challenge. Guys lined up for her, but she never kept them around. She left a lot of broken hearts in her wake."

Ben looked solemn; I'd almost have said chastised.

"So, Benjamin." Beckett sat back in her chair, her heavy winter coat zipped all the way up to cover the bottom of her chin. "What's your wish list? Give me your top three must-haves for the girl of your dreams."

"Bodacious, obviously." He cracked the words out like the lash of a whip, but his teasing grin was back in place. "A lot of fun to be around; she's gotta be able to take a joke." He paused then, like he was struggling to decide, and Beckett smiled at him.

"Four things, if you need them."

"Kind." He said it decisively. "Someone sweet, with a gentle heart—be real nice to have someone around who kinda liked me."

I pulled something of a surprised face and I watched Levi's eyebrows crawl up at the same time.

"And loyal—maybe shoulda said that one first. Gotta know that when I'm coming home to my woman, I been the only man on her mind all day long. Comin' home to her because she wants *me* and no one else."

"Good list," Ashley mused softly. "Yeah, you probably should have led with loyal, because that's your number one hangup, baby Benson: You don't trust anyone to do anything but fail you." Benjamin made a soft scoffing noise at her and she held up one hand. "Losing Mom fucked us up, guys. There's no question and no doubt. Look at how we all handled it—wallowed in it for *years*. It wasn't just losing her when she passed, but her decision to walk out on us. None of us have ever thought we were *good enough*, not for anyone—including Dad. Look what it did to us for years—is still doing, in some cases."

That made Levi swallow hard and Dan dragged one hand slowly down his face, the scraping noise making it clear he hadn't been friendly with a razor in a few days. I'd noticed, now that I was paying attention, this seemed to be his new normal.

"Think my coffee's frozen solid in the bottom of my mug," Dan mused, peering into the bottom of the ceramic mug and Ashley chuckled, holding up an insulated tumbler.

"Amateurs."

Everyone began to stand at the same time, working blood flow and warmth back into extremities, our breath hanging in the air like a bank of fog and we moved quickly to hug one another and say our goodnights. It was our unspoken understanding that the Benson family powwow was concluded for the evening and Levi took our mugs, saying he wanted to spend some time talking with Dad before he left for the evening.

Beckett and I hurried off the porch, toward my ratty old pickup truck. I lengthened the width of my steps and beat her to the passenger door by half a second, quickly yanking it open so she could slide in and give me an amused eye roll. I was pretty sure she secretly loved it when I made the attempt to be chivalrous, but she liked to give me a hard time. I'd never told her, but it was something Cait had never allowed, so after a time I'd stopped even attempting it, not wanting to start a fight. Cait's reasoning had always been that she was independent and didn't want to be babied; she hadn't been interested in my explanations about wanting to protect her.

I parked the truck in the garage again, snowflakes already falling from the sky to add to the huge white banks I'd plowed to the left and right of the driveway just that morning. I didn't love winter for all the extra work it brought, the extra layers, the time spent dressing and undressing and trying not to lose extremities.

"Jude." Beckett's voice was funny and I thought it was weird that she was standing at the garage door, looking out, rather than having rounded the front of the truck to let herself into the house through the side door.

"What is it, Tex?" I asked, my voice teasing as I stepped closer to her. If she propositioned me right here in the garage, I'd find a way to make that work and I'd do it happily.

"Someone was here."

My head snapped up, an alertness prickling down my spine as I stepped just outside the garage door. The light from the single strand of Christmas lights still hanging on the porch, on a ratty old timer, provided a weak multi-colored light that just barely made it possible to identify several sets of footprints in what was reasonably fresh snow.

"Bec." I said it very quietly. "Get back in the truck."

Without a word of argument she hurried to the passenger door and climbed back in while I quietly followed the tracks that led up the porch steps.

"Motherfuckers," I breathed softly, turning and hurrying back into the garage, turning over the engine and backing down the driveway like the hounds of hell were after us, because those footprints went in one direction—into my house.

I killed the headlights almost immediately, backing up by memory rather than sight, and I slowed as the truck came to the edge of the road, backing over the slight dip of the field driveway and through a drift, so that I was parked off the road itself.

"What are we doing?" Beckett's voice shook as I pulled out my phone, keeping it beneath the dash so it didn't illuminate our faces as I dialed.

"I'm calling Sal. If he's got some extra hands in town by now, we could use all of them. We're not going into that house until whoever went in there is escorted out in handcuffs."

She shivered when I said it and the line rang endlessly.

"Colson Creek PD." Sal sounded like he'd been asleep.

"You should be ashamed," I barked. "It's seven p.m., Sal. You sleepin' on the job?"

"You're the only excitement around these parts lately, Judah." It should probably have concerned me that he could identify my voice so easily. "Got me filling out all kinds of reports and answering questions that have no answers. I need a nap every now and then to keep up my strength."

"Well, round up some of your new pals and send them out to my place—thought they were supposed to be here already. Got footprints leading into my house but none exiting."

"How many sets?" He was awake now.

"Two that I saw, but I didn't stick around to check the back. Just saw footprints and got Beckett the hell out."

"Where are you now?"

"Parked in the field driveway across from the house, waiting to see if anyone comes out so I can hit 'em with the headlights."

Sal blew out a frustrated sigh. "And what happens if I show up with the cavalry and you've got an empty house? Makes me look like I'm entertaining hallucinations and nuisance calls."

Beckett's head turned toward me in the cab, a strange expression on her face and she shook her head slowly.

"Not a prank, Salvatore." I pronounced his name very carefully. "I don't fuck around when it comes to safety, and something's wrong here."

"Yeah, yeah. Let me drag some of these federal jackasses out of the Machine Shed and see what we can do about it. They weren't supposed to be on the clock until tomorrow."

Beckett's eyes rolled almost as hard as mine and I mashed the button to disconnect the call.

"That was an uncharacteristic response," Beckett said quietly as I dropped the phone onto the seat beside me. "Do we trust that he's going to do the right thing?"

She was voicing a concern that had just occurred to me, and silently I reached for her hand.

We waited in relative silence. I'd left the engine running, hoping we were far enough from the house that the sound didn't carry and I waited, my eyes trained on the house and the yard, trying to discern any dark shapes or shadows.

It was fifteen long minutes later when Sal's police cruiser, a hefty SUV, pulled into my driveway, followed by three dark unmarked cars. There was the sharp slam of several doors at once and finally I flipped on the headlights, pulling the truck back across the road and up the driveway to park behind one of the cars with Virginia tags.

"Weird they wouldn't just fly here," I said softly to Beckett and she raised one eyebrow, opening her door only when I opened mine.

"Stand clear," one of the men in a jacket with "FBI" emblazoned across the back barked at me and I bit back a particularly rude insult.

"Keys." I held up the key to the house. "Don't need some asshole breaking down the door." It was clear he didn't like that and I didn't much care. I jangled them in his direction like he was hard of hearing or slow, and he hadn't yet convinced me he wasn't both.

There were eight agents in total and Sal waited in his SUV, hands off because it was their jurisdiction now, and Beckett and I watched as seven drew sidearms and stood to the side, offering cover to the guy opening the door.

"The alarm," Beckett whispered, and I pulled her into my side.

"Pretty sure it's been deactivated already," I whispered back, and she nodded solemnly.

Lights flashed on in the house as the eight of them hustled inside and conducted a thorough sweep. Beckett let me pull her back to my front and I wrapped my arms around her, chin resting on the top of her head as we waited.

"Clear." Someone's voice rang out from inside the house after a few moments, and all of them came trooping back out.

"Check the back," I called.

Beckett went tense beneath my palms and I squeezed her shoulders gently and one of the men returned to a vehicle to pull a huge mag light out of the trunk. Three others did the same and they rounded the house, a muffled exclamation of surprise traveling back to us on the still night air. They were gone a long time, lights bobbing around in the wooded area behind the house, and Beckett's teeth started to chatter. "In the truck, Tex," I said gently, spinning her to face me so I could press a kiss to her forehead. Then I led her back to the driver's side door and helped her in, turning over the engine and blasting the heat while she shivered. "Going to see what they have to say first, okay?" I took her chin in one hand, to make sure her eyes met mine, and she nodded slowly.

"Not so sure I'd recommend staying here." They were all straggling back, putting flashlights away in cars, when one approached me: "Alarm system's fucked. There are footprints leading out the back of the house and into the woods, then they're just gone—they don't go anywhere."

"You find anything in the house?" I asked, a fist squeezing my gut. I couldn't keep her safe.

The man motioned for Sal to join us and he oozed out of his SUV like he'd been napping and his coordination hadn't quite returned.

"I think there's something both of you need to see," he said quietly into our little huddle, gesturing toward the house.

"I can't leave her here by herself," I said tightly, gesturing back toward the truck, and he nodded. He placed two fingers in his mouth and gave a short, sharp blast, gesturing to two of the agents who immediately moved to stand next to each door.

"This won't take long," he said grimly, "and I need you to think about who it is either of you might have pissed off. It's possible it's the escaped con, but I'll be honest, this might be even more personal. This looks to me like some kind of retribution that comes from a prior sexual partner—someone who's all twisted up about the way things ended, maybe."

I had no idea what made him think that, but Sal and I followed him into the house, where everything appeared to be in the order we'd left it that morning.

It was as he headed down the short hallway leading toward the bedrooms that I knew whatever it was, I wasn't going to like it. There was a strange smell in the air, the rich smell of iron that I'd recognize anywhere: blood, and I swallowed reflexively against the immediate nausea.

Standing just inside the doorway, trying to process the chaos in the room, the only thing I could focus on was the bed. A very careful half of it—Beckett's side—was covered in blood, two chicken carcasses resting at the foot. But it was the serial killer scrawl on the wall above the bed that made my heart catch. It stretched in huge, ugly letters over the entire headboard.

"Going to dust for prints." A voice broke through the thundering heartbeat in my ears and I nodded slowly. "Suggest you not touch anything for the time being. You have somewhere you can stay overnight?"

I nodded slowly, because it looked like Donna's unofficial bed and breakfast would be pressed into service once more.

"Like I said." The man gestured toward the wall. "Looks like someone's got a beef with you or your woman, but I gotta say that based on the size of those footprints in the snow, it's not a man we're looking for."

"How can you be sure?" My voice was scratchy, and he ran a slow hand over his face.

"Not certain, just an educated guess. Especially since there are two sets, around the same size, leading out the back and toward the woods."

That fit Beckett's narrative that Jason had teamed up with her sister, with one slight flaw: I had no idea whether Jason had tiny feet.

"This is likely someone you know," he said, and I caught the inference immediately. Someone *I* know. "Alarm was disabled, then disassembled entirely. Someone knew the code. And there were no signs of forced entry, making it likely that this person—these people—used a key to gain access to your home."

My eyes drifted back to the wall as I tried to process who it was that would do us harm, the bloody scrawl making goosebumps raise on my skin, the letters smeared on crisp white paint.

Traitor.

Chapter Twenty-Two

Beckett

Judah's expression was grim when he stepped off the front porch and walked toward the truck. I had been watching a few of the agents as they pulled things from the trunk of one of the cars, several kits, and I realized they meant to put in a long night, something that made my heart sink. I had allowed myself to be lulled into a false sense of safety the past few quiet weeks. There had been no additional sightings of my sister and the single tiny motel on the edge of town had no record of anyone named Beth, going back months—not that I expected my sister would have used her given name.

"I'll be back out to talk things over with them in the morning," he announced as he opened the door and I slid down the wide bench seat to allow him to slide in behind the wheel. "They'll be here most of the night, I'm afraid."

There was something he wasn't telling me, a new tension in his jaw and his shoulders, and I didn't have the energy to ask. I just nodded wearily, feeling the weight of the past twelve years pressing down on my shoulders. Somewhere I had slipped up. Somehow I had allowed my trail to stay just warm enough that I'd been located.

The cab was warm, the vents blasting hot air from the engine, but I shivered anyway. Judah noticed it out of the corner of his eye and he turned toward me, reaching over to haul me up tight against his side, something ferocious taking over his expression just before he leaned down the few inches to my mouth and kissed me hard. "Not taking any chances with you," he murmured. "We're going to find this piece of shit, and then you and me are gonna live happily ever after, okay?"

I felt a tear break the waterline and hurtle down my cheek and when he pulled back to stare down at me he brushed it away with his thumb. "That's a promise, Tex. You want to be in this thing with me, we're gonna do it right. *I'm* gonna do things right."

I had no idea what that meant, but I had a feeling he was thinking back over his time with Cait and berating himself for the things he felt he'd done wrong. Maybe he'd allowed her to live her life separate from him, in order to keep the peace. Maybe he hadn't fought for her the way he knew he should have. Whatever it was, I could hear the guilt in his words.

"A promise, huh?" My voice shook a little as I tried to lighten the mood just a little. "Sounds awfully serious, Benson."

"Is serious. Gonna marry you, Bec." His fingers curled into my hair, tugging almost to the point of pain when he made a fist. "I know a good thing when I see it; I'm no fool. We're putting all of this shit behind us and taking our second chance. Good things like this don't happen twice."

It sounded like things had been decided, and it made me smile just a little. Cade had never been as sure about me as Judah seemed, something that soothed my frantic heart.

There was a tap on the window and I jumped, something that made Judah lean in and kiss me once more, completely unruffled, before releasing me. He turned to roll down his window as Sal leaned into the truck. "They'll dust the house overnight and check out a few things." He gave Judah a tight look I couldn't decipher. "You headed back to the farmhouse?" Judah nodded shortly, a movement Sal matched. "Good. I have no doubt they'll be by in the morning; I'm sure there will be questions, and hopefully by then we'll have a few answers."

It wasn't late when Judah opened the door to let me back into the farmhouse, the familiar smells like a welcoming hug. This home was peaceful, a place where I felt safe, something I realized was mostly Donna's doing.

"Judah." There was a little surprise in Donna's voice as she hurried out of the kitchen in a thick bathrobe, a mug of tea in her hand. "What's happened?"

"Got some drama going on at my place." He grimaced a little when he said it. "Okay if Bec and I crash here for the night?"

"You're always welcome and you know that." The smile that stretched across her face was brilliant and impulsively I leaned forward to hug her, grateful for her kindness. Donna loved people, but she loved *her* people ferociously, something I recognized in each one of the Benson boys.

"You're good people, Ma." Judah pulled Donna out of my arms to wrap her in his own, kissing the top of her head and when he finally let her go she dashed a quick hand over her left eye. I had a feeling it was a rare moment between the two of them, not for any lack of effort on her part, but because Judah didn't let his feelings out often.

Donna led us up the stairs and into the room we'd stayed in previously, something that made me smile to myself. She didn't even try to put Judah in another room, she simply gestured toward the comfortable bed. "There are fresh towels in the bath and if you need anything else, you just put up a fuss." She patted Judah's cheek as she said it, and I wondered to myself how Erik Benson had been so lucky as to find this woman, all sunshine and care and kindness. She was a miracle.

The bathtub was an enormous clawfoot, something that seemed like it might be older than the house itself, and I watched as Judah leaned over and twisted the handles to start filling it. He gestured to the bathroom door, which I closed behind us and he straightened, his eyes on mine as he started to undress. I followed his lead, dropping the pile of smelly laundry on the floor before crawling into the tub to let the water finish filling around me. Judah climbed in behind me, his long legs bracketing mine as he pulled me back to rest against his chest and I sighed contentedly. This was my favorite place on earth, feeling the thump of his heartbeat against my neck, just below my left ear, his lips in my hair, his arms wrapped protectively over my chest.

"What did they find?" I finally whispered and he drew in a slow, even breath.

"Someone tore up our bedroom," was all he said, and though I knew there was something he wasn't telling me, I didn't want to know more. My every instinct screamed at me to pack my things and disappear; I had already overstayed my welcome and staying longer meant I was endangering the people around me. The people I was coming to love with an intensity that bordered on desperation. They had stepped into a yawning hole in my life, giving me family when I had none, something that both soothed and broke my heart.

We bathed slowly, refilling the tub with warmer water once when it cooled, my fingers starting to wrinkle, and yet he made no movement to get out. He seemed content to sit there with me, our feet tangled together, his heart a steady beat against my neck. It was a little terrifying, to realize that I had something with this man I'd never hoped to find.

The person who'd tried so hard to get under my skin and drive me away when I'd first arrived.

Someone who worked hard to hide such a tender, broken heart beneath all his bluster and grump.

I raised one of his hands to my lips and kissed the back of each finger. It wasn't sexual, it was a gesture of gratitude that I didn't know how to put into words, something I knew he understood. I needed him to know how I felt about him even if I feared using the words. Time with him was something I wasn't guaranteed, but I would greedily soak up every moment he gave to me, knowing the moments were precious.

The thought of staying wasn't what frightened me, it was that there was evil lurking here. It was something that had followed me, and I'd brought it right to the doorstep of the people I was falling in love with.

The water finally cooled again and Judah pulled me from the tub with him, wrapping me in a fluffy white towel before pulling several new toothbrushes from a drawer beneath the sink. "May as well put it in the holder." His smile was small and tight as he pointed to the toothbrush holder. "Looks like we might be here a while."

"I've made all your lives harder," I said quietly as I stood next to him, painting a stripe of toothpaste down the narrow bristles of the brush. "I never meant to bring this to you."

Judah stopped brushing and turned toward me, his hand on the handle, the toothbrush still in his mouth. He gave me a long look before turning to spit, rinsing quickly and slamming the toothbrush into the holder. "Beckett, if you hadn't shown up, I'd already be dead."

I stopped brushing too, frozen, waiting for him to finish the thought and he moved behind me, his eyes locking with mine in the mirror. "I was giving up in degrees, one bottle at a time. Every day was something to survive, but with you it's something to live. It's a gift and a blessing—you are—and whatever that cost, I will gladly pay it." His hands rested gently on my shoulders and he waited while I leaned over the sink to spit and rinse, then pulled me against him, my face to his chest. "You're more than I had ever hoped for ... this sounds so dumb. You're ... what was missing." His voice trailed off and I knew what it was that he wouldn't say, that he feared the happiness he'd found would be taken from him. He knew I understood that better than anyone else.

I grinned up at him, because those words meant more to me than he'd ever know. During the early years of my marriage to Cade, I'd struggled with our differences. We were polar opposites, his big, gregarious personality a complete foil to my quieter, more serious self. I'd viewed our differences as our strengths, but now I sometimes wondered if I'd talked myself into something that hadn't been quite the right fit, despite the fact I'd loved him with a ferocity that bordered on desperation. Underneath it all, I'd known I was hitting above my weight with him and I'd lived in the silent fear that I'd lose him to someone more worthy of his affection.

Slipping into the fluffy robe Donna had left in the bathroom for me, I waited for Judah to grab his and we shuffled down the hallway together, my hand gripped tightly in his. I could feel his concern. Was he worried something bad was going to happen to me, or did he feel about me the way I'd felt about Cade?

I wondered, as I drifted off to sleep in the circle of Judah's arms, just how I'd slept before. I could remember the long, sleepless or fragmented nights spent alone in my bed. This felt like completion; like it was what had been missing for just as long as I could remember.

"Cade didn't hold me like this," I whispered, my eyelids heavy, and I felt Judah stir behind me. His arms tightened just a little and his lips pressed to the back of my head like an encouragement to go on. "The authorities investigating afterward asked me if he was involved with anyone else. You could say they left no stone unturned." I paused, my stomach turning. I had refused to entertain the idea at the time. "If he was, I was purposefully blind to it. He ... traveled a lot for work."

"You never have to doubt me, Tex." There was a tenderness in Judah's voice that made me tear up. "I've been a goner from the start." He chuckled a little, and with those sweet words I twisted to kiss him before I let myself drift off to sleep.

The agents descended on the farm the next day, disrupting routines and complicating workflows, but Donna was in her element.

Erik joked it was time to install a second oven in the farmhouse as she pulled out tray after tray of cookies, muffins, cupcakes and scones. She kept fresh coffee going all day long and I had to wonder just how much investigating was getting done over the course of the day, since there were always several men in the kitchen.

Two of them asked to conduct a private interview with me in my office and Judah puffed up like a blowfish, indignant, something Levi did right alongside him. It made one of the men wince just a little; Levi was incredibly intimidating, a wide, solid 6'3" with a champion resting bitch face. I could tell it irritated Judah, to feel like he was the sidekick.

"Any particular reason you need to talk with her alone?" Levi's voice was extra deep and intimidating and Judah crossed his arms over his chest, like that was exactly what he'd been thinking.

"It's important that we ask some uncomfortable questions," the other man said. "There are some things that you might not want to hear." The look he gave me told me he knew just what Judah was to me and I watched Judah's face drop into an ugly scowl.

"Can't help but think someone might have dropped the ball here." The voice was easy and casual, but the insult was clear and I turned to see Erik leaning against the counter, arms crossed over his own substantial chest. "Interesting that our girl's been left to fend for herself—with no notification from any of the official sources. She's been living in fear for months and now you guys show up, half-assing an investigation." He gestured around the kitchen with an open palm, the criticism obvious: They were more interested in eating Donna's cookies than they were in getting to the bottom of anything.

"Mr. Benson, sir..." He gulped and I almost laughed, because Erik had just cowed the guy. "We'll do our best. It's in everyone's interest to figure out where this threat is coming from. No one will rest until Mr. Bachman is back in Ellis."

"Back?" Erik wasn't about to let the guy off the hook. He looked distinctly unimpressed. "Seems to me like he must've had some help getting out in the first place. You know how many people escape that facility?" The man shook his head slowly and one corner of Erik's mouth drew up in a grimace. I doubted he knew either, but he raised an eyebrow. "Odds aren't good for the inmates—heard once that guards are allowed to guarantee no one escapes. No investigations." He made an unmistakable gesture with one hand, index finger and thumb extended. "Don't know if that's true, but I'll run with it."

Both men turned. They'd been bested by a small town dairy farmer and they were salty about it, one of them fixing me with a bitter look. I gave him a short nod and held up my hand to Judah, a distinct *Down boy*, because I'd been through a lot worse than questioning with a few low-level feds.

The space heater was still on when we let ourselves into my office, the room surprisingly cozy despite the bitter wind outside, and one of the men crossed immediately to the small coffee maker in the corner.

"Gotta warn you," I called as he dropped in a pod, "chances are good Donna's coffee has ruined you for that."

He grimaced, but he brewed a mug anyway.

Nothing the two of them threw at me over the next hour was new. I'd lost my ability to feel offended years earlier, when the defense attorney had tried to accuse me of using my feminine wiles to lure Jason, then convince him to murder my husband. It had been like living in an alternate universe, one in which I'd repeatedly questioned my perception of reality.

"No credit cards, no phone—no movement from him on the grid since he escaped," one of the men commented to the other. "Just smart enough to stay off the radar."

"Or he's dead," I offered, a strange thought occurring to me. I'd hardly known Jason at all, certainly not as well as he thought he knew me, and the impression had been that he wasn't the sharpest tool in the shed. He had introduced himself to me once as one of Cade's work contacts, and from what had been dug up on him since, there was a tenuous connection. "It's possible there was an altercation with the other men or, depending upon where they crossed over, they could also have been taken out by a cartel." I shrugged. I was willing to entertain ideas they clearly weren't, because if he had wanted me dead I was certain I'd already be.

"Interesting take," one of the men said. "You know him well?"

"My sister knew him," I offered slowly, and two sets of eyebrows raised slowly.

"Sister?"

"Twin."

One of the men blew out a hard breath and they both sat back in their chairs as they pondered that little morsel of information.

"If you'd read the file you'd have known that, because that was right up front," I said quietly. "Everyone came in here convinced it was him, but what if it's her? Has anyone looked into the rumor she's in town?"

That prompted a whole new round of questions and one whipped out a small notepad to scribble down some notes. Then they both rose, tight-lipped. "Gotta go talk to the boss man," one announced and they marched quickly out of the room, leaving me with the space heater and a cold cup of coffee.

I had been working on some spreadsheets earlier in the day, pricing out some automations and making calls to the local auction houses to make sure they kept me top of mind when a big shipment came in, because by late spring I wanted to double the size of the milking herd. It was ambitious—insane, even—but I had some big ideas and Judah had already said he'd front it.

I was going to make this work.

To think I was going to get any more work done was ridiculous and I powered down the desktop, cleaned up the little coffee area and made sure everything was in the trash. There was a cold blast from behind me and I smiled to myself. Judah had probably lost his shit when the men came back to the house without me and I turned slowly, the smile falling off my face as I stared in horror at a woman I knew from photos on the walls in Judah's house. I swallowed hard, feeling the blood drain from my head.

"Cait."

Chapter Twenty-Three

Judah

"What the hell is wrong with you two?" I barked at the agents who'd let themselves back into the house moments earlier. They were deep in quiet, urgent conversation with their superior and one lifted his head to look at me, clearly confused. "Has it not occurred to the two of you that that woman is the reason you're here? You're here to protect her!"

Shoving my feet into my boots and snatching my jacket off the hook in the hallway, I rushed out onto the porch, a strange tingling down my arms and into my fingers. Something felt off and out of the corner of my eye I watched a large SUV turn out of the end of the long driveway and onto the road. I sprinted across the yard to the small office space that sat halfway between the house and the barn, yanking open the door to find the light on, the space heater running, but no Beckett.

For a moment I stood there, letting shock ripple through me. Beckett was gone, and I had *just* missed her.

Leaving things as they were, I slammed the door behind me and tore back toward the house. "She's gone!" I shouted as I opened the door, and I knew I looked completely wild. There was the pounding of feet as people rushed from different areas of the house and into the entryway, pulling on shoes and jackets, and I babbled almost incoherently as I tried to explain what I had seen.

I stood on the porch with hands in my hair as men tore past me, jumping into cars and tearing down the driveway toward the road.

"We're too late," I moaned, the adrenaline wearing off and a terrible weakness starting to steal over my body.

"We're not." Dad stepped out onto the porch behind me, slipping an arm around me to hold me up as my knees began to wobble. "They'll give chase and we're going to circle the wagons. We need to tear apart every possible detail we could have missed—because we know they're missing a lot." He made a face; it was clear he was unimpressed.

"Where are we going to start?" The panic was rising in my throat.

"We're calling your brothers," he announced firmly. "We're going to talk through *everything* and see if we can sort out the pieces together."

He led me back into the house, where Donna was marching across the kitchen and into the dining room, a grim look on her face, a huge bottle of whiskey in her hand.

"Benjamin." Dad already had his phone to his ear. "Need you to come by." A small pause. "Yes, now. I'm calling your brothers next." There was another pause as Ben responded and Dad barked, "Because Bec's gone." Then he hung up, scrolling quickly and tapping his phone to place another call.

"Come along, dear." Donna guided me into the dining room and placed a cup of coffee in front of me. I saw her eyes travel to the bottle of whiskey worriedly. She'd just realized what she'd done, and it made me smile just a little.

"No worries, Donna. Not gonna fall off the wagon now. Plain coffee's fine."

I cut myself off after that single cup of coffee, because I was already jittery, my heart absolutely hammering in my chest. I didn't want to be sitting still. I wanted to be in the truck, tearing down the road after that SUV, convinced nothing good was going to come of this.

"Which motherfucker's gonna die today?" Ben roared as he stomped into the entryway. He didn't bother taking off his boots and Donna didn't chide him for trailing snow through her house as he charged into the dining room like a bull on a rampage. He threw his keys down on the table and dropped heavily into the chair next to me, nostrils flared. He clapped me hard on the back before dropping his elbows onto the table and huffing out a huge puff of breath.

"Cavalry's right behind me," Ben said. "Levi just pulled in and Dan says he's only ten minutes out."

We waited in a heavy silence as Levi let himself into the house. I could hear him stomp the snow out of his boots on the front porch and Ben winced when he realized he was still wearing his.

"Dan can catch up later," Levi announced as he pulled out a chair and sank heavily into it. "Bring us up to speed."

Ben fiddled restlessly with his keys while I told them what had transpired at the house, the morning spent with agents searching the property and then interviewing Bec.

Something was nagging at me, something I couldn't quite identify.

There was a noise from the front of the house as Dan let himself in and he sank into a chair across the table from me, deep shadows still under his eyes.

"You're not sleeping," I said to him, hoping he understood that I was concerned.

"Temporary." He shrugged. "Getting used to an empty house has been rough."

I nodded, because of anyone I understood that all too well.

"Walk me through it," he said and I started at the top, but I paused when I came to the part about the SUV pulling out of the driveway. I reached for Ben's keyring, flipping through them slowly, something starting to crystalize.

"Where's your house key?" I asked him, my voice hoarse and he looked at me like I'd absolutely lost my mind. "The key to my house. I know you had one; each of you do."

"Fuck you talkin' about?" He snatched the ring from my hand, going through them.

"There were seven—now there are only six. You're missing the key to my house."

Ben looked like he was solving a complicated math problem for a moment. "Yeah, come to think of it, I never got it back after she dropped off that Christmas basket at your place." He was looking at me funny.

The color drained from Levi's face and he turned his face toward Ben. "You been keeping any company that might have an issue with our girl?"

Ben looked utterly confused. "Why would Cali have an issue with Bec?" He clapped a hand over his mouth the instant he said it, dropping his eyes to the table and I felt my jaw practically unhinge.

"Cali?" I could barely whisper, because I only knew one of those.

"Benjamin." Dad fixed him with a stern glare. "Do you mean you've been *seeing* your brother's sister-in-law? Explain what this entailed."

Ben hung his head in shame. There was a loud buzzing starting up in my ears when he responded, "You know what it means … the naked kind."

I could hear Donna reciting a rosary in the living room and I could understand the words swirling around me, but I couldn't piece together any of my own.

"You've been seeing Calista." I finally cleared my throat slowly, aware of what that meant Ben was doing with my sister-in-law. "Red underwear?"

Ben nodded slowly, his face turning the same shade as the bra that had been hanging on his kitchen chair.

"That means this has been carrying on for some time."

"Was, anyway." Ben shrugged. "Kinda on and off. Got the impression she wasn't real into me, or keeping me around for much. I was just sorta, uh..." He grinned sheepishly. "Rent-a-fuck, I guess. Worked for both of us for a while."

Donna drifted into the room with a plate of cookies and an odd expression on her face. She slid the plate toward the middle of the table, leaning over me to do so and when she straightened up she laid a hand on my shoulder. She looked like she was chewing on something, thoughts boiling away in her brain and I knew I wasn't going to like what came out of her mouth next.

"That's because she's been in love with Judah since they were kids." She shrugged when she said it and every pair of eyes around the table went wide, including my own.

"That's ridiculous." I scoffed and Levi raised one eyebrow slowly.

"That's actually not ridiculous." He leaned back in his chair, arms crossing over his chest. "Can't say I know what to make of it just yet, but it could be something. And now Ben's missing the key to your house, which was just broken into—manner of speaking. Doesn't explain the alarm, but it's a start." He chewed on his lip for a minute.

"She kept texting and asking to come over to sort through some of Cait's things and I kept putting her off." I hung my head as I tried to think things over. I hadn't heard from her in a while, so I'd put it out of my mind.

There was a weird suspicion forming in the back of my mind and I stood quickly. "I need to go check something."

"Coming with." Levi was on his feet and Ben jumped up as well, Dan's chair tipping over when he stood and started toward the front of the house.

"We'll be here." Donna grabbed both of my shoulders, gesturing with a nod toward Dad. "Anyone needs anything, you let us know and we hear anything, we'll let you know."

I dropped a quick kiss on her cheek, threw a salute at Dad and rushed toward the front of the house, shoving my feet into my boots and hurrying out the door after my brothers, all of them running for their trucks.

Levi was the first one out of the driveway and the rest of us followed after him, somehow all synched up without confirming anything with one another.

We were headed to my house.

No one stood on ceremony. Boots were stomped out on the porch, but the instant I opened the lock everyone rushed in with boots on, expressions of indignation on their faces. They'd taken this thing personally, furious that someone would dare snatch an honorary Benson, because that was what she'd become. In the months Beckett had been with us, she'd become their sister even as I'd tried to deny I wanted the woman for myself. I'd been the last to give in, finally letting her steal my heart, even if they'd let her in months earlier.

"Where are we looking?" Dan asked, and I drew in a slow breath.

"Gonna warn you all that the bedroom hasn't been cleaned. Gonna have to paint and get a new mattress."

Ben's eyebrow lifted. "Something you left out when you were bringing us up to speed?"

"Yeah." I swallowed hard and gestured toward the hallway that led back to the bedrooms. "Follow me."

"Fuck me sideways," Ben breathed as he took in the crude red letters on the wall and Levi paled at the sight of the blood-soaked bed. Dan was the only one who observed it all without a word, then nodded at me.

"What are we looking for?" Levi finally asked, running a hand over his mouth and I rushed over to Cait's closet, throwing open the doors and sifting through the clothing like a mad man.

"Judah." Ben's voice was firm. "Tell us what to do."

"Missing," I muttered, a weird sense of calm stealing over me. "Half of her stuff is missing—her wedding dress is gone."

Dan rushed out of the room and I knew he was calling Dad.

"No, Jude. I know that look." Levi held up one hand. "We're calling Sal and he can rally the scattered troops. You're not going over there by yourself."

"We really think Cali had some part in this?" Ben looked dazed. "We sure she's that kind of crazy?"

I didn't know what to think anymore, but I knew it was time I paid my prior sister-in-law a visit.

Chapter Twenty-Four

Beckett

My head ached, a steady throbbing on the left side that made me pause to evaluate the best I could, aware something felt sticky. I couldn't lift my hands to check, since they were cinched tightly behind me and I tried to stretch out slowly, my feet pressing up against a wall a short distance away. It was too dark to see, but the space felt small and cramped and I tried to calm the wave of panic that tried to steal my breath and send me down the spiral of a panic attack.

Slow, deep breaths calmed the buzzing in my ears and from the rhythmic motion and the chill, I guessed I was in the trunk of a moving vehicle. That made my breath catch again, because the last thing I remembered was a horrible smile on the woman's face before the world went dark.

It must have been hours before I felt the vehicle make a turn and there were voices just outside. I stayed quiet, waiting, having already searched the small space for something I could use to defend myself and coming up empty.

There was a sudden, sharp blast of light and cold air, and arms reached in to haul me out.

"Where are we?" My knees were weak and I stumbled as I tried to stand up, my balance off-kilter with my hands tied behind my back.

"That's not something you need to worry about." The voice was familiar and I squinted, confused when Beth stepped up alongside Cait. "Make it quick." She gestured toward an outhouse and I squinted, realizing we were at some sort of roadside rest stop.

Cait snipped the band holding my wrists together and gestured toward the small stall. "I'd suggest you move quickly."

Beth walked me to the stall and waited outside while I did my business. There was no running water and the wipes were empty, something that made me grimace before I stepped back outside.

I was frog marched back to the parking lot where a car and an SUV sat side by side. Cait was closing the trunk on the car and I noticed that it had no license plates, something that made me tilt my head as I thought. It was a movement Beth caught immediately and she chuckled. "If you think they're going to find you, you're dead wrong."

It was the dead part that worried me, because I'd never known my sister to make idle threats.

She shoved me into the back seat of the SUV and Cait climbed into the front passenger seat, clipping her belt as my sister took the driver's seat and reversed the vehicle.

"Finally," Cait breathed, sliding a hand over her head and I watched in horror as she pitched a handful of golden-red hair in my direction. The long wig landed next to me with a plop and I sat staring at the back of her head and the dark brown hair the wig had been covering.

"You're not Cait," I croaked, and it was my sister who laughed. The other woman didn't answer me, content to lean back in her seat and watch the world go by as we tore down the highway. It was a long time before she turned to look at me over her shoulder, the same small, sinister smile in place.

"You're right, I'm not. But just like her, you stole what was mine."

What the hell was she talking about?

I squinted at her in confusion and my sister shook her head. "You're going to have to spell it out, Calista. To this day she still thinks she lost her family because Jason was obsessed with her." She made a snorting, smirking sound and I felt all the blood drain from my head.

"What are you talking about?" My voice was weak. "He staked out the property. He watched us for months. He admitted to it on the stand."

“Oh, Beckett.” She clicked her tongue a few times. “You really just never could figure things out for yourself.”

I was still trying to figure out how these two had linked up and why.

“I thought you were Cait,” I said to the other woman, who audibly smirked but she didn’t turn to look at me.

“I’m not her twin—” she hooked a thumb toward my sister, “but I’ve been known to pass for her. Nothing like you two, though—it’s almost uncanny.”

I sat back, waiting for one of them to offer more information, but they were tight-lipped.

“We’re going to Texas,” I finally said as I watched the road signs whizz past and the woman in the passenger seat nodded.

“Won’t be the last thing to shock you.” She threw a grin over her shoulder, something that made me uncomfortable when my sister laughed.

“Why?” My voice cracked on the word.

“Because we both know what it was like to have to wait for all those years...” the woman mused and my sister barked a short, sharp “Calista!” like that was already too much, but the other woman didn’t take the hint.

“My sister stole him when we were kids.” She turned in her seat and sat watching my face. “I waited. Bided my time. Tried out one of the brothers to see if the Bensons are all they were cracked up to be.” She held up one hand and grinned at Beth. “Spoiler alert: they are.”

There must have been an expression of distaste on my face, because I could feel my nose wrinkling up. "Shame on you. Ben's already screwed up; you didn't have to stir the pot."

She shook her head at me, but she didn't argue.

A sick feeling churned in my stomach, because whatever awaited me at the end of this trip, I knew it wasn't good. I also knew what it would do to Judah to realize I was gone, to think that I'd left or had been taken and it made me sick to realize that Calista hadn't even been on anyone's radar. There were no clues for anyone to even begin looking for me.

I leaned my head against the window and tried to calm the nausea spreading up my trachea. There were so many unanswered questions I didn't have the energy to ask, and for a moment I let myself sink into despair.

Chapter Twenty-Five

Judah

"This part has nothing to do with the FBI." I ground out the words furiously as Sal tried to be the voice of reason.

"Whether or not you want them on this, they're involved now and they're not going to quit. They went on some wild goose chase all the way into Wisconsin today, chasing down an SUV that matched the description you gave. Scared the shit out of a family of four."

I shook my head. "Someone sent us the flunkies."

"Gonna need a search warrant for your sister-in-law's place." He sighed, running a hand over his face. "See if we can gather any clues."

"Ben has a key; he's there now."

"He has a key..." Sal repeated the words slowly before the penny dropped, disbelief flitting across his face. "The only time

I'd have to say it's been beneficial that boy can't keep it in his pants."

"Dan's with him, to see if he can get into her computer."

Sal shook his head at me slowly. "Unorthodox, Benson. It doesn't look good."

"Not exactly illegal," I argued. "And you know as well as I do that this means she's in danger, Sal. If her sister's in on this..." I felt a cold chill run through me. "She wants to make her pay for some perceived wrong and I don't know what Calista's issue is, but that's probably a double helping of crazy. We'd have never seen that coming."

I couldn't sit still after my talk with Sal and I knew he'd have his hands full making calls once I left, so I hurried back to Beckett's little office and started digging through files. There had to be something to work with, and it hit me like a bolt of lightning that she'd mentioned a cattle shipment to an address in Texas.

"Find anything?" Levi looked as wrecked as I felt when he wrenched open the door and stomped into the small space, frustration radiating off of him. I knew he had a lot going on with his custom furniture and restoration business, but he would never complain about the time this was stealing from him.

"Almost." I was sifting through her notes, flipping through pages of a notebook, checking her contacts on the desktop and the small sticky notes she left everywhere. She had some kind of organizational system, I just didn't know what it was. "If her sister was involved, I think she's being taken to Texas and I know there's an address in here somewhere." My fingers scrambled across the stack of invoices and papers in her Incoming tray, flipping through them faster than my brain could register the information.

"Here." I snatched a paper from the stack, a piece of notebook paper with an address hastily written, one I plugged into a search engine to bring up photos. "It's a ranch in central Texas—looks run down from the photos, but I think this is where our cattle were shipped. Willing to bet just about anything..." I let the words trail off as I pulled up another window to access property records, pausing as I took in the date it had last been sold.

Levi was watching me closely and he saw it when my jaw dropped. "What is it, Jude?"

"Can't be right." I shook my head, refreshing the page, but the information remained the same. "Says the land was purchased almost thirteen years ago by Cade and Beckett Langston."

Levi's right eyebrow crawled up slowly. "That makes no sense."

I sucked in a sharp breath. "Hope you're up for a road trip."

Let me tell you what the drive from Minnesota to Texas is not: short. The two of us took turns behind the wheel, driving as fast as we dared. No luggage, no food—not so much as a change of clothes. We simply jumped into Levi's truck and went tearing down the driveway and out onto the highway.

The trip gave us plenty of time to talk, but neither of us seemed to have many words. I knew he was as concerned as I was, having promised we would keep her safe and we'd done anything but.

"Ben and Calista." He shook his head slowly as we left Nebraska, crossing into Kansas. It was late and we were both tired, enormous cups of coffee shoved into the console from our last fuel stop. I was still trying to wrap my head around it, too. It went some way to explain why Ben had been so protective of the identity of the woman he'd been sleeping with: He knew I wouldn't approve.

It was another hour before I spoke. "What if she can't ever let go of him?"

Levi could read my mind. "Bec wouldn't do that to you. She wouldn't feed you a whole pack of lies like that. She wouldn't steal from us, either." He shook his head resolutely. "No, whatever this is, I think she was blindsided and I don't think she has any more answers than we do."

I crossed my arms over my chest, watching the flat countryside of Kansas blur past as Levi pushed the truck harder than any patrolling officer would appreciate. I couldn't help but worry we were too far behind, having found what we needed too late, and I certainly didn't trust the ragtag band of agents to handle things.

"Don't borrow trouble," Levi said gently, reaching across the space to squeeze my left shoulder. "We'll get there in time."

"We have no idea what we're walking into. We don't know why they're taking her there."

"Yeah, we do." Levi's lips flattened out. "They're going to hurt her, Jude—maybe worse, after they get whatever it is they want from her."

"Worse?" My brain wasn't working.

"Yeah." He tapped the fingers of one hand on the wheel. "Have some cartel worries, based upon proximity."

"Thanks." I reached over to punch his shoulder. "Makes me feel so much better."

"Nah, we're reasonably prepared," he said, something fairly cryptic, and my thoughts drifted to the huge toolbox built into the back bed of his truck.

"Hope you've got a shovel," I said, "because we might need to dispose of a few bodies."

"No shovels—got plenty of firepower, though. Counting on the shovels being on-site."

The last thing we needed was to get pulled over, and Levi shot me a tight smile like he knew what I was thinking. "No worryin' yourself over there—Constitutional carry all the way there."

"Not for what you're packing."

He waved a hand dismissively. "Be fine."

I knew a few things about my older brother, and one thing was that he was a weapons expert. This man did not fuck around and find out, but he took care of those who did. He was the perfect person for this trip.

"Never did tell me what you did in the service," I said casually, aware that he was avoiding my fixed gaze.

"Reason for that." He was utterly calm. "Information most people can't handle."

"I mean, killing people for a living. That much is obvious. Otherwise, you'd share stories about your days in the service and beyond."

"No idea, bro. You have no idea and you don't want to." He almost sounded remorseful.

"That's why you let her go." It had just occurred to me. "You thought you were damaged goods, so you let the love of your life walk away without a fight. Levi, holy shit ... how have you lived with that all these years?"

"She wanted out." His voice was tight. "She wanted to chase her dreams and so I let her. It just turned out I wasn't in them."

I had never seen my brother cry. I had never seen him rage or break shit when his wife left. Instead, I'd watched him buckle down, devoting his life to his daughter, straight as an arrow.

"You miss her?" I couldn't help but ask him, even though it had been decades.

"Every fucking day." The words were vehement.

"Really, still?"

"Always."

I stopped talking for a while; this was already a lot of words for us. But I remembered the deep depression he'd dragged himself out of when he'd returned from the service to find his young wife had left him, leaving him to raise their infant daughter. I had been righteously indignant for him, furious with her, ready to hate her as soon as he gave me the go-ahead, but he never did. He had remained steadfastly in love with that woman, going back as far as I could remember, even if I hated her on his behalf.

"Yeah, well ... we gotta fix that as soon as we get this sorted out." I meant it, even if it was kind of a ridiculous thing to say. I had no idea where he stood with his ex, all these years later. I just knew that I had once liked her for him—before her family got in the way.

"You still love her." I couldn't help it. I could see the sadness in his expression even if I could only see one side of his face.

"Never stopped, Jude. She was the one, even though I lost her."

"Fuck." I slapped the door, angry for him, because Levi was the most loyal person I knew. He deserved happiness. "Don't know how, but we're gonna fix it."

He gave me a small smile and when he said "You first, brother," it made something ache inside my torso. He deserved a woman who loved him without question, and for him I'd always thought that would be Hannah; that she'd find her way back and fix what she'd broken. But here we were, decades later, and she still lived halfway across the country.

"Got a real bad feeling about this," I said quietly. "I haven't figured out why Bec was a target."

"Might not be much of a reason—" he took a chug from his huge coffee cup, "least not one based in reality. But we don't have to know the answer now, we just need to get to her and make sure she's safe."

"And eliminate the threat," I said through pursed lips. "No more of this bullshit. I'm tired of living with this hanging over our heads."

We fell silent again, the sun finally beginning to peek over the horizon, and Levi stopped again for fuel. I resupplied the coffee and bought some sandwiches, then I took over driving. We were mere hours away, having pushed hard the entire trip, and my heart started hammering as I took the last turn that led up a long, winding drive toward the property in question. It was set back so far from the road that I couldn't see any buildings, squatty trees lining the drive and obscuring most of the view, and Levi placed a hand on my forearm. "Don't like it; we can't see what's coming. Find a spot to pull over and park out of sight. We're going the rest of this on foot."

I pulled the truck into a stand of trees and over the course of the next five minutes, I watched my brother transform into someone else entirely. He slipped me a handgun but the case he pulled out of the toolbox was without a doubt not something that qualified for concealed carry or just about anything else. It was a specialty piece, with a complicated scope, and I watched him begin some kind of an emotional—and maybe even human—shutdown process as he checked it over.

The two of us moved almost silently through the trees, keeping the driveway in our peripheral vision to the right, and finally the trees opened into a large clearing, several large outbuildings and a modest house sitting atop a slight hill.

"House is the most secure space and allows for the best vantage point of the property." Levi was so quiet, I almost didn't hear him. "Likelihood is that they're keeping her in there."

I folded over my knees, panic rising, my breaths erratic and uneven, pinpoints of light starting to dance in my vision.

"Hey." Levi put one hand on the side of my neck and I realized he was taking my heart rate. "Gonna need you to take some deep breaths and talk yourself off that ledge. Won't do her any good if I have to carry you out of here first."

I wasn't cut out for this and I knew it, whereas Levi was absolutely in the zone. He'd crouched down and had a small pair of binoculars out, a slow smile stretching over his face. "Cavalry's already here, Jude. We're just the auxiliary team. They must have sent the big boys this time." He held up one hand in a gesture and seemed satisfied that communication had been established, whereas I had no idea what he was looking at. I hadn't seen so much as the reflection of the sun off a pair of glasses.

"What are we waiting for; you talking to ghosts?" I hissed, well aware there was a reason I wasn't fit to be the leader of anything. I had the patience of a hungry bear coming out of hibernation.

"We're waiting for their signal, because we're not in charge here. And if we're told to stand down, that's what we'll do. I don't need to be digging any bullets out of you." He removed the binoculars for a split second, just long enough to give me a piercing look.

I'd been known to charge into situations in the past, with little heed for instructions or safety.

"So ... what, we just sit here and wait?" I knew I sounded like a toddler throwing a tantrum, but I was a man of action. I wanted to rush the house, break down the door, and carry Bec out over my shoulder.

"Fools rush in," he reminded me. "Tactical operations are all about recon. Running into unknown potential danger is a great way to die young, and I'm pretty sure all of these guys would like to go home at the end of this—including you. Getting yourself injured or killed doesn't help her, Jude."

"Fucking hate this." I sank into a squat next to him, furiously chewing on my lip. I could already taste blood.

The minutes dragged by and Levi kept the binoculars pressed tight to his face, his head turned just enough that I knew he was watching the treeline on the other side of the deep yard. It made me wonder how quickly Sal had placed the call and whether this was really a new team. I hoped so, because we needed some competent guys on this side of things.

Guys with guns and cracking aim, not handfuls of Donna's cookies.

Levi held up a hand, keeping it close to his body so as not to attract attention, making a complicated set of small motions.

"You jabbering in Special Forces?" I teased, because none of us would ever know what he'd done during his first stint in the Army but I was reasonably certain he'd taken private security contracts over the years, because my niece Jessa had been in school for what seemed like decades and had no student debt.

"Getting by." He smiled a little, the binoculars still sealed to his face, and I took my first deep breath. He was the right man for the job, far better suited to the situation than myself.

"What's the plan?" I asked irritably, eager to tear into someone.

"Wait until nightfall, when we can send up a drone."

"Fuck me. We can't wait here all day. What if we're too late?"

"We need to know how many people are in that house, Judah. We need to know where they are so that we're not taken by surprise."

"Heat signatures?" I asked and he gave me a slow nod. It made me sigh in frustration and I dropped slowly into a seated position.

"Thought it'd be warmer," I groused, pulling my jacket a little tighter and Levi chuckled.

"Texas winters can be almost as brutally unpredictable as Minnesota," he whispered and I shot back, "It's bullshit." My blood sugar was already starting to drop; it had been hours since we'd eaten sandwiches while driving.

With a slow, spare movement, Levi reached into some kind of secret pocket and produced a rectangular packet, handing it over to me.

"This better not be some thirty-year-old MRE," I whispered, and he snorted.

"You're welcome."

It was dry and dusty and tasted like mildewed peanut butter, but I ate it, making sure Levi saw my disgusted expression as I did.

"Perspective, Jude," was all he said quietly. "It's uncomfortable, but this is what most of it is: waiting. Assessing. Measuring and identifying the moment. I can almost guarantee you're more comfortable than she is right now."

That sobered me real fast and when the front door to the house flew open, Levi's hand twisted into the back of my jacket to keep me from shooting to my feet. "Down, boy." His voice was still quiet and I watched as Beckett was shoved out of the house, tripping on the rough treads of the porch, a blindfold over her eyes, her balance compromised by the fact her hands were zip tied behind her back.

"Think it's just the two women," Levi said quietly, and he held up a hand very slowly, signalling something.

"Bitch," I muttered bitterly. It was applicable to either of the women holding Beckett, but my vitriol was focused on the one I knew: Calista, marching Beckett toward the yard while pressing something into her back that I presumed was a small handgun or a knife.

Beckett's sister stomped out of the house with a spindly wooden chair, slamming it down in the middle of the yard and Calista produced more zip ties from a pocket, directing Beckett to sit before she secured her ankles to the chair legs.

"The fuck are they doing?" I fumed, rage crawling all hot and prickly over my skin, like a swarm of fire ants.

"Not sure yet," Levi muttered. "Don't like it."

There was a low hum in the distance and I sucked in a breath. "Get down, Levi—truck coming our way."

Chapter Twenty-Six

Beckett

I wasn't sure how long we'd been at the house, my sense of time beginning to warp with the loss of sight and sensation in my limbs. I was severely dehydrated, my thoughts fuzzy, my stomach threatening to start digesting some of my internal organs if I didn't eat something soon.

"Told you we had another surprise." Calista chuckled as the ties around my ankles went so tight, they bit into my legs.

In the distance I could hear a big engine and tires eating up a dirt road, the sound drawing closer though the blindfold effectively blocked out even a hazily-filtered glimpse.

"What's in this for you?" I finally asked, a sharp slap stinging my cheek, the blow hard enough to force my head to the side.

"I'm helping to take out the trash." Her voice traveled toward me from a distance and I knew then she hadn't been the one to slap me. "You have a job to do to set things right and now that I've helped deliver you, my part of the bargain is up. I get paid and get to go home to my man."

"Benjamin?" I laughed with more bravado than I felt. "Haven't you noticed he chews up women and spits them out? He'll never keep you around."

"He was a nice distraction." She sounded a little dreamy. "But you know better than that."

Judah, then.

"He won't touch you with a ten-foot pole." I couldn't help but scoff when I said it. "He wants nothing to do with you."

There was a clucking noise from my sister and a truck pulled into the yard, stopping some distance away before the motor was cut.

"Took you long enough." My sister's voice was teasing and playful, something that made goosebumps stand up along my arms.

The sound of heavy boots thudding on dirt were magnified by the fact I couldn't see the person approaching me and a rough palm rested against the side of my face. The person didn't say a word, squatting down in front of me, close enough that I could feel body heat, and I choked on a swallow when I drew my first lungful of a smell that had been imprinted on me years earlier.

The blindfold was yanked off in a single, sharp motion, some of my hair ripping out with it and I sat blinking furiously, my vision blurry as I took in the broad man squatting before me. My voice cracked when I let the name drop from my lips, terrified and hurt and confused all at once.

The anger, I knew, would come later.

"Cade."

"Princess." His smile was the slow, easy one I remembered, fine lines around his eyes and mouth and across his forehead that hadn't been there before.

"I don't understand." I shook my head, aware of the triumphant smile on my sister's face as I stared at Cade's handsome features. "You're dead."

"Only to some folks." He chuckled, leaning in to kiss my cheek, and a cold lightning bolt of horror stabbed my stomach, spreading down my legs and into my toes in sharp electrical shocks. "But you were supposed to be. Funny how that worked out for both of us." He rocked back then, his elbows braced on his knees as he traded a look with my sister.

"Care to explain yourself?" A voice I knew and loved rang out from the treeline and I watched as Judah charged across the yard, shouting. "Don't much appreciate you gettin' all familiar with my wife, asshole."

I wasn't sure whether the sensation I felt inside was one of breaking or melting, something happening to my heart when he used the word of possession.

"Really, now?" Cade smiled again, something cold and flat, and I watched Calista's face go completely white as Judah barreled down on us like an angry bull ready to gore someone. "I suppose the fact I had a death certificate helped maintain some mystery, though you can imagine that was with some difficulty when we consider there were no remains." He picked up his hat, running fingers through the dark waves now shot with silver before resettling it into place.

"Like to know just how it is you two own this place when you died just days after the closing." Judah was towering over Cade, fury radiating from him as he tried to step between Cade and me, shielding me.

"Almost worked it all out." Cade pushed easily to his feet and held out a hand to Beth. I felt something click into place in my brain when their fingers linked, the fog of a horrible suspicion finally sharpening into something clear. "That fool Jason went and fell in love with our Beckett and spared her. Completely fucked the plan, and I had to go into hiding." He shrugged. "*I* was supposed to be the survivor. The beneficiary." His teeth gleamed when he smiled and I let my head tip forward, bile churning in my gut. There was a strange glint in his eye when he said "Beth and I purchased this property once we were able to confirm a substantial inheritance was left to each daughter. Unfortunately, my girl suffered a crisis of conscience at a very inopportune time and you had her committed."

I turned my head, sure I was going to be sick, and Judah reached a hand behind himself to cup my face in a curled palm.

"I was named the executor of her trust when she was committed," I said hoarsely, and Cade nodded slowly.

"Hell of a complication that you weren't dead, and committing Beth really threw a wrench in our plans. Made for some unnecessary financial struggles and I've had to jump through some hoops." He gestured around us. "Beth couldn't exactly maintain your identity with both of you still running around. Been trying to find you ever since she was released; had some fixing to do, especially once we found out my life insurance policy had been paid out to my wife." He smiled down at my sister and she leaned into his side. Almost a mirror image of me, it was like looking at a photo of Cade and myself, only to realize how one evil soul had attracted another. By now they'd been together longer than Cade and I had ever been.

"The cows," I stuttered, weirdly desperate to fit the last missing piece into the puzzle. "What became of the cows?"

"Please." Calista swiped a hand furiously through the air—I had forgotten she was standing nearby. "I would have taken the whole damn herd if you had given me a few more days."

Judah and I were the only ones facing the tree line and I tried to keep a straight face as Levi crept closer, a vicious weapon pressed into his shoulder, his eye dropped to a site as he moved closer and closer to Cade.

"Why?" I croaked, forcing myself to look at Calista, keeping my eyes trained on her so as not to attract any attention to Levi.

"You never wanted me, Judah." Her pretty face took on an ugly sneer. "I was the faithful one. I didn't cheat on you every time I went on those stupid chartered flights. Those boys weren't even yours."

I felt the shock run through Judah's body and I turned my head to kiss his palm, his hand beginning to tremble.

"Why?" It was Judah's turn, a pain in his voice like I'd never heard.

"She wanted more and you wouldn't give it to her." She shrugged. "The irony is that her death made you obscenely wealthy. I just took a little of what was yours in order to get by. I was going to start over with that money, until a better offer came along."

I had some idea of what that better offer was, but the couple standing in front of us couldn't be trusted and I wasn't sure Calista knew that.

Cade grunted in surprise as Levi pressed the rifle into his back. "You try anything funny and this bullet's exit point is through your heart."

The woods exploded with sound and motion and I watched in horrified slow motion as Cade's hand darted toward the waistband of his pants and a shot rang out. He crumpled to the ground and when I registered Levi's astonished expression, I saw the small sidearm in Judah's hand. Beth froze, her hands slowly going into the air and Calista screamed, throwing herself down on the ground.

My brain filtered out the sound and I watched a silent movie in horror as the property was swarmed by men in tactical gear, guns raised, several trucks tearing into the yard as someone dropped to his knees to take Cade's pulse, while two others kept guns trained on Beth and Calista, shouting directions at them that my brain couldn't unscramble.

"You fucking idiot." They were the first words to filter back into my ears and Levi threw his arms around Judah, squeezing him so tight I didn't know how Judah could breathe. There was a panicked expression on Levi's face, his eyes suspiciously shiny, and when he released him both men turned to me, Levi dropping down onto one knee to pull a knife from his boot. He slid the flat of the blade carefully beneath the tie on each leg. I winced against the additional pressure of the blade beneath the tight ties and with a quick flick of the wrist, he snapped each band before moving around to free my hands.

"They were gonna hurt you, Bec." Judah's voice shook. "I couldn't let it happen. Wasn't gonna let him take you from me." He dropped to his knees in front of me and took my face in both of his big hands, covering my face with hard kisses, his eyes every bit as shiny as Levi's had been.

"I don't understand." My head shook back and forth, my eyes trained on Cade's still body. "He did this. My husband destroyed our livelihood. Our lives. Our family." My voice shook. "Why?"

"Knowing the answers won't make it hurt less, baby. He let you live with the belief he was dead for almost thirteen years—that's fucked up." Judah scooped me up in his arms and Levi sighed heavily.

"Got some questions to answer or a body to bury—maybe both. Won't be leaving anytime soon."

"He was already legally dead." Judah shrugged, but he looked haggard. "Maybe the law will see the sense in keeping it that way. Hell of a lot less paperwork."

Judah carried me to one of the trucks parked in the yard and wrenched open the back, pulling out a medical kit to see to the cuts and bruises on my wrists and face. He cleaned me gently, applying ointments and bandages while men swirled around us in a sea of chaos and cursing. Then he twisted open a huge water bottle and I drank like a camel, hardly stopping for air.

We answered questions for hours and a medical examiner zipped Cade into a body bag. I was still in shock, staring at the place where he'd crumpled to the ground, the dirt where he'd fallen boasting an ugly black splatter.

It was late that night before we were finally granted clearance to leave, having answered an endless barrage of questions from officers and agents, and I watched as more police vehicles pulled into the yard and Calista and Beth were tucked into the back of separate cars and driven away. It was too much all at once and, weak with hunger, I let Judah hold me up. By then he was tense again, tight-lipped and worried, and when someone suggested I should be taken to the hospital for an exam and an IV, Judah snarled at him like a rabid dog. "I've got her. She's not leaving my sight."

I had been passed from one person to another over the course of the afternoon, Judah always at my side. The story was told and retold countless times, reports taken, heads nodding and lips drawn in tight, flat lines. There was nothing pretty about this story, something that opened up an old wound for both myself and for those who remembered what had happened that night in May, all those years ago.

Levi and Judah pulled up the center console in the front seat and tucked me between them as Levi drove, and Judah pulled me into his side, his arm around me, his lips in my hair.

"Stopping in the next big town," Levi said, his voice worn and scratchy. "Think we could all do with a good night's sleep."

"Need to call home and let everyone know," Judah said quietly and Levi chuckled.

"They know we've got Bec. I told Dad about your boneheaded move and he's promised to give you a proper beating once we get home."

"It's Donna I'd be worried about," I teased softly and there was gentle laughter from both men.

Levi pulled the truck into the parking lot of a roadside motel, the *M* burned out on the sign. I didn't care. I hadn't slept much in the past few days and I knew Levi and Judah had driven straight through to find me.

"Get some rest." Levi tossed Judah a key after checking in. "We'll stop at a Walmart or something in the morning and buy a change of clothes so I don't have to smell myself the rest of the way home." He grimaced and I threw myself across the space to hug him.

"Thank you, Levi. I don't ... I just ..."

"Beckett." His eyes were full of kindness and understanding when he held me at an arm's length before drawing me back in to wrap me in a full hug. "It's what we do for any member of our family, and this one's chosen you for himself." He gestured toward his brother. "You're a Benson now, sweetheart."

Judah grumbled something unintelligible behind me and I chuckled as Levi released me, turning to find him giving his brother a heated look.

"Too tired for a shower," Judah mumbled, the lock sticking a little and he gave the doorknob a wiggle, leaning his shoulder into the door to unseal it, and it gave with a pop. "Just want to hold my girl and go to sleep."

I had to agree that sounded like the only thing I was capable of at this point, and I turned on the light only long enough to take off my shoes and socks, draping my coat over the back of the chair while Judah stripped off his coat, kicked off his boots and folded back the bedspread. We both crawled in and I flicked off the bedside lamp before curling into him, our legs scissored together, hinged at the knees, our arms wrapped tightly around one another. I felt him draw an enormous breath and knew he was thinking of how differently things might have gone, a thought that was terrifying in its depth of emotion and fear.

"I love you, Judah." I whispered it against his chest. "I've been so afraid to say it."

"Love you back, Tex." He hummed happily, his arms tightening around me as he pressed a ferocious kiss to the top of my head. "Keepin' you forever, baby. Suppose you guessed that."

There were things to process, I knew, something that filled me with dread. I would never understand what had broken in

Cade's brain; what made it okay to have our loved ones murdered.

"Think we should have you talk with Ash," Judah murmured into my hair. "This is gonna knock you sideways, baby. She can refer us to someone, another trauma therapist she trusts."

I hummed in agreement, my throat raw with tears I couldn't shed. He twisted my body to spoon me from behind, tucking his knees into the backs of mine, his arms wrapped tightly around me. With that I let my eyes drift shut, our breaths already growing deeper as both of us fell into an exhausted sleep.

Chapter Twenty-Seven

Judah

We took a slower pace driving home, but I knew Levi was eager to get back to work and honestly, I was ready for life to settle into a more comfortable, predictable rhythm. I was fairly certain the investigation wouldn't be marked complete for a long time to come and I anticipated it causing some difficulties, but knowing Beckett was safe was enough to make that worth it.

It was the middle of the night when we pulled into the yard, the barn light filtering weakly across the cold, open space and Beckett sighed. "I'm ready for this snow to melt."

"You'll like our Minnesota springs," Levi said amiably, running a hand over his tired eyes. "Just gonna be a while before it gets here."

“I’m thankful I get to see one,” she said softly, leaning over to kiss his cheek before sliding back and pressing her face into my neck. Her voice was muffled when she said “Plan on seeing a lot more of them, thanks to the two of you.”

Levi shrugged easily. “Family,” was all he said, giving me a look I could well interpret. “Now you two get on inside and let Donna fuss over you. Get some rest. Big changes coming here and now you can focus on building this thing up for the two of you—maybe some talks with Ash.” He looked worried, something that passed between the two of us that Beckett caught as she leaned back into his arm.

"I'm never going to have the answers, Levi. Beth wanted to ruin my life and she almost succeeded. I'm not letting her steal the rest of my joy."

"Sick." He swallowed hard. "Won't ever understand how a woman could steal her sister's husband or convince him to do away with his family."

"I'll never know if that's what she did." She shrugged slowly, straightening once more and linking the fingers of her right hand through the fingers of my left. "But I've mourned for almost thirteen years now. My mom's not coming back." She choked for a moment, drawing in a deep breath. "Rebecca's not coming back. My only way is forward."

Levi nodded slowly. "The only way," he agreed quietly. "No other options."

The two of us picked our way across the icy patches of the yard with care. Winter was hanging on hard, a brutal blast of wind nearly knocking us off our feet.

The front door flew open as we climbed the porch steps and Donna snatched Beckett away from me, pulling her into such a tight hug that she squeaked. Dad just shook his head at me before doing the same, hugging me so hard that I thought he'd snap my ribs and I could feel his chest rising and falling with deep inhalations. "Foolish boy," he said softly. "No question how you feel about her, willing to put your life on the line like that."

The two of us crawled into the huge cast iron tub in the bathroom and fell asleep together in the warm water, Beckett's body cradled by mine. For the first time in months I felt a sense of relief, the lifting of an unnamed fear, and when the water grew cool and it woke me, I helped her from the bath and wrapped her in a fluffy robe before carrying her off to bed.

Truthfully, I couldn't wait to get my girl alone again, to kiss and worship every inch of her glorious body, but that would not be happening in my father's house. So I settled for pulling her naked body against mine, the skin-to-skin contact soothing something inside of me as we drifted off to sleep beneath the heavy down duvet.

Sal was out to see us the next morning, with an awful lot of questions, and he warned us to expect a visit from a few of the agents who'd decimated Donna's cookie stash the last time we'd seen them. Jason hadn't yet been located and it turned out interagency communication wasn't all that great, so there were some holes to fill for another supervisor's report.

That morning was the first time in a very long time I felt like the weight of worry, grief and anger had been fully lifted from my shoulders. I couldn't stop smiling, the realization that this true second chance was a gift I wasn't about to squander.

Beckett started implementing things that very morning. She was on the phone, scribbling frantically, negotiating and arguing, and I took myself out to the barn to help the hands with the morning milking. I had something to propose, keeping the two of them on with an increase in pay to manage the morning shift and hiring another set of workers for the evening milking. Beckett's plan to double the herd would come into play soon enough, once we had accommodations for all those cattle.

Over the following weeks, Minnesota began to thaw. Neighbors started to drop by, nosily enquiring about next steps, as news was beginning to spread around town that there were some big changes taking place at the Benson farm. I was reasonably certain I could thank Roy for spreading the word. The man had never met a piece of gossip he didn't take to.

Dan had taken it upon himself to have my house cleaned by a company he used on smaller residential jobs. We returned home to find the bedroom repainted and completely rearranged. The furniture had been removed, replaced with new pieces, something I understood he'd done to give us a fresh start. It was a relief to find that it didn't bother me, and I watched Beckett take it in with a sweet smile.

It was nearly June by the time the first stage of Beckett's plans took effect and Dad had been outside every day to supervise the goings-on, astonished by the equipment she'd had brought in and she patiently answered his questions.

We had contracted Ben to install a number of items on the farm, to perform some necessary repairs, and to keep an eye on him in general, something I didn't think he'd figured out just yet. Most mornings he showed up wretchedly hung over, stumbling into the house for a plate of something to settle his stomach and a giant vat of coffee.

Most days Beckett found her way to him eventually and I watched from a distance as she stood talking to him, probably helping him to unwind the knots in his spirit that kept him caught up in such a ridiculous cycle. It was enough to make me text our sister with some regularity, expressing my concern over the fact Ben was spiraling hard.

"Thought he was going to stop drinking," I remarked to Dad quietly one day as the two of us sat on the front porch. Ben was across the yard, his body halfway under a tractor while Beckett squatted down next to him, occasionally reaching into a red steel toolbox to hand him another wrench.

"Think the Calista thing threw him for a bigger loop than any of us expected," Dad remarked easily, but I could tell he was worried.

Calista was spending a nice, long vacation in a federal facility, along with Beth. She had been charged with a laundry list of things, kidnapping being only one of them, and Beth's charges guaranteed she would no longer be a menace to anyone but her cellmate.

Charges against me hadn't been pursued, but questions had been complicated, extensive, exhausting, and there were nights I saw it happen all over again behind closed eyelids.

Beckett had listed the property she didn't know she owned, and there had already been two viable offers. She was weighing each of them carefully, negotiating, as she did so well. I worried sometimes it meant she was keeping herself too busy to process the wave of grief I knew threatened to swallow her up. I felt her struggling with it sometimes at night, doing her best not to give in and crumple the way I had.

For a time I had seriously considered selling my home—maybe purchasing a lot on the farm from Dad, in order to put up a new house. But in the end it was Bec who talked me out of it. She wanted to stay in the house that contained some bitter memories, in order to replace them with new ones.

There were still a lot of unanswered questions when it came to Beckett's sister, but Levi's cartel fears hadn't been unfounded. One of the agents assigned to the case eventually uncovered a deal brokered by Cade, to have both Beckett and Calista delivered to a team in Laredo once Beckett had done her part to release any remaining funds to Beth. While her sister had been bold enough to purchase property masquerading as her sister, she hadn't managed to convince anyone she was the executor of the estate.

I was struggling with my own questions, trying to sort out how long Cait had been unfaithful to me and how it was that she'd managed to conceive not one, but two children who weren't my own. I sat for long hours staring at their photos, the little boys I'd loved so dearly that it made my heart bleed to see their faces even now. It was true they looked a great deal like Cait, but with no way to run genetic testing now, I would never know the truth.

I had been so incredibly blind.

It was my suggestion to Sebbe that we increase our visits, and I met with him routinely every Tuesday and Thursday for an hour at a time to unwind all the shit stored up in my head. I refused to take it with me going forward, having realized this was a true second chance at life and the only one I would get with a woman I didn't deserve but loved like hell.

Truthfully, I was a little worried about how Beckett was handling things. She was going on with everyday life like nothing had happened, like she had compartmentalized that part so she didn't have to deal with it. Every time I tried to talk to her about it, she shut me down with a shake of her head and said she didn't want her past tainting our future.

It seemed new details were still coming out every few days about the complicated mess we'd found ourselves in. We'd largely buried the hatchet with the Avila family, who were more than happy to sell their land to us when Beckett approached them about expansion, something she didn't tell me about, using money from the sale of the ranch to nearly double our acreage. It had knocked me on my ass, to realize my fears were unfounded; that she was all in.

Hugo Avila apologized to her for "the state we left your house in," and sent her home with two young steers to make up for the calf they'd butchered on her front lawn, having initially hoped that violence and blood would encourage the family to sell.

It turned out that Calista had been the one to lead Beth and Cade right to us, in a weird twist of fate, when she contacted the Lang Haul Cattle Service, with an office in Cedar Rapids, Iowa, with no idea that Cade Langmore was Beckett's not-at-all-dead husband and the man had a few bones to pick. He'd been looking for Beckett, high and low, for years.

Beth's arrival in town meant she took some time to familiarize herself with our farm and Beckett's little cabin, thanks to her new tour guide, Calista, and from what we could put together, it had been the two of them terrorizing Beckett.

Cade had remained in Texas, running his multi-state hauling service, waiting for the women to bring his erstwhile wife to him.

Not only was I thankful Levi and myself had acted quickly, but that Sal had gotten on the phone and demanded the FBI send a skilled team to the address I'd left out in the open, on Beckett's desk in her office. If he hadn't done that, chances were good things might have gone a different way that day.

Ben was completing a test run on an automated feeding system for the calf pens when I walked into one of the new livestock barns, looking for Bec one bright, sunshiny day. He had been unusually quiet lately, withdrawn, not the ridiculous, gregarious brother who sent stupid shit to our family group text. In fact, he hadn't been texting at all for the past month or so.

"Almost lunchtime," I called to let him know I was coming up behind him and he turned slowly, his eyes bloodshot and tired. It worried me to see him looking so haggard, a repeat of what I knew they'd all gone through with me.

"Not hungry," he said quietly, turning back toward the system to make an adjustment.

That was impossible, and I drew up alongside him and hung over the top pole that constituted a row of feeding slots. I said nothing, waiting for him to finish making adjustments, to say something, to look at me–anything.

"Want to tell me about it?" I finally asked, hardly surprised when he shook his head. It bothered me, to know he was hanging on by a thread and he wouldn't tell anyone why.

"Ben." I blew out a big breath, because I was just going to go for it. "Were you in love with her or something?" It made him turn his head to look at me again, but his expression was flat.

"In love with who?" He scoffed. "You know me, Jude. I don't do that mushy shit."

"Was pretty sure I didn't either," I offered, leaning down to scratch a calf's nose when it poked its head through the feeding slot and started to chew on my pant leg. "Turned out I was wrong. And whatever this is, it has to stop, because we're losing you, bro. Not gonna stand for it." I might have hiccuped a little, emotion making a weird bubble in my throat when I thought of what it would do to us to lose part of our family, and Ben was a big, big part of it.

"Couldn't even if you wanted to." He made a scoffing sound, but he kept his head turned resolutely away from me and I knew I'd gotten to him. "Just ... eh, you know. Tired of doing this thing alone, I guess. Every day a little more of the same; kind of getting old, with no one to go home to." He sighed and I kept my surprised expression to myself, because Ben had never expressed an interest in being anything but single. He'd been pretty resolute about playing the field for as long as I could remember, going all the way back to high school. Women had always fallen at his feet and he'd had his pick, but none of them had been able to tie him down.

"You find someone you'd *like* to go home to?" I asked cautiously, and when his shoulders slumped I knew I had my answer. "Holy shit, Benjamin." I couldn't help myself. "Who is this miracle worker?"

"Fuck off." I saw just the corner of his mouth lift a little and I tapped into patience I didn't know I had, waiting for him to explain himself. It took a long time and finally he couldn't stall any longer. He snapped the lid shut on a fuse box and shoved a few small tools into the carpenter's pouch he wore over one hip.

"You know Roy has a daughter?"

It seemed like a total non sequitur, but I knew it was a clue, so I looked at him a little strangely. "Yeah, I suppose. She wasn't even close to my age, so I didn't go to school with her—didn't know her at all. Did you?"

"Yeah." He nodded slowly. "A couple years behind me in school. Couldn't even stand the sight of me." He grinned.

"A challenge, huh? The one that got away?"

"Oh, she had *no* time for me." His grin grew wider. "Feisty little shit, even then."

"And now?" I liked where this was going. Perhaps the universe had produced a woman who could keep Ben on his toes.

"So much worse now. Attitude like you wouldn't believe."

"And?" I just couldn't leave this alone.

"And she's buddy-buddy with Donna."

"Since when?" I could feel my eyebrows hitching upward. Had Donna been holding out on us, or was she the matchmaker?

"Since she moved home and the two of them see each other every week at church." He winced a little when he said it, and I couldn't decide whether to be shocked or to burst out laughing.

"Mother Teresa's got you all wound up in knots," I said.

It wasn't a question.

"Somethin'," he admitted. "Can't sleep. Actually thinkin' about going to church with Donna and Dad on Sunday."

"Good." I wasn't about to poke fun, and he turned his head quickly to look at me. I knew he'd been expecting me to start laughing at him. "It's about time you ironed yourself out for someone who's worth it. Anyone who makes you want to be a better person is worth your effort." And wasn't that just a lesson I'd learned the hard way?

"Roy's gonna plant an IED in my driveway," he groaned, and that got me to laugh.

"Guessing she's old enough that he's given up the gatekeeping by now," I said, and he shot me a skeptical look.

"Speaking of old enough..." There was an evil gleam in his eye and I turned, leading him out of the barn and into the sunshine of a late spring day. "You gonna make an honest woman out of my sweet girl anytime soon?"

The truth was that I'd had the ring for the past month, but a part of me worried she wasn't ready. I wasn't sure she'd processed what had happened in Texas, and part of me was still dealing with the guilt I felt for being the one to put a bullet in the man she'd mourned for years. She had never blamed me for it; she didn't talk about it at all, even when I asked if she'd let Ashley make a recommendation.

"Not sure that's what she wants," I finally said as he fell into step beside me. Donna's front porch was already covered with potted plants that she still brought in at night when she worried it might get too cold.

"Heard it said she wouldn't mind trying for a baby Benson or two, but she's worried there's not much time left on her clock—she might've been the one to say it. Not so much a grapevine thing." He raised one eyebrow at me. "But you knock her up without tyin' her down proper and we both know Donna will kill you with her bare hands—maybe strangle you with her rosary beads. Oh, I like that better." He barked out a short, sharp hyena laugh.

The stupidest grin stretched across my face as I thought about what it would be like to start a family with Beckett. It would be a redemption of sorts for both of us. A beautiful new life together.

"Love her an awful lot," I admitted quietly.

"Knew that by day three." I couldn't tell whether he was teasing. "No way you were gonna stay mad at her—too pretty, for one thing. Smarter than you, too, and I bet you couldn't stand that."

He had me there and even I could admit it.

"Dan says he has news," Ben said as we climbed the porch steps and untied our boots. He kept his voice down. "My money's on the divorce."

"Too soon for it to be finalized, don't you think?" I asked, having no idea how long it took to finalize something like that, but I knew Lindsey wasn't the sort to make things easy on anyone.

"No idea," he said, "but if he's bringing it up you know it's something big. You know him: Jackass keeps his cards close when it comes to that woman."

This was true, and it was something I'd never liked. Not that I'd felt Dan excluded us because of her, but that she'd always encouraged it. He'd always been somewhat unavailable to us during their marriage, because she'd argued that she was his first priority and his family was second. She wasn't wrong, but she wasn't willing to accept that it meant she was a part of our family.

She drew lines where we'd never had any.

My girl was in deep conversation with Dad when we walked into the kitchen and whatever it was, I watched him wrap her into a tight hug. It was something she softened into, reciprocating with a sweet look on her face, and it struck me like a lightning bolt that I had never seen Cait interact with either of my parents that way. She had never accepted Donna or Dad as her own, like Beckett had, and it filled my heart with gratitude to know how strong the love was between all of them. This woman had blended seamlessly into the group of people I loved most in the world, accepting them and all of their craziness as her own.

"Looking a little stunned, Jude." Levi socked me in the arm and I snapped out of it, surprised to find him in the kitchen on a weekday. He'd been traveling a lot lately, completing restoration projects and hauling custom pieces all over creation. Business was booming for him and it made me happy he'd finally settled into something that truly gave him joy.

"Thinking on some big life changes." I grinned at him when I said it and he nodded at me, an affirmation, because he could read my mind.

"Approve of a life change like that—do you both some real good." He smiled.

It was a miracle Levi hadn't been put off marriage altogether, but underneath such a stern exterior I had a feeling he was still a hopeless romantic. After all, I didn't know many other men who'd carried a torch for the same woman for thirty years, but he'd never deviated.

"Suppose you could officiate?" I asked, and he chuckled.

"Bec might have some objections to that, so I suppose you should ask her first. Then we'll talk."

I could feel eyes on me and I looked up to see her watching me with a sweet expression on her face. She was waiting for me and I finally closed the gap between us to press a kiss to her mouth. We had been incredibly busy the past few months, between the conclusion of the investigation, the sale of the property in Texas, making major changes to the farm, and now implementing the new milking schedule with twice as many cows.

The cows Calista had sold had been traced through the hauling company's records, split off into several small groups and sold to farmers in North Dakota. We filed a lawsuit to recoup damages, but I didn't anticipate seeing a check anytime soon.

Things had been changing in big ways and we had new contracts to show for it, along with exclusive products and fancy new branding. Bec had been working herself into the ground to make this farm a success, which meant there hadn't been a lot of time left for some of my favorite things. We were too tired at the end of each long day, falling into bed together after a shower, our eyelids snapping shut the instant we hit our pillows.

"Yes, Levi can officiate," she whispered into my ear just before her lips met my neck and I pulled back slowly to look down at her.

"Woman, you have supersonic hearing."

"I was starting to worry you'd never ask." Her smile told me she hadn't been worried at all. "I have to grasp at straws when I find them."

"Well, that settles it then." I felt like my chest might explode from the joy that bubbled inside. "Suppose this family better start planning for a wedding."

There was a startled noise and a crash behind me and I knew Donna had just cut herself while slicing bread, and Dad had dropped the stack of plates he was carrying to the table. I lifted my head to take in the room, everyone frozen like they were in suspended animation, staring at us. Donna had a hand to her mouth, Dad looked like he might have shit his pants, Ben was grinning like an idiot, and Levi looked downright gleeful. Officiating for his siblings' weddings was becoming a real tradition for him.

"Suppose that settles it." I looked back down into Beckett's eyes as I said it, cupping her face in both of my hands. "Gonna add a Benson to the family, and I'm not giving this woman a chance to tell me no."

"Judah." Beckett swatted my shoulder playfully just before pushing up on her tiptoes, sinking her fingers into my hair to hold my head in place. "You were my choice from the start, you beautiful idiot." She kissed me hard. "The answer was always yes."

Chapter Twenty-Eight

Epilogue

Six Months Later...

"This family really has a thing for winter weddings," my sister mused as she pulled on warm boots beneath her bridesmaid's dress. "At least you two are actually getting married inside."

Considering it was the middle of December, it hadn't exactly been a surprise when over a foot of snow had been dumped on us in a pre-Christmas blizzard. For that very reason we hadn't even been willing to consider an outdoor wedding, even though there was a pristine hayloft on the new barn we'd finished just before the first really hard freeze.

"Need a Benadryl or something; church weddings make me itchy," Ben complained, fingers going beneath his tie like it was choking him.

"That's not allergies, it's the weight of your sins," Dan called from the kitchen, where he was hunched over his laptop. He had been working like a madman lately, even more so than usual, throwing all of his time and energy into his business rather than things like getting back out there now that Lindsey was officially his ex.

"At least you have a full staff now," Levi mused, "so you can step away to do things like get married." He grinned. "Knew Bec could pull it off, but I didn't think she'd have things humming along this fast. Got to admit I picked a good one." His grin grew wider—shit-eating, really—and I rolled my eyes at him.

"Yeah, yeah. Whatever. Picked a real powerhouse."

It was true. Beckett had saved the farm, but she'd also saved *me*. She claimed I'd saved her as well, but she didn't say those things when anyone else could hear her. She saved the sweetest things for me, alone, late at night when I held her in my arms after showing her how much I loved her.

We had made my house our own, a home filled with happiness and routine, two new kittens tearing the fuck out of our furniture. Bec found them on the farm one day and promptly decided to bring them home, and I swear to you she treated them like they were our children. They adored her, but they liked to pounce on me and scare the shit out of me in the middle of the night.

The kittens had been something healing for her. She was meeting with a therapist Ashley had recommended, once a week, working through the betrayal. She was dealing with the loss all over again now that it was in a different light, something that made me hope she reached the anger stage soon because that was all I ever felt when I thought of the asshole who'd cheated on his wife and took her family from her.

I had finally proposed to her properly, about a week after the kitchen ambush, and she'd let me sweat it out for about thirty seconds before she knocked me over and had her way with me.

Best proposal ever, thank you very much—or acceptance—whatever. Since it ended with a naked *yes*, I took that as a win.

In early September Sal had driven out to the farm to pay both of us a visit. I happened to be in Bec's office going over some records with her when he showed up to let us know that interagency efforts had resulted in locating Jason and the case would finally be closed. It seemed that he had indeed crossed into Mexico and would no longer be a problem, because he'd been identified by dental records.

It was that day I knew Beckett had truly put things behind her, because I watched her shoulders square on a deep breath and slump with an exhale, like she'd let go of a huge weight.

Cade had been left to the state. Beckett refused to claim his body and as a result, neither of us had any idea where he was buried. It was for the best, she said, that he was completely forgotten and, seeing what he had done to his family, I had to agree.

The wedding wasn't huge; we'd only sent out about fifty invitations, but the reception promised to be a real shindig.

Word had gotten out in town that it would be hosted at the Benson farm, and Donna was making use of one of the new buildings. She and Dad were practically party planners these days, filling it with heaters, tables, and string lights, and she'd been cooking and baking for weeks. She'd bought a new deep freeze for the occasion, one that lived in the garage alongside the first one she'd already had in place, and she'd been stocking it a little more each day.

Bec had asked Dad and Donna to walk her down the aisle, something I thought was a nice touch. I knew she had adopted them as her own parents, and sometimes I thought she was closer to them than any of their natural children. It was good for them, and I thought it healed something in Donna, who rarely saw her own kids, so she'd given all of her love to us instead—and God knew how we'd needed it.

The church was nondenominational, since we couldn't exactly marry in Donna's parish, neither of us identifying as Catholic. And while I couldn't have cared less where we were married, so long as the woman finally took my last name and I could call her "wife," she said she wanted to do it right. So we did. Right down to the rice, which I picked out of my hair and my ears for the next five hours.

Our service was quiet and serious. No one saw fit to tease us after the things we'd seen in the past years and months, and when the pastor told me I could kiss my bride, I gave it everything I had. I bent her back into a deep dip and poured every bit of myself into that kiss, something that left her wobbly and unfocused when I brought her back up for air.

What she didn't know was that I'd planned a proper honeymoon, and with a solid staff in place to oversee the daily operations of the farm, we could get away for a few weeks so long as we remembered to bring a laptop to check in occasionally.

I had planned for two weeks of sun, sand, and delicious food.

It went without saying that thanks to a private bungalow, we'd be naked just as often as I could convince her it was a good idea.

I liked my chances.

"Happy for you, Jude." Dan looped an arm around my upper back and squeezed me tightly. I had noticed he'd had maybe one or two drinks the entire evening, and he'd turned down several women who'd asked him to dance. "Feel like you finally found the right one—just took some false starts, didn't it?"

"Suppose you know a thing or two about that, huh?" I didn't mean it in a mean-spirited way, and I knew he understood.

"Better than most," he agreed, smiling as Levi held out a hand to Donna and led her out onto the dance floor. Dad was too deeply engrossed in a conversation with Roy to notice.

Both of us chuckled when our eyes drifted to Ben, arms crossed over his wide chest as he glared daggers across the room. "Must be Roy's daughter?" I asked Dan, having never met the petite brunette.

"Yup." Dan chuckled. "She is *so* much more than Ben will ever be able to handle. I've suggested to him that scaling Everest naked might be a slightly easier undertaking than trying to win over that one."

"Be good for him." I was feeling magnanimous this evening. "Someone to give him hell for once, instead of just rolling over."

"Literally." Dan groaned. "That boy's had it too easy his whole life. He should have to work for it for once."

"Anyone catching your eye?" I asked, easily tipping back my glass of sparkling water. Dan had never been a player, but these days I was pretty sure he and Levi had joined the same order because they were so celibate, it was possible their virginity had grown back.

"Work," he said, his lips going tight. "The only woman in my life looks suspiciously like my hand." He shrugged. "I don't have the time and honestly, I don't have the fight in me. Lindsey took just about everything." I knew he meant more than just tangible possessions.

She'd also taken his spirit.

"Don't rule it out." I looked across the room to see Beckett laughing, her head thrown back as a blonde woman I didn't recognize leaned close to say something to her. "Trust me, the weirdest shit happens when you least expect it."

"Got that right," he said, his expression telling me my little platitude worked both ways.

Donna had returned to her table and the blonde that had been talking to Beckett crossed the space to catch Levi's attention, and finally I recognized her as one of his former sisters-in-law. It made me uncomfortable for him, wondering if when he saw the woman, all he thought of was his ex.

"Suppose you'd better get back to your bride—think I'm gonna fuck with Benjamin for a minute." Dan smiled wickedly and I knew he was genuinely happy for me. The tinkling sound of cutlery on glass swelled to a din in the space as he moved away and I took the cue, hurrying back to my wife, unable to keep the smile off my face. She was a knockout in a simple gray dress. It was cut to hug her gorgeous figure, something off-shoulder with no flashy details, but something at the back she said was a mermaid train.

All I knew was that it drew just about every eye in the room to the gentle sway of her hips when she walked, something that made me think of things that did not involve churches or parties or the eyes of others.

"You look like you want to eat me." She giggled when I drew close and swept her back into my arms. To be honest, that very thought had crossed my mind, something that made me wiggle my eyebrows at her and she squealed. "Judah Benson!"

"Yes, Mrs. Benson?" I couldn't get over how much joy it brought me to say that, something that made her smile too.

"Behave yourself—at least for now." She leaned in and kissed me, something soft and sweet and full of promise that made me anticipate what would happen once I took her home.

I pressed another kiss to her mouth and an appreciative murmur made its way through the room.

"Deal." I hiked up one wicked eyebrow, a still photo flashing through my head of what my first wedding had looked like. It made me pull her close again and whisper, "On one condition."

When Beckett thought I was up to something, she could level me with just one look and I watched one of her brows slowly begin to rise.

"We open the discussion about working on some baby Bensons." I almost held my breath when I said it, because I was only mostly sure she was on the same page. I had always figured talking about kids was something for couples in their twenties, not their forties.

She shook her head at me slowly, a sweet smile on her face and I stood waiting for her to explain why she looked both amused and serene. She stepped close to me and wrapped her arms around my neck, leaning up to whisper, "In that case I think we have about a seven-week head start."

"The fuck?" Ben roared, and a shocked silence descended over the room filled with people, some of whom preferred a little more Jesus and a few less f-bombs. I jerked my head so quickly to the side, convinced he'd overheard Beckett, that I felt a tendon catch and snap. Instead, I saw Dan leading a pretty little brunette out to the dance floor, completely ignoring Ben, who looked like he was chewing on nails.

"Another one's about to bite the dust," Beckett whispered in my ear with a chuckle. My eyes were still darting between Benjamin and Dan, trying to decide whether I needed to run interference. "You think?" I asked, confused, because Dan had shown more interest in the table linens than any of the women at the reception until just now.

"Not that one." She gripped my jaw gently to twist my head toward Ben. "That one. Dan's poking the bear."

I laughed hard enough that Dad's gaze was redirected from Ben to me, and I shook my head within Beckett's grip. "Nah, baby. That one'll never fall."

My wife didn't say a word, just tipped her head to one side with a little smile, and I wondered what else she knew that I didn't.

"Well, Mr. Benson, I suggest you brace and fortify, because our little sapling's just been taken out at the knees."

Finally convinced Ben wasn't going to maim Dan, I turned my full attention back to Beckett, watching her pantomime a tree falling. *Timber*, she mouthed.

I kept her close, still knocked sideways by her whispered admission, completely terrified but more than anything, hopeful. It was a foreign feeling, warm and wonderful, and I folded my wife into my arms to lead her through one last dance before I stole her away from our adoring public.

When it came to her, I wasn't going to waste a single minute.

- The End -

Other Works

The Atholton Series

Forsaking All Others - (Seraphina & Mateo)
The Battle Back Home - (Aaron & Harlowe)
All The Days After - (Noah & Eve)
The Things I Can't Say - (Asher & Olivia)
When I Had Nothing - (Thomas & Natalie)

Men of the First Brigade

Unexpected - (Jack & Daphne)
Unforgiven - (Scott & Mia)
Unwelcome - (Brandon & Giulia)
Unstoppable - (Alex & Lauren)

Unrequited - (Lincoln & Ava)
Undeniable - (Adam & Madelyn)
Unrecognizable - (Michael & Claire)
Unconditional - (Gerald & Emerson)
Unforgettable - (James & Gemma)

Wolf Mountain Ranchers

Something Lost - (Mark & Lana)
Something Broken - (Travis & Ashley)
Something Gained - (Jacob & Emily)
Something Sacrificed - (William & Genesis)
Something Saved - (Grant & Morgan)
The Something Smutty Book Club - Wolf Mountain Novella

Colson Creek

We All Fall Down - (Judah & Beckett)
The Greatest of These - (Dan & Charlie)
The Wages of Silence - (Levi & Hannah)
The Weight of Ashes - (Benjamin & Tristyn)

Acknowledgements

If you've been with me for a while, you know that this has been a marathon, not a sprint. (Your girl is tired, but invigorated.)

Over the past year, the incredible growth and support I've seen from new team members and new-to-me readers has been astonishing. I've been so thankful that a ragtag band of blue collar ranchers pulled people into their orbit and wouldn't let them go. It made me realize how much I love the small town aspect, and it won't surprise many of you to find that this series is even more of a return to my roots than The Wolf Mountain Ranchers. Write what you know and love, right? And it turns out I love small towns, tight-knit families, and broken souls.

Huge thanks are due to my tireless, patient beta readers, Heidi, both of "my" Nicoles, Jadin & Carly. You're constantly put upon by my tight (and often blown) deadlines and yet you work tirelessly to save me from myself.

A special shoutout to Michelle Healy, who has established herself as my savior in shining armor. Girl, I don't know what stars aligned to bring us together, but whenever something good happens I can trace it back to you! Thank you for sharing so much of your knowledge, your advice, and just talking nonsense with me when you know my brain is fried.

To my wonderful ARC team, most of whom I feel I can call friends: Thank you for sticking with me. There are so many good books out there and I am so honored that you would choose to give me your time and support. I cannot tell you what a tremendous encouragement it has been to watch this team grow and to know that you love these characters like I do.

To my street team: Ladies, what would I do without you? With your help, the word is getting out. Thank you for your patience, your friendship, and your eternal willingness to jump in with "What do you need? Let me help."

And to anyone reading, whether you've been here the whole time or this is your first experience with one of my books: Thank you. I hope you've loved it here and will stick with me. I couldn't do this without you.

www.ingramcontent.com/pod-product-compliance
Lightning Source LLC
LaVergne TN
LVHW041058080826
845145LV00007B/1618